Praise for Eternity Between Us

"In *Eternity Between Us*, Stephenia H. McGee displays not just her passion for history, but her respect for it. Thoroughly researched and convincingly told with the detail readers are sure to appreciate, this tale brings a turbulent time to life with nuance and sensitivity."
JOCELYN GREEN, award-winning author of the Heroines Behind the Lines Civil War series

"Stephenia H. McGee kept me turning pages to see what new scrapes Evelyn could get into. Samuel was a worthy hero perfectly suited to his vocation, in spite of the "thorn in his side" that seemed to thwart him at every turn. Through Samuel, Evelyn comes to realize that everything is not all black and white, nor is it simply blue and gray. And sometimes even those we think are loyal are the most cunning and devious of all. Readers who enjoy Civil War stories and strong women who aren't afraid to dive into the fray will enjoy *Eternity Between Us*."
CBA bestselling author PAM HILLMAN

"Set amidst the Civil War in the south, *Eternity Between Us* takes readers on a journey filled with suspense, danger and known enemies—and a love that finds a way to bloom despite all opposition."
DAWN CRANDALL, award-winning author of The Everstone Chronicles series

D1091939

"McGee once again brings her authentic Southern historical style reminiscent of *Gone with the Wind*, weaving a tale filled with action, intrigue, and characters who warm your heart."
MISTY M. BELLER, bestselling author of the Heart of the Mountains series

"Stephenia H. McGee has a thrilling way with words. Her novels both inspire and enthrall, and I for one am hooked after chapter one. This newest novel, Eternity Between Us, is no exception. As soon as I met Evelyn and Samuel, I couldn't read fast enough. I had a strong feeling these characters were going to find an everlasting love despite their slow start! McGee is an expert in all things Civil War, so you will learn some fascinating historical facts as you follow the intriguing plot. Five stars from me!"
SHARLENE MACLAREN, Author of the Forever Freedom, Tennessee Dreams, and Hearts of Honor Series

"Stephenia McGee has written another page-turner! I thoroughly enjoyed reading *Eternity Between Us*. The character development is fantastic and Ms. McGee's research for this book was extensive—and it's quite evident as the story unfolds. The plot keeps readers sitting at the end of their seats, wondering what's going to happen next to Evelyn, Samuel, and other characters. If you love Civil War romance, this book is a must-read!"
ANDREA BOESHAAR, Author of Shenandoah Valley Saga

"*Eternity Between Us* grabbed my attention from the first paragraph. This is a story that will sweep the reader up in the turmoil of the Civil War with a romance between a Yankee physician and a Southern belle. It was a story I hated to see end."
PATRICIA BRADLEY, Inspirational Readers' Choice Award-winning Author of the Memphis Cold Case Novels

Eternity
Between Us

Eternity
BETWEEN US

Stephenia H. McGee

By The
Vine Press

Cover Design: Carpe Librum Book Design
Cover Model: Period Stock www.PeriodStock.com

Library Cataloging Data
Names: McGee, Stephenia H. (Stephenia H. McGee) 1983 –
Title: Eternity Between Us / Stephenia H. McGee
356p. 5.5 in. × 8.5 in. (13.97 cm × 21.59 cm)
Description: By The Vine Press digital eBook edition | By The Vine Press Trade paperback edition | Mississippi: By The Vine Press, 2018
Summary: When Civil War erupts and more than uniforms meld into shades of gray, can love span the divide that tears the country asunder?
Identifiers: LLCN: 2018907212 | ISBN-13: 978-1-63564-035-9 (trade) | 978-1-63564-037-3 (POD) | 978-1-63564-036-6 (ebk.) | 978-1-63564-039-7 (large print)
1. Civil War fiction 2. Christian historical 3. Christian Romance 4. Clean Read Historical 5. Historical Romance 6. 1800s Historical Fiction 7. Spies and Espionage

To Mamaw
For all the things you've taught me
over the years.
Those times spent canning tomatoes, learning to sew and
cook, and our long talks on the porch are more precious to
me than words can express.
Thank you for always being there for me.
I love you.

"*Between* us and those former friends

exists a divide as deep and wide as eternity."

Rose O'Neal Greenhow, Confederate Spy

One

Martinsburg, Virginia
July 4, 1861

They were here.

Evelyn Mapleton gathered her courage and stood at the parlor window to listen. The sound came first as a steady growl accompanied by the *rat-a-tat* of drums and squealing trumpets, upending the precarious calm of a town poised on the knife's edge of war. An unnatural thunder rumbled through the air, carrying with it not thoughts of rain but of smoke and trepidation.

With each pound of the nearing forces, Evelyn's heart quivered. One single thought kept cadence in her mind, bringing with it a chilling fear that turned her stomach to lead.

They were here.

The vibrations trembled through the house, rattling Aunt Mary's porcelains and coaxing the other members of the family to gather in the parlor alongside Evelyn in the scant hope there might be a measure of peace found in company. The oppressive heat thickened in the house, Aunt Mary having been too nervous to let in even a timid breeze.

For the two days since the Yanks defeated Jackson at

Falling Waters, Evelyn had stayed sequestered in her aunt's townhome on South Queen Street, waiting for the inevitable. Now it came, with raucous laughter and barking voices to accompany the rumble of drums, a most quarrelsome and discordant attempt at victory's song. Half of Martinsburg would surely join them, while the rest of the divided citizenship had likely either abandoned their homes or was now hiding within them until the trouble passed.

Evelyn peeled back the curtain and stared outside. Would Daddy's warnings about the invaders come to pass? She tightened her hands into fists. She must be brave and fulfill the promise he'd coaxed from her before he'd left her again.

Pulse fluttering, she gazed down the town's empty street for as far as she could see. How long would it be until the sound gave way to the sight of those who caused it? How many would descend upon them like locusts, destroying all they touched without conscience?

"Evelyn! Come away from that window at once!"

Evelyn let the lace curtain fall and looked over her shoulder at her aunt's pale features. At thirty-eight, Aunt Mary was the same age Evelyn's mother would have been. Daddy had promised his sister was a fine lady of pristine character, and she would provide for Evelyn what a lone man never could.

Unfortunately, his news reports stated the Yanks gave no heed to such things, and no deference would be given to the genteel. Brutes, the lot of them, Daddy had said.

The terrible fears Daddy had printed in his newspaper articles reflected in Aunt Mary's eyes, so Evelyn pried herself away from the window and withdrew into the shadows of the parlor. Little Lara clutched her mother's skirts, her sweet face buried deep into Aunt Mary's sage gown. For her sake, Evelyn pasted on a smile. "Not to worry, Lara. They will soon enough pass. We're safe in here."

Lara lifted her eyes to Evelyn for a few seconds, then managed a small nod before seeking out her older sister's gaze as well. Isabella remained too engrossed in plucking at her immaculate gown to notice. Evelyn inwardly sighed. Did her cousin ever truly notice the child?

Lara's grip loosened on Aunt Mary's skirt but did not release entirely. Aunt Mary gave a small dip of her chin in appreciation for Evelyn's necessary deception and pulled the girl closer. "How many of them do you think there are?"

She'd heard their neighbor, Mrs. Grady, boast that nearly fifteen thousand Yanks had swarmed through the valley, and at least three thousand had crossed the Potomac to trample into Falling Waters. Evelyn wouldn't be surprised if every one of those, if not more, had come to seek their revelry in Martinsburg. But she wouldn't further distress her aunt by saying so.

"No more than a few hundred, I should hope. Let us pray they will be on their way quickly."

Aunt Mary seemed relieved, and Evelyn told herself the lie was as much of a benefit to her aunt as her previous one had been for little Lara.

Isabella lurched to her feet and paced around the parlor, her hands flying nervously about her throat. Golden curls hung limp at her temples and sweat glistened on her forehead. Her bright blue eyes landed on Evelyn, and her rosy lips pulled back from her teeth. "They have come to murder us all!"

"Isabella!" Evelyn grabbed her cousin's elbow and pulled her close, her voice lowering. "Do not frighten your sister."

Isabella's eyes widened in shock and she glared at Evelyn, then sank onto the settee, her breath coming in rapid flutters. Evelyn sat next to her and stroked the back of her hand. Though close in age, the cousins were opposites in most everything. Where Isabella had sunshine hair and ocean eyes, Evelyn's thick locks fell in cascades of raven black, and she studied the world through eyes the same deep brown as her mother's. Isabella thrived on the attention her beauty drew, while Evelyn ever found herself blending into the walls and remaining unseen. Today, however, none of their clashing personality problems mattered.

Regardless of the many things separating them, for the moment the only thing of consequence was the fearful song that grew louder, slipping through every crack in the house and snaking its way across the frayed nerves of the family huddling in the parlor.

The sound of scurrying feet sent Evelyn's senses into a dither until she caught sight of Lizzy bounding into the parlor, her arms filled with a mound of red cloth. Sweat dripped down her ebony face and darkened the stiff collar of her brown dress. Her dark eyes darted over each lady of the household, landing on Aunt Mary who sat with Lara clutched against her.

Lizzy waved a piece of the red fabric at them. "I done got the flag, mistress. What you wants I should do with it?"

Aunt Mary stared at her and offered up not a word. Evelyn looked to her cousin, who should have been next to speak, but Isabella had taken to wrapping her arms around her middle and rocking herself, her lips moving silently.

Evelyn swallowed. Daddy's flag. A symbol, he'd said, of the pride of their cause. When she'd dared to ask what pride that meant for those who had no stakes in the argument of slavery, he'd lectured her about tariffs, taxes, and Lincoln's agenda.

Gunfire cracked outside, and Lara whimpered. Evelyn's pulse raced, her heart hammering in her chest. She'd promised she'd be brave. She'd promised to help in any way she could. But despite reminding herself to make it so, her quivering hands indicated she'd likely fail Daddy again.

Would the invaders breach the house or merely continue their contemptuous parade through the streets? Word had spread like wildfire that the Federals had defeated Southern forces at Falling Waters two days ago and had planned their march into Martinsburg for today, the fourth, where they could celebrate the eighty-fifth birthday of a fractured nation with drunken gasconade.

The sounds of their impending arrival cast all thoughts of propriety away. Evelyn rose. "Lizzy, take that secessionist flag and hide it somewhere. Then, gather the other servants and find a place to stay out of sight."

The older woman hesitated a moment and then bobbed her head and slipped away on silent feet. The rumble now turned to a steady pounding, and Evelyn pushed aside the urge to cover her ears against the thousands of Patterson's Yanks who would soon swarm around the house.

Overcoming a fraction of her fear, she dared to move the curtain a smidgen, needing to glimpse these scallywags that reports throughout the South had warned were capable of every manner of outrage. Daddy reported the soldiers had been raiding homes, stealing and destroying property, and committing unspeakable acts against defenseless women.

A blur of blue cut through the yard and stilled her hammering heart. Breath left her body, and for a moment, Evelyn stood frozen. Then she blinked, and in so doing, forced her mind to process once more. The Yanks had arrived, and her Uncle Phillip and cousin, Paul, were away with Jackson's Second Virginia Infantry. If she did not take action, her relatives may soon be another unsavory line in one of Daddy's news reports.

She whirled around and hurried to her aunt's side.

"Where is the pistol?"

Aunt Mary regarded her with glazed eyes.

Evelyn shook her shoulder. "The pistol, Aunt! I must have it!"

Aunt Mary shuddered as though coming free of a trance. "It's in Phillip's study. He left it in the desk drawer."

Evelyn hiked up her skirts and ran through the house, nearly tripping on the corner of a rug. Her shoes clomped across the wood floors, sounding too much like the incessant drumbeat outside. She threw the door to her uncle's study wide and snatched the drawer in his carved desk open, pulling it clean out of the furniture.

The drawer hit the rug below, its contents shifting around in her haste. She pushed aside a stack of envelopes and found the metal of a Colt pocket pistol gleaming in the late afternoon sunlight. Fingers shaking, she plucked it from its place. Glad of her father's insistence she learn to handle a weapon, Evelyn flipped open the revolving chamber and counted three bullets inside. She sucked in a quick breath and slipped their only means of protection into the pocket of her yellow gingham skirt and hurried back to the parlor.

The sound that had laid siege to the town had now grown to a cacophony of bugle blasts, disjointed songs, and shouts of victory. The wood frame of the house trembled like the women inside it, trinkets on the shelves in the parlor quivering. Sweat gathered at the nape of Evelyn's neck and slid between her shoulder blades as she rejoined her family.

She took up her place by the parlor window once again and tried to remain still, lest any movement draw the attention of an unscrupulous soldier.

Evelyn feared her father had made a grave mistake. He'd told her to continue staying with Isabella after they'd concluded their studies at Mount Washington Female College and to do her debut with Aunt Mary's society friends in Washington. But by the time her season came to an end, the threats of war blanketed the country. Then after what happened at Fort Sumter, Daddy refused to let her stay with him, even though it was what he'd always promised. Travel, he'd said, would be dangerous with the stirs of combat causing young men to grow hot with battle fever and sully themselves with desires for war.

She pried back a piece of the curtain, and this time her aunt did not reprimand her. She could see them now. Loose lines that didn't hold to any respectable formation barely contained the men waving bayonets and hollering about Yankee Doodle on his pony. Gun carriages clattered across the pavers, mechanical reapers that tainted the once quiet streets of Martinsburg.

They came in droves, singing, swaying, and having the audacity to hoist a flag that boasted the stars of thirty-four states even though eleven of them had chosen to leave.

Sovereign states had the right to dissociate with the union they'd freely joined, didn't they? How had they reached a time when fellow Americans celebrated the invasion of their neighbors? Evelyn shivered, the sight of so many untamed men causing her stomach to sour.

Aunt Mary's blue china vibrated behind the doors of the rococo hutch, their tinkling the only sound that came from within the house. All the doors had been locked and the windows secured. Now all she could do was pray the men would pass them by. Wave after wave came, their steel flashing in the sunlight that dipped farther toward the dust stirred by the passing of boots.

Evelyn pulled heavy air into her lungs and held it as the crash of shattering glass mingled with the sound of children's screams. Such noises were now too close to allow them to keep up the pretense of safety for Lara's sake.

Evelyn dropped the curtain. "Aunt! We must hide. They will soon—"

The front door erupted with a thundering of pounding fists. Evelyn thrust her hand into the pocket of her dress and retreated farther into the parlor.

"Come, Lara. We must hide," Aunt Mary whispered, her voice wavering.

Isabella lurched to her feet, her eyes wild as she flung her hands into the air. "I cannot abide this!"

Evelyn grasped her cousin's arm. "Abide it or not, it is coming. Best you keep your wits about you."

Her cousin stared at her in disbelief. Never once had Evelyn spoken to Isabella in such a manner, but now was not the time to maintain a lady's demure deference to her betters. Her aunt and uncle had been kind in their treatment of their niece, feeling for her after the loss of her mother and Daddy's frequent absences. Because of this, Evelyn had allowed her cousin her whims and air of superiority and had never once bucked against her. But now she held the only means of protection they had and was the sole one who could use it. She could not allow Isabella's histrionics to endanger them further.

"Let's find somewhere before—"

The front door gave way with a splintered crash.

Men spilled into the house. Tracks of sweat cut paths through their filthy faces, and their wild eyes bounced around the entry before landing on the huddled forms of the women.

A great big man stepped in front of his counterparts and flashed a grin through his yellow beard. His eyes glazed like that of a man who had found too much brandy. He loomed closer, his heavy boots thudding across the floor as he stepped into the parlor.

Evelyn took a step back and put her fingers under her nose to ward off the smell of sweat, dirt, and drink that wafted off the scoundrels.

The big soldier's eyes focused on her, and he laughed, a coarse sound that made her fingers tremble over the secret concealed in her pocket. "You're one of the rebels, aren't you?"

Evelyn let out a long breath. She would not let this devilish brute see her fear. Better she stand her ground and hope to not make herself an easy target. "We are not."

The big man scratched at his greasy hair that fell in heavy locks over his ears. Evelyn took a small step forward, broadening her shoulders as she prayed for courage she did not truly feel. "We have not rebelled," she said, using Daddy's words. "We are merely defending our homes against invasion."

The humor left his flat face. He sneered, and no fewer than six others pushed in closer behind him. Evelyn's pulse raced as her cousin groaned. Then suddenly, Isabella was pressed up behind her.

"She speaks only for herself!" Isabella whined. "My mother and sister and I want nothing to do with the rebellion."

The soldier crossed his arms over his broad chest. "Are there any rebel flags in this house that would prove you a liar?"

Isabella trembled and Evelyn felt her sway. She tried to catch her, but Isabella's knees crumpled, and she dropped to the floor.

Aunt Mary wailed and darted to her daughter's side, fanning Isabella's face in desperation.

Evelyn stepped in front of them, hoping their vulnerability would be shielded behind the volumes of her skirts and, thus, would persuade the ingrates to forget about them.

Another of the men stepped forward, a reedy fellow with brown hair and probing eyes. "We'll get to hoisting the stars and stripes over the house, then."

"You will do nothing of the sort." Evelyn pointed a haughty finger at them, hoping they would be reminded of any lessons in gentlemanly manners they may have been taught as youths. "You will remove yourselves from the premises and, as gentlemen, will leave us be. What consequence are a couple of hapless women in a town you have already conquered?"

The broad one roared with laughter, and before Evelyn could react, he shoved her aside. Evelyn caught herself on Aunt Mary's bookshelf and sent framed portraits and crystal figurines crashing to the floor. Thankfully, she kept her footing.

The beast knelt and wrapped a beefy arm around a still woozy Isabella, who pressed a hand to her head but remained conscious. She cried out as he shoved Aunt Mary aside, hauled her against him, and pulled them both to standing though Isabella's toes barely skimmed the floor. Then his slackened lips aimed at hers.

Horror lit Evelyn's veins on fire. She could not stand by and see her cousin ruined! In one thud of her heart, Evelyn planted her feet, whipped the weapon from her skirt, cocked back the hammer, and trained it upon the man's hulking figure.

"Release my cousin!"

The man turned one eye upon her, and, catching sight of the pistol, stilled in his advance.

Then he grinned.

In that moment, life seemed to slow. Evelyn could feel each beat of her pulse. The trembling in her fingers stilled as her blood boiled. Men scrambled, a tangle of torsos and limbs shifting in front of her and obscuring her target.

Her finger curled around the trigger, the cool metal smooth against the heat of her hand. She drew a breath and held it, settling the end of the barrel in line with the wolf who once again descended upon her cousin.

The recoil came first, a great snap of power that transferred up her arm and jolted through her shoulder. Then came the scent of smoke and the acrid burn of gunpowder. The crack of the weapon echoed in her ears as it erupted against the horrors unfolding around her.

The man's grip loosened, and Isabella pulled from his grasp. He swayed, crimson slowly seeping from the tear in his blue uniform jacket. He stared at Evelyn with his mouth agape. She watched him as he crumpled, vaguely aware of the men who'd shifted to attack her. Her eyes remained focused on the barbarian as the stain on his jacket widened. She watched him clutch at it, his fingers staining red. Then his body fell to the floor with a sickening thud.

Evelyn trembled and dropped the gun from horrified fingers, shocked as it smacked against the boning in her skirt and slid across the floor. Through the buzzing in her head, she heard screams that surely came from her family, but they seemed miles away, lost in the thrum of blood in her ears.

Two

Washington Infirmary
Washington City
July 4, 1861

*S*amuel Flynn pulled in the caustic scents of human waste, blood, and disease through his nose, held it for a moment, and then let it back out with a sigh he hoped his patient would not notice. The smells turned his senses, but he would not let them master him. He'd worked too hard to fall victim to his own nose. Yet, the ailment ever sought to undo him despite the years he and Father had spent praying against it.

Samuel peeled back the thin blanket and assessed the skinny form of this moment's patient and mentally recited what he'd learned. Nicolas Jones, eighteen, meant to report to training after being released from the infirmary. Eighteen looked to be an exaggeration. Samuel swept aside Jones's auburn hair and pressed the back of his hand to the boy's forehead. No fever.

He lifted one eyelid wide. "Pupils are not dilated. That is a good sign."

Worry flashed in that brown eye in the instant before Samuel let the lid fall. Jones had found his first tastes of battle by way of an angry mob deflecting volunteer soldiers from reporting to Washington.

"I believe you will soon be on your way to join the other recruits."

Jones stared at him as he checked the pulse at his wrist, neither resistant to Samuel's probing nor necessarily helpful. Not that Samuel expected anything different. Jones had been apathetic since he'd arrived some weeks ago. Samuel hadn't let on to Dr. Porter he'd begun to wonder if some of the symptoms stemmed from avoiding joining the men drilling. Perhaps the rage of an angry mob had given Jones second thoughts about joining the actual fray.

Samuel stared down at him and tried to ignore the man retching in the corner of the room. "If you do not wish to volunteer, that is none of my concern. But you cannot take up a bed in the ward with naught but laziness as your ailment."

Jones's eyes widened. "Yes, sir."

Samuel grunted at this further proof Jones had understood and regained mental function after his head injury. Samuel understood the boy's fears, but could not stomach cowardice wrapped in deceit.

Finished with his assessment, Samuel nodded to one of the Sisters of Mercy, who was cleaning vomit from the floor, and quickly made his way through the large chamber of the Washington Infirmary. He sucked air through his mouth, grateful his curse had not yet betrayed him here.

Not for the first time, he wondered what would happen if these halls ever became filled to the brim with wounded soldiers bursting with the pungent odors of rot and death. He would no longer be able to conceal his weakness.

He ground his teeth. As his father's only son, he *would* carry on the legacy before him, even if he had to fight his every breath to do it. With a patient or two at a time, he could manage. With the numbers this pressing war threatened, it would be all the more difficult. A hospital physician he could not be, but a country doctor to families, well, that was a dream he could achieve.

Physicians and students from the wards joined him in the hall, wiping their hands on aprons and nodding to one another in greeting as they made their way toward the midday meal.

"Ho, there, Dr. Flynn!"

Samuel paused and waited for Marcus Hammond to catch up, giving the short, pudgy man a slap to the shoulder.

"A title neither of us has yet to claim, Mr. Hammond." Samuel chuckled.

"But soon enough, my young friend. Soon enough."

Though only twenty-five years to Samuel's twenty, Marcus was not the only medical student or attending physician to make note of Samuel's age.

But though he was younger in years, Samuel did not lack in training. None of the others had toiled at a doctor's side since the time he was old enough to feed and dress himself.

Marcus pushed his round glasses up on his nose. "You've only your final assessments remaining, Samuel. Surely Dr. Porter will sign you into full commission within the month. I'm quite surprised he hasn't already."

Samuel cast a sidelong glance at his friend. The two had entered into their medical studies at Columbian College around the same time and often had found themselves tending the poor on many of the same occasions. They'd settled on a comfortable friendship, at least as much of one as could be had in the little free time afforded to them.

"Let us hope that's true." With any luck, Samuel could complete his studies and return home before the army found a greater need for the infirmary than a few bruised volunteers.

Marcus broke into an excited grin. "Word is we defeated Jackson at Falling Waters."

Samuel had heard the news from a few excited fellows in the east ward. "I hear the cry of 'onward to Richmond' from nearly every window each night on my way home. The people are restless."

"Indeed. It's a grand and noble campaign."

"Noble, most assuredly. Though I still hold the conviction that abolition can be accomplished without bloodshed. It's foolish to think violence will bring about a merciful cause."

"Nothing of greatness is ever accomplished without bloodshed."

Marcus's words wove an odd mix of humor and resignation, and as they rounded a corner, Samuel declined to respond. Regardless of the noblest reasons, war never seemed a grand thing to him. It meant death and suffering. And now it came when he was too near finishing his medical training for him not to become a part of it. Could not the Lord see fit for him to carry out his calling quietly?

Samuel shook depressing thoughts from his mind and took a place at the table. They passed the day's portion of crusty bread, beans, and salt pork. One thing was certain: the charitable ladies of the city only extended their grace to the poor so far, and unless a lady over-prepared for a party and found herself with half-eaten abundance, the meals at the hospital were barely palatable.

"You haven't listened to the first syllable I've uttered, have you?"

Samuel discreetly eyed Marcus. A rounded man with soft features and thick spectacles, he looked the part of the kindly family physician.

Samuel swallowed a bite of tasteless meat. "You were extolling on the specifics of the battle."

Marcus blinked. "Quite right."

Samuel could easily guess the topic even though he hadn't been listening.

"So, then," Marcus prompted, "what do you think?"

Samuel chewed a chunk of dry bread and washed it down with tepid black tea. "What do I think about what?"

Marcus groaned. "I knew it." He stabbed his meat and paused with the morsel halfway to his mouth. "If you ask me, McClellan better start moving. Greeley has the right of it in those headlines. We cannot allow that Confederate congress to take place."

Samuel nodded along. "Surely this rebellion will be quelled within the month." If not, he may not be able to control his condition long enough to receive his physician's title.

"Let us hope that is so," Marcus agreed. "Those arrogant fools need to be put in their place with swift assurance."

After finishing the rest of the meal in companionable silence, Marcus wiped his mouth and rose from the table. Samuel bid him a pleasant afternoon and downed two more pieces of bread to coat his stomach before he quit the dining area and finished his duties of changing bandages, checking the medical supplies, and collecting soiled linens.

Then he turned his attention to the best part of the day.

In the western wing, the sound of childish giggles greeted his ears. While open to the soldiers who found themselves at the hands of unruly Southern sympathizers, the infirmary still maintained its original purpose of caring for unfortunates who did not possess the means to procure medical aid.

The children clustered together in a row of metal cots with threadbare mattresses. They battled various sicknesses, some of which were cured with simple rest and adequate nutrition. He paused at the door for a moment, watching them while they were unaware of his assessment.

One little girl spied him and the volume in the room quickly rose. Samuel's lips curved. Even in their illness, the little ones demonstrated joy.

"Mr. Flynn!" Young Benjamin's pale face split into a wide grin as Samuel neared. "Have you come to give us a tale?"

Samuel drew his brows low in mock seriousness. "I don't know, Benjamin. That depends on if you have minded the sisters today."

The boy made a face and crossed his arms over his gown. "They want me to stay in that bed all day."

Samuel indicated where Benjamin stood with bare feet. "Which is where you should be now."

The boy glanced at the other children currently sharing the space, but they kept their eyes downcast. Benjamin huffed. "A man shouldn't be confined to a bed." His voice rose in indignation. "Nor be forced to wear an infant's gown all day!"

Samuel rubbed his chin, the day's worth of whiskers rough against his fingers. "I'd say you have a point there, sir."

Benjamin beamed. "Then you'll tell them right good, won't you, Mr. Flynn?"

"Well, now, let's see." Samuel tapped a finger on his chin. "A man has certain responsibilities, wouldn't you say?"

Benjamin's forehead creased. "I reckon he does. But what's that got to do with wearing gowns and lying about?"

Samuel ignored the comment and pretended to ponder. "Yes, truly a man has many responsibilities." He fixed the boy with a serious stare. "And what are you responsible for, young man?"

He wrinkled his face. "I ain't but nine." He shrugged. "Least, that's what they say at the orphanage. But I don't believe them."

Samuel didn't allow him to digress. "Well, now, you said a man shouldn't be in bed all day in his gown, didn't you?"

Benjamin drew his eyebrows together but gave a stiff nod. "So?"

"Then we established a man has responsibilities, correct?"

He nodded again, this time more reluctantly.

"So, Benjamin, as a *man*, what responsibilities do *you* have?"

Benjamin glanced at the girl to his left with ashy brown hair and big eyes. "I got to take care of my little sister."

Samuel sank on the bed next to the boy and gripped his bony shoulder. "And if she stays in bed and gets her rest and gets better, what do you think is going to happen?"

Understanding lit his eyes. "Then the nuns are goin' to send her back to the orphanage."

Samuel waited.

"And if they do"—his voice dropped so as not to alarm his sister—"then Emily won't have no one to look after her."

Samuel patted the boy's shoulder. "Like I said, a man has responsibilities. What do you think might be the best course of action so you can be certain you are there to care for her?"

"I got to get better," he said without hesitation.

Samuel rose and turned to the shelf on the opposite wall to reclaim the worn book he'd been reading to the children. "Best you get on that, then."

"Can't *make* it happen," the boy grumbled.

"Perhaps not." Samuel thumbed through the book to his place. "But you can listen to those who have more knowledge about something than you do and follow their advice. A man has no shame in following wise orders and making himself stronger, now does he?"

Benjamin puffed his chest. "No, sir. Ain't no shame in that." With the determination and pompous movements rivaling any soldier drilling in the fields outside the city, the boy marched to his bed and settled himself in it.

The other children pulled their covers about them while Samuel sat and opened to the next chapter. Their excitement settled as Samuel read, his voice rising and falling as he recounted a swashbuckling tale of adventure on the high seas. In those precious moments, they forgot their ailments as their imaginations tasted the salty air and vanquished every foe. And then, all too soon, the chapter came to an end.

"Please, sir, won't you read a bit more?" The soft voice of Benjamin's sickly sister stirred his heart. The little one seldom spoke.

"I wish I could, Emily, but you know the sisters will soon be here to make their rounds, and we don't want to interfere. I think I smelled a tasty stew for tonight."

She looked to her brother, who gave her a brave nod, and then smiled sweetly. "Tomorrow, then."

"Tomorrow." He patted a few heads and ruffled Benjamin's hair before replacing the book and turning to leave.

A soldier stood waiting for him in the doorway, a small fellow with narrow shoulders and facial features a touch too soft for a man. He waited stiffly as Samuel approached, his crisp blue uniform still new. "Are you Mr. Flynn?"

Samuel caught the scent of lye soap and mint. "I am."

"The head physician said to come to you to procure our supply of quinine and calomel."

Samuel stepped past him and motioned for the man to follow him down the hall. "What supply? I already sent the allotment for the military medical staff."

The soldier kept his eyes downcast as though he feared he

might trip in the empty hall. "Dr. Porter said to prepare crates to send with us."

Samuel's skin prickled and he paused. "Crates?"

Now the man looked at him as though he were daft. "Yes. Dr. Porter said you were in charge of counting the supplies and would be the one to prepare the crates."

Samuel resumed walking, leading the way to the supply closets. "Forgive my questioning, Mr...?"

"Frank Thrash. *Private* Frank Thrash."

"Private Thrash, none of the other men who came to supplement their supplies have ever asked for this much medicine at one time. Is there an outbreak among the ranks? Perhaps some of our staff could help."

"No, sir." He leaned closer, his voice dropping to a conspirator's whisper. "The boys are well and hearty and ready to march."

Samuel's pulse quickened as they rounded a bend and came to a stop in front of the supply storage. Fifty thousand men, regulars and volunteers, had converged on the capital, and for nearly two months had trained for something Samuel had continually prayed would not come to pass.

Samuel opened the door and kept his face impassive. "Marching? Part of your drills?"

The soldier straightened to his full height, which fell short of Samuel's by several inches and squared thin shoulders. "We march to Virginia, sir."

Samuel's chest tightened. McDowell would move thousands of unprepared men hot with war fever across the invisible divide that fractured the land. An invisible line that now separated him from his sister Nellie and made her husband an enemy.

Declining a reply, he lifted a crate and ignored the smell of dust, chemicals, and wood shavings. Private Thrash waited in the doorway as Samuel filled it with small paper pouches of calomel. How would those recruits fare once the dysentery came upon them? He'd had a theory for some time that small organisms in the water could make men sick, but no one seemed to give his idea any thought. But then, they couldn't smell the differences in the water as he could. Those green boys would stop at any creek during their long march and scoop up handfuls of tainted water. Then their bowels would revolt.

His face must have settled into a scowl, because the young soldier clapped him on the arm. "Not to worry now, Doc. Our boys will be back soon. Once we take Richmond, this will be over."

Samuel thought to offer a perfunctory smile but found his lips lacked the gumption to do so.

Private Thrash leaned to help him pack the pouches, his clean scent mixing with the stringent smell of the calomel. "Some of the boys are worried this will be finished before they get to see any action. Me, I just want to set things to rights and get home."

Samuel nodded, but he didn't worry the action would be over before the men got to see it. He worried the action would engulf them all, and thousands would descend upon the quiet halls of the Washington Infirmary in a bloody mass of needs he felt ill-prepared to combat.

Three

Martinsburg

*T*he sound intensified, a keening wail that knifed through her very bones and caused them to quiver. All of Evelyn's eighteen years narrowed into sharp focus—a childhood spent in the company of various relatives, followed by years of study at Washington Female College meant to prepare her to be a proper lady fit to run a husband's household. Disjointed memories of an oft-absent father converged upon her senses, pricked with the veiled tolerance of those he'd thrust her upon.

In that moment, when her aunt and cousins' horrified screams pierced through her mental fog and the reality of her actions slammed into her heart, Evelyn knew she would never be the same. The passive girl who'd sought to blend into the walls had shattered when the wolves invaded.

Daddy had been right. She *could* be brave. Now, for once, perhaps she could finally make him proud. She must never again let her guard down, not for an instant, or she would most surely find herself at their mercy. Defiance settled in her chest like a heavy weight. She would accept what came next. They would demand blood for blood.

She was ready.

"Only cowards shoot women." Evelyn flung her arms wide. "Now, shoot!"

She shut her eyes and waited for the pain to come. For cowards they most surely were, fiends who preyed upon helpless women and children under the guise of war.

Lara's whimpers quieted, and in the lull that followed, Evelyn listened to the quick intake of jagged breaths. She opened one eye, and then the other. The brute lay at her feet, alive and clutching his chest. His companions followed her gaze and, in so doing, must have come to their senses as well.

In a sudden surge of awareness, one man shouted orders and another wrenched Aunt Mary's heavy velvet curtain from the window. With it they fashioned a makeshift litter and stretched the cloth underneath the fallen man. They hoisted him from the four corners and then abandoned the house.

Evelyn stood there for moments that seemed to stretch into eternity as she willed her trembling to cease. She'd done it to protect them. If she hadn't acted he would have...

She'd done the right thing. Hadn't she?

She retrieved the weapon from the floor. Evelyn turned to look upon her aunt, who returned her gaze with an odd mixture of horror and appreciation, and then slipped the pistol into her pocket. She drew a long breath and closed her eyes. Let the consequences come. At least her cousin had not suffered a manner of violation that would ruin her.

Arms slipped around her waist and pulled her tight, and Isabella's customary scent of rose water still found its way into Evelyn's nostrils even under the shroud of sweat and fear.

"Thank you, cousin." Isabella clung to her with a fierceness her cool demeanor had never once demonstrated. "He wanted...wanted to..." Her voice dissolved into a sob.

Evelyn returned the unexpected embrace, feeling stronger. "There now. You're all right. We'll be on guard every moment and—"

Lizzy's screech pulled her from her attempts at comfort.

"Mistress! Oh, Mistress, they's goin' to burn the house! They's piling stuff against it!" The maid fanned her face, her wide eyes darting around the room as though at any moment the flames would engulf them.

Evelyn set her teeth and stepped away from Isabella.

"Oh, Mistress! What we goin' do?"

Aunt Mary fanned herself. "Fetch my writing box. I will send immediate word to their commander. Surely such lawlessness will not be tolerated."

Lizzy seemed apprehensive but hurried up the stairs.

Evelyn turned back to Isabella. "Go tell Able to get ready. He'll need to run the message for us post haste."

Isabella blinked rapidly. "What?"

"I said—"

"I know what you said," she snapped, the color in her face returning and making her cheeks a mottled red. "But since when do you think yourself in a position to order me about? It's bad enough you started giving directions to Lizzy."

Evelyn's mouth fell agape. "Now, Isabella, take hold of yourself." Isabella had suffered a shock. She merely unleashed her fear and anger in the wrong direction.

Isabella crossed her arms. "I will not let this madness make you—"

"Enough!"

At Aunt Mary's sharp word, they both quieted.

Aunt Mary rubbed her temples, suddenly seeming much older. "Isabella, this is not the time for this discussion. Your cousin is right. We must have the missive delivered quickly. Hopefully, it will be in time to save our home."

Isabella cast another hard look at Evelyn and strode from the room with a stiff spine. Her cousin acted out of fear and not rational thought. Surely Isabella did not direct the loathing burning in her eyes toward Evelyn. It was meant only for this horrid situation.

"Aunt Mary, I think we should start gathering things and—"

"No!"

Evelyn stared at her, then dared further. "Didn't you hear what she said?" When Aunt Mary didn't respond, Evelyn stepped closer. "We can't stay here. They're going to burn the house."

Aunt Mary lifted her chin, the look in her eyes not unlike what had clouded Isabella's. "I do not expect you to understand, but this house has been in my husband's family for two generations. I'll not abandon it. They simply will not burn a house with ladies inside. We need only to send word to an officer. A gentleman will not stand for this outrage and will come to our aid."

Evelyn snapped her teeth together. They would not burn…? Had her aunt already forgotten what had almost happened to Isabella? Well, if Aunt Mary wished to delude herself into thinking this situation called for customary genteel proprieties, then Evelyn would have to take charge once more.

Without another look at Aunt Mary, Evelyn stepped over the scattered ruins of the front door and out onto the porch. The sea of blue now thinned to a mere trickle, and the few remaining Yanks on the street paid her no heed.

To her left, the Grady's house appeared untouched. Three homes on the other side of the street seemed to have fared no better than Aunt Mary's, broken windows a testament to the army's devastation. Had they chosen randomly, or had they sought out the homes of Southern sympathizers?

She lifted her hand to shield her eyes from the dipping sun and scanned the lawn. No one gathered rushes or limbs. Perhaps Lizzy had been mistaken in a fit of terror.

A scraping sound drew her attention, and Evelyn stepped down and made her way past Aunt Mary's hydrangeas and to the side of the house. There she found two men neatly stacking boughs against the wooden slats of the house.

"Hold!"

The men paused in their foul deed to look up at her for an instant before resuming their task. A fellow with short, dark hair stacked the sticks in his arms against the house and then accepted another from his companion. The second, a man of short stature and an unappealing face, stuffed leaves into the crevices.

Driven by desperation, Evelyn lifted her wide skirts and stomped her way across the lawn. "Did you not hear? Stop this madness at once!"

The taller one narrowed his eyes. "You must be the one who shot him."

Forcing her tongue to work against the dryness in her mouth, Evelyn spoke calmly. "And I suppose I was to stand idly by while a robber disguised as a soldier sought inexcusable liberties with my cousin?"

To their credit, they had the manners to appear embarrassed. The dark-haired one stared at the ground while the other looked everywhere but at her.

She flung her arm wide. "Is this what we can expect from the Federal Army? Marauders who ravish and burn helpless women?"

The short one blanched. "Miss! We are not—"

"Not what?" Her words came out in clipped measure. "You are not wanton men who, upon not being satisfied with their victory on the battlefield, then decided to burn the homes of defenseless women and children?"

The taller one frowned and Evelyn stepped closer, the burning in her blood scalding away her fear. "Blackguards!"

He snarled and turned to resume his task, slinging another stick against the house with a solid crack.

Slowly, she pulled the pistol free from her dress and lifted it. "As you already know, I'm capable of using this."

The men stilled. Evelyn lifted the gun higher, not sure now what she planned to do with it. Shooting one man had been little more than a frantic mistake. What would Daddy say if he saw her like this? Would he be horrified? Or pleased she'd learned something from his lesson?

The gun wavered in her hand, and she used the other to brace it. What if they both lunged at her instead of running away? She'd have to shoot the tall one first. Perhaps in the knee. She didn't want to kill him. Her gaze drifted to the other man. If the first one fell, she might have a better chance staving off the second one. With his porcine face and shifty eyes, she doubted he would pose as much of a threat.

The short one's gaze suddenly darted away from the pistol and over Evelyn's shoulder.

Before she could turn to see, something slammed into her. The pistol flew from her grasp, and she struck the ground with a crunching sound she hoped only came from the boning in her skirts. She tried to expand her protesting ribs, but a heavy weight landed on top of her, grinding her face into the dirt.

She struggled but could not dislodge it. Raw panic surged. Evelyn found her breath and screamed.

Her attacker grunted and rolled off, allowing the boning in her skirts to spring free, exposing everything beneath them to anyone who stood behind. Mortified at her indignity, Evelyn scrambled to her knees to hide herself beneath the spread of fabric. Her breathing came so rapidly she felt dizzy. She forced herself to calm. She could not succumb to flutters and leave herself helpless.

Her gaze darted across the grass. The miscreant who'd fallen on her rolled to his knees and scooped her pocket pistol from the ground. He smothered its pearl handle beneath his meaty paw and cast her a crooked grin. She summoned her anger and fanned its flame, finding its heat preferable to the bitter cold of terror. She glared at him.

"Much obliged," the short man with the pudgy face said, running a hand across the back of his neck. "We appreciate you not letting her shoot us."

Evelyn remained still as the men stared at one another and then down at her. What would they do now?

The man holding her uncle's pistol rose and tucked the weapon under his belt. "I happened to be passing by and saw her take aim." He shook his head as though he were sorely ashamed. "These rebel women have been giving us all kinds of trouble."

Evelyn produced a most unladylike snort, and their attention shifted to her once more. "And what, sir, do you think your northern women would do if their homes were invaded and all manner of outrage was sought against them?"

The man tipped his cap back and studied her, then shrugged. "Probably not leap to shooting."

Evelyn scoffed at his idiocy. "No appeal to a gentlemanly nature was heeded. Words not even a fallen woman should hear were showered upon the innocent. Then those men sought to commit the most horrendous of crimes against women. Surely you can see how any woman could become distraught under such circumstances."

His gaze held not the first touch of sympathy, nor did any of them show proper shame at having a lady at his feet. None had offered to help her up. Defeated, she wrapped her arms around her middle and lowered her head. Perhaps she could at least distract them long enough to keep them from burning the house while Aunt Mary sent a missive.

Though, if the men she'd thus far encountered were indicative of the whole of the army, she doubted the officer in charge of this chaos would offer much aid. She sat there for some time while the sun sank, sending the final rays of dusk to creep across the lawn and dip her farther into shadows.

The men exchanged names and company information, blessedly ignoring both her and the house. Evelyn tried to remain as still as possible so as not to garner their attention, but her petticoats and underpinnings were damp and her knees ached from being held beneath her. She shifted slightly and dared a glance up at them, but the men had fallen into some lively conversation and paid her no attention. Perhaps she could stretch her legs out...

"What's the meaning of this?"

A booming voice cut through the men's laughter, and immediately the three soldiers snapped their heels together and drew up tall. Evelyn turned to see a distinguished man stalk into the yard. She let her gaze drift from the newcomer's polished boots, up his stark blue pants, over a belted jacket, and finally to a staunch, stern face with a refined nose and neatly combed hair.

Had he come in response to Aunt Mary's missive?

He returned her gaze. "I received a report that a lady of this house shot Private Meadows."

Her insides twisted. Of course he hadn't come to save the house. He'd come to arrest her. Choosing her words carefully, as they would surely decide her fate, Evelyn gave a solemn nod. "I felt it was the only course of action that would keep him from..." Her voice hitched. She cleared her throat. "Sir, your men broke down our door, spoke rude remarks and threatened a huddle of frightened women, and then that man who was shot, your Private Meadows, put his hands upon my cousin and sought to ruin her."

The man's face contorted, and he looked sharply at the men behind her. "And these men were present during this offense?"

"No, sir. These are the men who arrived just after and conspired to burn the house."

"Jones!" the man roared, not removing his steely gaze from the stony men.

Another soldier jogged around the side of the house and snapped his hand up to his face before standing at attention. "Yes, sir?"

"Remove these soldiers and have them await my instruction."

"Yes, sir!"

Evelyn watched in disbelief as the officer called for other soldiers and more men in blue swarmed about the house. They dispersed from the yard with the offenders in tow, the one who'd knocked her to the ground complaining he hadn't been trying to burn anything.

When they were gone, the officer extended his hand.

"I'm afraid, sir, that it will take more assistance to remove me from the ground." Her cheeks warmed. "I cannot get myself righted in my hooped skirts, and some of the feeling has gone from my feet."

Compassion sprang to his eyes, and with as much dignity as possible for such a humiliation, he reached under her arms and lifted her to her feet. She found it necessary to cling to him for a moment until she thought she could stand on her own, and then stepped away.

"I thank you, sir. Both for your assistance and for taking

31

those men away."

He offered his arm. "If you will come inside, miss...?

"Mapleton."

"I have some questions for you."

Evelyn allowed him to guide her back into the house, where her aunt and cousins sat nervously in the parlor. What had they been doing all this time while Evelyn sat on the lawn? Aunt Mary's eyes widened as Evelyn entered on the officer's arm, but Isabella kept her gaze trained on the carpets. Little Lara clutched a rag doll to her chest and stared at Evelyn in horror.

"Ladies," the officer said, removing his arm from Evelyn's grasp and indicating she should select a seat. "I'm General Patterson. It's my understanding that an unfortunate event occurred with some of my men, resulting in the wounding of Private Fredrick Meadows."

Wounded? Evelyn's heart fluttered. She hadn't killed him?

As though sensing her question, General Patterson sought her gaze. "The bullet landed in his shoulder, and the surgeons are tending it. If gangrene doesn't take him, he should survive."

More relief than she should feel for the rapscallion flooded her heart.

"Now, madam," he said, indicating that Aunt Mary should rise. "Would you recount the events that occurred?"

Aunt Mary fiddled with the brooch at her throat as she told the ghastly tale. When she'd finished, he posed the same question to Isabella.

Isabella's eyes filled with tears. "It's as Mother said. That horrible man and his fellows spoke to us in a most crude manner, and then he put himself upon my person with the intent to ruin me."

"Forgive me, but, how exactly do you know that was his intention?"

Isabella's face crumpled, and she turned away.

"He wrapped his arms around her," Evelyn interjected, "hauled her against his body, and was in the midst of attempting to put his mouth upon hers when I called out for him to stop."

The general gave a small nod. "You warned him you would shoot?"

"I told him to stop and had my gun aimed at him. I'm rather certain he understood my meaning."

"Yet, you shot him anyway."

A surge of fear swelled, but she forced it down. "He had the audacity to grin at me, and then tried to proceed with his vile intent despite my warning. So, yes, I shot him."

General Patterson studied her for so long that Evelyn had to bolster every smidgen of her courage not to wither under his gaze. "Given your reasoning," he finally said, "I shall declare this a closed matter."

Her breath left her lungs in a wave of relief.

The general tugged his wide brimmed hat down upon his head. "And to be certain that such an event does not occur again,"—he sought and held Evelyn's gaze—"I will place sentries about the house for your...security."

His words indicated protection, but his tone seemed to hold another meaning. Evelyn frowned, though Aunt Mary did not seem concerned.

He quickly turned on his heel and left them in the stunned wake of his declaration. Evelyn rose and watched him gather his men and exit through the gaping wound that had once been the door. He shouted orders and two men in blue positioned themselves at the base of the porch.

General Patterson addressed his men, though his eyes

rested on Evelyn. "Be sure to escort Miss Mapleton at any time she needs to leave home. We wouldn't want harm to come to anyone."

His meaning clutched her stomach like iron bands. She would not be arrested, but neither would she be free.

She stood on the porch and watched him leave. Then, accepting defeat, she turned back into the house.

It would seem she'd just become a prisoner.

Martinsburg
July 14, 1861

*F*aint wisps of music wafted on the evening breeze, so bright and cheery they tempted Evelyn's foot to tap. She rose from her writing desk, the early evening shadows making her lines of script harder to see. Leaving it for later, she moved to her bedroom window, where the air felt laden with moisture and the gentle breeze seemed weighted in its effort to lift the edges of her curtain.

Voices mingled with the chords of a pianoforte, and somewhere nearby a mockingbird trilled. Evelyn leaned against the window frame and watched the street below. It almost seemed like a normal evening, where people laughed and collected in groups that would soon visit the Grady house for a time of fellowship and dancing.

If she wanted, Evelyn could pretend all was well. She could join Aunt Mary and Isabella's charade and merely act as if life had returned to a semblance of normalcy. And, in a sense, perhaps it had. Since Patterson had set his guards, life had settled into a strained lull. One where people tried to forget their worries and sorrows in the haze of company, music, and dance.

But all had changed for her. She could not return to the timid girl she'd been. She'd protected Isabella, but her aunt and cousin still seemed displeased with her every word and action. Would not even her courage esteem her in their eyes?

Though, to be fair, she'd also caused their enemies to take up residence on the property. Evelyn watched people gather below, the increasing feeling of restlessness plucking at her.

Perhaps if she could do something to help a cause she'd previously not taken up, all would be forgiven. She plucked at the curtain. But had she not fully taken their side, a side which Isabella had denied, when she'd shot that soldier? It seemed that, too, had not been enough.

Though she'd discounted the reports in Daddy's increasingly infrequent letters, it seemed he'd been right about the Yankees.

She brightened. Why worry over her aunt and cousin? Was not her true place at her father's side now that she was a woman? If she proved her dedication to Daddy's cause, would he see her as a woman who could aid him rather than a child to be handed off to others to rear?

Evelyn watched the Yankees below as a trumpet cast bright tunes into the humid air. Wicked beings, Daddy had warned, with their unjust taxes and selfish constraints on sovereign states.

Her anger stirred. Their march into Martinsburg proved it true. Naught but a barrage of useless scoundrels who wouldn't be satisfied until they had pillaged, plundered, and otherwise squeezed the life out of them all. And not on the battlefield, but here in their very homes.

These same men who had swarmed their streets and broken into homes and businesses now strutted about like invited company down for a cordial visit rather than devils the residents should seek to oust with both prayers and prodding.

The music grew louder, and the conquerors would soon enjoy their dancing next door at the Grady house the same as they'd done the three nights prior. Merely ten days of occupation, and Martinsburg seemed to have forgotten the fear it had felt when the army marched in. Businesses had reopened, and from what Isabella said, were glad to receive Federal silver and gold instead of Southern shinplasters.

The stars and stripes hung from windows in the square, and Federal sympathizers openly boasted as though they'd forgotten Martinsburg hung in a precarious position. Evelyn watched the soldiers for a few more moments and then turned from the window to light a lantern. Resting it on her desk, she set about twisting and pinning her dark locks into an intricate style.

If the Blues were going to frolic, then by goodness, she would make use of it. Wouldn't her father be surprised when she sent him information for his news reports?

She donned a set of silver earbobs and clipped her mother's pearl necklace around her throat. Evelyn studied herself in the mirror, turning to the left and right. Perhaps a little more...

She allowed the drape of her rose gown to slip down to the edge of her shoulders, careful that she displayed only enough creamy skin to intrigue, not entice. As a final touch, she slipped a flower into her waves of hair and turned from the mirror.

Her writing desk held the letter she'd thrice tried to compose to inform Daddy of her situation. Perhaps after this evening, she'd have something he'd relish knowing. And even if she gathered nothing of import, he'd surely be proud to know she did not cower.

She slipped a pair of gloves over her fingers and stepped

out into the hallway. Though Evelyn closed her door with a soft click, Isabella's own door across the hall immediately flew open.

Her cousin stepped out, narrowing her eyes. "Where are you going?"

Evelyn tried to step around her. "To the party."

Isabella grasped her elbow, her nails digging into Evelyn's skin. "Are you mad? What will Mother think?"

She pried her cousin's hand away and tried to keep bitterness out of her tone. Did they not see that her care for her family was exactly what had driven her to this? "I *am* thinking of her. And you, for that matter."

Isabella rolled her eyes. "By making yourself a fast girl with the Yankees?"

Heat crept up her neck and warmed her ears. "Isabella!"

She folded her arms over her silk day gown. Then she lowered her voice. "Evie," she drawled, using a pet name Evelyn hadn't heard since childhood. "You know what those brutes will try even if a lady doesn't give them the first nip of encouragement."

Evelyn's throat tightened.

"So," Isabella said, her voice strained, "what do you think is going to happen with you going over there dressed like that?"

Evelyn studied the concern in her cousin's eyes, warmed by the notion that Isabella was worried over her safety. "I do appreciate your concern, but—"

Isabella's eyes turned icy again. "But nothing. You will *not* earn such a reputation while you are staying here." She jutted her chin. "You going to dance with the blue bellies is unseemly and will reflect poorly on me. No Southern gentleman of good standing is going to want to take on the scandal you are placing on my family. Can't you see that?"

Scandal? Evelyn pressed her lips into a tight line and refused to comment. Isabella stared at her for several moments, the spark in her eyes growing sharper with each breath Evelyn took. Still, she stood there, wondering exactly what Isabella would do if she continued to defy her. She held her cousin's gaze, no longer feeling like the inferior girl who should lower her eyes and meekly do as she was told. No, that girl had been lost with the crack of the revolver and the unrelenting truth of what she was capable of.

Finally, however, Evelyn inclined her head, and tension slid off Isabella. She kept her voice serene. "It's not my intention to cause you any distress, though I find your concerns unwarranted. I'm only trying to find a way to aid our boys in gray."

Confusion turned Isabella's icy eyes to a stormy blue. "By dancing? Mother and I are working on organizing a supply collection. It's a terrible bother, but—"

Evelyn patted her arm. "There, see? You do your part, and I'll do mine by sending Daddy any information he can use."

Isabella started to relax, then stiffened again as words Evelyn should not have spoken sprang free. "Don't worry, this invasion will soon be over and you can go back to your parties and fripperies."

Isabella blinked rapidly. "What did you say?"

Evelyn hurried to undo what Isabella would rightly deem an insult. "We were discussing how we are all trying to quickly see this invasion ended so we could return to normal life."

Isabella started to nod, and then paused and narrowed her eyes. "When did you become so slippery?"

"Slippery?"

Isabella pointed a finger in her face. "Avoiding answering me and slipping other items of discussion into the conversation to distract from its true intent."

Perhaps if her cousin had ever truly taken the time to know her, Isabella would not have asked such a question. Pushing down the rather hostile thought, Evelyn tried a smile instead. "Again, you misread my intentions. I didn't mean to confuse you."

Isabella scrunched up her face, her beautiful features twisted into an unattractive scowl. Then she spun around and stomped into her room, slamming the door for good measure.

Evelyn stared at the door for a few heartbeats, surprised not only at her cousin's actions but her own as well. Had the threats around them turned them both into people they were not, or had it merely peeled back the layers of carefully crafted mannerisms to reveal the truth underneath?

A question for another time. She slipped down the stairs unnoticed, and then out into the heavy evening air.

She made it down the porch and part way across the lawn before one of the sentries appeared at her side. "Good evening, Miss Mapleton."

The sight of the man's easy smile turned her stomach against the deception she would work, but she reminded herself it must be done and plastered on a smile of her own. "Why, good evening, Private."

He tipped his bearded chin toward the Grady house, which glowed with cheerful candlelight. "Going to call?"

"I thought on it. It's rather lonesome sitting at home all day."

He laughed. "I'm sure."

Evelyn slowed her steps to more easily allow him to take

her side as he was commanded to do. Though he but obeyed orders, being followed about like a toddler with her nanny grated. "But I'm sure you know all about that. Seeing as how you are stuck here with me."

A guarded expression had his features tightening, so she produced the practiced laugh a lady used when she needed to charm her company. "Oh, I cannot tell you what a relief it is to know we can yet frolic despite this unfortunate division. I should thank you for your escort, even though you do not freely give it."

His shoulders lowered slightly, and she watched him from the corner of her eye as they slowly ambled down the walk.

After a moment, the lines around his eyes crinkled with a smile. "It's my pleasure, miss, orders or no. Though you truly have naught to fear. The citizenship has prospered under our protection and I believe the danger of rebel uprising has passed."

Evelyn bristled under his poor choice of words, seeing as it was his fellows that had raided homes, but kept her expression serene. "Indeed. Tell me, are you lonesome, Private Harrison, this far away from home?"

He offered his arm to escort her through the gate and onto the street, and she let her gloved fingers slide onto his sleeve with the lightest touch possible.

"It's only for a short while."

"Still, I know your ladies at home must miss you terribly."

Private Harrison chuckled but gave no other reply.

Evelyn grappled for a topic of polite conversation. "How do your boys fare over at Rich Mountain?"

He seemed more comfortable with a less personal topic, which suited Evelyn perfectly. "Well and good," he said, lifting a hand in greeting to another soldier as they passed. "Restless, I hear, but that's the way of it."

"I can imagine four thousand men sitting about camp would grow rather restless."

"And that much more for the *seven* thousand there."

Evelyn withheld a gasp. Seven thousand! Three thousand more than the rumors stated. This could be information her father would covet. But was it true or merely an exaggeration on the soldier's part? She produced a fan and waved it at him playfully. "Oh, come now, no need to embellish the numbers to one little lady."

He steered her toward the neighbor's gate, where two lanterns hung from posts like oversized fireflies. "You wound my pride, Miss Mapleton. The numbers are true."

She tucked the information away. Not wanting to rouse his suspicions so that he could be lulled into saying more another time, Evelyn gave a little shrug. "Oh, very well, but let us discuss something more interesting. Do you suppose someone will play the fiddle this eve? I've always adored the fiddle."

The lanky fellow gave a wide grin, and if not for the fact that he kept ranks with rapscallions, might have been considered handsome. "If they do, will you promise me a dance?"

Evelyn made a show of a loud sigh. "Perhaps I may consider it, if you promise not to dog every step I take." She pointed her fan at him. "It makes it difficult to enjoy a moment of pleasantness with other ladies when there are men so closely about."

He gave a small bow. "Certainly, Miss Mapleton. I will see to your safety from a distance, so as not to disturb your feminine discussions."

"Why, Private Harrison, you may be becoming my favorite sentry."

He grinned and handed her up the steps. "Here we are. I'm going to have a cigar on the porch with the lads while you enjoy your female company. Then I hope for that dance."

She snapped open her fan and looked at him over the top. "And you shall have it."

She ducked into the crowded house before he could say anything more and let the mask of a giggly girl slide from her features. Mrs. Grady had not invited Evelyn's family to an event since Uncle Phillip and Paul had joined the Confederate Army. Would she make a scene when she saw Evelyn here?

She walked slowly along the foyer wall, giving little notice to the fine molding and glittering chandelier as she made her way deeper into the house. Perhaps this was a foolish idea.

Isabella was probably right. What useful information could possibly be worth the risk of their neighbor's wrath? Despite being on opposing sides of a war, Aunt Mary would be furious if Evelyn stirred Mrs. Grady's ire. The lady was too prominent in society.

The woman's voice carried down the hall, and Evelyn's pulse quickened. She should duck inside the library and wait until her neighbor passed, then hurry out.

She slipped through the doorway into the room where several soldiers gathered in groups in front of floor-to-ceiling bookshelves talking and puffing pipes or cigars. A few of the Federalist women moved about, giving her the confidence to scurry farther inside. She stepped behind one group of older gentlemen, officers by the looks of them, and perused the

43

books on the shelf.

"And then Lincoln told him the Rebs were green, too," one of the officers said, the cigar in his mouth muffling some of his words.

"All those volunteer boys are green. Complaining about blisters from their boots and pestering one another about when they will get to see more action."

Evelyn ran her finger across the leather spine of a book, trying not to seem out of place.

"Green or not, that Congress cannot be held."

She filtered through the information in her head. The Provisional Congress would be held on the twentieth of this month. It would be the first time it would take place in the new nation's capital of Richmond.

One of the other men spoke, but his words were lost under the hum of guests and the jaunty tunes of the twenty-first Pennsylvania's regimental band.

Curious, Evelyn started to step closer when a feminine voice stilled her and sent a shiver of dread down her spine.

"Why, Miss Mapleton, what a pleasant surprise to find you in my home."

Evelyn fashioned a honeyed smile upon her lips as she turned. "Mrs. Grady! Forgive me for not seeking you out sooner. I have only just arrived and found myself distracted by your books. I've read all of mine, you see, and well…" Her words trailed off as the hostess eyed her.

Evelyn found her fan and waved it in front of her heated cheeks. "I hope you'll forgive my intrusion. I could not resist the music."

The slender woman smiled, but Evelyn couldn't tell if it was genuine. "Of course, dear. I'm sure any young lady would tire of being sequestered at home."

"Yes, ma'am." Evelyn did her best to remain still, unsure what she should say to the hostess who had not invited her into the house.

Gracious lady that she was, Mrs. Grady gave a small nod. "Well, it's good that you came. Now you can see that what happened at your aunt's home was not indicative of our boys." She patted a gloved hand against her perfectly styled hair, only a few strands of silver giving away her age.

"Yes, ma'am. I've found those posted outside my door to be friendly." The truth. Though what that meant in light of Daddy's declarations she couldn't be sure.

Mrs. Grady offered a bright, if somewhat oddly triumphant, smile and cupped Evelyn's elbow. "How about you come join the ladies in the drawing room? My daughter is about to entertain us while the men enjoy their tobacco. Then, we'll have desserts and dancing. Won't that be lovely?"

Evelyn followed the woman away from the bookshelf, relieved she hadn't disgraced her aunt by being ordered out. "Yes, ma'am. That sounds simply delightful."

Mrs. Grady did not let go of Evelyn's arm until she had her securely seated in the drawing room, and then glided away to speak with her guests.

Feeling out of place, though that wasn't unusual, Evelyn settled into the plush chair and waited for Miss Grady to entertain them. The space was filled with handsome furniture and gilded frames that boasted the family's ample means. Floral paper graced every wall all the way up to the thick, carved molding where the walls met the ceiling. Overhead, a chandelier dripping with crystals bounced light from dozens of tapered candles.

Evelyn listened as the ladies around her twittered, none of them seeming to have noticed her presence.

Stephenia H. McGee

"Oh, have you seen Miss Simpson's new gown? Why, what *was* her mother thinking?" one dour woman said, clicking her tongue.

"Then you add a pinch of grated cinnamon before you bake it," said a woman to her left.

"Well, I heard that as soon as he returns, Michael Banks is going to declare himself for Sara. You wait and see."

Evelyn toyed with the fringe on her skirt, for the first time realizing that she'd listened in on people who took little notice of her for most of her life. Perhaps she truly would make for a good partner for Daddy. People said all kinds of things in the presence of one of no consequence. Could that be true of newsworthy things as well?

A few moments later, the women quieted as Miss Grady began to sing. Evelyn supposed she had a pleasant voice, but she wouldn't be starring in any opera houses.

While the others listened with rapt attention, Evelyn let her gaze drift around the room, flitting from face to face like a restless butterfly. Did any of the women here hold Southern sympathies? Impossible to tell. How did one know whom to call enemy when they all just looked like neighbors?

Daddy had said not to be fooled. Those radical people believed the Northern siege on Southern raw goods in order to make New England factories more profitable was of little consequence.

The singing finished and sweets were served. The time came for dancing. It took but a shy lift of her gaze, and two men immediately scrambled in front of her to ask for a turn around the floor. Without Isabella's beauty to overshadow her, she may actually have an abundance of dance partners. Evelyn smiled and allowed the first fellow to take her hand.

He spun her around the dance floor, and by the time she

finished twirling with him and then three others, she could almost forget these same men in blue could also be wolves.

Breathless, she was about to declare she required a rest when Private Harrison strode from the crowd.

"My dance, Miss Mapleton?" He gave a small bow.

Evelyn fanned herself. "Oh, I wondered if you would come. I fear I have grown quite wearied."

"Not too wearied for one final dance, I hope?"

"Only one."

He laughed and took her hand, guiding her out into the middle of the dance floor as the band struck up a waltz. He settled his hand on her lower back, and she touched her palm to his. They flowed through the box pattern she'd learned at the female college.

"Well, now, let's see. What topic of discussion will interest you, Miss Mapleton?"

Evelyn gave him a mischievous smile. "I'm interested in politics."

He moved her back and forth, his steps sure. "Not a normal area of concern for a woman."

"Perhaps not. But when one's father is a newspaper man, a lady could find herself more interested in the topic."

"Are you close with your father?"

The unexpected question brought a sting of tears to her eyes, and she had to blink them away.

"I apologize," Private Harrison said quickly. "I did not mean to be too personal."

Evelyn shook her head. "No, it's quite all right. I simply wish this fighting was over and I could join him as planned."

He spun her around and then settled back into step. "Not to worry. We will crush Richmond before they can hold their congress, and that will be the end of it."

Evelyn let a bemused smile turn her lips. "With the way things look, I fear that is naught but wishful thinking."

"It is not!" He barked his defense, his eyes sharpening. "Lincoln has ordered McDowell to move out of Washington."

She studied the young man in front of her, wondering if the information he gave was of any importance. Surely if a private knew these things, then Confederate officers did as well. Finally she opted for a tip of her head, and he relaxed once more.

The song ended and he escorted her through the house where she bade Mrs. Grady a good evening. Outside, the warm July night came alive with the sounds of crickets and frogs. Evelyn studied the stars glittering overhead. Oh, to live in such oblivion to the heartache of mankind.

As though sensing her melancholy thoughts, Private Harrison remained blissfully quiet until he brought her to her door.

"I thank you for the dance." He doffed his hat. "And I do hope that you will get to see your father soon."

Even though he wore colors that made him her father's enemy, Evelyn gave him a genuine smile. "I thank you. Good evening."

He returned the pleasantry, then slipped down the porch steps. Evelyn let herself inside and made her way up the dark stairs and into her room, her feet tired and her heart burdened.

She settled at her desk and stared at her missive. Should she tell Daddy what she learned? Or should she merely be honest with him that she felt unwanted and unloved at her aunt's house and beg him to fetch her?

The idea tempted, but it would be ungrateful of her and

only cause Daddy further distress. Sighing, she blew out her candle and prayed she'd find a way to be more to her family than an unwanted burden.

Five

July 16, 1861

The last of the ladies' trunks slid into place on the back of the carriage two days later. Evelyn waved her fan in front of her sweat-glistened face and avoided looking at her cousin. Where her relationship with her aunt and cousin had been pulled taut, it now felt close to rupturing.

"I suppose you will miss all your suitors." Isabella's bitter tone sliced through the sounds of the carriage's rattling tack and the horses' stamping hooves and jabbed her tender emotions.

Aunt Mary had been furious when Isabella told her Evelyn had gone to the Gradys' party, and her aunt had declared Evelyn was forbidden to leave the house.

But then without much warning, Patterson suddenly pulled his men from Martinsburg, leaving only the First Pennsylvania to maintain order. With the removal of the sentries from the house, Aunt Mary immediately announced they would be leaving to visit relatives in Front Royal, inadvertently relieving Evelyn of her imprisonment, if not the shroud of their disapproval.

Evelyn let her eyelids droop along with her shoulders.

"Why must you hate me so?"

Isabella mumbled something indecipherable but decidedly snide. Her fresh scent of rosewater drifted on the breeze, an inviting smell quite contrary to the razor-sharp pickets that had been erected between them.

"Hate you?" Isabella snapped open an ivory-handled fan and drew Evelyn's gaze. Her eyes were pools of ice under drapes of honey-colored eyebrows. "Really, Evelyn. What a ridiculous thing to say."

Evelyn studied her cousin, resplendent in her plain cobalt traveling gown. "By what other word would you name this bitterness?" The words popped out of her mouth as though of their own accord, and Evelyn seamed her lips lest they seek further damages.

"You are impossible." Isabella rolled her eyes over the lacy tips of her fan. "I know you are selfish, as your actions clearly show, but I didn't realize you were hampered by dull wits as well."

A sharp prick pinched somewhere deep within her, and Evelyn could only stare at the young woman who was not simply family, but one with whom she had once longed to share a deep friendship. What had happened in the years since their girlhood?

"You truly don't see it, do you?" Isabella's shoulders slumped, much of the haughtiness slipping from her like a borrowed cloak. "I really shouldn't expect so much of you. Even though you were allowed to attend schooling with me, your breeding doesn't hold up to the expectations this family is under. I shouldn't blame you for something you have no control over."

Had Isabella apologized and insulted her in a single breath?

"However." Icicle eyes probed her, and Isabella seemed

to draw her superiority around her once more. "Your actions have brought us to a head. Your shameless flaunting with the enemy *must* come to an end. Whatever it is you are doing that you think is helping, I assure you it is not. You are doing nothing but hurting this family." She softened and offered a slight curve of her lips, though Evelyn had begun to suspect these fleeting glimpses of tenderness were pure fabrication. "Please, Evie, do try to understand this has dire effects on mine and Lara's futures. This sort of behavior cannot continue when we reach Front Royal. I simply could not bear it."

The rustle of Aunt Mary's skirts indicated she'd joined them behind the carriage. "Yes. It is past time we had this discussion, I'm afraid."

Aunt Mary regarded Evelyn with a mixture of reprimand and sorrow. It was the disappointment, rather than the reproof, that felt like a brander's iron.

"Forgive me, my dear." Aunt Mary took Evelyn's hand and squeezed it. "The traumas that befell us seem to have affected us each in different ways. I'm guilty of hiding away, refusing to see that the world of my youth no longer exists." She released Evelyn's hand and gestured toward her elder daughter. "Isabella has let her fear over an uncertain future turn her inside out, and even Lara has withdrawn into herself."

The sudden gentleness of her aunt's tone released a well within her, and it surged up to leak out of her eyes.

"I know that you are adrift," Aunt Mary continued, the motherly tone one Evelyn had once longed for. "Your mother is gone, and my brother, God bless him, did the best he could with you. We have tried to give you the same advantages as Isabella, but I fear your"—she hesitated and then waved a hand—"your upbringing may have hampered those attempts."

Evelyn clenched her teeth, not sure if her aunt truly meant comfort or not. The woman had a way of wrapping insults in velvet and serving them on a silver platter.

"So," Aunt Mary said when Evelyn offered no response, "I have realized that the subtleties of our station are often out of your grasp. Therefore, as a kindness to you, I will speak frankly."

Evelyn ran a dry tongue over her lips.

Aunt Mary straightened herself, looking not unlike an officer about to deliver orders to his men. "Holding friendly conversations with lowly soldiers is unseemly. Attending parties you were not invited to shows low breeding. For heaven's sake, Evelyn, you are gaining a reputation. Now, you may not have a care for your own reputation, but reputation may be all Isabella and Lara have left. When this nasty war is finished, and let us pray it is before we are reduced to poverty or worse, then a pristine reputation may be all my daughters have to secure their futures." Her blue eyes glistened. "Please, tell me you understand this."

Guilt stabbed her heart. Had she been consumed with trying to do something, anything, to help that she had put those she loved at risk? Evelyn drew a breath that seemed to hitch like wheels over rough cobblestone. "Forgive me. I never intended to cause you any distress. You and Uncle Phillip have done much for me. I only wanted to do something to help."

Isabella placed a hand on Evelyn's shoulder. "We are but women. It is not for us to dabble in these things."

Evelyn slumped, her attempt at perfect posture forgotten. "But surely we cannot sit by and do nothing while the men in our family risk their lives."

"And we will not." Aunt Mary gestured to the carriage,

which waited on their pleasure as the driver patiently stood by the door pretending not to listen to their conversation. "We're going to my husband's family in Front Royal and will be of use there."

Evelyn tilted her head. "What use?"

Aunt Mary waved the question away like a pesky mosquito. "We will find something of value to occupy us, I'm sure." She pinned Evelyn with a sharp gaze. "Something that does not involve inappropriate relations with strange men. Do I make myself clear?"

"Yes, Aunt. Abundantly."

Aunt Mary smiled as though the matter were settled, but deep within Evelyn's churning heart, it felt anything but.

"Good. Then it's past time to be on our way."

Aunt Mary called into the house for Lizzy to bring Lara out, and the child quietly clutched her doll and gained her mother's side while Aunt Mary once again relayed instructions to the servant for the care of the house during their absence.

Then, in a flutter of skirts and petticoats, Aunt Mary, Isabella, and Lara were situated in the carriage. Evelyn hesitated. Her father had told her not to travel, and with the coldness her family had shown her, she wasn't all that interested in being locked inside the carriage with them.

"Evelyn!"

Aunt Mary's clipped use of her name had her scrambling inside without the driver's assistance. She plopped onto the plush seat as he closed the door behind her.

They clattered down the cobbled streets along with several other conveyances that Evelyn suspected were also filled with people hoping to move farther away from Federal control. A burr of worry wriggled under her skin until she could no longer contain it.

"Aunt Mary?"

Her aunt turned from the window, her smooth features and perfect hair a testament to the breeding she claimed was better than Evelyn's own. How that was possible when Aunt Mary and Daddy shared the same blood and Mother had been a lady of quality, Evelyn didn't know.

"Yes?"

"Daddy did not wish for me to travel because he said the warring states would make passage dangerous—"

"Worry not," Aunt Mary replied, dismissing the question. "We will be safe."

Evelyn said no more, wondering which of them would prove correct. For the sake of her raw nerves, she hoped Aunt Mary was right.

Travel proved far easier than she'd expected, and the farther they journeyed from Martinsburg, the more Evelyn decided Daddy had been overly cautious. By the time they'd traveled the forty miles to Front Royal, she was sure of it.

Front Royal extended past the carriage windows in a most picturesque village, nestled snuggly between the surrounding mountains like a young bird in its nest. They clattered to a stop in front of the Fishback Hotel, where they were immediately greeted by a young man in a pressed suit.

"Mrs. Lawrence," he said, extending his hand to Aunt Mary to assist her from the carriage, "I have been instructed to see you and the ladies to the cottage in the rear. You will be more comfortable there."

Aunt Mary stepped down with the lightest touch upon his hand as possible. "Thank you. And where is my husband's brother?" She glanced around, obviously expecting they should be greeted by someone of greater importance than a rather willowy-looking employee. From her place in the carriage, Evelyn had a better view of the young man than she did of her aunt, but she didn't have to spend much imagination to picture the look that graced Aunt Mary's features.

The young man offered something by way of an excuse and then helped Isabella, Lara, and Evelyn down in turn before clasping his hands behind his back. He had a friendly, open face that was neither plain nor handsome, and Evelyn thought him rather pleasant. Especially since Aunt Mary was now glowering at him.

He offered her a smile all the same and lifted his hand toward a small pathway that led behind the large whitewashed inn. "Mr. and Mrs. Lawrence are preparing for your arrival. If you will please follow me, we will see that your trunks are delivered to your rooms posthaste."

They followed him around the building, the sounds of rumbling carriages, nickering horses, and laughing children fading as they stepped behind the hotel and through a small garden. Fresh blooms in an array of whites, pinks, and reds fragranced the air with sweet scents that added to the pleasant nature of the carefully tended area. Evelyn filled her lungs, and her shoulders relaxed.

It would be good to be away from Martinsburg for a time.

Evelyn lifted her gaze to the unadorned building that would serve as their temporary home. Slats of wood coated in white paint formed a flat, rectangular structure with a squat roof and not the first shingle of porch for protection from the rain. Windows, delicate curtains flitting in the breeze, dotted the front of the structure on both floors.

Cozy, if not noteworthy.

The blue door, which matched the shutters flanking the windows, opened, and a heavyset woman stepped out into the late afternoon sun. She held up a pale hand to shield her eyes from the light, and her soft features spread into a smile.

"Ah! There you are. We had begun to worry." The woman bustled from the house, the pearl buttons on her embroidered coral gown shining like little white orbs.

Aunt Mary hurried forward and extended her hands. "It's good to see you, Hattie. I'm only sorry it cannot be in Washington."

The woman gave Aunt Mary's hands a gentle squeeze. "Harold and I are glad to have you. Surely these unpleasant circumstances will only last a short time. Lord willing, our home there will be just as we left it." She turned to the three standing on the walk. "Ah! Isabella, my darling, you are as beautiful as ever."

Isabella grinned the first real sunny expression Evelyn had seen on her in weeks. Yes, the reprieve from Martinsburg would do them all good.

"It's lovely to see you as well, Aunt Hattie. I have missed you."

The lady turned next to little Lara. "And my precious one!" She leaned forward, and two silvered blond curls slid forward on her cheeks. "I heard tell that Uncle Harold has some sweets in his pocket for the prettiest little girl at the hotel."

Lara's blue eyes widened.

"Go on in now and see him. I'll wager you are just the distraction he needs."

Lara squeezed her doll and went into the house, her gait much too controlled and smooth for a child on her way for sweets. At that age, Evelyn would have skipped around the adults and bounded inside like a deer. But then, perhaps that was the kind of thing Aunt Mary meant when she said Evelyn didn't understand the ways of their station.

As the girl slipped inside, Hattie turned her attention to Evelyn. Her honey brown eyes remained friendly but lost most of their sparkle. "And this must be your brother's child. Evelyn, is it?"

Evelyn dipped her head. "Yes, ma'am. It's a pleasure to make your acquaintance."

The woman studied her for longer than Evelyn deemed normal, and she found herself wiping damp palms on her skirt.

"If you please, Hattie dear, we are travel weary and would be delighted to be afforded the opportunity to freshen up."

Hattie blinked and turned quickly from Evelyn. "Oh, of course! Come now, we've had the rooms readied for you."

The woman swished into the boxy house, Aunt Mary at her side. Evelyn and Isabella followed. After a brief tour of the parlors, study, and dining space, they ascended steep stairs to the upper level. Aunt Mary and Lara took one room, while Evelyn and Isabella were to occupy the other. Evelyn smothered the hope for her own space just as the same sentiment seemed to play across Isabella's features.

The rest of the day passed in the uneventful chatter of a family who barely acknowledged Evelyn's existence. By the time the evening meal ended, a pulsing throb had gathered at her temples, and she excused herself from her cousin's half-hearted offer of a game of checkers, preferring to call an end to the day. Isabella performed the customary regret, and they went their separate ways.

As Evelyn slipped under her sheets, the memory of Hattie Lawrence's continued study of her pricked at her senses. Throughout the day, the woman had cast furtive glances she must have thought Evelyn didn't notice.

Evelyn rolled to her side. The last rays of the day's light crept through a small slit in the drawn curtains and cut a silver swath across the rose-patterned rug that spanned the divide between Isabella's bed and her own.

Aunt Mary must have told her sister-in-law all about her unwanted niece. Evelyn threw the thin blanket over her head. Still, even under their disdain, Evelyn could not turn her mind from finding a way to help and proving herself to her father.

But, as Isabella had oft reminded her, she was merely a woman. Such matters were left to men.

Evelyn huffed. Well, as the only man who had a care for her had abandoned her, then she had no choice but to find a way to prove Isabella wrong.

Washington Infirmary
July 22, 1861

*L*ittle Benjamin clung to Samuel's neck and wailed, refusing to let the nun take him. He smelled of damp hair, fresh linen, and childhood. Samuel turned his body and removed the boy from the scowling nun's reach.

"Mr. Flynn! We have to get these orphans out of the beds. They are coming!" The desperation in the elderly woman's voice matched that in her faded brown eyes.

Benjamin sobbed against his shoulder, and Samuel clutched him tightly. "I shall take them, Sister. I do not mind."

She grabbed Samuel's arm, the tips of her bony fingers digging through the cloth as she leaned closer. "You're needed here. Saints preserve us! They say more than a thousand are coming."

Samuel tried to ignore the dryness that crept up the back of his throat and robbed his mouth of moisture. A battle at Bull Run had ended in disaster for Federal troops. The broken and battered were on their way.

"Don't send me back!" Benjamin wailed, his drops of

sorrow wetting Samuel's shirt.

The nun huffed. "Two weeks ago this boy grumbled over everything in this infirmary. If you stop coddling him, he'll give up on these theatrics."

The muscle in Samuel's jaw ticked, and he turned his back on the impatient tap of her leather shoe. Amid the chaos of the scrambling nuns, physicians, and medical students, Samuel knelt and eased Benjamin's head from where he buried it against Samuel's neck. Grasping his shoulders, he stared earnestly into the boy's eyes. "Benjamin. I need you to be strong for me now. We must think of Emily, mustn't we?"

Benjamin blinked, his deep green eyes shimmering. "Emily doesn't want to go. She was crying all morning."

The nun skirted around him and put a hand to her hip. "What nonsense is this?" She clicked her tongue. "Children wanting to stay in a hospital. We need to go." She hooked Benjamin's elbow and pulled.

Benjamin screamed and tried to snatch his arm away. Samuel set his teeth and prayed God would grant him patience. "A moment, please, Sister. It will be easier for you if I can calm him."

The nun hesitated for a moment and then, apparently seeing his logic, released the child and turned to usher the other urchins out of their sick gowns and into threadbare clothing.

"Please, Mr. Flynn," Benjamin whimpered. "We don't want to go yet."

A strange tightness coiled around his chest and squeezed. Children muttered under the nun's instructions, some sniffling and others stoically following command, their eyes dim. The joy that had permeated this ward during the past weeks dissipated. Soon this place would be filled not with children's laughter but with the screams of the wounded.

Samuel focused on Benjamin. *One issue at a time.* "Why?"

Benjamin chewed his lip. He tried to bury the toe of his cracked shoe into the floor. "We like it here."

Samuel cocked his head and attempted a smile. "In the hospital where you must lie about in bed in your infant's gown?" He tried for humor, hoping the memory of one of their first days together might bring a smile to the boy's tightly pinched lips. When more tears gathered instead, Samuel gave him a small squeeze. "We haven't much time. Please, tell me what's the matter."

He sniffled and lowered his voice. "The children ain't kind to her. They poke fun because she don't talk much, and they say her eyes are too big. They call her mouse face."

Samuel sat back on his heels, knowing full well children could be relentlessly unkind. "But she has you to look after her." He patted Benjamin's shoulder, hoping that somehow the inadequate gesture would give him the strength a child so small shouldn't need. "She will listen to your words more than theirs."

Benjamin's eyes searched Samuel's as though he would find answers there. "The nun said we was getting too big. They'll send us to a girls' home and a boys' home now."

Sorrow twisted Samuel's stomach. Fear and uncertainty laced the boy's quiet words, speaking volumes in naught but a few syllables. He looked frail, his eyes too full of sorrow and understanding for one so young. Samuel's mind scrambled. Then, in a moment of irrational emotion, he scooped the boy from the floor and turned to the nun. He couldn't let them be separated. Didn't she see the children needed each other?

The sister held Emily by the wrist, and the little girl stared at the floor. Dressed in a faded blue skirt and blouse with her hair hanging limp about her shoulders, she seemed more like a worn doll than a child.

Samuel glared at the elderly nun. "Are you sending these two to different orphanages?"

The sister eyed him. Then her gaze darted to Benjamin clinging to his arm. "I trust the boy is ready now?"

Samuel clenched him tighter. "You didn't answer my question. Is it your intention to separate these children from the only family they have?"

She glanced between the siblings and gave a small dip of her head. "It is the way of things."

A way Samuel did not want to accept. "But they have only each other."

Compassion filled her eyes, replacing the impatience that had swarmed there ever since Samuel had insisted on helping in the children's ward until the wounded arrived. "As the children get older, it's better they are separated." Her tone pleaded with him to understand, to think about all the issues that could arise with housing restless youths together. "It's best they each learn to be respectable men and women without the complications of joint living quarters." A gentle smile tempered her angular features. "They'll see each other again."

Samuel pressed his lips together. It made sense. They would be cared for. The nuns might seem prickly, but they tended to the people no one else wanted. The Washington Infirmary gave proof of their persistent, if not always tender, care. The children would be safe, fed, and clothed. It would be for the best.

He set Benjamin on the floor, and a great emptiness enveloped him.

Lord, what is this feeling? Help it to pass. This is for the best.

Benjamin turned from him, defeat etched in his countenance and in every tremble of his small shoulders. He took his sister's hand, squeezing it gently. Emily's large brown eyes skewered Samuel's heart. She took a small step forward.

"Thank you, sir," she said softly, one of the handful of times she'd offered more than a smile. "I liked your tales."

"Come now. We must be going." The nun tugged on Emily's arm, and she dropped her gaze to the floor.

Samuel struggled for words, but inexplicable emotion pasted his tongue to his palate.

Benjamin wouldn't look at him. The pressure that had squeezed Samuel sprouted thorns and pricked at him until he could barely breathe. A wild thought seized him and he tried to toss it aside.

Wisdom, please, Father. Remove these feelings as I have asked you to remove the smells.

Emily looked up at him one last time, and a glimmer of tears coated her eyes. Those large, expressive eyes that took in too much and let out too little. What would life be for this little one, separated from the only person who would guard such a tender heart?

Samuel's stomach twisted, and this time, it had nothing to do with the smells filling the room.

The children gathered together, and without a glance back, the nun shooed them toward the door.

"Wait!"

The nun turned to him, questions in her eyes.

He rubbed the back of his neck. "If someone were to claim the children, would they be allowed to return to the orphanage together for a short time while arrangements could be made?"

The nun's eyebrows lifted, widening her eyes. Samuel didn't look down at the children, afraid of what he might see in their eyes. His pulse beat too rapidly as it was. What was he thinking?

The sister must have thought the same. She studied him.

"Sir, unless a family has been found"—she shook her head—"we cannot foster false hopes."

Movement shifted around the nun's simple skirts, and Samuel glanced down. Two small faces peered up at him. Emily's eyes filled with a guarded wonder, Benjamin's with disbelief. Precious little ones, already wounded. Had he not sworn to heal wounds to the best of his ability? Had he not promised to do all in his power to care for those who needed aid? Samuel's pulse slowed. Peace gurgled through him, easing his heart's gallop.

He smiled. The nun frowned. The children stared.

"I cannot say that I have any experience with children, but I promise I will provide for them and care for them to the best of my ability." He spoke to the nun, but kept his eyes on Benjamin. "I'll need a lot of help becoming a guardian, but I am willing to learn."

Benjamin's eyes widened, and he swallowed hard, looking away as tears fell down his softly rounded cheeks. He'd been well for more than a week now but had managed to fool the nuns into thinking he had to stay. Now, Samuel better understood why. Emily still suffered a slight cough, and little Benjamin had done what he had to in order to stay by her side.

"You...are you certain?" the nun asked, drawing his gaze back to her face.

Strange as it seemed, he was. He reached down to ruffle Benjamin's hair. "Of course. Why, I must speak now for such fine children, or surely someone else will soon whisk them away."

The nun stared at him for several moments, then finally gave a small nod. "Very well, then. I will take them back to St. Nicholas Orphanage for one week. But only one. If they are not retrieved by then—"

Samuel lifted his hand to stay her words. "I will be along to fetch them as soon as we tend the incoming soldiers and I secure a nanny."

A light sprung up in her eyes, and the nun turned to gather the other children, shooing them toward the door. Samuel dropped to his knee and stared at his two new charges. Were they as nervous as he?

Emily slowly stepped closer, lifted a tiny hand, and placed it on his cheek. She cocked her head and blinked at him.

Benjamin shifted his weight, his little hands shoved deep into his trouser pockets. "She wants to know if you mean it."

Knowing the question came from both of them, Samuel nodded against her tiny hand. "I do, Emily. A night or two at the orphanage, and then I'll be along to fetch you both. You have my word."

"Why?"

Benjamin's question hung on the air as heavily as that same word spoken from Samuel had earlier. His entire life had shifted in mere moments. He decided on simple honesty. "I couldn't watch you go. Not knowing that you would be separated and I would never see you again."

Benjamin sniffled and then squared his shoulders. "We will be good for you. I promise. We won't make you want to send us back."

Sorrow twisted him to think a boy so young would consider such things, but he offered Benjamin a smile. "I could never send you back. Then who would listen to my tales? I look rather foolish reading to the furniture. You are saving me the trouble of my neighbors thinking me mad."

Benjamin stared at him, but little Emily giggled. Then the children were ushered out, leaving him for the briefest of moments in the silence of the empty children's ward.

No sooner had they gone than shouts rang out through

the building, heralding the arrival of those unfortunate boys who'd found more action at the hands of the Confederates than they truly wanted. Reports had reached the hospital yesterday evening about a shattered army, a defeat, and endless scores of injured men heading home to Washington.

They'd spent a hurried morning trying to prepare, moving the poor out and readying beds for the hundreds—some said more than a thousand—wounded soldiers who would arrive on wagons, buggies, and blistered feet.

Girding his courage for what he would face, Samuel breathed a prayer for strength and, for what seemed the millionth time, that he would not be able to smell. He stepped from the room that would no longer be the children's ward and into the chaos of the hallway. Soldiers stumbled in, some shouting orders, others slumping against the wall.

For a moment, Samuel could only stare. Covered in mud, they sullied the halls and scrubbed floors, their scent a wall of sweat, blood, and filth that slammed into him and made his head spin. He placed his hand on the doorframe to steady himself.

"Flynn!"

Samuel turned to see Dr. Porter shouting at him, his face red above his neatly trimmed beard. Cold blue eyes bore into Samuel, assessing his every failure. Of all the students under his guidance, Dr. Porter liked Samuel least.

Samuel pulled himself away from the steadying fortitude of the door. "Yes, doctor?"

Dr. Porter flung his arm toward the mass of men. "Have you not eyes, man? We have work to do! Gather the rest of the bandages."

"I already placed adequate supplies in each ward, ready for the nuns."

Dr. Porter pushed past him, aiming for an officer at the

end of the hall who half dragged a man with blood caked in his hair. "However much you placed, it will not be enough!"

Samuel hurried the other way. He slipped a key from his pocket and thrust it into the supply closet door. Sister Mary Abigail had warned that with this many men about, they might think to help themselves rather than wait for proper care and advised the room always remain locked. The key turned and Samuel ducked inside.

Merely two crates of clean cloth strips remained. He stacked one on top of the other and heaved them from the room, glad for his father's insistence he always chop his own cords of wood to keep strong. After pausing only to be certain to lock the door behind him, Samuel lifted the crates once more and made his way through the throng pressing in the hallway.

Physicians shouted to officers and tried to separate the men into groups based on the varying degrees of their conditions. Samuel picked his way through the men ordered into the main wing and located Sister Mary Abigail.

She tucked a graying lock under her wimple and calmly motioned him to the bed of a man clutching his gut and moaning. Samuel stepped over the leg of a man who'd dropped to the floor when he could drag himself no farther.

"Set them over here, Mr. Flynn. The sisters and I will clean wounds and wrap them. All the physicians are to go to the western ward."

She hurried away, the last clean scent trailing behind her. He reached down to haul the man from the floor onto the nearest bed, taking care to position him on the mattress. The man never stirred, though from injury or exhaustion, Samuel couldn't tell. Sour musk clung to him like a shroud, and Samuel had to hold his breath until he finished removing the man's boots and tucking them under the cot.

In the western ward, the metallic scent of blood clung to patients and doctors alike, the latter gathering those who would need sutures or amputations.

Taking a place by Dr. Porter, Samuel waited for instructions.

"You! What's your condition," Dr. Porter asked one dirty fellow with three missing buttons and the distinct smell of a man who had been struggling with dysentery.

He held up a hand that had been wrapped in a cloth. Crimson and black stains caked the wrap. "Lost two fingers."

Without a word, Dr. Porter waved him to the left. The man shot a look at Samuel, then cradled his hand in his other arm and turned away. Knowing his duty must take precedence over his heaving insides, Samuel decided this soldier would be his first. He took a step closer, the smell of something putrid rising in the air and sticking to his nostrils.

Forcing himself not to recoil, he placed a hand on the soldier's upper back and guided him over to an open bed.

The man sank, his wide shoulders slumping.

Samuel instructed one of the nuns to fetch him a pan of water.

"I am Mr. Flynn." Best to get right to business and keep himself focused. "If you'll allow me, I'll see to your hand."

The soldier glanced up at him, wary eyes set in a sweat and dirt stained face. "You're not a physician?"

"Nearly. I'm in the final days of completing my studies."

The man hesitated and then shrugged, holding out the hand. Samuel unwrapped it, holding his breath against what he found inside.

Torn flesh hung around the snapped bones of the man's trigger and middle finger, the first of which still had mud caked onto the white bone.

Samuel breathed through his mouth, though it did little

good. "You did not wash this?"

"No time. Grabbed a cloth and wrapped it up, then did my best to get out of there."

He rotated the soldier's wrist. "And you had no time for washing at any point during your march back to Washington?"

The man shifted. "Didn't want to see it."

The nun returned with water and clean bandages, left them next to the bed, and hurried off on another mission. Samuel turned the soldier's hand over, noting most of the bleeding had been stemmed by caked dirt and blood. "I'll have to clean it, remove the broken bone fragments, and then stitch the skin back together."

"Will I be able to shoot again?"

"That I cannot say. You'll lose both fingers. The first at the center knuckle, and the second at the base of your hand."

He seemed to accept this and waited as Samuel ignored the screams and moans of the other men filling the room. *One patient at a time.* He shut off his nose and breathed through his mouth, but still the overpowering thickness gagged him.

He swallowed the shame and bile and gathered the supplies he would need. The soldier inhaled the chloroform Samuel waved under his nose, and then relaxed back against the mattress. He grunted in pain a few times, but mostly remained still as Samuel removed the dirt, blood, and broken bone from his hand.

Some minutes later, Samuel stitched flaps of skin together over the stubs of the missing digits and then wrapped the hand in a clean cloth. As long as he kept his gaze narrowed on his task and breathed slowly, his head remained clear enough to perform a single duty. Perhaps that would be the key to success.

With bolstered confidence, he gathered his supplies and

left the man to rest, keeping his gaze on the floor as he turned to the man on the next bed. Before he could lift his eyes to assess his needs, the soldier rolled to his side and retched.

Blood and stomach contents spilled over Samuel's shoes. The smell exploded on his senses, his own stomach violently rebelling. Samuel stumbled backward, and an involuntary quick intake of air sent fetid vapors down his throat and caused his head to swim.

His stomach lurched.

No. Samuel clenched his arm across his midsection as sweat popped out on his brow and slid down the side of his face. This couldn't happen. Not now.

He forced leaden feet forward, past the heaving man, down the center of the aisle, and past doctors scrambling for supplies. Dr. Porter reached for him, then called his name.

The edges of his vision became fringed in black, and heat clawed up his spine. Somehow, he managed to push past groaning soldiers in the hall and to the rear door of the hospital. He gulped for fresh air, praying it would soothe the roaring storm within.

Rather than a sweetened breeze, only the bouquet of damp earth, horse manure, and waste greeted him.

Help me.

He doubled over, and shame consumed him as his stomach emptied.

Seven

Front Royal, Virginia
July 29, 1861

*E*velyn's needle came to a sudden stop, pricking her finger and drawing a drop of crimson in the process. She discreetly drew a handkerchief from her pocket and dabbed the tip of her thumb while the woman across the parlor hurried on.

"Yes, that's exactly what I heard. Can you believe it?"

Aunt Mary set her material in her lap and gave the woman dressed in olive silk a gentle shake of her head. "Honestly, Mrs. Camden, I really cannot."

Evelyn kept her chin down and looked at the other women around the room through her lashes. Six of them had gathered for a sewing circle in Mrs. Camden's impressive home, though Evelyn suspected the women came for gossiping under the guise of fellowship rather than the professed mission of stitching new shirts for Confederate soldiers.

Mrs. Camden, a vibrant-looking woman of middling years, bobbed her head enthusiastically, her tightly pinned lace cap stifling a mass of gray and brown curls. "Oh, but it is true."

Mrs. Swanson, the other lady of around the same age, nodded in much the same fashion, the pair of them reminding Evelyn of two carriage horses tossing their heads for a lump of sugar.

Mrs. Camden waved long fingers at Mrs. Swanson. "Tell them, Mrs. Swanson. It's quite fascinating."

Aunt Mary spoke before the other woman could get a word past her thin lips. "Come now, I've known Margret Greenman for years. My daughter spent much of her season in Washington under the lady's care. I cannot imagine such a thing to be true. It's merely prattle, I'm sure."

Her daughter *and* Evelyn. Evelyn thought about the time she'd spent in the company of a woman who was as near to royalty as Washington could boast. Such cunning and connections did not seem out of the lady's reach.

Evelyn glanced at Isabella, who regarded Mrs. Camden with open curiosity. "I don't know, Mother. Mrs. Greenman *does* know everyone who is anyone in Washington. It seems possible."

"Oh, pish posh," Hattie Lawrence said, setting aside her work as well. "So do I. I don't see what that has to do with the matter."

Isabella focused on her aunt. "I can see how such connections might lead one to take such measures, especially if one had information they knew could save our men's lives."

Hattie's forehead creased, and Evelyn wondered what thoughts had plowed such furrows.

"I'm telling you," Mrs. Camden insisted, reinserting herself into the conversation. "It's quite true. Isn't it, Mrs. Swanson?"

The reedy woman glanced at Aunt Mary before she spoke, as though wondering if the younger woman would forestall her words again. When Aunt Mary pointedly settled her gaze on the linen shirt in her lap, Mrs. Swanson spoke, her nasally voice filling the bright yellow parlor with more excitement than the day of sewing had thus far provided. "Yes, it's true. My husband says that Margret Greenman *is* responsible for sending word to Beauregard's headquarters and giving him the warning he needed to prepare. She is pivotally involved with our victory at Manassas."

"How did she accomplish it?" Evelyn interjected, her own needlework forgotten.

Aunt Mary cast her a scathing look. "We should not continue such wanton gossip. This sort of thing is naught but fanciful hearsay. To think a woman of fine standing would do such a thing." She gave a derisive laugh. "Why, it's ridiculous."

Mrs. Swanson turned up her nose, her eyes flashing. "On the contrary, Mrs. Lawrence. It's quite understandable that she would want to use her extensive connections to aid in our victory. Why, I can hardly think of how anyone would *not* use whatever advantages she had at her disposable to aid our boys."

Evelyn's heart fluttered. Had that not been her very thought? She'd sent her missive on to Daddy with the information she'd learned at the Gradys' party. Had he received it? Would women be sitting in sewing circles talking about how a newspaperman's information had altered another battle?

Aunt Mary lifted her eyebrows but said no more. Isabella glanced between her mother and the petite woman who'd challenged Aunt Mary and pressed her lips together.

Daring her aunt's wrath, Evelyn spoke up. "Do you know, Mrs. Camden, how exactly she accomplished such an amazing feat?"

Mrs. Camden smiled and turned her attention on the only

one of the Lawrence family who shared her interest in the matter. "Oh, yes, Miss Mapleton. It's quite an intrepid tale."

Evelyn waited while the older lady folded her needlework away and focused on the telling. She took her time in doing so, as though she relished the attention focused on her. She patted the cap on her head, straightened her floral print skirt, and then settled her hands in her lap.

"They say Margret Greenman has gathered a collection of scouts to aid in her efforts." Mrs. Camden leaned forward, her voice ripe with the implications of her words.

"Scouts?" Hattie interrupted. "What do you mean, scouts? Like frontiersmen that kept a lookout for those filthy redskins?" She cast Evelyn a look Evelyn couldn't place.

How odd. What association did Evelyn have with frontiersmen?

"No," Mrs. Camden replied, drawing out the word. "A scout is someone who works in an unofficial capacity gathering secrets, like a spy, but one not associated with the military. These are regular folk who keep alert for information that may be of use to our army."

The word *spy* slithered through Evelyn's ears and set her heart to quickening. Had that been what she'd done when she listened at the Gradys' party? Would passing that information on to her father label her a spy?

Aunt Mary mumbled something, and Evelyn had to bite her tongue to keep it from prodding the woman to hurry and tell more. Mrs. Camden seemed to sense her thoughts, however, and appeared to enjoy the sense of urgency swirling underneath Evelyn's carefully controlled features.

"Now, I dare say no woman in Washington knows more men of power and influence, both from the Southern and Federal causes."

Hattie seemed to bristle at this, but thankfully, kept her

opinion to herself.

"So then," Mrs. Camden continued, ignoring the thinly veiled looks of disgust from Hattie and Aunt Mary. "Mrs. Greenman came up with this marvelous idea. She tucked a message inside a little silk purse." She paused to put her hand to her throat in a most dramatic fashion. "And then she weaved that right into a girl's hair! Why, I bet those pickets never suspected a thing!

"Then this little scout, Miss Sophia Dole, she makes her way from Washington, through the Federal camps at Georgetown, and stops for the night at a plantation near Langley. They say the next day she rode on to Brigadier General Milledge Luke Bonham, who faithfully took the information to Beauregard who then sent a courier directly to Mr. Davis!"

The women continued to chatter about the victory at Bull Run near Manassas and the way they had staunchly stopped the Yanks' march on to Richmond.

"Well, then," Isabella replied, taking up her needlework once more. "Since the Federals were unable to make their move on Richmond, then perhaps this will be finished by summer's end."

Aunt Mary smiled. "Yes, indeed, dear. Surely come winter they will give up on this hapless invasion and leave us in peace."

"If you think that is going to happen, then you don't know men." Mrs. Camden chuckled, leveling a look at Aunt Mary.

"Why, I—"

"Oh, but I do believe it's time for tea," Mrs. Camden lurched to her feet, spilling her partially finished shirt to the floor. "Wouldn't tea be nice, ladies?"

Evelyn glanced to Aunt Mary, whose cheeks had flushed

pink, and watched as she schooled her features back into the refined grace of a high-bred lady. "Why, I would love a spot of tea. Thank you for your hospitality."

The other women offered their thanks as well, and after a few tensely quiet moments their hostess returned and settled back into the sewing circle. "Have we heard any news of our wounded?"

"Oh, yes," Mrs. Swanson said. "We must not forget our brave boys. In fact, the general in command has fixed his gaze upon Front Royal to set up a hospital."

"I have it on good account," Mrs. Camden supplied, "that they should be arriving any time now."

"Oh, my." Evelyn glanced at the women wasting time with sewing when they should be slicing these linens into strips to use for bandages. "Should we not be preparing to help?"

"I'm sure there are people who handle those types of needs," Aunt Mary stated, using the tone she utilized whenever she considered a matter beyond contestation.

"Actually," Mrs. Swanson said, her thin lips parting in a smile, "it's one of the things Mrs. Camden and I hoped to discuss with you ladies today."

Before anyone could respond, a Negro slave girl in the final stages prior to womanhood entered the room balancing a silver tray topped with a fine tea set and a platter of sliced bread and peeled fruits. She settled it on the low table at the center of their sewing circle and then silently slipped out of the room once more.

Mrs. Camden lifted the etched teapot and proffered a cup. She poured for each lady in turn and then passed around the cream and sugar before offering the refreshments. Those who had not done so already set aside their respective projects and sipped quietly for a few moments before Hattie replied to

Mrs. Swanson's comment.

"Am I to understand that you wished to speak to us about a hospital? You don't suppose the army will wish to commandeer the inn, do you?" She spooned a few blackberries onto a small painted plate and sprinkled them with sugar.

Mrs. Camden regarded her over the top of her silver-rimmed teacup. "There are many who have already volunteered their spaces to care for those who are risking life and livelihood on our accord."

Evelyn sipped her tea and waited to see what response Hattie would provide. To say no to offering her family's inn for their soldiers would label her unsympathetic to the cause, but to allow it would cost the family income.

"We will be in need of volunteers for nursing the boys as well," Mrs. Swanson inserted into the thickening silence.

"I'll help," Evelyn piped up. From the corner of her vision she saw Aunt Mary narrow her eyes, but she forged on before her aunt could raise a protest. "Surely lending aid in the hospital would be a productive way for a lady to support the cause?"

To her surprise, it was Hattie who offered support. "Why, certainly! We women are adept at bathing fevered brows and soothing away pains. And I'm sure some of the boys would like for a lady to pen a word home for them." She smiled sweetly at Evelyn. "Such service seems quite fitting for you."

"Yes," Isabella said, settling her cup on its saucer. "Surely even I could pen a few letters. If Father and Paul were in such a position we would want a kindly lady to write on their behalf."

Evelyn held her breath as Aunt Mary studied Isabella. Perhaps she had a better idea of what drove Isabella's unexpected response than Evelyn did. Regardless, Evelyn was happy to find some way that she and Isabella could work together to contribute.

Aunt Mary finally slathered on a smile that did not reach her eyes. "Why, of course, darling. It's generous of you to sacrifice your time. I'm sure there will be some fine officers who would be most grateful for your charity."

The other ladies added their shallow praise as well, as wide as the gulf but only as deep as the dregs remaining in her tea cup. Evelyn set her refreshments aside and inquired after how they would begin their duties.

"They've come! Hurry, ladies! We are wanted immediately!"

Evelyn had scarcely entered the garden outside the cottage behind the Fishback Inn when Mrs. Camden's fervent call broke the still gray of early morning light the next day. Isabella closed the door behind them, her sensible brown dress the most subdued Evelyn had seen her cousin don in some time.

Birds offered their morning reveille, flitting from branch to branch in the pleasant manner of creatures unaware of the goings on beneath them. Evelyn tied her bonnet ribbon under her chin with quick fingers and rushed to Mrs. Camden.

The older woman's cheeks puffed with a cherry glow as she waved her ungloved hand at them. "Hurry now, girls. The wounded are arriving, wagonloads of them, and we shall have our hands full within the quarter hour." She spun back around without further greeting or instruction, leaving Evelyn and Isabella no choice but to hurry after her.

The street in front of the hotel gave credence to Mrs.

Camden's warning, with a mass of rumbling conveyances clogging the road. Two-wheeled vehicles with open sides gave glimpses of men lying inside before they hurried past. Larger, four-wheeled carriages with canvas walls that had been rolled up to their roofs were stuffed full of men in dirty uniforms.

Her feet stumbled over themselves and brought her to a shuddering halt just before a pair of bay horses veered to the edge of the road. She stepped back. Dirt spun up from a cavalcade of churning wheels, sending it swirling around the press of people until it thickened the air and made the carriages look like dirty vegetables boiling in a vat of dust stew. How many of them were pushing into town before the day had taken its first full breath?

Isabella tugged on her arm. "Come on, we're losing Mrs. Camden."

Not that it mattered. One only needed to follow this mournful parade to deposit herself at the correct location. Mindful of the danger, they ducked into the crowd, weaving their way among horses and carriages and men clutching bloodied arms to their chests. Like fish caught in the current, Evelyn and Isabella bobbed along in a river saturated with the ripe scents of animals, sweat, and blood.

Thankfully the hospital was not far from the hotel, and after a few harried moments, they had gained entrance to the large wooden structure. Evelyn barely stepped across the threshold when Mrs. Swanson thrust a white cloth at her and tossed another to Isabella.

"Quickly, girls. Pin these aprons on. The beds are already filling."

Evelyn tied the apron strings behind her back and then took pins to secure the upper flap to her bodice. The moans and cries of men perforated her ears and made even such a simple task difficult. Her fingers trembled, and it took two attempts to clip the apron into place.

"What will we have to do?" Isabella asked over the clamor of voices, concern causing her voice to reach a higher pitch than usual.

Mrs. Swanson gave aprons to more girls with freshly scrubbed faces who seemed not long from their beds. Women tied their strings, watching the commotion in the hospital with varying degrees of astonishment.

"Wash, dress, feed, comfort, and nurse them for the next weeks if not months," Mrs. Camden replied. She spoke brief words of encouragement to each of the women who entered the hospital looking pale-faced and wide-eyed.

A cluster of twenty or so ladies gathered, and Mrs. Swanson ushered them into a small gaggle in a far corner of the main ward and pitched her voice above the commotion. Gone was the quiet woman who'd allowed Aunt Mary to step over her words. This lady stood with a calm self-assurance that belied the building chaos around them.

"Ladies, we have before us an opportunity to care for our dear boys who have fought bravely for us at Manassas and have brought us a great victory! Remember that you are a soft touch, a gentle voice, and a friendly face that is desperately needed after the untold horrors of battle. You'll need your wits about you and an abundance of compassion. Remember your efforts here are of dire importance."

Women nodded along, and Evelyn's blood stirred.

"Find a doctor or nurse in need of assistance and spread yourselves among the beds." She clapped her hands together. "Let us begin!"

As Mrs. Swanson hurried off, Evelyn was met with the stares of women looking equally as confused. Were they to receive no further instructions? No details on their duties?

She had no nursing experience. How, then, was she to tend a wound, or reduce a fever, or assist a doctor? Her stomach suddenly turned, the impossibility of her task sending her insides into a hurricane of turmoil.

Isabella clutched her elbow. "What are we to do?"

As her cousin had received precisely the same amount of instruction as she, Evelyn could not find a proper way to answer the question. The tumbling mass of men washing through the hospital was like a wave of bloodied gray.

"I suppose we follow instructions whenever they are given and do our best to be of service. We'll just have to spread out among the beds and try to assess what is needed."

Isabella gave a small nod, and they moved through the rows of hospital beds, drifting in opposite directions. In a matter of moments they were separated by the sheer volume of bustling nurses, volunteer women, and colored servants entangled in the knot of humanity pulsing between the hospital beds.

Evelyn situated herself at the head of a row of beds that extended the length of the great hall. Each row contained tidy beds with sheets tucked in nicely, the white cotton waiting to be soiled with the mud and crusted blood of hundreds of wounded men. She took her place and stood stiffly, hoping her presence appeared calmer than the waves of inner turmoil tossing her about like a ship in a disgruntled ocean.

She had no business here. How could she think to care for any of these? She didn't know what to do. What if she made one worse or he died under her care?

A shiver ran along her spine. She was inadequate. Completely and utterly inadequate.

There was no time for such self-doubt, however, as rows of carts outside continued to unload their sad cargo at the door.

For a fleeting moment, the selfish wish that she could return to the inn bubbled to the surface. Evelyn pointedly extinguished it. These men were in dire need of any care they could receive, and her lack of training did not have to hinder her willingness.

A woman hurried by, dipping a wide brush into a bowl and flinging droplets of water all around the floor and at the foot of each bed. The cloying scent of some type of cologne mingled with sickness and blood in a paltry attempt to mask the odors that no sweetness could disperse. Instead, the abnormal combination succeeded in further twisting Evelyn's stomach.

Her feet remained rooted to the floor, her gaze locked on the soldiers as they flowed through the open doors. Some came on stretchers, others were merely cradled in hearty men's arms. Those who fared best staggered in on crude crutches, some dragging useless limbs.

Unmoored by a desire to help, even if she didn't rightly know how, Evelyn drifted between them as they fell haphazardly into the beds, her senses raw with the swelling pain that clouded the room as thick as smoke. To her left, one soldier lay, still and silent, as another draped a covering over his face.

Orderlies soon clogged the inflow, insisting that each man's name and rank be recorded before he could seek his rest and examination. Doctors pointed men in one direction or another, quickly assessing injuries and directing them to various locations. The beds near the front filled quickly as groaning men settled weary frames. And still they came, until the hall was full of wounded humanity. Those able to stand leaned against and then slid down the walls into huddled forms gathered along the fringes of the ward like the unraveling edges of a beaten rug.

Evelyn turned as a stretcher pushed against her, aghast to see the man upon it had lost his arm at the elbow, the remaining limb a mass of bloodied flesh and bone. Her heart hammered so rapidly she thought she might faint. The back of her throat burned, and the urge to run pumped through her veins.

No. She must cork these feelings. She was here to work, not worry or weep.

No sooner had she admonished herself and girded her strength than a woman with a stoic expression stepped in front of her. Appearing to be in her mid-thirties and dressed in the stained attire of one who might know her way around this debacle, the woman assessed Evelyn in one sweeping glance. She must have been somewhat satisfied with what she saw because she thrust a bowl toward Evelyn's middle. "Here." She dropped a bar of lye soap into the bowl with a little splash. "See to washing."

Without further direction, she hurried on to another task.

Washing. She could do that. Bathe the sweat and blood from wearied faces. Evelyn took the bowl and rag and knelt at the first bed, her wide skirts pooling around her. Tomorrow, she would wear fewer petticoats and forego her crinoline cage. Such fashions hindered her movements.

The soldier before her was as young as her cousin Paul. Aunt Mary had pleaded with Uncle Phillip that seventeen was far too young to be scarred by war. In the end, however, both father and son had gone to do their duty. Did this boy have a mother who had pleaded for him not to fight?

What would that mother think to see her boy, his face coated in dirt and crimson that flowed from a gash along his hairline? He stared at Evelyn with sandy-brown eyes haunted by shadows and deep set with exhaustion.

Brave Boys, the paper had called them. And they must

surely be, for Evelyn could not fathom the courage required to face the prospect of shell and shot that could tear a body to shreds.

She dipped her rag into the tepid water, wrung it, and dabbed at the boy's brow in the most motherly fashion one her age could muster. "There, now. We'll get you cleaned right up."

The boy merely continued to stare at her, the wide inner circle of his eyes not seeming to fully recognize her presence. Perhaps whatever had caused the gash on his head had knocked free some of his senses. Or maybe he'd merely suffered a great shock at the unimaginable horrors he must have seen. Determined to draw his mind anywhere but back to the battlefield, Evelyn refrained from seeking answers a newspaperman's daughter yearned to know. Instead, she spoke of the pleasantness of Front Royal and how soon the men would surely receive a good meal. He would welcome that, wouldn't he?

Still, he made no reply, and when she had finished cleaning his face and gash to the best of her ability, she turned to the next man on the line of beds.

The same woman who had given her the bowl of water returned, pushing auburn locks away from her sympathetic eyes. She looked down at the boy Evelyn had washed and gave a gentle shake of her head. "Come, my dear, you must wash quickly and much more thoroughly. Have the men remove socks, coats and shirts, and scrub them well. Put on clean shirts..." She thrust a pile of linens against Evelyn's chest, disrupting the bowl of water. "And then the attendants will finish the...*sensitive areas* and lay them in bed."

Before Evelyn could protest, the nameless woman was gone again. Heat crept up her neck at the thought of removing a man's shirt. Had she been asked to dance a jig for their entertainment, or give them a shave, or do any number of other ridiculous things, she would have likely been less staggered. But to have to disrobe strangers at a moment's notice?

She drowned her scruples in the dingy water of her wash bowl and resolved to do anything—well, within fathomable reason—they asked of her. What was the sacrifice of her feminine sensibilities in the face of what others had suffered? One quick glance around the crowded ward, and she was assured that many other young ladies had found themselves with the same task. How had Isabella fared with such a request?

She glanced at the next patient on her row, and seeing him regard her much too closely, turned her back on him once more. Better her first attempt at such necessary humiliation be with the boy who seemed rather oblivious to her actions.

Clutching her block of soap with determination, she assumed the most businesslike air she could garner, and set herself to the job. She separated her feelings from the task as much as possible, reminding herself that these things must be done and telling herself to think of the young man as a brother who needed motherly tending. With that in mind, she managed to wash all but his waist and legs, and after a fair amount of struggling, got him into a clean shirt that contrasted roughly with his mud-stained pants.

With a flaming-hot face, Evelyn turned to the next man on the line. She calmly instructed him to remove the necessary garments without a single glance at his face. Only after she performed all of the washing as quickly as possible and had him buttoned into a clean shirt did she look into his eyes.

He smiled shyly at her and then turned away his gaze. "I

thank you, ma'am, for doing such an unpleasant thing without causing me more embarrassment than necessary."

Evelyn dipped down and settled herself on the bed, her aching feet glad for the moment of reprieve. A laugh bubbled up from her at the ludicrous nature of the conversation, and the soldier joined her in it, his beard dancing as he did.

"We'll do what we must to save ourselves from this Northern aggression," she teased, "be it shooting or washing."

He chuckled again, calling her a right and good patriot, and then his eyes drifted closed. She laid his soiled clothes on the floor at the foot of the bed and readied herself to move down the row.

She further numbed to the task with each man in line, and soon one face melded into dozens of others. At some point, Evelyn lost count of how many men's bare torsos she had sponged. Boots, socks, and feet were naught but a mass of mud. She dutifully tended each one as she imagined a tidy mother might see to washing rambunctious boys on a Saturday night. Some took it like sleepy children, their exhausted heads lolling to one side or another. Others looked as grimly scandalized as she felt, and even a few of the roughest in appearance colored like bashful girls.

At one point in the dredges of the relentlessly long day, a man with a gunshot wound to his face asked for a looking glass and she was able to scrounge one up for him.

"By goodness," he said, rubbing at where Evelyn had dressed his swollen face as best she could. "That's too bad, it is. I reckon I wasn't a bad looking chap before, but now I'm done for. What woman will have want of a man with a thunderous scar?"

Evelyn knelt beside him. "Here, now. Don't you know a woman cares more for the inner being of a man than his outer appearance?" At his doubtful expression, she shed her attempt at humor and gently laid a hand on his arm. "Take heart. I'm sure your lady back home will see it as a mark of honor. Such a scar is but a badge won in great bravery and service."

His eyes glistened, and he squeezed her hand. "Thank 'ya, ma'am. For saying so, even if it probably ain't true."

She gave him a gentle smile and moved on until she came to the end of the ward and collapsed behind a stack of linens consisting of cut shirt-sleeves, bandages, and towels. Her back ached, she hadn't had the first snip to eat all day, and her head felt light.

A doctor found her there some moments later and tugged her to her feet. "Ah, miss, you look as though you will drift away before you make it home to your bed."

Evelyn blinked up at his face, a face lined with years and set with eyes that held the knowledge of the pain of life. She gave a weak nod. "I'm sorry, doctor. I sought only a moment of rest."

He patted her shoulder and turned her toward the door. "It's nearing on midnight. Most of the girls have long since gone. You've done all you can for today."

Several moaning men were still swathed in dirty jackets. "The work is not yet done."

He guided her around the beds and to the center aisle of the ward, pointing her toward the door. "It's never done. But if we do not rest, we will be unable to take up the task again on the morrow."

Resigned to the wisdom of his words, Evelyn placed one heavy foot in front of the other, and with only a vague sense of her surroundings as she navigated through a fog of exhaustion, found her way back to the Fishback Inn.

Eight

Washington Infirmary
August 7, 1861

*S*amuel watched a chaplain amble through the ward with his hands safely tucked away in his pockets lest he inadvertently touch one of the men he passed. The lanky fellow floated about like a ship without mooring, vaguely offering words of encouragement that held little warmth. Should not a man of the cloth be kneeling in prayer, touching shoulders in encouragement, and offering peace to those who desperately needed to commit themselves to the Lord before their days on this earth were spent?

If Samuel did not offer these men a measure of hope, then who would? Certainly the chaplain seemed disinclined to do so. Samuel made a mental notation to ask one of the officers if another chaplain could be had.

"You see that fella there, doc?" the man in the bed to his right asked, drawing Samuel's attention.

Samuel returned his gaze to the patient before him, the faint putrid scent of infection tickling in his nose. He ignored the soldier's question and leaned closer to the man's shoulder, where the stump of an arm remained. To anyone else, including the patient, it seemed Samuel merely examined the bandages. In truth, he allowed his nose to confirm what he already suspected.

The smell increased as he leaned in and breathed deeper. Perhaps this time, he would treat it without consulting Dr. Porter first. Then, maybe he could prove his theory. If he could treat the infection before it showed any visible signs, he could stem it off before it ran rampant through the body.

Unfortunately, no one believed him. And without any visible evidence on the last patient, Dr. Porter had declared Samuel's proclamation of infection unwarranted and denied the man treatment. Samuel's insistence that the man had an infection despite the doctor's diagnosis also seemed to further demean him in the doctor's eyes, something that had festered since his sickness had driven him from the ward the day the swarms of wounded arrived.

He'd taken pride in his ability to control it since, but his lack of appetite and the constant heaving of his stomach had shown up in two tightened belt loops.

An unfortunate complication for one in his position, though it did bear a singular positive. Rather than the curse he'd always believed would seek to ruin his destiny, he'd discovered his senses were so attuned, that, if he were able to separate the smell of infection from the other scents, he could detect it early.

He eyed the current patient, though he contemplated another. A matter of days after he had reported the man's infection to Dr. Porter, the fever started. Dr. Porter had treated him, but the infection had already taken hold, and the man passed within the week. He'd hardly spoken to his attending physician since. Samuel could only imagine what the man must think of him.

"Doc? Did you hear me? I asked if you saw that fellow over there."

Samuel pulled back the dressing on the wound, causing the soldier to wince. "I'm currently occupied with your condition. I'll see to the other patients in turn."

Mumbling something under his breath, the private shook his head. "No, Doc. You don't want to be treating *that* one."

Samuel tugged another strip of cloth free, exposing the neat rows of stitches that folded the skin over the sawed-off humerus. "And why is that?"

"He's a Rebel deserter. Hang him!" He nearly spat the words. "It's a blasted shame to fetch him in here right alongside us. Better they go right on to prison for their treason. Don't matter if they signed any loyalty papers or not."

The clean wound showed only a faint edge of angry red around the suture lines. Still, he was rather certain… Samuel leaned closer, narrowing his eyes for good measure.

The patient shifted, and the anger in his voice turned to worry. "What's wrong?"

"Just inspecting your sutures."

"Dr. Porter don't ever look that close on them." His voice lifted a notch. "Did you leave your spectacles some-place?"

Samuel sat back and wrapped the bandages around the stump. "How often does Dr. Porter check your wound?"

He shrugged his good shoulder. "He's checked it twice since he robbed me of my arm. Why?"

To tell this man his suspicions would only cause him unnecessary worry. "I'm still receiving the final portions of my training. I ask a lot of questions."

The soldier relaxed against his pillow. "Fine, then. I don't suppose being a case to study can add any further humiliations on top of what this stump already affords me." He laid his hand across the top of the sheets a score of laundresses had

93

worked tirelessly to keep clean.

Samuel took a glance around the ward still packed with men suffering from various sorts of ailments. Some had been patched up and returned to their ranks, but those with more serious injuries were still taking their rest until they were deemed fit to return to service. His current patient was not the only one to be missing a limb. If anything, this man suffered an unfortunately common condition.

He tried to compose words that might lend the man some comfort, but before he could string together the thoughts to do so, the bark of his name drew his attention.

He recognized Dr. Porter's voice rumbling through the ward like an engine down the tracks. Samuel promised to check on the private later and stepped away from the bed, dreading what reprimand would come now. Ever since the day he'd run out of the ward, Dr. Porter had delayed signing off on Samuel's training. He should have received his final release weeks ago.

Then again, he could hardly blame the man. Dr. Porter was charged with training physicians worthy of the title. Samuel was well aware of the doctor's strict attention to detail and ardent insistence that all men under his training be fit for service.

Any doctor who lets his patients see him run away in fear isn't a physician they can trust.

While Samuel did not disagree with Dr. Porter's words, it had not been fear that had driven him from the hospital. But a doctor who could not stomach the smells of blood and bile would be far worse, and so he had endured what he had always known would come. Now he could only hope his years of training would not end in vain and leave his father disappointed.

Worse, he could not continue to take his father's stipend

beyond his schooling. If he couldn't soon earn his way as a physician, what would he do to care for the children he'd adopted? He had no other skills that could provide the life he'd promised.

"Yes, Dr. Porter?" Samuel stepped into the center aisle that ran between the beds in the ward.

Dr. Porter tugged on the lapel of his jacket, the lines around his eyes seeming to have grown deeper in the past weeks. "Come with me." He motioned toward the door at the rear of the ward that led to the section of the hospital that contained his office. "I need to speak with you on a matter of some importance." Without waiting for a reply, Dr. Porter turned sharply, his coattails flying out behind him.

Samuel silently followed him toward his office off the East wing. Nurses and volunteers thinned in this section of the infirmary, and only a single nun swept dust from the corners of the hall. They had sprinkled lavender water about in an effort to control the smells that were daunting even to them.

He passed her with a small nod and received a brief smile before she continued with her task, her long skirts moving as much dust as her broom.

Dr. Porter stepped into his office and motioned for Samuel to take a seat before closing the door.

"How is your father?"

"Well," Samuel said, "though I'm sure he is eager for me to return and help with his practice."

Dr. Porter grunted and stepped toward his desk. The office was neat and tidy, as one might expect from a man like Dr. Porter. His desk contained stacks of papers that were evenly spaced, and jars of ink were arranged in a straight line.

"And your mother?" his voice seemed to thicken. "How is she?"

Samuel tilted his head. "Uh, well, sir."

The doctor took his seat, pulled the chair up to the desk, and folded his hands on top. He stared at Samuel a moment, as though looking for something in his features. Finally, he said, "It's my sincere hope that you have overcome your aversion."

Dread mingled with hope and slashed at one another without a clear victor. Samuel focused on keeping the battle from manifesting on his face and waited for the doctor to continue.

"I have watched you closely, and, well, if nothing else, I daresay you seem downright determined."

Why did the man seem surprised by the statement? "It's always been my intention to be a practicing physician, sir. That determination has driven me through these years of study and practice and will continue to drive me to continuously seek the best care for my patients. Despite any difficulties I've had, no other profession appeals more to me."

Dr. Porter stroked a thumb over his graying beard. "That I can clearly see."

Relief sent his dread into retreat. Perhaps he had redeemed himself after all.

"Still, I'm not convinced."

A muscle in Samuel's jaw twitched, and heat churned in his chest. Would one lapse cost him everything? It hardly seemed reasonable. He struggled to keep the bite from his tone. "I should hope that evidence of how a man overcomes his failures would be a better testament to his character and abilities than the failure itself."

To Samuel's surprise, Dr. Porter's features lightened in a rare smile. "I'm rather pleased to hear you say so, because that is my thought exactly."

Samuel's thoughts stalled, all words fleeing from his grasp. The man spoke in riddles!

"I don't believe this war will be over in a matter of weeks," Dr. Porter continued as though he had not just hung all of Samuel's ambitions over a cliff and dangled them in front of snapping lions. "The disaster at Bull Run is proof of it. I fear that before long we will be in dire need of surgeons who can command hospitals and take charge of the chaos that will blanket us."

He offered another smile and further deepened Samuel's confusion. "Therefore, I've been charged by our government to see that we have as many able physicians as possible." His gaze sharpened. "And perhaps with the proper guidance you have been denied, you could be better than expected."

The room seemed to slow into a long moment of drawing in a breath and releasing it out. "I, uh, thank you, sir."

Dr. Porter stroked his beard, his expression returning to its customary stoicism. "You have decent organization skills." He held up his hand and touched his forefinger. "You're fairly responsible." He touched the next finger. "Your determination is without rival." He poked another finger. "And you are skilled. With my guidance, you could be exceptional, son."

Samuel's mouth dried. What had caused this change? Yesterday the man seemed to barely tolerate him. Today he called him *son*.

The doctor sat back in his chair, a strange glitter in his eyes. "I'm sure your father would be pleased to see how well you do under my care."

Was that mockery in his tone? Samuel waited, but the image of his career hanging before the lions did not dissipate. If anything, he felt the line holding him aloft was being lowered farther over the cliff's edge.

"But you battle something I fear will eventually be your undoing."

And there it was. Samuel braced himself.

"I cannot endorse you only to have you crumble before this nasty war runs its course."

The line unraveled, spilling all he had worked for to be gobbled up simply because God had cursed him with this blasted nose. If he could cut it from his face and continue his life free from its havoc, he surely would.

Lord, how will I feed the children?

A nervous tick started somewhere in his toes, made its way up his leg, and came out as a tapping of his foot. When Dr. Porter lifted his eyebrows, Samuel forced himself to remain calm. Even facing such devastation, he must not let go of his professional control.

"Forgive me, Dr. Porter. This news has caused some distress."

"Distress?" The man had the audacity to chuckle. "Mr. Flynn, you have not been listening. I'm saying I would like to make you my second in the infirmary. I can give you far better opportunities here than if you returned to"—he cleared his throat—"well, if you return home."

Samuel stared at him. He was quite certain that had not been what the man had said.

"But you see, I yet fear you may not hold up under the charge, and I wouldn't want my fine young doctor to crumble under the pressure because I heaped it upon him too soon."

The words beat upon Samuel like pounding rain. Dr. Porter thought him capable enough to appoint as his second, yet in the same breath deemed he would fail in the position. He shifted his feet, trying to make some sense of his reeling thoughts. "You have not yet signed off on my studies." A less than subtle reminder that it needed to be done. "Surely you would appoint a licensed physician with credentials and experience, and thus my own readiness would not be of consequence."

"One would think." He straightened a perfectly spaced line of writing utensils. "Yet even this soon surgeons are being stretched thin. The army is woefully unmanned in medical staff, and the fighting has barely begun. What do you think will happen when every encampment and battle-bordered town is overflowing with wounded and sick men?"

"I'm sure I do not know."

Dr. Porter folded his hands once more, his features growing grave. "Dr. Fields defected to the South and Harold and Edward went with him. Dr. Engels will be moving to a new hospital and Dr. Floyd decided to retire. The students, except for you, of course, have moved on."

Samuel rubbed the bridge of his nose. Every teaching doctor from the university would be gone, leaving only Dr. Porter and the army surgeons.

"As you can see, this infirmary will soon be under the command of hastily trained army surgeons who have little to no knowledge about all of the duties involved in running a hospital. I worry that without a firm hand and attentive eye, the patients will only suffer further."

Samuel could certainly see the problem, but failed to see the solution.

Dr. Porter regarded him closely. "I've given this matter a great deal of thought ever since you first showed up in my hospital. Why do you think, in addition to being in charge of the supply closets, I put you at the helm of rationing out medications and organizing the nurses and volunteers?"

"Punishment for running out on you when the wounded first arrived and minimizing my unsupervised time with patients." The words slipped free from his lips before he had the good sense to catch them.

Dr. Porter shook his head. "No, son. I assure you that was not my intention."

Samuel clenched his hands and willed his mouth closed.

"I wanted you to learn how to manage a hospital as well as tend the patients in it. I'd thought someday you would find the training useful. It's an extra area of study I've not given to other students, but"—he spread his hands—"let's just say you're special."

Samuel shifted, unsure how to respond. The man seemed to waver in everything he said.

"Tell me, what did you plan to do after your studies, had it not been for this war?"

Samuel straightened. He thought the man knew his plans, but he answered anyway. "Help my father run his practice." He admired his father more than any other earthly man and could think of no greater ambition than to match his father's compassion and skill and work at his side.

The doctor sighed. "As I thought." He cleared his throat. "Well, I hope you will soon see you have better options. Until then, I have decided to send you to General Smith."

The air in the room seemed to thicken, the scents of leather, faint pipe smoke, and the ever present linger of the lavender water the nuns insisted on sprinkling around the building washing down his throat. "Beg your pardon?"

"McClellan's army has issued a request for temporary field surgeons, and I'm sending you. You'll take supplies and spend a few weeks with the Army of the Potomac and return to the infirmary when Dr. Nielson arrives to his post at Chain Bridge."

Confusion swirled in Samuel's chest, threatening to choke out his words. "I don't understand." Had the man not said he wanted Samuel to help him run the infirmary? Now he would send him away?

Dr. Porter leaned forward, his face oddly earnest for a man who had issued banishment. "I'm providing you an opportunity. If you stayed here, you would merely finish your final training, and then you would return home with the papers you need to practice under your father."

Precisely what he had in mind.

"Instead, I'm giving you the chance to serve your country and see if you truly have what it takes to be the surgeon I believe you can be. Any doctor who can serve in an army tent will be a different man at the end of it. I believe that is exactly what you need."

Silence settled on the room in lieu of whatever enthusiastic reply Dr. Porter seemed to expect. A field tent with the army? Close confines with men who would not have the opportunity to bathe? Where sickness was sure to run rampant?

Dr. Porter cleared his throat once more. "You leave immediately."

Samuel shook his head. "I cannot."

The lines in Dr. Porter's forehead deepened. "I don't think you understand. This is an opportunity for you, but it's also a requirement."

"I understand perfectly, but it doesn't change the fact that I'm responsible for two children. I cannot leave them for an extended excursion, no matter what intentions you have behind it."

Surprise widened the doctor's deep-set eyes. "You have children and did not inform me?"

Samuel held the man's gaze. "I didn't know it had any bearing on my work."

"Did a deceased relative leave you in this position?"

"No, sir. They came from the orphanage."

This time Dr. Porter stared at him with open astonishment. "You took on two orphans during your studies, in the midst of war, with no wife to care for them?"

Coming from the man's lips, the logic did, indeed, sound rather absurd. But logical or not, seeing those children's guarded eyes soften during the limited amount of time he was able to spend with them was worth it. Even if Mrs. Tooley's services were straining his accounts.

"Yes, sir. I did."

"You should have come to me first. I would have advised you."

Samuel struggled for a reply.

"Have you at least secured care for these children while you are at the infirmary?"

"I have."

"Live-in services?"

Samuel could see where this conversation headed. "Yes, but they should not be left for several weeks when they have just started to settle into their home."

Dr. Porter grunted. "And how do you suppose the men serving in the army feel about leaving their wives and natural-born children at home while they put their lives at risk for as long as is required of them?"

Guilt nipped at him. Of what merit were his convictions about keeping the country whole if they were cast aside as soon as it required something of him? "I understand."

"Very good then. I knew you would come to my side of thinking." Dr. Porter smiled and slapped the top of his desk. "You leave tomorrow. See that your affairs are in order."

Samuel rose and turned to leave, then paused with his hand on the knob. "Private Reilly needs to be treated for infection."

The doctor scoffed. "Nonsense. He's healing fine. I checked his stump yesterday."

"Even still, the infection has started."

He rose and came around his desk, narrowing his eyes. "He appears hale and hearty. Tell me what you've seen that causes you to think otherwise."

"I didn't see it." His hand tightened on the doorknob, and he held Dr. Porter's intense gaze. "I can smell it."

Dr. Porter cocked his head but did not label him mad.

"I know it sounds strange, but I am telling you it's true. Please, treat him. Treat this one and see if I'm not correct."

The doctor hesitated then offered but a small nod. "I'll give him a thorough examination."

Knowing he would receive nothing more, Samuel left the office. His footsteps fell heavy down the hallway, each one seeming to thud as leaden as his heartbeat.

How was he to tell the children he'd just adopted that he was leaving them?

Front Royal, Virginia
August 25, 1861

*E*velyn swiped the moisture from her damp cheeks and tossed another load of soiled linens into the pile for the laundresses. Weeks had melded into one another until she felt as wrung-out as the threadbare sheets drying on the line. She'd washed bodies, written letters, and ferried meals and coffee to and fro until the blisters on her feet had long since turned calloused.

Miss Alice Avery, a pleasant young woman who had taken to Evelyn's side since Isabella had abandoned the hospital two days into their duties, dumped another load into the pile. The nearest laundress, a dark-skinned girl of no more than twelve, regarded the growing pile with tired eyes.

"I reckon those poor girls have their hands full of it." Alice gathered a loose lock and pinned it to the rest of her mass of chocolate-brown curls that ever tried to defy their confinement.

"No more than the rest of us, I dare say."

Alice gave a knowing grin. "That's the truth of it. I never worked as hard at the farm as I have washing and tending those men."

Evelyn had done little physical labor prior to her weeks volunteering at the hospital, and her body bore the aches to prove it. But more than the soreness that plagued her limbs, her heart grew restless. Weeks she'd waited, and still no word from her father. What had happened to him?

Alice wiped her hands on her apron. "I heard one of the generals would be coming by tomorrow to check on the men. Any who are able to get out of their beds on their own are going to return to duty."

Evelyn shifted her attention to the young laundress and gave her a sympathetic smile as she dropped her soiled apron into the pile. She'd worn it for three days, but when Sergeant Reynolds lost his supper in her lap, it was necessary to find a replacement. She felt sorry for the wash girls, but was more than glad to be separated from the garment. "Nonsense. Just because they can stand doesn't mean they need to go back to drilling and marching. How are they to heal?"

Alice shrugged and made her way around another heaping pile of soiled bandages waiting to be burned. Flies buzzed around it in swarms. Why wouldn't the laundresses do the burning first? Surely smoke was preferable to flies.

"I don't know," Alice replied. "No one asks my opinion on such things."

Nor did they care for Evelyn's, though she had often enough given it. They made their way out of the wash yard, and Alice fell into step at her side. The girl twisted her hands together as though something buzzed about in her brain as incessantly as the flies around the bandages.

Sure enough, Alice sucked in a quick breath and spouted hurried words. "How well do you know Mrs. Greenman?"

"Not well."

"You did spend time with her, though, right? She was one of the ladies you visited during your social season."

Evelyn halted and looked at the girl, who stood an inch or so shorter. For all of Alice's wild hair, she was lovely with a smooth complexion and clear brown eyes. Isabella would dub her pleasant, though not beautiful. "Why the sudden interest in my social season, Alice? Do you have plans on securing one yourself?"

"Ha!" The wind snagged another of her locks and sent it scurrying across her thin nose. "Don't be daft. What farm girl has any cause for a social season? Silliness, if you ask me."

Evelyn studied the young woman who had become a much-needed friend in the shared trials of tending the wounded. Perhaps she was right. Once, Evelyn had longed for her season, hoping it would equalize her in her cousin and aunt's eyes. Now, she wondered if such preening was naught but foolish pride and desperate plays for a man's attention. What were they? Fillies paraded about at auction? The absurdity of it made her laugh. "You're right, of course. But this is not the first time you've asked me about Washington."

During the past three days, Alice had peppered her with various questions about Washington, her social season, and now Mrs. Greenman.

Evelyn put a hand on her hip. "If you have no interest in presenting yourself to society, what reasons do you have for all these questions?"

Alice glanced behind her at the women working the washtubs and grabbed Evelyn by the elbow. "Come with me."

Evelyn planted her feet. "We have work to do."

Alice tugged. "It can wait a few moments. This is important."

Too intrigued to refuse, Evelyn allowed Alice to lead her farther from the wash yard toward an open area away from the range of any listening ears.

"What's this about, Alice?"

Alice grew still, her eyes more intense than Evelyn had ever seen them. "I need to know what you know about Mrs. Greenman and her spy ring."

Evelyn scoffed. "I know nothing of it other than the rumors I've heard flying about town ever since Manassas." She frowned. "What makes you think otherwise?"

"You and your cousin are the only ladies I know who have met her in person."

"I'm sorry I can't tell you more, but anything she has to do with spying is beyond my knowledge. I still don't know if any of those rumors are actually true."

She turned to walk back to the hospital to help with settling the men in for the night, but Alice grabbed her hand in earnest. "They say she has couriers running notes from Washington all the way to Richmond." Her eyes sparkled as she leaned closer. "And I aim to help her."

Evelyn's heart quickened. "That's too dangerous."

Alice bounced on the balls of her feet, making her appear all the younger. "Don't you want to do more to help than wash filthy men?"

Evelyn hesitated. She'd felt satisfaction in her work at the hospital, but it wouldn't gain her a place at her father's side.

"You know Mrs. Greenman," Alice pressed. "You can introduce me to her."

The girl was mad. What Alice sought to do would see her captured and possibly killed.

The breeze picked up, sending dust clouds to play around the hems of their skirts and tug strands of hair free. Evelyn tucked it behind her ear. Perhaps she could get her friend to think it through and see the foolishness of the idea. "And what, precisely, do you think to do if I did introduce you?"

Alice lowered her voice, though no one stood near. "Just

what I said. I'm going to Washington to be a courier for Mrs. Greenman."

She said it as though it were the simplest thing in the world, as though it were not a harebrained scheme with no real direction or thought-out course of action. "And your plan is to waltz up to Washington alone and unprotected and announce you'd like to be a spy?"

"Shh!" Alice glanced around. The clearing in which they stood separated them from the orderlies who toted bodies to the dead house and from the washing women who likely had no interest in their discussion.

"This is foolishness. We need to get back inside."

"Please. Just listen."

Despite her better judgment, Evelyn paused.

Alice latched on to her hesitation. "I won't be alone. I'll have you. You are all the protection we will need."

Suddenly, Evelyn wished she hadn't confided in Alice about what had happened on Independence Day. She'd been tired, worn down with the tending of men, and the guilt and anger in her heart had bubbled over and found a willing ear.

Feeling older than eighteen years should, Evelyn's shoulders sagged. "How old are you, Alice?"

She stiffened. "Old enough."

"How old?" Evelyn insisted with more annoyance than she'd intended.

Alice squared her shoulders. "I'm sixteen. Not much younger than you."

Evelyn crossed her arms, the feeling of maturity fleeting with the childish gesture. "And how do you know my age?"

"Miss Lawrence told me." Alice lifted her chin as though the pronouncement was one to be proud of.

Evelyn glanced at the sky, where the thickening clouds portended rain. "I wasn't aware you were friends with my cousin." Why the thought rankled, she couldn't be sure.

Alice barked a laugh that seemed to mirror a hint of the bitterness Evelyn had often tried to smother within herself. "Of course we're not friends. She'd never be friends with the likes of me. But"—her grin returned—"she did answer a few of my questions."

Worn down by Alice's insistence, more likely. Evelyn turned back toward the hospital. "We've dallied too long."

Alice grasped her hand. "Wait! You haven't said if you'll go with me."

Evelyn paused. Part of her longed for the adventure. But it simply wasn't practical. "We are making a difference *here*."

Alice looked doubtful, and Evelyn had to wonder if her words were more for the over-eager girl or herself. "This is where we are needed."

"Please, just tell me you'll think on it." Alice squeezed Evelyn's hand and let it go. As she turned away, her soft words floated on the restless breeze. "I'll be leaving soon whether you join me or not."

Evelyn followed her friend back to the hospital, where they resumed their work. She'd soon have to figure out a way to convince Alice to change her mind, but right now she had too much to do.

She headed to gather a fresh basin and bar of soap when a young man entering the hospital caught her attention. He stood near the entry with a small black bag in hand. He was dark-haired and of an average height, with a plain face that probably didn't draw many eyes. But there was something about the way he studied the ward that caused Evelyn to approach him.

"May I help you find someone?"

He shifted his regard to her. "I'm a dentist. Anyone in need of service?"

"Others have already come, but you are welcome to ask one of the doctors."

"Perhaps I'll just ask some of the fellows."

Evelyn shrugged. "Suit yourself."

He bounded away, his gaze darting around as though he looked for someone. Curious, she followed him.

He moved through the hospital, asking men their names and taking note of any who said they had need of a dentist. Then he came upon Tim Holloway and dropped his dental bag at the foot of the private's bed.

He glanced around to see if anyone watched him, but didn't take note of Evelyn. Then the dentist removed something from his jacket and passed what looked to be a folded paper to Tim. They whispered low words Evelyn couldn't hear.

A few moments later, the fellow hurried out without examining a single tooth. Evelyn watched him go, then promptly went to Tim.

Tim Holloway was a towheaded fellow who hailed from Martinsburg. Evelyn had met him in passing at various neighborly gatherings, and since he'd ended up in the Front Royal hospital, she'd taken many of his letters to the postman. Putting on a smile, she settled onto his cot.

"In need of a dentist, Private Holloway?"

His eyes widened. "Um, I thought so, but turns out I was wrong."

She hitched her eyebrows. "And how do you know that since he didn't look in your mouth?"

Tim paled.

"What's really going on?"

He shook his head.

She lowered her voice. "You can trust me."

He stared at her for several moments, then sighed. "Your

father is a newspaper writer, isn't he?"

"Yes." Though that had nothing to do with dentistry.

"Then maybe you're the best to tell. Even if you *are* a woman. Not like I can do it myself anyway."

"What are you talking about?"

Tim leaned closer. "A new secret service is bringing in recruits. Ordinary people who aid in the transfer of information. One of the resourceful ways they operate is by running columns in the newspaper to coordinate their movements and plans."

Evelyn nearly laughed. "How secret can something be if you take out an advertisement for it in the newspaper?"

"The messages are coded. They announce arrivals and departures by advertising under previously determined aliases. If you don't know what to look for, you would never see it."

Ingenious. Did Daddy know about such things? "What does that have to do with you and the dentist?"

"He's not really a dentist."

She should have known.

"He's a part of a secret group that calls themselves the Knights of the Golden Circle."

A strange tingle ran down her spine. Why did a name so full of light give a feeling of darkness?

"We've been friends for many years. He thought I would be returning to duty and said he could trust me to get the dispatch to the right place."

Evelyn sighed. "You didn't tell him."

"Should have. Was too ashamed."

She kept her gaze from wandering to where his missing foot was hidden beneath a thin blanket. Tim Holloway wouldn't be returning to duty.

"Will you do it?" He slipped a paper from underneath him and showed her an advertisement for employment.

"I cannot." She rose. "Surely there are other ways of aiding the cause than such clandestine tomfoolery."

Tim's face reddened. "It's not tomfoolery. They even have a doctor line that runs from Washington to Richmond. Clever, really. They send doctors, both real and fashioned, to carry the messages. It's a grand idea, seeing as how medical men can move around at all hours without raising suspicion, and they carry bags that can be used to smuggle all kinds of items."

Evelyn put a hand to her temple. "Women spies and fraudulent doctors? What has this war brought us to?"

Tim leaned forward and grasped her skirt, desperation in his eyes. "If I don't do my part, then the mission will fail."

"Why didn't you think of that when you told him you would help, knowing full well you could not?"

He released her. "If you will not aid me, do you know anyone who will?"

Evelyn's gaze sought out her friend and watched her carry linens through the ward. Perhaps it would be just the thing to curb Alice's desire for adventure without her trying to undertake a dangerous trip to Washington.

She looked back to Tim. "I may have just the person."

Isabella turned up her nose. "I will not."

The rain fell in buckets outside the square dwelling they'd called home since coming to Front Royal. It beat upon the glass like hundreds of tiny fingers beckoning for her to return outside and to the hospital. Soon after her talk with Alice, the rain had started, and it hadn't let up in the two days since. The streets had turned to mud, and when the doctor sent her home with strict instructions to rest today, that mud had clung to her shoes and hem in clumps.

"The worst of it's over." Evelyn twirled the thimble on her thumb. "The doctors and nurses see to the wounds."

"Still." Isabella shivered. "I'll not go back. Mother says I don't have to."

"You won't have to do any washing."

Isabella sighed. "Please. Can we not simply spend an evening in companionship?"

Evelyn blinked. Isabella wished for her company? For the first time in weeks, she would be present for the evening meal with the family. She'd spent nearly every waking hour at the hospital, from dawn's break to deep into the night. Had her cousin actually missed her?

She held her tongue, not wanting to spoil the sentiment even though she wanted Isabella to return to the hospital with her. She could see how Isabella would shy away from the messiness of it all. But things were different now.

Isabella set aside her knitting. "Evie, I just can't." Before Evelyn could reply, her gentle tone dissipated and became steeled with arrogance. "It's simply too much for a proper lady's delicate sensibilities."

Evelyn withheld the unladylike snort that would have undermined her argument. "That isn't true. Why, many ladies have offered their services. It is a small price asked of us when the men are giving their bodies and lives."

"I'll still not go." Isabella frowned at the window, the diminishing light causing gray shadows to cling to her floral print skirt. She rose with the grace of one who put the utmost care into her appearance and fetched a lantern.

Evelyn watched her light it and set it on the table by her parlor chair, then tried a different approach. "Surely you could visit for an hour and write a few letters? That would not stress you overmuch." She tried to keep sarcasm from darkening her tone, but it pricked her words all the same.

"I will not be present with half-clothed men for any reason." Isabella glared at her, all traces of their fleeting moment of tenderness gone. "There are plenty of low-bred girls about who can write for those who are not educated enough to do it themselves."

Heat crept up the back of Evelyn's neck and tingled along her hairline. She tried to keep her voice soft. "Many are fine, educated gentlemen who have had the unfortunate luck of losing a hand or arm while trying to defend the rest of us."

"That's not my concern. Such are the consequences of men's quarrels. Women are to remain quietly at home."

Evelyn frowned. "You don't have to just sit around and remain helpless."

Isabella wrinkled her nose. "There you go sounding all high and mighty, as if you have any right to be. Do you ever grow tired of poking at anyone who does not do as *you* think is right?"

Evelyn sat back, her cousin's words hitting her like a slap to the face. "Excuse me?"

"You heard exactly what I said. You pick your words to make me sound heartless simply because I do not do things the way you would have me do them."

The hypocrisy of the statement scalded as surely as if she'd been doused with the contents of a frying pan. "Oh, no. Surely you are correct. I don't suppose I have *any* idea what it feels like for someone to shoot condescending words in my direction because I didn't speak, or walk, or *breathe* as deemed appropriate by the infallible Lawrence women."

Isabella tossed her knitting to the floor. "Why, you ungrateful little—"

"Is everything all right in here?" Aunt Mary stepped into

the parlor, the drum of the rain on the roof having muffled her approaching footsteps.

Isabella glared at Evelyn before scooping up her knitting and plastering a fabricated smile across her face. "Everything is fine, Mother. How was your day?"

Rather than taking a seat, Aunt Mary stood by the window though she surely couldn't see anything past the waterfall cascading from the high-pitched roof. "Well enough, I suppose. Lara's reading is improving, and she seems to find some enjoyment in her dolls, but I fear she's terribly homesick."

Isabella's voice returned to its usual velvety timbre. "I'm sure she'll be fine. We must only endure a little longer."

Evelyn doubted that, but held her tongue.

Aunt Mary turned from the window and lifted one corner of her mouth. The expression was so marred with sadness, however, that one could scarcely consider it a smile. "I have decided we will return home."

Isabella clapped her hands. "That's wonderful news, Mother! I'm sure it will be good for us."

"I've already spoken to your aunt and uncle. Should the Yanks descend on us in Martinsburg again, we'll simply return here. But unless that happens, there's no reason we should stay on."

"What about the hospital?" Evelyn interjected, though no one cared for her opinion. "They need our help."

Aunt Mary turned to her as though seeing her for the first time. "There are plenty of women in Front Royal. It's not our concern."

"Not our...?" Evelyn squeezed her hands in her lap in the hopes that all of her frustration would find anchor there and not worm its way into her words. "Aunt, do not your husband and son fight? What if they ended up in a hospital?

Wouldn't you want—"

"Do not dare to speak to me about my husband and son!" Her gaze turned incendiary. "I know more of their sacrifice than you ever could."

The rest of Evelyn's statement died in her throat, and she merely stared at Aunt Mary. Did she not see that hiding from the reality of this war would do her no good? Pretending they were not under attack would not keep the forces at bay.

Aunt Mary glared at Evelyn with eyes as sharp as bayonets that held nary a tone of motherly affection. But did they ever? Despair writhed in her stomach. What had she ever done to gain such distaste? Had she not always tried her best to earn the love of the family that had taken her in?

"We will be returning to Martinsburg day after tomorrow." Aunt Mary's cool tone slipped across the room and stabbed her. "When we return there, you may wait for your father to retrieve you."

Despite the undercurrent of the words, Evelyn's heart swelled. "Daddy is coming for me?"

"You will send word for him to do so."

Evelyn rose from her chair and stepped closer to Aunt Mary. "But I haven't heard from him in several weeks."

Aunt Mary glanced at Isabella, who had forgotten her knitting and was watching them closely. "A letter came two days ago. He's going to Washington."

"I have high hopes my letter will reach him there," Aunt Mary said, "through our mutual friend Mrs. Greenman."

Evelyn took a breath but had to pause to wet dry lips before she could speak. "He wrote and you didn't tell me?"

Isabella waved a hand. "You're never here."

Aunt Mary remained stoic, but her gaze roamed down Evelyn as though she hadn't spent years in her company. "No one can say I didn't try. Truly I did, but with all that is

Stephenia H. McGee

happening, I can no longer bear the responsibility. I regret my failing, but no amount of training can account for your unfortunate heritage. The time has come for me to return you to your father."

The woman spoke in strange circles, hinting and retreating, baiting and abandoning. Evelyn rubbed her temples, wishing she would speak plainly. "What are you talking about?"

Aunt Mary shook her head, her lips pinching together.

"My heritage? What does that mean?" Her voice tightened. "Surely you don't hold my mother's death against me."

Turning her gaze out the window once more, Aunt Mary seemed years older than she had mere months earlier. "Not her death. Her birth."

"What?"

Aunt Mary clutched the cloth at her throat. "She was..." She shook her head and lowered her voice. "Of Indian descent."

Evelyn stared at her, the faded memory of her mother surfacing. Her long black hair. Her deep-brown eyes. Beautiful.

Red splotches decorated Aunt Mary's cheeks. "She was a half-breed. My father warned Douglass not to marry her, but my brother wouldn't listen."

Tears burned Evelyn's eyes, but she refused to let them fall.

Isabella gasped. "But she's as pale as I am."

Aunt Mary looked away. "I did all I could. Now I must focus on my own daughters." She straightened. "Besides, you are a woman now, and can make your own way. Perhaps your father can find a husband for you in Washington, since I was unable to secure one for you during your season."

Evelyn could scarcely breathe. Her own family shunned

118

her because one of her grandparents had been an Indian? For this secret she had suffered years of feeling that she could never do enough, say enough, *be* enough for her aunt?

Could she return to Martinsburg with them and await word from her father? Or would the animosity that defied logic continue to thrust her farther into isolation?

Nothing she could do or say could ever change the blood in her veins. And even if she could, she wouldn't. She would never want to erase her mother's fingerprints.

Evelyn lifted her chin. "Then perhaps I should go ahead and begin my journey to Washington instead of waiting for him."

Alice's plan tickled the back of her mind. Could she and Alice travel together to Washington and then seek her father together? She studied her aunt. Regardless of their current animosity, surely her aunt would never allow such a thing. Surely.

Aunt Mary heaved a sigh. "I wish it were possible, but it would be irresponsible of me."

Not concern or love. Merely obligation and responsibility. Evelyn lowered her eyes and assumed the docile stance that had once gained her fleeting approval. "Then with your permission, I'd like to wait here for him. I feel I'll be of more use at the hospital than sitting idle in Martinsburg."

Aunt Mary stared at her for what felt like an exceedingly long moment, relief clear in her eyes even if it didn't come from her lips.

Finally, she gave a curt nod. "Very well, then, since that is your wish. I will speak to Hattie, pay for your room, and leave you a small stipend." She lifted a finger and aimed it at Evelyn as though she were a wayward child. "But you will see to your hospital duties and keep out of trouble. I'll not have you give Hattie any reason to regret her hospitality.

Don't forget you're my responsibility, and your actions fall back on my good name."

"Yes, Aunt." Evelyn excused herself from the room, plans already digging for a foothold in the swarming sting of rejection.

As she took heavy steps to the upper floor, Evelyn breathed a prayer for strength for what would come. She passed Hattie in the upper hall with a cursory nod, which the woman returned with a veiled expression. Did Hattie know of her heritage? Did she despise her for it as well?

Alone in her room, Evelyn gave a quick glance at her belongings, counted the currency she had in her reticule, and contemplated a risky decision. Perhaps Hattie would not have to tolerate her for long.

Fairfax County, Virginia
September 7, 1861

A breeze stirred the hair around Samuel's ears and sent tendrils playing across the top of his collar. It carried with it the richness of freshly dug dirt, the hint of rain, and the tang of horses. He stood on a small hill some yards away and watched. His medical bag grew heavy, though it paled in comparison to the weight that settled on his heart.

Soldiers in blue toiled in various groups performing a myriad of tasks to prepare themselves for the threat of attack. The lush land rolled out beneath their tearing boots, a jaunty green carpet that had once been the bed of fertile crops. Now it would be tramped and muddied underfoot as the great Army of the Potomac ground it under its heels. Washington must be protected, even at the cost of lives, land, and crops.

He should make his way down to the dwelling at the rear of the activities and announce his presence, but still he hesitated. The faces of two small children swirled in his mind, rooting his feet to the ground. Would they be proud of his efforts, or would they see his duty as abandonment? Benjamin had merely studied him with guarded eyes while Emily patted his cheek goodbye.

They would be well cared for with the widowed Mrs. Tooley. She was a kindly woman in her late middling years who seemed to find contentment and purpose with the children. Having lost her own twins soon after their delivery and never having birthed any others, Mrs. Tooley poured out her mothering tendencies on Samuel's children. Soon, he hoped, they would blossom under her patient care. Her quick response to his advertisement had been a blessing to them both.

Before leaving, he'd penned a missive to his parents, letting them know the trip they'd planned to come meet the children would have to be postponed until he was able to return to Washington. He explained Dr. Porter's reasoning for sending him to stay with the army and requested his father continue to pray Samuel would be healed from his condition.

The wind shifted north, scattering leaves and bringing the first hints of cooler weather. Samuel transferred the weight of his bag to his other hand and made his way down the hill.

He'd reached the flatland when a fellow with a full beard and a rifle aimed at Samuel's chest called for him to stop. The picket threw up his right hand.

Samuel removed his cap and tapped it against his left knee, as he'd been instructed to do. The picket lowered his gun, the signal indicating Samuel was not an enemy.

Samuel produced the proper papers, which the soldier scanned before nodding for him to continue. Having passed this odd manner of acceptance into camp, he was struck by the interesting things men had to come up with in attempts to differentiate friend from foe when no outward sign could distinguish a man's loyalties.

McClellan's army noted him as he passed deeper into the settlement, several tipping up caps and stopping to watch him with curious stares. He continued with the purpose of one who had cause to be here and strode down a narrow lane lined with canvas tents flapping against the persistent breeze. Would one such dwelling be his home during the coldest months of the year? Would he be stuck here that long?

Small campfires smoldered after the noon repast, giving off wisps of smoke that tickled his nose and disguised some of the scent of unwashed bodies. Camp Griffin appeared to be little more than a bivouac in some unfortunate farmer's field, and Samuel sincerely hoped the men would find better ways to gird themselves for the winter than the thin walls of canvas tents.

He passed dozens more of the flimsy structures before he came to the cluster of outbuildings surrounding the farmhouse he'd first spied from the hill. He'd barely entered the more civilized section when a man stepped in front of his path.

Tall and muscular with sandy-colored hair and a wide face, the man held up his hand as though the rest of his body blocking the way had not given adequate indication he wished for Samuel to halt. "Ho, there."

Samuel tipped his hat. "Good day, soldier. I've shown my papers to the picket."

The man chewed on a sliver of wood stuck between his lips and assessed him with narrowed eyes. "What's your business?"

"Medical staff, sent down from the Washington Infirmary. I'm to see the division commander General William Smith."

Satisfied with nothing more than those words, the bulky fellow tossed a finger over his shoulder, indicating the large farmhouse beyond. "He's in there."

The soldier turned away. Samuel watched him disappear behind a smokehouse and then continued on to the farmhouse.

Wide and sturdy with an inviting porch, the home seemed the type of place where a man could build a good life for his family. A pang of regret for the fellow who'd accomplished such a goal only to see it trampled under war jabbed him. They must all sacrifice something to see the evils of slavery diminished and the country remain whole. For some men it was the demise of their dreams and aspirations; for others it would be their homes and land. For the soldiers, it could be their very lives.

Samuel rapped on the front door of the whitewashed home. After a moment, another soldier opened it and required the exchange of the same question and response as the last man. Only then was Samuel led inside and told to wait.

The front receiving area was as inviting as the exterior promised, with tasteful furnishings and portraits of honest-looking people hanging in carved, if not gilded, frames. Wood floors burdened with soldiers' dust stretched out in long planks beneath his muddy boots. What did the family think of having these men in their home? Did they still abide within, or had they abandoned it?

"Are you the doctor?"

Samuel turned at the sound of the voice. An officer, who by the looks of him, Samuel assumed to be General Smith, stepped from the room to the left. The man stood maybe an inch or two shorter than Samuel with thinning hair combed to one side and a mustache that blended into the pointed hair hanging from his chin.

Samuel bent forward slightly at the waist and held his cap in front of him. "I've not completed my final rounds of hospital attendance, sir, and therefore as of yet haven't received my title."

The man narrowed his eyes. "But you've had training?"

"Yes, sir."

"What kind?"

Pleased the officer seemed to care enough to take stock of any man claiming to be a medical practitioner, he held no animosity for the barked question. There'd been too many quacks who'd attended a few lectures and fancied themselves doctors before the American Medical Association had started implementing higher standards. His father had served on that board and had strong opinions on the matter. Those same opinions carried through to his only son.

"I have completed my apprenticeship, lecture series, and dissection courses, and I'm near to finishing my final year in hospital rounds under the guidance of Dr. Porter of Columbian College. Upon his signature, I shall receive my commencement papers and my physician's title."

The officer motioned to another man, who had stepped up during Samuel's answer. "That sound about right to you?"

The other man turned stony eyes on Samuel. "I suppose. Though I would wager any spy worth his salt would take the time to know something like that."

Spy?

Samuel reached into the inner pocket in his jacket. "I have a letter of introduction from Dr. Porter in addition to my pass."

General Smith chuckled. "Then why didn't you say so?"

Samuel withheld his retort that he hadn't been given the opportunity and merely handed the document into the officer's waiting palm.

He scanned the contents, nodded, and gave it back. "Good. You'll report across the chain bridge to Benvenue and to General Winfield. They are setting up a hospital over there."

Without further instruction, Samuel was ushered out the door.

"Are you sure about this?" Evelyn pressed her back into the trees and watched the men down below. "We could just go on to Washington."

Alice laughed. "You've changed your mind already, have you?"

Evelyn brushed dirt from her skirts. "This detour wasn't part of the plan." Though, if she were honest, the thrill of the road, the freedom from the constant expectations, and the fresh air had done her spirit a world of good. Perhaps that came from her mother's blood. The thought made her feel closer to the mother she never really knew.

Alice touched her hand. "I'm sorry. That was unkind of me."

Alice glanced around the wooded area, her wild mass of curls looking more like they might if the two of them had camped out of doors rather than spent their nights nestled in the hospitality of Southern sympathizers.

Not for the first time, Evelyn wondered how Alice had so deeply ingrained herself into a secret society that it took care of their traveling needs. She didn't like the idea of being indebted to them for it. "The plan was to go straight to Washington. Once we find my father, he will take care of us."

Alice picked at the tree bark. "You see them down there?" She flung the bark in the direction of the soldiers.

"Of course I do." Evelyn glanced at them. Men prowled along the length of a grand bridge, its sturdy beams and fine construction an obvious asset to guard.

"That's an awful lot of Yanks, Evelyn. Don't forget what happened to you in Martinsburg, or how many men you tended who suffered at their hands. What I'm asking you to do today is important."

The Federals had been fortifying for miles surrounding Washington. They might have to pass through the whole of the Army of the Potomac to reach Margret Greenman, and Alice intended to make use of it.

"What if they see us?"

"What threat are two women? They might not notice us. We'll pose as girls looking for laundress work. Word is there are plenty of such women around the camps." Alice smirked. "And I've heard tell most of those women offer more to the men than just clean britches."

Evelyn ignored the comment and settled down in the edge of the woods to watch. "And why is it I need to be the one to find this doctor?"

Alice looked down at her. "I told you. I have to make contact with the nearby Confederate camp. As I'm certain you won't want to do that, all you have to do is take what the doctor gives you, and then give it to me." Alice smiled. "You won't even know what it says, so you can't be accused of anything."

"Tell me the signal again, just to be sure I don't get it wrong."

Alice grumbled something about Evelyn's lack of memory and then plopped down into the leaves with all the grace of a ragged hound. "He will have a doctor's bag. Watch for him to shift it to one hand, and then the other. Then he will drop it to the ground. Once he does, you approach him."

Evelyn stretched her legs out in front of her. "But how will we know he's the right one? What if you're wrong and this isn't the place?"

"I'm not." Alice plucked a fallen leaf from the ground, its yellow tint the first early signs of autumn. "The system hasn't been wrong about anything else, so I don't see why it would be any different now."

They settled into silence. Evelyn couldn't guess what her friend contemplated, but questions and concerns swirled around in her own head enough for both of them. Were they about to get themselves into trouble so deep it would drown them?

A howl of laughter caused them to startle and they turned their eyes to the men down below who joked and lounged as though they'd forgotten their enemy resided not far from here.

"It's almost time." Alice rose and brushed her skirts.

Trepidation scurried through Evelyn's veins, but she steeled herself against it. Daddy had been right about the Yanks, and Alice had gotten them this far. She could do her part.

Alice flashed a sunny smile. "Let's get started."

Samuel kicked up dust as he walked. He tried lifting his feet and settling them down flatly, but it made little difference. The dust swirled under his boots and clung to the legs of his trousers. The air received it gladly and carried it up for a dance before returning it to the ground somewhere behind him. Some particles refused their proper place, however, instead insisting on dancing into his face.

He swatted it away as best he could and moved forward. Perhaps it truly would be better to be in nature with the dust and the scents of earth than the press of bodies in the infirmary. This assignment might do him good after all.

Tent hospitals, while sparse, allowed for an abundance of fresh air. And fresh air would certainly do him good. He breathed deeply, and by the time he reached Chain Bridge, he'd fostered a patriotic hope that buoyed his steps.

The bridge was impressive. Wide and stout with curved beams, it resembled a fancy garden arbor on a grand scale. An impressive passage worth guarding from Southerners who would have to cross it to reach Washington.

Samuel stepped under the arching wood. Proud men in blue uniforms carried weapons ranging from sabers to rifles as they paced the bridge waiting for any sign of Rebels. Some merely stood along the length of the structure, keeping their eyes focused on the churning water below, ever vigilant for any sign of danger.

He moved closer to the railing and followed one bearded man's gaze. The Potomac provided a grand barrier, indeed, and Samuel certainly didn't envy the soldier, even an enemy one, tasked with crossing it without the aid of a well-made bridge. The soldier nodded to him, as though they had shared the same thought.

He stepped off the wood beams and onto the dirt on the other side. In a few moments, he was in nature once more and the tense watch for the enemy could easily be forgotten along the quiet road to the hospital. Wildlife scurried thither and fro, the scampering of a squirrel's feet a rhythmic beat to accompany the chorus of birdsong.

Then the wind shifted, and on the breeze wafted a fragrance that spoke of nature, yet did not belong. It bloomed with hints of sweet honeysuckle and lavender. His steps slowed. Lye soap, and something else. He hesitated and breathed deeper. Something more tingled along his senses. Something he could not place.

He planted his next step and whirled around. But the path behind him was empty.

Eleven

*T*he hairs on the back of his neck stood on end. The wind shifted, and the enticing fragrance that had stirred him disappeared. The woods standing sentry along the edges of the road held fast to their secrets. Still, Samuel remained rooted to his position, his senses alert to danger.

Would a rebel emerge from the underbrush to slay him where he stood? Samuel shifted his bag to his right hand, held it for a moment, and then decided to pass it back to his left. If a hot-blooded Southerner popped out of the trees, better he have use of his dominant hand to defend himself.

A flash of cornflower blue caught his eye, and then a slip of material passed between the trees. He narrowed his eyes. A skirt? What woman would be slinking about in the woods?

The swath of blue drew closer, materializing into a silhouette of a woman. He stood there like a fool, mesmerized by the sway of fabric as it drew closer. He watched as the details emerged, captivated.

The skirt hung limp, unencumbered by the fashionable hoops women of means touted. No frills or pomp, but no thick line of muck coated the hem. Why he should notice such a thing, he wasn't entirely certain.

His eyes drifted farther up. The skirt narrowed at the top, and the fabric swelled over womanly curves. The graceful arch of a feminine neck rose from a high neckline, supporting a face hidden in shadows. Like a fairy from one of Emily's storybooks, the woman hovered in the cover of the woods, watching him as surely as he watched her.

He dropped his heavy medical bag.

No sooner had it hit the dirt than she took another step forward. He waited, not wanting to frighten her. For surely a creature as timid as this offered no cause for alarm. The shadows of hanging limbs dappled across her form until she stepped free of their embrace.

Hair as dark as a raven's wing swept away from a face free of a temptress's paints. Wide, dark eyes stared at him, hidden for the briefest of instants behind the sweep of lashes. She drew her lower lip between her teeth and took another step toward him, twisting long pale fingers together.

A striking woman. With the contrast of her creamy skin and raven hair, he was again struck by the thought of a fairy. Her complexion was smooth, and the lines of her face pleasing. But it was her eyes that held him captive all the way to the moment she stopped a few paces from him.

Deep as pure cocoa, they sparkled at him with intelligence, bravery, and determination. Were he truly standing on a page of Emily's book, surely this arresting creature would be called the *Lady of the Mist* or the *Queen of the Wildwood*.

The thought brought an unexpected turn of his mouth. Queen of the Wildwood. Emily would fancy that.

Lady Wildwood stepped closer and offered a tentative smile. Her lips parted, and the strong and confident voice one would expect of a fairy tale queen broke the silence and the strange spell surrounding them.

"Are you the doctor?"

He lifted his eyebrows. Had she been waiting for him? "I am."

She glanced down at his medical bag. "You have it, then?"

"Have what?" He reached down and picked up the black leather satchel that contained the whole of the supplies Dr. Porter had allowed him to take. As much as he could fit in one medical bag, Dr. Porter had said. And so Samuel had packed it full. Hence the weight that had caused him to need to shift it from one arm to the other. "Are you in need of medicines?"

She cocked her head, and those expressive brown eyes darted all around him. "I thought you would know what to give me."

Suspicion cut through his fascination with the Wildwood Queen. Something was amiss. "Oh?"

She stiffened, as though he had disrespected some unknown sensibility. Curiosity prodded him on, so he played the game to see where it would lead. "Right. Of course."

Suspicion flared in her widened eyes, and she took a step back. "You're not him!"

He reached for her. "Wait!"

Evelyn took another step back and then spun around. She'd been mistaken! The brush of fingers swept along the back of her arm and she yelped, springing forward.

Dirt kicked up around her feet as she lunged back toward the woods. She darted under the cover of low-hanging branches, her feet churning through the fallen leaves and making too much of a ruckus. If he wished to follow her, he would have no trouble in doing it.

She ducked under a limb, and then another, her lungs heaving with exertion. Whoever said that proper ladies did not run had never found the need to escape a man.

Footsteps pounded behind her.

"Wait!"

The man's voice cut through the woods around her, but she had no intention of heeding his call. Whoever he was, he certainly wasn't the man Alice told her to find.

And that wasn't good.

She lurched around a sturdy oak, lungs burning with the effort of each breath. Her skirt snagged on the claws of branches and slowed her progress. They tugged and ripped, shredding fabric and leaving strips of it behind.

She gasped, her throat searing with each gulp of air that could not cool her lungs. Her stomach rolled. Still the man's heavy boots pounded behind her. She darted behind another tree and glimpsed salvation.

A massive oak stood like a king among its subjects, its trunk wide enough that two of her would have had a hard time clasping hands around it. Stumbling, she flung herself behind the tree and pressed her back against the bark.

She tried to listen, but she panted so heavily that she could hear naught but the rapid flow of air in and out of her body. Evelyn closed her eyes and prayed he would not see her. Her heart pounded in her chest, beating against her ribs like the Yanks trying to burst into the house.

She couldn't be caught by one of them out here in the woods. If the vile brutes would mar a lady in her home before a cluster of witnesses, what would one of those Blue Devils do to a woman alone in the woods?

Her hands searched for the comfort of Uncle Phillip's pocket pistol. But a Yank had long since taken that.

Panic, cold and icy, perforated the burning in her chest. A flash of movement, and a hand reached out and cinched her wrist.

Evelyn screamed.

Startled, Samuel released his hold and stepped back, raising both hands in the air. "Easy, miss. I don't mean to frighten you."

She patted her hands along the upper folds of her skirt and stepped away from him. Her chest heaved after her dash through the woods, short as it had been. The material over her bosom rose and fell, and he had to snap his eyes back to her reddened cheeks to keep his gaze from resting too long.

She stared at him, black hair all tangled and hanging in disarray around her face. She looked like a frightened child. Vulnerable. He took a step closer, meaning to dispel her concern.

Her eyes hardened, and she planted her feet. She drew her shoulders back, and the vulnerability left her features. She glared at him. "What…" She sucked another breath. "What do you want?"

Samuel rubbed the back of his neck, wondering the same thing himself. He'd dashed after her without the first thought. Now that he'd caught her, he had no idea what he aimed to do next. "I thought you might be in trouble."

She took another step back and bumped against the stately oak. "Liar."

Samuel paused. Venomous little sprite. He held up his palms and took a step away from her. "I'm not going to harm you."

Her eyes narrowed into slits. "Forgive me for not believing you."

Samuel tossed his thumb back over his shoulder. "What was that about?"

"What?"

He sighed. This was foolish. He had things to tend to. Whatever purposes the Queen of the Wildwood had were her own. It had nothing to do with him. He shrugged. "Suit yourself. But if you have a loved one in need of the medicine you asked after, I would be willing to give you some."

Her mouth pressed into a line, and she seemed to consider his words. "Why would you do that?"

"Because, despite your odd behavior, I'm a doctor, and it is my duty to offer aid to any who have need of it."

Her breathing slowed as she studied him, and he wondered if she would bolt. He waited, watching her assess him. What did she see that caused her to look intently upon his face?

"Very well. But you'll walk in front of me, and when we arrive at the road, you'll remove the medicine from your bag and leave it on the ground."

He almost chuckled. "Such demands, lady. And what makes you think I will adhere to them?"

She lifted her shoulders. A tear had ripped the top of her dress, leaving a flap hanging open at her arm. "Do or don't. It makes little difference to me."

She was as likely to run as not, but Samuel gave her his back all the same. He needed to get to General Winfield and stop dallying with this madwoman in the woods.

He wound his way through the underbrush, picking the easiest path back out of the forest. Pieces of her cornflower blue gown clung to the tips of briars and brush, and he wondered if some of her anger at him sprouted from her ruined dress. But then, it was hardly his fault she raced through the woods.

No noise followed him, at least that he could hear over the crunch of his own boots, but the scent of honeysuckle and lavender was as clear an indication of her presence as heavy footfalls would have been.

Evelyn kept several paces behind the man's retreating form, lest he think to whirl around. Even if he did, she wouldn't be able to outrun him. If he had no intention of manhandling her, then why did he chase her into the tangle of the woods? Did he truly only want to help her? Why would he bother?

She stared at the back of his head, as though her eyes could see through the hair that curled around the top of his collar and thereby read the thoughts encased behind them. The color of a river stone, his locks were a deep brown shot through with auburn strands. His shoulders were fairly wide, tapering to a slimmer waist, indicating strength was hidden under his jacket. Could such a man truly be a physician?

The doctors she had seen were usually into their graying years, and even those who weren't were spindly, or bespectacled...or, well, not like this. This man appeared more a blacksmith than a doctor.

Another reason not to trust him. But she'd missed whoever Alice had sent her to find, and her friend would be furious. If this man was willing to give her medicines, perhaps Alice would forgive her.

He stepped out of the woods and ambled to his belongings as though he fully expected they would still be right where he'd left them. She scanned the road, but saw no signs of any Federal blue. They must be there somewhere, though.

He lifted a small box from his bag and placed it on the ground. "What ailments do you need a cure for?"

She ignored his question and waited at the edge of the trees. But rather than repeat himself or be annoyed, he merely regarded her with calm assurance. His confidence rankled her.

"Who are you?" The words slipped free, though she knew better than to try to engage him.

"I could ask the same of you, miss. Why is a lady hiding in the woods?"

She forced herself to keep his gaze, even though it surely allowed for him to see right through her. "These are dangerous times, as you know. A woman is at constant risk."

Surprise, and then concern, played across his cleanly shaved features. This was all very confusing. He had clearly given the sign. He'd gone farther past the bridge than he was supposed to, but she'd figured he'd had his reasons for it. Then he'd stopped, looked around for his contact, and proceeded to exchange his medical bag from one hand to the other before dropping it to the ground. Did he yet test her to see if she were truly his contact?

"Are you in danger now, miss? Has someone sought to harm you?"

He did not test. She'd merely foiled the mission. She took another step away. He made no move to follow her, though he surely could have caught her.

"Miss, I'm sorry for whatever trouble you've found yourself in. I apologize for not being able to offer you proper aid, but I must get on to patients who need me." He gestured toward the little box on the ground. "But there are medicines for stomach ailments and infection in there. Please take it for whoever needs it."

He cast her one last apologetic look and turned and

walked away.

Evelyn stood there long after he'd gone. When all remained quiet, she darted to the center of the road, scooped up the box, and then ran back into the woods. With one hand clutching her skirts and the other holding fast to the box, she leapt over an upturned root.

A flash of movement to her left sent a stab of fear through her gut. He'd circled back upon her! She darted in the other direction when a harried female voice caused her feet to stumble.

"Evelyn!"

She halted and spun, finding only Alice. She blinked, trying to be sure her friend stood there and not another.

Alice scrambled over to her. "Evelyn! For heaven's sake, what are you doing?"

"I...I thought you were a Yank."

Alice let out a breath that stirred the curl hanging across her brows. "Whatever gave you that idea?"

Evelyn simply shrugged.

Alice's eyes sparkled. "You got it!" She pointed to the box in Evelyn's hand.

"No, I'm afraid not." She glanced around, still not sure if they were safe. "Come on. We need to get away from here."

Alice frowned. "What do you mean?"

"I approached the wrong man."

Alice frowned. "Then what's that?"

"He was a doctor, but not the right one." She pressed her fingers to her temple, which had begun to ache. "He gave me this medicine because he thought I needed it."

"That doesn't make sense. If a doctor gave you something, then it was what we were after." She smiled. "You did well!"

Evelyn bit her lip. That couldn't be right, could it? She

139

didn't tell Alice about her flight through the woods. If Alice had what she wanted, then it didn't matter. And if Evelyn had gotten it wrong, then they would know eventually. For now, she was simply glad it was over.

Twelve

ire from dozens of campfires lit up the valley like an inverted sky. They dotted the fields, twinkling with a merriment unsuited for such foul company. Evelyn set her teeth. She was tired of being afraid. Alice was right. Those Yanks down below were all the same as the miscreants who had invaded her aunt's house in Martinsburg, and any schemes worked against them were earned.

Thinking of her aunt caused her empty belly to tighten. Surely by now Hattie had alerted Aunt Mary that Evelyn had chosen to go to Washington without escort. Did she and Isabella worry?

She shook the thought away and decided it didn't matter. Why did she always strive to please a woman who would never care? No, better she put her efforts into Daddy's cause.

Alice's features were barely visible in the moonlight, but her voice was firm. "If we keep our heads low and move around like we are supposed to be here, no one will notice us."

Though doubt refused to release its hold, Evelyn squared her shoulders. "Very well."

They skirted farther to the left, carefully stepping over branches and upturned roots. A cool breeze portending a harsh winter kissed the back of her neck and sent a shiver down her aching back. They huddled among the trees, watching like orphans on the outskirts of a king's feast.

A score or more of women buzzed around a huddle of campfires, tending pots. Roasting meat turned over flames as smoke wafted lazily in the air. A shift of the breeze, and the sizzling smells caused Evelyn's stomach to complain. She pressed her hand into her belly but didn't succeed in stifling either the grumbling or the ache.

Evelyn glanced around in the dark and picked up a fallen limb. "Here, gather some wood."

"What? I can scarcely see." Alice shifted in the shadows, her skirt skimming over rustling leaves.

"And what do you suppose those women will think of us strolling out of the woods? At least if we have some wood, we can look like we've been gathering it for the fires."

"Oh! Marvelous idea." Alice stooped to gather a few branches, and the two of them stumbled around in the dark. It was a fragile plan at best, but better than nothing.

When they had a sufficient armload, Evelyn thrust her chin toward the camp even though she knew Alice couldn't see her. "All right then, let's go."

Faint music intertwined with the delicious aroma, and coupled with the dancing firelight, the camp held an atmosphere that made the place appear almost festive. Evelyn ignored the thud of her heart and kept her chin down, walking straight toward the encampment as though she belonged. Alice tripped behind her, nearly dropping her load.

The warm circle of light beckoned, offering a safe haven of comforts that at the moment seemed less the enemy than the woods. They drew nearer, and the sounds of the crackling fire, the high pitch of women's laughter, and the hum of conversation slithered into her ears and promised security for the paltry price of betrayal.

Women of various ages milled around, some wiping their hands on their aprons, others unclipping linens from a line. They laughed as they worked, either forgetting or ignoring the shabby conditions brought on by bivouac camps. They did the women's work that men, even in war, deemed either menial or unnecessary, contributing in their way to the comforts of those they cared for. Evelyn could respect that notion. Despite their loyalty to miscreants, she could esteem any woman who gave of herself to such a degree.

However, as for the women who saw to the men's other needs...

She shook her head, trying not to gawk. Such women were not hard to spot, their raucous laughter and Jezebel eyes as telling as any signpost. They drew men deeper into the sanctuary of women, their hands lingering a second too long on a sleeve. With a disgusted grunt, Evelyn turned her face away as one shapely woman didn't try to hide pulling a soldier into her tent.

Such a woman would not be of any aid. Evelyn scanned the more respectable camp followers until her gaze rested on a lone lady tending a fire slightly removed from all of the others. The woman's gray locks were pulled back into a matronly knot at the base of her neck, giving her a practical and efficient appearance.

Evelyn turned her head slightly to whisper to Alice. "Let's try her," she said, gesturing to the matronly woman.

Without giving herself time to change her mind, Evelyn stalked forward, Alice's steady footfalls behind her. The kindly looking woman tended a crackling fire, its light shooing away shadows. Evelyn gazed at her feet as they poked out from her skirts, then followed them all the way into the edge of the glow of the stranger's campfire. She lowered the stack of wood in her arms, and a second later, Alice dumped hers next to Evelyn's.

The limbs hit with a thud, one rolling into the edge of the flames.

The woman startled and dropped her wooden stirring spoon. "And who might you be?"

Evelyn clasped her hands in front of her and kept her gaze on the woman's well-worn hem. "A laundress, ma'am. My sister and I have brought you more firewood."

"Oh?"

Had Evelyn dared to look up into the woman's face, she was certain she'd have seen distrust color the woman's eyes.

"And who sent you out in the dark to fetch it?"

Evelyn's pulse quickened at the suspicion thickening the woman's tone. She shifted her weight from one blistered foot to the other. "No one, ma'am. I just thought…" Her words trailed off.

This had been a terrible idea. What had she been thinking? Lured into the dangers of a Yankee camp. She took a step back. "We'll be going now."

The woman's hand shot out lightning quick and grabbed Evelyn's wrist, causing her to yelp.

Alice mumbled something, but Evelyn didn't look at her. Her gaze locked on the matronly woman who stared at her with hooded eyes. She looked Evelyn up and down as though contemplating what to do with her. Would she sound an alarm? What would they do then?

To her utter astonishment, the woman released Evelyn with a sigh. "All right, girls. The truth now." Her voice softened, and she offered a grandmotherly smile. "Where did you two come from?"

Evelyn glanced at Alice in the firelight. Her hair was falling down on one side of her head, and dirt streaked her cheek. Evelyn withheld a groan. How had she not noticed how pitiful they appeared? And after her run through the woods, she must look much worse than Alice. No wonder the woman suspected them.

"We…" Evelyn twisted her hands together.

"Just looking for work, ma'am," Alice said.

The lady glanced at Alice, then returned her regard to Evelyn. "Come now, child." The woman stepped closer, her words gentle. "It's all right."

Evelyn blinked, caught off guard. "We, uh, we came from Front Royal." She sensed, rather than saw, Alice stiffen beside her.

Time slowed as the woman studied them, their fate held in the balance. Cicadas buzzed a constant hum against the pop and crackle of the fire.

Finally, the woman chuckled. "Did you now? From the looks of you, I'd say you had a time of it."

Evelyn stood a little taller. "We did, ma'am. We are trying to make it to my father in Washington. Just yesterday we, um, *escaped* across the river."

The woman shook her head, her hand fluttering to her heart and resting on the gingham fabric that covered it. "Oh, you poor dears. What has this country come to? Those hotheaded fools making it so that young ladies have to run through the woods to escape their marauding."

The words caught her off guard. Had secessionist soldiers acted in the same horrendous manner as the Yanks? Impossible. Daddy reported unbiased news, and surely he would have mentioned such a thing. She sought to keep the confusion from her face as Alice answered for them.

"It has been a difficult journey."

"Why, of course it has, child." The woman's eyes pooled with pity. "Those intolerant traitors don't care for anyone but themselves and their own greed. Why, the tales I've heard would turn your blood cold."

Evelyn's jaw fell open, but she snapped it closed. The woman patted her arm and then addressed Alice. "My goodness, girl. You look like something's gone to nesting in your hair." She waved a hand at them. "Come along. I'll get you a pot of water warmed, and you can get washed up."

Relief swarmed through Evelyn's stomach. "We couldn't possibly trouble you."

"Of course you can. That's why I'm here."

Evelyn allowed the woman to shoo them toward a nearby canvas tent. "Pardon?"

The woman laughed. "It's just the way of it." She lifted the flap and motioned them inside.

A large rug covered the grass underneath, creating a cushion and barrier against the dust. A narrow bed stood against one wall. The lamp hanging from the highest point in the center of the tent cast dancing light across a neatly spread quilt. A miniature stove stood against the rear with a pipe lifting through to the top of the wall and then disappearing outside. A sturdy trunk with metal banding completed the furnishings.

"I'm Ida Johnson, but you can just call me Ida." She looked at Evelyn expectantly.

Seeing no reason not to give at least their Christian names, she pointed to her friend. "This is Alice, and I'm Evelyn."

The woman waited for a moment. When neither of them said more, she shrugged. "Good, then." Ida turned and rummaged in a crate sitting near the stove and pulled a kettle from underneath a cloth. "I think a little tea is in order." She eyed them. "I've some nightdresses you can borrow in the trunk. Best we get those gowns washed, too."

While they gaped at such open hospitality, Ida bustled out of the tent, letting the flap fall behind her.

Alice scuttled to Evelyn's side, her eyes wide. "I can't imagine that could have gone any better, do you?"

Evelyn tried for a smile, but wound up only stretching dry lips instead. "No. I suppose not."

"Hello?" A voice called from the other side of the tent flap. "May I come in?"

They glanced at one another. "You may," Evelyn replied.

The flap parted, and a woman with a long blond braid draped over her shoulder entered with a tin plate. "It's not all that much, you having missed the evening meal and all, but it's something." She lifted the plate toward them.

Alice accepted it. "Thank you kindly, ma'am."

The woman nodded and slipped out of the tent once more. No sooner had she gone than Alice plucked a slice of bread from the plate and shoved half of it in her mouth. Aunt Mary would have had a conniption if she saw Evelyn do such a thing, but hunger had a way of slaughtering propriety. She plucked a slice for herself and barely chewed before swallowing it down.

By the time Ida's shadow crossed the rug once more, the plate had been cleaned of nearly every crumb. Ida said nothing, offering only a smile before setting a pot of steaming water by the little woodstove. "Wish there were a tub for you, girls, but a rag will have to do."

Alice giggled. "Clean water is more than enough to ask for, ma'am. We thank you kindly."

The older woman smiled, a gap between her front teeth making her all the more charming. She pushed her wrist against her brow and surveyed their dresses. "Just toss them out of the flap. I'll see they get a good boiling. If the weather holds, you should be able to wear them by afternoon."

The thought of being left with naught but a borrowed nightdress sent Evelyn hurrying to grab Ida's arm before she could go. "I thank you, but how are we to go about tomorrow without gowns?"

"You may stay here and rest until they're dry. I don't have but the one bed, but I'll fetch some extra blankets for you from some of the girls. They won't mind."

"Why are you out here?" Evelyn's question came softly, spurred by curiosity over how someone so hospitable kept company with an invading army.

Ida wiped her hands on her skirts. "With the camp, you mean?" At Evelyn's nod she continued. "My boys are in this army. I didn't see any reason to sit at home and fret over it when I could come with them. I don't see them much, mind you, but I know I'm helping them." Ida's gaze felt heavy. "I might ask you the same question, my dear, though I think I know."

Evelyn somehow managed to keep her features impassive. "Oh?"

Ida laughed. "Come now, you don't think you're the first little gals to come looking for their sweethearts, now do you?"

Evelyn shook her head. "Oh, no, we…"

Ida's face grew stern. "Then don't go looking for one who isn't already yours. Too many girls are getting their skirts in a twist, thinking they are doing good for these boys and letting the threat of battle get them to thinking they best find all the fun they can."

Heat crept up Evelyn's neck and seared into her ears.

"Now, then." Ida's businesslike tone signaled the conversation was over. "I'll get you some gowns if I can find some you can borrow. Otherwise, you'll be sitting here until yours dry."

"And then?" Alice asked.

Ida shrugged. "Then, we'll talk about what tasks you'll do to earn your keep."

An hour later they were washed, wore borrowed night-dresses, and sat working the tangles out of their hair with a comb.

Alice's fingers tugged on Evelyn's hair, twisting her hip-length locks into a braid before securing the bottom with a strip of twine. "This sure beats sleeping in the woods."

"I almost thought we were going to have to," Evelyn whispered.

Alice gave a playful tug on the knot of twine. "Don't fret, *sister*. You've done very well."

A surge of pride welled in her chest, and Evelyn twisted on the rug to properly face Alice. "You think so?"

"Of course. Why, a little longer, and you'll be a heroine women prattle about in their sewing circles."

Evelyn smiled. Perhaps so. And then wouldn't Isabella be surprised? She curled her arm under her head and lay back next to Alice on their pallet. In a matter of moments, the swaying lantern overhead blurred and then disappeared behind the curtain of sleep.

The next day, Ida bustled in with two gowns, shoes, and of all things, crinoline cages. Evelyn rubbed grit from her eyes and stared at the bundle of things Ida tossed on the bed. The light warming the canvas walls and the sounds of the commotion outside indicated they'd slept well past dawn.

"Here now, aren't you in luck?" Ida beamed, her cheeks dimpling. "Looks like some of the boys found a couple of trunks in an abandoned house." She gestured toward the pile of fabric. "Now, Mrs. Lotta Pickers has claims on these things, seeing as how it was her husband who found them, but you girls can borrow them for the day 'til your own things are good and dry."

Evelyn rose and fingered the fine fabric of a lavender dress. "And these things were taken from someone's home?" She ran her hand down an embroidered corset. "Won't the lady that owns these be sore to find her things missing?"

Ida grunted. "Don't be silly, child. Those rebels have long since run off."

Evelyn exchanged a glance with Alice that Ida didn't see. Alice's features hardened, making her young face appear far more mature.

The older woman scuttled about, cooing over the fine clothing. "Now, you'll look like good and proper ladies when you go see the captain today."

"Captain?" The word seemed to stick to the roof of Evelyn's mouth. "What captain?"

Ida snatched the blankets from the floor. "All the camp girls have to talk to the captain, dear. He's in charge of making sure everything runs smoothly." She cast a glance over her shoulder. "And with as pretty as you two are, we need to make sure everyone has the right impression. 'Twas providence that sent this trunk in the nick of time, it was."

She helped them dress and fawned over each piece of the finely made clothing, and then before Evelyn had time to formulate a proper plan for this turn of events, they were ushered out of the tent, her wide hoops barely squeezing through the opening. The idea of wearing such fashions in camp seemed utterly ridiculous.

She'd given up on looking like a well-to-do lady when she'd started tending wounded. Why in blazes would she want to strut around an army camp in such a getup? It served precisely the opposite purpose of what she aimed to accomplish—going unnoticed.

Alice swished along beside her, a rose gown buttoned all the way up to her throat. The woman who owned these things had been blessed with a figure neither she nor Alice possessed. The bosom of Evelyn's gown was too loose where it should have been fitted to her smaller curves, and the waist of the bodice pulled against her middle despite Ida's lacing the corset underneath up tight.

She crossed her arms, aware that every woman in the camp stared at her as she tried to make sure the wide hems didn't brush into any fires. Not only was wearing the cane-reinforced skirt making her conspicuous, it was downright dangerous.

"Ida, are you sure we need to be dressed in this fashion?" Alice tugged her lace collar, concern clearly etched across her forehead. "None of the other ladies are dressed in this manner."

Ida spoke without turning. "None of the other girls are going to present themselves today."

Evelyn didn't like the way that sounded, but she had little option other than to move forward. They made their way through the women's lines of drying uniforms, socks, and blankets, and then passed into the decidedly masculine portion of the camp. By the time Ida finally came to a halt outside one of the larger canvas structures, Evelyn felt certain her face must be the shade of a mulberry.

Ida said a few words to a knobby looking guard with wispy hair, and in a moment an officer with a pointed chin and probing eyes exited the tent.

His eyes roamed over them, and Evelyn had to force herself to keep from shifting under his intense gaze. "Came out of the woods, you say?"

Ida nodded. "The poor dears escaped over the river. Came from Front Royal, and from the looks of them, had a time getting past all those Rebs."

The captain gave a curt nod. "What skills do you have?"

Evelyn laced her fingers. "We can do any manner of womanly efforts, sir. Mending, washing, cooking..." She trailed off on that last part, as she had doubts anyone would want to eat anything made by her hand. But then, she had no intention of staying long enough for anyone to find out.

"Nursing?"

"We've tended to wounded before," Alice piped up.

Evelyn tried not to grimace. Didn't she see such an answer would lead to questions about when and where they'd gained such experience?

The captain seemed not to notice. He spoke to Ida as though she and Alice were not standing there. "Send them to General Winfield. They can serve at the hospital and boost the lad's spirits." He turned on his heel and disappeared back inside his tent.

Ida gestured they return to the women's area. "Very good, girls. Now, see, you did well."

Evelyn thought to disagree, but there'd be no point. She simply turned her lips into a fabricated smile, too relieved the man hadn't asked further into their nursing experience to be annoyed at this ridiculous pageantry. Why did they need to be dressed in such a manner to answer a single question from an officer?

As they were ushered back through the camp the way they had come, Evelyn's eyes roamed the men, taking note of their condition, their numbers, and the lines of their camp.

Campfires smoldered, sending smoke curling around canteens, boots, sabers, and various other items the men left scattered around. Why, the boys at the hospital in Front Royal complained that they didn't have enough supplies, and here were the Yanks tossing things about.

An idea formed. A wild, foolish idea. Evelyn stepped to the side, the hem of her skirt sliding over a musket. For an instant, the weapon remained hidden under the wide circle of her dress. Her lips quirked.

Come evening, she would help to remedy that problem.

"You're brilliant!"

"Shh," Evelyn hissed. She cut her gaze to Ida's bed, but the woman's soft snores continued undisturbed.

Alice bobbed her head, the movement sending her curls swaying. She lowered her voice. "The Confederate camp isn't that far. We could at least make it to the outskirts. How'd you ever think of such a thing?"

Evelyn grinned. "Didn't you see all those things scattered about?"

"I did." The light of a full moon seeped through the thin walls of the canvas tent, giving Evelyn enough light to see the contemplation on Alice's face. "But that doesn't mean they're still out after dark."

Evelyn scooted closer, casting another look at Ida. "But worth a try, yes?"

"Yes." Alice winked and tugged on a pair of boots and hooked the buttons. "I knew you would be great at this."

A few moments later, Alice grabbed a blanket and Evelyn peeled back the tent flap. Clouds hung low in the sky, breaking up the moon and leaving slivers of pale light across the ground that resembled cast-aside swords. Campfires had smoldered down into a glow of embers, creating circles of red that contrasted with the silver filtering from above.

Somewhere in the distance an owl called to its mate. Frogs croaked in their nightly gatherings. Evelyn strained her ears to sift through the noises, but no human sounds disturbed those born of nature. Evelyn waved her hand behind her, gesturing that it was safe for Alice to follow, and then slipped out.

Evelyn stood in the bands of silver and waited. It took two long, controlled breaths and a smattering of rapid heartbeats before she felt safe to continue. Alice moved around Evelyn's side, her white shift seeming to have a faint glow in the moonlight and making her appear like an apparition.

Evelyn shoved the haunting thought aside and skirted the nearest campfire.

Keeping to the shadows, Evelyn crept through the camp, surprised to find not a single soldier sitting with his weapon at the ready to fire upon an intruder. Such pickets must all be positioned outside the camp itself. How they had managed not to find one when they'd first approached baffled her.

Alice grabbed Evelyn's hand, her palm cold without a glove to ward off the night's chill. "I don't see anyone."

"And they've left their stuff out." She gave Alice's hand a quick squeeze. "Quickly, gather what you can. But don't take everything from one tent, as that might make them suspicious."

The clouds hid whatever expression Alice may have had, and Evelyn hurried to the nearest soldier tent before either of them could change their mind. Inside the canvas structure, a man snored so loudly that she scooped up a bayonet, a box of shot, and a carving knife without making a single sound that could have been heard over it.

She continued slinking from one tent to another, pilfering items left around the campfires and propped against trees. A twinge of guilt nipped at her heart, but she shoved it away.

Thou shalt not steal.

Evelyn ground her teeth. Thou shalt not murder, either, yet war was what it was. Her sin seemed the lesser of the two. And if by playing a lady Robin Hood and stealing from the Yanks to give to the Secessionists who were grossly under supplied, well, then…

The argument crumbled away. Evelyn set her teeth and turned herself to the task with more vigor. She would do what she must, even if it seared her conscience.

Some of the Yanks had been daft enough to leave rifles and pistols out of arm's reach while they snored in idle tents. Such the better. By the time Evelyn finished moving as deep into the camp as she dared, she'd gathered a rather large pile of items. Taking one final armful, she crept back to the wide branches of a pin oak, its boughs not sufficient enough to hide her clandestine movements from the eyes of heaven.

Evelyn gently placed a metal pot on top of the pile of stolen goods and surveyed her work, waiting for Alice to appear. The biggest question now would be how long it would take them to get these things secured. They wouldn't have much time.

A shimmer of white slipped past the nearest tent. Evelyn remained still so as not to startle Alice as she approached.

"Did you find enough?" Alice whispered, laying two rifles next to the rest of the stash.

"Yes. Now let's hurry and roll this up."

She grabbed the corners of the borrowed blanket, trying to make as little noise as possible. Alice grabbed the other end, and together they maneuvered their way around the tents. Each rattle made her heart skip. At any moment a man would see them.

But no forms emerged from the soldier's tents, and no bugle blast signaled thieves were creeping among the ranks.

They made it back to where Evelyn had previously stashed skirts behind the laundresses' washtubs when she'd gone to do private business just before bed. Chest heaving, whether from fear or the exertion of the load, Evelyn lowered the bulging blanket behind a large tub and dropped to her knees.

"We did it!" Alice said, her excitement bringing her voice above a whisper.

Evelyn tossed her a ball of twine. "We're not finished yet. Best not to count our fortunes prematurely."

Alice snagged the string and grabbed one of the hooped crinoline cages. They cut slits in the fabric around the boning, and then with careful loops and a lot of knots, set to tying four sabers, two muskets, six pistols, a cooking pot, three canteens, five knives, and sundry smaller items to the hoops of each one of the skirts.

By the time they'd finished, Evelyn's fingers were shaking from both the cold and the tedious job. She'd thought at any moment someone would discover them, but no one stirred.

The items were secured and the two of them encased in their weighted fashions by the time the sky began to lighten. Evelyn pulled at the string holding up the crinoline. Even with her corset, the skirt was so heavy it squeezed her middle like an anaconda.

Alice turned in her gown, holding out her hands. "Well?"

No one would know by looking at her that Alice carried as many items as a sutler. "Walk easy. Too much movement and something may rattle."

"Best we get moving before camp awakens, then."

"Yes." Evelyn lifted her face to a sky the same color as

the gunmetal hidden beneath their skirts. "We've a long and difficult walk to the other camp with all this weight. It will surely slow us."

Evelyn ignored her conscience once more and told herself the sin was worth the good it would bring. Then with stealthy steps, she lifted the stolen supplies and hastened toward the maw of the woods.

Thirteen

Benvenue Stone House Hospital
Fairfax County, VA

*S*amuel hid his smile and made another notation. The men were doing well, indeed. The seventeen of them seemed to be rather comfortable, their spirits lively in the coolness of early morning. Distracted from their ailments, some read the paper while others played whist, checkers, or chess, all while loudly discoursing the war news.

He had taken quickly to his duties here, finding the running of the small hospital refreshing. Samuel made a point to speak to each of his patients, find ways to bring forth a chuckle, and be assured their spirits were seen to as well as their bodies. Perhaps Dr. Porter had been right. He'd found a sense of purpose here, and with the brigade surgeon ill, had found himself immediately in the position of running the hospital.

"What in the devil have you got here?" The voice boomed across the walls and incited an immediate lull in the jovial mood. Soldiers who were able stood, and all turned their attention on General Hancock.

Since the officer addressed Samuel, he stepped forward. "My hospital, General."

He grunted, curling up one side of his mouth. "A brigade that looks a sure sight better than those outside drilling. Where are your sick?"

What manner of nonsense did he allude to? "They are here, sir."

"Well, this beats anything I have seen in the army. If you give soldiers such beds and comforts as this, you'll have every man in the regiment in the hospital within the month!"

"It's my experience that a rested soul as well as body restores a patient to health. With a little mirth, a fresh breeze, and an air of cheerfulness, one finds that conditions are greatly improved. You'll soon have men hearty and eager to return to their ranks."

The general scoffed and then pointed a finger at him. "They will not shirk their duties, regardless of your babble. This is war, Doctor, or have you forgotten? We are not here to see to the tenderness of the soul. Any soldier who is able to stand will return to work. He will not be lying about playing checkers."

Samuel eyed him, refusing to be intimidated. "If he is able to perform his duties without causing a regression in his illness, then he will most certainly be returned as soon as he is able."

General Hancock gave one last glance around the ward and then stalked from it. As though fettered to his boots, every last sense of light-heartedness was dragged out of Samuel's patients and through the door with him.

For the remainder of the morning, Samuel tried to restore their spirits, but found the task much more daunting than it had been prior to their superior officer's arrival. What made a man come into a hospital and demean the improved condition of the sick and injured? Samuel's jaw tightened. He was no soldier and didn't have to bow to the whims of a sour general. What could the officer do? He needed Samuel's services too much to send him back to Washington, and he could not court-martial a civilian.

Determining not to let the general's rancor affect his own mood, Samuel set himself about his work seeing that the patients were tended, the hospital kept clean, and any odorous obstacles kept at bay. He set a smile on his lips that would surely seep into his countenance and made his rounds.

"How do you fare, Private Miller?" Samuel scanned over his notations and then set them aside, turning his full attention on a patient with a waning case of typhoid. Samuel's senior by at least two decades, the soldier's features bore the lines of his years.

He swept a lock of chestnut hair from his brow and shifted himself to sit up in his bed. "Right good, Doc," he replied, looking at Samuel with eyes finally free of the fever that had plagued them. "Seeing as how I managed to survive the typhoid."

"Indeed, you have." However, he was in no condition to be returned to digging trenches, no matter what the general decreed. "Your condition is much improved."

"Wish I could get a furlough to go home to my wife. Would do me a world better to be in her company than yours." He smiled. "Meaning no offense to you, Doc."

Samuel chuckled. "None taken."

He leaned back against his pillow, his hand caressing the letter under his palm. "She didn't want me to volunteer. Said it would be naught but a death wish. But it was my duty, you know?"

The vision of two little faces lit in Samuel's mind's eye. Perhaps he did know. "It's for a noble cause that we make such sacrifices."

The private's features turned pensive. "I thought that,

too. Now I'm not rightly sure."

"Certainly, it is. We must be willing to fight to abolish slavery. It has no place in this country."

Private Miller wagged his head as though Samuel was a boy who'd said something naïve. "You abolitionists. All that hubbub you people created sure gave old Abe a good selling point for war."

Samuel's jaw tightened. "The abolition of slavery is the apex of the conflict. The Southern states refuse to see it abolished."

"Perhaps. Either way, seems a mite more noble thing to fight for than taxes."

Samuel's brow lowered. "These do not sound like the words of a patriot."

Private Miller rubbed the graying scruff along his jaw. "Don't get all up in arms, Doc, I'm only saying what's true. Ain't like I believe any man should be a slave. Me, now, I volunteered because I truly am deeply invested in the cause. There's no question that we must fight for government instead of anarchy. No good can come of turning our forefathers' nation into two hostile countries."

"No, it most certainly cannot." Samuel turned to leave.

"And yet, I wonder…If the government can tell the sovereign states they no longer have the right to leave the Union, then what else might they soon take under control?"

Of no mood to enter a political debate and with duties to attend to, Samuel offered a rueful shake of his head. "A bridge to cross at a later date, yes? For now, we must keep the country whole and eradicate the evils of slavery."

The older man nodded. "An evil institution, yes. But there still be times I would rather leave them that partake in such sins to face their judgments without me." He turned sad eyes back onto the letter he clutched in his hand, and Samuel stepped away.

War was an ugly thing, and he feared it would get uglier as it ripened. He tamped down his annoyance, knowing the man spoke from the ache of missing home. But they must not compromise, and they must not stand idly by. Who was to say that this fight was not, in fact, the judgment meant for taming the greed that fueled such an evil institution?

State's rights, taxes, and government control were all minor issues, mere twigs burning alongside the log that was the issue of slavery. Surely anyone could see that. Theirs was a most noble cause, brought to a head by good men fighting in a valiant army. As such, they could only prevail.

Samuel finished his ministrations, instructed the nurses on the dispensing of the noon meal and the afternoon care of the men, and then stepped out into the pleasantly temperate day. Sun skittered through the boughs hanging over the green lawn and cast dappled shadows across the blades of grass. Soon, they would wither as the days grew shorter and colder.

He exited the yard and made his way around the tents of the Fifth Wisconsin, nodding to men as they set about their various duties. Across the chain bridge, he approached the army's main encampment. The scent of strong lye soap and the sound of feminine voices drifted on the breeze as he neared the women's section at the rear of the camp. He needed to speak to Mrs. Johnson about sending one or two of the laundresses to the hospital. He had need of someone to scrub the floors and help the nurses change the bedding. Keeping the men in clean bedclothes did much for their health.

Even the nurses thought him excessive, but keeping his ward in pristine condition not only helped the men, it kept his weakness at bay. The aroma of roasting meat mingled with the strong smell of the soap the closer he came to the women's domain.

Set apart from the rest of the camp, the women who trailed the army had set up a tidy area of tents smattered with cooking fires and bubbling pots of laundry. A blessing they were, these wives, sisters, and friends of the men who served.

Mrs. Ida Johnson's voice rose above the general din of the camp. "And I told you, Lotta, I haven't seen them!"

Samuel neared where the two women stared at one another, both with hands set firmly on hips and looking like two roosters about to flap their wings and extend their talons.

"You're the one who let 'em take it." The red-haired woman crossed her arms. "My man found it, and it belonged to me. You had no right."

Mrs. Johnson made a face. "They were in need, and you said you didn't mind."

The other woman tossed her head, looking rather like a high-strung filly. "I said I would be willing to help some girls in need. You never mentioned anything about letting them wear my gowns!"

Samuel resisted the urge to roll his eyes. Such venom for a couple of borrowed dresses? He would never understand women and their fripperies. He cleared his throat and stepped nearer. "Excuse my interruption, Mrs. Johnson, but may I have a word with you?"

The older woman turned to him with tired eyes. "Certainly, Doctor." She glanced back at the fiery young woman and wagged her head. "We'll talk about this later."

The younger woman cast Samuel a scathing look and stalked off.

"Never you mind her. She's up in arms because she had laid claim to some Rebel woman's finery, and now it's gone and run off."

Samuel didn't wish to be dragged into such nonsense, but

the manner of the statement, and the tone in which the woman delivered it, piqued his curiosity. "Pardon?"

"These two girls came out of the woods. Pitiful, they were." Her hands flew about rapidly as she spoke. "All covered in muck and looking like they had been through a terrible fright."

Samuel stilled. He'd seen a lady coming from the woods once before. Had the Wildwood Queen visited the camp? "And they stole that woman's clothing?"

Mrs. Johnson waved a hand. "Heavens, no."

Samuel couldn't explain it, but he felt a sudden surge of relief.

"They needed a good bath and some rest. I got them cleaned up and took them to the Captain for assignment. In fact, they were supposed to be going to the hospital. But then…" She shrugged. "They up and disappeared. Haven't seen them since last night."

"Odd." Samuel glanced toward the edge of the woods as though he would see the sprite standing there. "Tell me, what did these women look like?"

"Well, one was but a wisp of a girl, with wild curly hair and eyes a mite too big for her face."

Not the lady he had met on the road, then.

"The other was a couple of years older with hair as black as soot and a complexion that didn't look like it had ever seen much of the sun. Said they escaped from Front Royal."

A strange excitement pitched through him. She had returned, only to disappear again. What kind of woman made her home in the woods? The notion of a fairy-tale creature captured his imagination once more, but of course that was all foolishness. What logical explanation could be had for such behaviors?

A curiosity he might never satisfy. "I've come to ask for

women to help clean the hospital."

Mrs. Johnson touched the lace on the little cap pinned to her head, eyes round. "That was the job the captain gave those two girls."

"Then send others, would you?"

At her nod, Samuel turned and made his way out of the women's area, careful not to let his eyes linger on any lady lest she think him interested in the service he knew some offered...services that had naught to do with laundry and meals.

He picked his way around the camp, then came past the guardhouse for the Fifth Wisconsin Volunteers. He'd set his course for the hospital when a commotion sent up a wave of shouts from the other side of the camp. Men dropped their shovels and axes and ran in a swarm of blue.

Samuel followed them, his gaze darting from one man to another, trying to figure out what sort of turmoil had them moving with more vigor than he had yet seen.

Were they being attacked?

Samuel snagged the arm of a young fellow who barely seemed old enough to be called a man. "What happened?"

The soldier turned and walked backward. "Was a skirmish."

"Where?"

He turned and started to jog away, throwing over his shoulder, "They attacked the survey party."

The implications hit him all at once. Skirmish meant fighting, which meant wounded. He must get back to the hospital before any arrived.

Breaking into a jog, he dashed across the chain bridge where soldiers' voices rose with clamor and reached the stone house as two men entered with a stretcher.

A soldier lay on the fabric, his cries mingling with the

tang of blood in the air. Samuel thrust open the door and called for the nurses to prepare the beds and make ready. It took but a glance to assess the damages.

The soldier's jacket was torn to shreds, and his flesh hung in strips that revealed a hint of the ribs underneath. "Ready surgery!" Samuel called, indicating the soldiers should take the man to what had once been a dining room and now served as his operating space. He would have to dislodge the shards of metal and stem the bleeding if the man had any hopes of survival.

"Doctor! There are more coming through the gate."

Samuel ignored the slight nurse who possessed too flighty a countenance to be suited to such work. It mattered not how many would come. He would tend them by order of need, and this man's need was paramount. He pushed his sleeves up and turned his attention to the surgery, calling for instruments, linens, and water.

They stripped away the soldier's jacket and shirt, and his best nurse, Mrs. Fanning, bathed away the blood. Though try as she did, it continued to seep.

"Get me the chloroform."

Someone passed the bottle and a rag into his hands, and Samuel applied a dose into the cloth, held it over the moaning man's mouth and nose, and sent him into the comforts of sleep.

It took at least an hour for Samuel to remove the foreign objects, repair a cut vein, and marvel that a miniè ball had missed the man's heart by a mere half finger's width.

Leaving the final bandaging to the nurse, he stepped out of the surgery room to evaluate the rest of the wounded. Fortunately, it seemed only a few soldiers with minor injuries added to the number of patients, and his two nurses had them in hand.

A woman's wail broke through his assessment of his hospital. He swung his gaze to the entry, where a lady in a resplendent lavender gown knelt on the floor, her dress a great pool of fabric around her.

Black hair spilled from its pins and hung down her back, mingling with the tumble of silk and lace. Samuel's breath caught, and for the first time in his memory, the smells seemed to dissipate.

The Queen of the Wildwood.

The strange sprite who had stolen dresses and kept to the woods. He hurried toward her, ignoring the call of one of the nurses.

As he drew closer, he realized the mound of fabric came from two gowns rather than one. She held another woman against her chest, her sobs muffled against the other woman's great mass of tangled brown hair.

Samuel knelt and placed his hand on her shoulder, her trembles sending a gush of something through him. It was akin to the feeling of protectiveness he had over little Emily, yet such an emotion had no place in this circumstance. He removed his hand.

The woman did not react, but continued to sob over the one in her lap.

"Miss?" He reached out to gently shake her shoulder. "Come, release her so I may look upon her injuries."

His words seemed to startle her, and she jerked her head up. When their eyes met, hers flew wide with recognition.

"You're…" The Queen of the Wildwood heaved a ragged breath. "Oh, is she dead?"

Samuel had to pry the lady's fingers from her companion in order to get a look at the injured woman's face. He leaned in, putting his ear near her nose. Breath, though faint, still flowed from her body. He leaned back on his heels. "She lives. What injury did she sustain?"

The black-haired woman watched her friend with tearful eyes.

"If you don't tell me what happened," Samuel said impatiently, "then I cannot tend her."

She didn't look at him. "The men started fighting. We didn't know they would be there." She shook her head, sucked in a gulp of air, and then…something shifted.

Before his eyes, the trembling woman disappeared. With a hardening of features and the stiffening of her spine, a different woman now sat before him. Warm brown eyes turned cold and bore into him from a stony face. The transformation was so abrupt and so complete that Samuel nearly flinched.

"I'm not sure what happened." Her matter-of-fact tone held not a hint of emotion. "We were traveling the road this morning. Then men were forming ranks near us, and then suddenly they were fired upon. Chaos erupted. I turned around, and Alice was on the ground. I called for help, but no one came. It wasn't until they gathered the wounded some time later that someone hoisted her up for me and brought her here." Her eyes darted around the room as though looking for the man who'd aided her. "He said she was dead, but carried her here anyway."

Samuel placed his fingers under the patient's jaw. Her pulse beat rhythmically. "Did you see this lady—"

"Alice."

"Did you see Alice get hit with anything? Are there open wounds?" Not that he needed to ask. The scent of blood didn't cling to her. Only moss, earth, and the faint tinge of rosewater.

"As I said, one moment she stood by my side and the next she lay in a heap on the ground. I suspect she may have fallen as we tried to get away, but she remained on the ground and I couldn't rouse her."

Samuel eased his fingers into the tangle of curls that covered Alice's head, and in a moment found the cause of injury. A large knot formed on the back of her skull, like an egg that had been cut in half lengthwise and plastered against her scalp. "She's sustained a blow to the cranium."

The Wildwood Queen bit her lip, and Samuel's eyes snagged on her mouth before returning his gaze to her guarded eyes. "I didn't mean for her to get hurt."

He nodded and released his hold on the patient, then called for one of the hearty soldiers who still milled about to help him. With the aid of a reedy man who was stronger than he appeared, Samuel lifted the unconscious woman from the floor onto a nearby cot. He would have her moved to the privacy of the upper floor as soon as he had the hospital in order.

He stepped back over to the heap of light purple material and offered his hand. "I will see to her once I finish my rounds."

The sprite grabbed his hand, her luminous brown eyes filling with fear. "You must see her now!"

He gave a slight tug, and she lurched to her feet. Samuel extracted his hand from her grip, uncomfortable with the way such a mundane thing affected him. "There are soldiers who require care first." There was little he could do for a bump to the head, besides allow the woman to rest, as he had already done.

He walked away before she could argue, distancing himself from her troublesome presence. But even as he did, something in him wanted to cast responsibilities and logic aside and yield to the whims of the Wildwood Queen.

Fourteen

The air in the hospital—formerly a home—crawled with tension, fear, and mistrust. Well, at least it did for Evelyn. Did any of them know what she'd done? Had a weapon she'd stolen from one of these men led to him ending up here?

Evelyn watched as the stout young soldier who had carried Alice the three miles back from Lewinsville knelt over a fallen compatriot. Was this ward any different from the one in Front Royal? Nurses darted about, removing blue jackets and bathing dirt from open cuts, and Evelyn put her fingers to her temples, sank to the floor next to Alice, and grasped Alice's limp hand.

Was it that easy? Shed the color of their coat and they were the same underneath? It couldn't be. These men were devilish fiends. Then why did they look more like tired, bedraggled, men who suffered injuries the same as the boys in gray?

Their moans mingled with ones that came from somewhere deep in her soul. Watching the man who had carried Alice lower his head in prayer over his injured friend broke something within her. Had she been wrong? Had she heaped the sins of one man upon all who wore the same color as he?

And had Ida been right, as well? Were men from *both* sides capable of the atrocities Daddy had only attributed to the Yanks?

Here sat not marauders as she'd believed, nor evil men as Alice and Daddy had labeled them. They were as much husbands, sons, sweethearts, and friends as the Southern boys. Did the women who sent these loved ones to battle weep any less than Aunt Mary? Suffer any less? She squeezed Alice's hand tighter.

She'd convinced herself they were evil and deserving of the sins she'd committed, making excuses and finding an easy target for the anger churning in her heart. Had her theft helped mothers lose sons and wives become widows?

The doctor walked among them, giving them encouragement as he saw to their mental as well as physical well-being. A contradiction. A Yank with a heart. Something Daddy said didn't exist.

But he was wrong. Memories of the lighthearted private who had stood watch over her in Martinsburg drifted to mind. The young man had not been evil. He'd treated her with respect and dignity despite the fact they clearly stood for opposing sides.

Had she merely found an outlet for anger she could not direct elsewhere, and so she'd made devils out of men? Evelyn clutched the fabric at her neck, tears burning their way across the back of her throat and finding release through stinging eyes. Stealing to make her father proud and pouring hatred on strangers would not ease the true ache of her heart.

The truth, cold and bitter as unnecessary death, surfaced from the depths where she'd long buried it. Daddy had abandoned her under the guise of safety and education. Aunt Mary had never been the mother-figure Evelyn desperately longed for, and Isabella had always looked down on her.

Her deeply buried anger had bubbled and festered. She'd first found her courage in order to defend against sinful deeds, but then that courage had somehow deteriorated into something much less gallant. Under the guise of courage, she'd baited her cousin, defied her aunt, and hated people she didn't even know. She'd taken all that was discontented within her and found something to heap it upon.

If she were honest with herself, the Yanks were just easier to hate than those she loved. They were easier to blame for her problems than blame herself.

She gazed at Alice, tears blurring her vision and distorting her friend's face. Was she herself naught but a selfish termagant bent on having what she wanted at the expense of others?

She released Alice's hand and drew her knees to her chest.

Try as she might, she could not keep the wracking sobs from overtaking her. She pulled her legs in closer, wishing nothing more than to be as small as possible. To disappear unnoticed.

A warm hand enveloped her arm. "Miss?"

Evelyn shook her head, pressing her eyes into her knees until it hurt, trying to stop the torrent that sprang free.

"Miss?" The doctor's voice, smooth as a river stone, breached her defenses and offered comfort. "Your friend's not dead. She merely needs rest. I'm confident she'll wake in time."

She lifted her head. The doctor stared at her, concern in his eyes. Would this handsome Yank be compassionate if he knew she'd stolen from Federal soldiers? Shot one?

His hand squeezed her shoulder, and an irrational thought surged through her. He didn't know her. Not a single thing. She could be anything in this moment.

"I…" She swallowed hard, trying to regain a pinch of

composure. "Forgive me. I am...undone."

Compassion warmed his eyes, which held traces of green mingled with brown as soft as a fawn. "Perfectly understandable. You've been through an ordeal. I daresay any lady would be undone by such things."

Even though she'd said the same thing herself, his words chafed. Evelyn pulled away from him and swiped the moisture from her face. Naturally, he thought a woman could not handle the same circumstances as a man. Not without turning into a sodden heap of uselessness. She lifted her hand so that he might assist her to her feet, glad that she'd dropped the hoops, which were still laden with supplies, at the outskirts of the Confederate camp.

As soon as she stood properly upright, she extracted her hand from his and tried to ignore the sensation his touch sent scurrying up her arm. She squared her shoulders. "No, it's not acceptable, lady or otherwise. These are times in which a person must set aside personal emotions and do one's duty."

He lifted his eyebrows.

"Again, I must apologize." She glanced around the ward and then back down at Alice. "I'll stay near until she awakens." He opened his mouth to respond, but she continued without giving him the option. "But until then, I shall make myself of use. I have experience tending wounded."

He regarded her with open curiosity, seeming unconcerned with hiding his thoughts as they played across his face.

"I would like to offer my services, if you have need of them."

The doctor rocked back on his heels, his eyes narrowing. She kept his gaze, hoping he wouldn't see her own uncertainty clawing to break free.

"I appreciate the offer. However—"

"But—"

He held up his hand. "Please, miss, if you don't mind, I'd like to know a little about you before sending you to work among the men. Especially after the day you've had."

Evelyn swallowed her words. His reasoning was sound.

"Now, Lady Wil—" He clamped his mouth shut and then quickly spoke again, as though he thought hurrying his words would erase what he'd almost said. His gaze sharpened. "What's your name?"

What had he been about to call her? Did she remind him of another? "My name is Evelyn Mapleton." She kept her hand at her side.

He dipped in a small bow. "Samuel Flynn."

A strong name befitting the man who bore it. She turned her gaze away from him, afraid to look too long upon the fine contours of his features.

"May I ask where you've served as a nurse?"

Evelyn glanced at the slow, shallow rise of Alice's chest, so faint she could barely see it move. "I'm not a nurse. I washed, cleaned, fed, and helped change bed sheets. I didn't tend wounds, replace bandages, or assist in operations."

He nodded along, seeming to listen and consider her words. "And where did you perform these duties?"

She withheld a sigh that wanted to escape her lips. "Front Royal."

"I see." The lack of malice in his voice caused her gaze to dart to his. The utter lack of condemnation in his eyes held her there. "I will be glad to have a lady who understands the needs and is capable of handling them. I'll send Nurse Fanning to you momentarily."

Evelyn watched him leave, too stunned to say anything. Here he'd had another opportunity to cause her undoing, but had simply walked away.

The room, large as it was, seemed smaller for the presence of a man like that. How could one such as he be in favor of government control and suppressed freedoms? She shoved the thought aside. He'd not had her hauled off, though surely knowing she'd tended men at Front Royal had given her loyalties away. Because of that, she would do her best in tending his patients.

Yanks or not.

"Miss Mapleton, I presume?" A woman, plain of features and of average height, addressed Evelyn with an impatient wave of her hand.

"Yes?"

"I'm told you wish to help?"

"I do."

"Good. Please come with me." She turned, the click of her sensible shoes as stiff as her spine.

Casting one more glance at Alice, Evelyn followed the nurse through the ward, out a rear door, and into an adjacent stone building. The nurse opened the door to the structure, and a wave of heat rolled out.

"The men will need to be served their meal soon," the nurse said, gesturing that Evelyn should enter the kitchen. Then she hurried away without waiting for a response.

Inside, a skinny woman covered in flour puttered around the stove. Better to serve meals than to have to wash grime from partially clothed soldiers.

The scrawny woman ushered her through the door. "Come, come, love. We've much work to be about." She pointed to an apron hanging from a peg inside the door near a barrel of potatoes.

Evelyn tied the strings around her middle and waited for further instruction, assessing her surroundings. The small kitchen teemed with crates of root vegetables and onions.

Sacks of flour and cornmeal had been shoved against the walls, and corn husks littered the floor. Despite the disarray, trays of golden loaves and sweet-smelling confections covered nearly every work surface. The cook might not be an organized woman, but she seemed talented.

With a cheerful attitude misaligned with the chaos of a cluttered kitchen, the cook sang softly to herself as she pulled a tray of small muffins from the oven. The scent made Evelyn's stomach rumbled, reminding her she'd not had a midday meal.

The cook laughed. "Oh, you poor dear. You nurses get busy with your treatments and forget your own body needs tending as well." She nodded to a basket filled with corn muffins as she set more on a wide plank table, filling the only open space. "Go ahead and grab you one, and then you can help me assemble the trays."

Evelyn plucked one of the fluffy yellow muffins from the stack and took a bite of the sweetness.

The cook watched her with a crooked grin that made her angular face undeniably friendly. "Good, ya?"

Evelyn smiled and swallowed. "Very much. Thank you."

"Sure, sure, love." She wiped her hands on her apron. "Get you another if you want. Won't do a lick of good for you to go fainting for lack of nourishment."

Without a single care about Aunt Mary's admonitions on a lady's appetite, Evelyn snagged another and popped the entire thing into her mouth.

Taking a survey. Looking for an occupation site. Blasted Rebels fired on us from hiding. Fragments of information about the skirmish

dappled the ward and clung to any ear willing to hear. *The Rebs are cowards. They didn't announce themselves with a blood-curdling yell prior to attacking.*

Samuel listened to it all, processing each thing as well as a man who had never seen a battle could. It seemed that one of their survey crews had gone into Lewinsville, which was in enemy territory, to scout the location. At some point, General J.E.B Stuart and the First Virginia Cavalry learned of this excursion. The Rebels crept through the woods, coming not a hundred yards from the men left standing on the road while the officers preformed reconnaissance.

Then the Rebels attacked, and the Federals were forced to retreat until their heavy artillery could cover them.

All the information that the men spouted Samuel took with nods and simple words of encouragement until his hospital, filled with frustrated, sick and gallantly wounded men, settled in for the evening. They had been washed, stitched, and wrapped, and only the one man had required surgery. His duty to the army complete for the moment, Samuel turned his attention to the one patient who didn't belong.

A slight girl with hair as wild as a treed bobcat's slept peacefully in a cot as far away from the men as he could get her without losing sight of her. Her companion was nowhere to be seen.

Miss Evelyn Mapleton.

The name lacked the absurd fancifulness of the Wildwood Queen, but sounded both resolute and feminine. Not unlike the lady herself. A mystery, indeed.

He rolled the name around in his mind as he checked Alice's pulse. The girl's eyelids fluttered, and her lips moved. Samuel leaned in closer to catch whatever request she might have.

"Watch. They'll be coming."

What? He leaned back to look at her face, but her eyes remained closed. She must be mumbling words within her dreams. Despite the oddity of such a statement, it nevertheless infused Samuel with hope. If she could dream and speak, then surely she would soon wake.

Leaving her to slumber, he stepped away. Between the customary scents that engulfed the hospital, the gentle hint of honeysuckle carried with it the hearty aroma of bread and meat. By the time Evelyn arrived with the serving tray, he stood by the door to receive her.

"Good evening, Miss Mapleton."

She balanced the tray with the ease of one who'd been trained in the art of graceful movements. Her posture perfect, she gifted him with only the slightest upturn of rosy lips before passing him by. Too intrigued to look away, he watched as she dispensed bowls of soup and corn muffins. Her gaze never turned to him but darted to Alice a dozen times before her tray emptied.

He stood in the doorway as she made to leave. Brown eyes lingered on him in question, but her lips did not part. After what seemed a rather long stalemate, he stepped to the side and extended his arm.

She passed him without word or expression. He found himself watching her once more, and yet again had to remind himself to refocus his thoughts.

What in creation had gotten into him?

Fifteen

Washington City
September 21, 1861

*M*rs. Margret Greenman, looking every bit as refined and superior as Evelyn remembered, stared at them while she stirred her tea. Evelyn and Alice had finally made it to Washington to call upon the widow who'd only months ago been a part of Evelyn's social season.

Had it only been months? So much had happened, it seemed years. She smoothed the russet folds of a silk gown she'd purchased upon their arrival. It had cost more than expected, and Evelyn worried that if she did not find Daddy quickly, her limited funds would soon come to an end.

She fingered her mother's pearl necklace draped across her neck, hoping she looked the lady Mrs. Greenman would expect. The silence thickened, broken only by the click of the widow's spoon in her delicate cup.

On the blue parlor settee next to Evelyn, Alice kept her gaze on her folded hands. Alice had recovered splendidly, thanks to the dedicated care of Doctor Samuel Flynn. The thought of him caused an irrational stirring in Evelyn's chest, not unlike the prolonged stirring their hostess used with her tea.

"These tarts are delicious, Mrs. Greenman," Alice said, interrupting the awkward silence. "Thank you."

"Certainly."

She seemed disinclined to inquire about the nature of their visit, leaving Evelyn with the familiar feeling of being out of place. But after all she'd been through, finding herself seated in the parlor of a well-to-do Washington lady who looked down her nose at her didn't intimidate Evelyn the way it once had.

"Miss Mapleton, does your aunt know you're here?" Mrs. Greenman's delicate brows lifted with the question. A woman two decades her senior, Margret Greenman was fetching beyond her youth. Little wonder the widow had charmed information out of many a Washington politician.

Evelyn held her gaze. "I left word. I decided I would go ahead and meet Daddy here rather than wait for him to travel to Front Royal to fetch me."

Mrs. Greenman turned shrewd eyes onto Alice. "And you, Miss Avery? Are you also looking for family in Washington?"

"No, ma'am. I'm only after the cause for which I've devoted myself."

The lady gave no expression in regard to such a declaration, neither in surprise nor excitement. She merely accepted it with the stoic grace of one of her social standing.

Knowing full well Mrs. Greenman would frown upon Evelyn prodding her for information, she kept her lips seamed despite her inward squirming to know what had become of her father.

"As I recall, Mr. Mapleton is a member of the press," the lady said, drawing the matter out.

Evelyn's heart quickened. "He is. You've spoken with him?"

Mrs. Greenman set her gold-rimmed teacup on a delicate saucer. "I have not. Though the government has soundly silenced all men of the press in Washington. Well, except those paid from its coffers."

Evelyn exchanged a worried glance with Alice. "What do you mean?"

"I mean that the hirelings of the government press have exercised their ingenuity in mystifying the people."

To this, Evelyn could garner no response. It seemed, however, that Mrs. Greenman had no need of one in order to continue her discourse.

"Shameful, it is. They misrepresent things from every angle. Why, it's acceptable to recount the gasconade of those who fled from imaginary foes, yet they deem it unnecessary to describe the forlorn condition of the returning soldiers who had gone forth to battle flushed with anticipated triumph they did not find." She steepled her fingers. "Rather, we must read reports of how General Burnside, on the morning he sallied forth, was said to have required two orderlies to carry the flowers showered upon him by the women of Northern proclivities. Meanwhile, the voices of the people call out for the *where* and *why* of the disasters of this war. But, alas, the government knows that if this discontent is allowed to gather strength, it might well hurl them from their present lawless eminence to the ignominy they merit."

What did any of that have to do with Daddy? "My father would not propagate such tactics. He is a man set on delivering the truth." Despite niggling doubts, she would not think otherwise until she'd had opportunity to speak with him.

Mrs. Greenman's eyes sparked. "And hence, his voice has likely been silenced. I've not seen the first byline with his name."

Evelyn could feel the color draining from her face.

Mrs. Greenman held up her hand. "Now, I am not saying any harm has come to him. Merely that men who seek to report the truth of our present circumstances are not allowed to put such opinions into print."

"Surely that is unethical," Alice quipped. "It can't be as bad as that."

"Do not be naïve, Miss Avery. This is not the Washington City of years past. Ruffians fill the streets. Insults, curses, and blasphemy rent the air on any given hour. Many of the decent citizens left the city as rapidly as the means of transportation or conveyance could be obtained."

A weight, heavy as a cannonball, settled in Evelyn's stomach. She'd finally made it to Washington, but seemed no closer to locating her father. She'd been certain Mrs. Greenman would tell her his whereabouts. Propriety set aside, she leaned forward.

"You received a letter from my aunt, did you not?"

Mrs. Greenman lifted her eyebrows. "I've received hardly any correspondence of late, and nothing from Mary."

"Aunt Mary sent you a letter asking if you knew where my father resided in Washington. When we asked to call, I was hoping you would know his whereabouts."

The lady's eyes softened. "I'm quite sorry, Miss Mapleton. I did not receive such a letter. Had I, I would have put forth an effort to locate him." She shook her head. "It comes as no surprise, though, given the deplorable state of things in this city."

Tears burned at the back of her throat. What was she to do now?

"It's brave of you to stay," Alice stated, breaking the silence and affording Evelyn a moment. She twirled the fringe of her dress around one finger. "It's my desire to aid you in the good work you do, and if you don't mind my boldness, that was the reason I traveled to Washington. I aim to join you."

Mrs. Greenman rose and closed the parlor door. Upon her return, she offered a smile that spoke mostly of pity. "Be careful the words you speak, Miss Avery." She looked to Evelyn. "Regrettably, the person to whom your aunt addressed the letter likely had more to do with its disappearance than the mere upheaval. I have acquired the attention of some rather determined men."

Knowing she didn't mean suitors, though the widow probably had an ample supply, Evelyn leaned closer.

"Men have been set upon my heels like starving hounds, dogging every step I make into town. At first I found it rather amusing, some overzealous Northern sympathizer thinking he had discovered me. I once thought a Secessionist with a kindly heart merely sought to offer me some kind of protection. But, alas, a missive from my dear friend, Senator Wilson, indicated he felt as though he were being watched with *hawkeyed vigilance*. I have come to believe their snooping is of a more nefarious nature. I have been followed, and my house watched, by those emissaries of the State Department, the detective police." She sipped from her teacup once more, seeming no more unnerved by this declaration than if she had merely informed them of the weather.

Evelyn's skin crawled with the sensation of being watched, and she glanced toward the window.

"Yes, they have most certainly seen you enter, mark my words. What you do with that now is up to you."

Evelyn clasped her hands. "And what do you think they will do to us?"

Mrs. Greenman waved the question away. "Nothing. They have merely set upon me to cause irritation and perhaps frighten me away from my work. But as they have not found the first shard of evidence, what shall they say? Mrs. Greenman is entertaining women in her parlor?"

Alice giggled, but Evelyn found no humor in the statement.

Mrs. Greenman admonished her with a haughty sniff. "Be on guard, Miss Avery, because they are as shrewd as snakes. Why, the first acts of the Republican President were to violate the express provisions of the Constitution. Those things set in place by the wisdom of our forefathers for the protection of the rights of the citizens. Those rights have been suspended, all under the plea of military necessity. The law of the land has given place to the law of the despot."

"It was not easy entering the city," Evelyn allowed, her disquiet growing with each passing moment. "Even after we made it past all the pickets and finally reached what we expected to be the civility of the city, we came upon more than a few drunken soldiers who expressed no remorse at sending a lady stepping into the ditch." She shook her head. "And that was the better part of it."

"Indeed, Miss Mapleton. They've had to close the schools, as it is not safe for the children on the streets. I ask you, what kind of army is that?"

Weeks ago, a scathing retort would have jumped from her lips, but after spending many hours under the benevolent direction of Doctor Flynn and tending Federal wounded, Evelyn couldn't quite form a response. Where she'd at first thought the issues clearly defined, it now seemed rather complicated. She clutched the fabric at her middle, the turmoil within making her stomach sour.

"An unholy army, that is the truth of it," Alice said, casting Evelyn a curious glance. "Such lawlessness should not avail itself upon the citizenship."

A knock sounded on the door, startling all three women. With a proper excuse and apology, Mrs. Greenman rose. Why she had no servant to respond, Evelyn couldn't fathom. No sooner had their hostess swept from the room in a swish of silk did Alice turn to her.

"Heavens, Evelyn, what has come over you?"

"Pardon?"

Alice fanned her face as though Evelyn's behavior had caused her flutters. "Why, you hardly seem the same woman who gave me the secret codes in the newspapers and smuggled supplies beneath her skirts. I'd thought your help in the Yankee hospital was a ruse necessary while I healed, but now I'm not certain." She gestured at Evelyn. "Now you seem rather like one who stands with one foot on each side of the divide."

Evelyn resisted the urge to squirm, realizing there was an undeniable truth in Alice's statement. When had such a shift occurred?

How could a person set a foot on each side of such a divide? Deep and wide as eternity, there would be no spanning it. One must choose to stand on one side or the other, lest she find herself tumbling into the abyss in between.

"What do you want?" Mrs. Greenman's elevated voice slipped into the parlor during Evelyn's prolonged silence.

Alice scurried to the door, leaning close. Alarmed, Evelyn hurried after her, grasping Alice's hand to pull her back.

"I have come to arrest you." A man's voice, cold with authority, made Evelyn's breath catch.

They're going to arrest Mrs. Greenman? With us here in the parlor?

Alice turned to Evelyn with wild eyes, the identical thought apparently having occurred to her. Evelyn tried once more to tug Alice away, but Alice shook her head, her eyes hard. She pointed to the door and then set a finger against her lips.

Resigned, Evelyn forced herself to breathe slowly and strained her ears toward the voices in the foyer.

"By what authority?" Mrs. Greenman remained calm, not a hint of concern in her genteel voice.

"By sufficient authority, madam."

"Oh?" Evelyn could hear a strain of humor in the intrepid lady's voice. "Very well, then. I shall see your warrant."

The man mumbled something Evelyn could not quite decipher, only the chilling words *State Department* slipping into her itching ears. Suddenly more footsteps pounded into the parlor, reminding Evelyn of when the Yankee soldiers had stormed into Aunt Mary's house. The terror of that day bubbled up like a pot of water over a roaring flame, and she stepped back away from the door, snatching at Alice's reluctant frame.

Alice yelped and stumbled back toward the settee, her eyes alight with indignation. Evelyn placed a finger to her own lips and settled herself on the seat, indicating Alice should do the same.

Once she was seated, Evelyn whispered, "Act as though you are naught but a dainty lady of vapid intellect having tea with a family friend. Give no hint you have any understanding of what's happening. If all else fails, rally your feminine indignation that men should act in such ungentlemanly ways."

Wide-eyed and darting glances toward the door, Alice nodded. No sooner had they taken up their teacups and fabricated smiles than the parlor door swung open. Men poured in, and before Evelyn could turn a single thought into words, she and Alice were rudely seized by two stern law officers. Without preamble, the men positioned the two of them along one side of the parlor while they hauled Mrs. Greenman through the door. The matron shot them an apologetic glance but spoke not a word.

A tall fellow with a mustache that swished when he spoke announced himself as Captain Dennis. With a loud and authoritative voice, he demanded to know from whence the two of them had come and the nature of their presence within the Greenman home.

Evelyn lifted her chin and donned her most affected air of superiority. "We have come to have tea with a family friend. I did my social season with Mrs. Greenman, and I'm delighted to call upon her while I am in Washington to see my father." She pinned him with a cold stare. "A pleasant visit you have brutishly interrupted."

He merely snorted and barked orders to more men, who filed into the room as though they had exploded from a beehive outside the door. "Take them all to the back parlor."

"What do you intend to do?" Mrs. Greenman inquired, her hands clasped tightly in front of her.

"We aim to search," another bearded man said. He crossed into the parlor with a victorious air, as though he had captured some great prize. Evelyn recognized his voice as the one at the door who'd not been able to produce a warrant.

They were led to another parlor. With its masculine furniture and polished cherry desk, it must have belonged to Mr. Greenman. The smell of pipe smoke no longer lingered in the air, but Evelyn could imagine that it had once permeated the leather furniture and clung to the books lining the wall.

Watching in a surreal awe, she and the other two ladies remained silent under the keen eye of their guard as men unceremoniously stripped the bookshelves and upturned the contents of the desk. The widow observed the crime without a trace of emotion as they pilfered through her husband's things. Finally, after what seemed an unending expedition where they unearthed nothing, they marched the women to the library.

The scene unfolded in this room much as it had in the other. Every private letter was scrutinized as though it were dangerous correspondence. The men gave no heed to a widow's affection for such items, and crumpled or tossed them aside. It was upon this disrespect that Mrs. Greenman's face pinched.

Later, they were moved upstairs. It seemed the three of them were to accompany the marauders upon their ransacking mission through every room in the house. Evelyn could only guess the reason was to see if some slip of expression or gasp of alarm might alert the searchers that they had stumbled upon a sensitive location.

Mrs. Greenman suffered the indignity with grace. It was not until they were marched into her bedroom did the ordeal reach the height of indecency. Mortified, Evelyn watched the scallywags upturn the matron's bed and strip her wardrobe. Soiled clothes were pounced upon with avidity and mercilessly exposed. Evelyn turned her face away, the heat in her cheeks surely no rival to what must be burning upon Mrs. Greenman's face.

Still, the woman uttered not a word as her desk was stripped of papers. Even torn sheets in the receptacles were carefully gathered and scrutinized. Mrs. Greenman observed all of this with keen eyes, and Evelyn marveled at her composure. Had someone set their hands upon her own underthings... Why, she could not even finish the thought!

"There are many papers which speak treason," the man who'd not brought a warrant stated, regarding Mrs. Greenman with sharp eyes.

Alice seemed to bristle under the words, though no one

had spoken to her. She stepped next to Evelyn.

Mrs. Greenman drew a deep breath. "I'm a Southern woman, Mr. Peterson. Born with revolutionary blood in my veins. My first ideas on State and Federal matters received consistency and shape from the best and wisest man of this century, Mr. John C. Calhoun. These ideas have been strengthened and matured by reading and observation. Freedom of speech and thought are my birthrights, guaranteed by our charter of liberty, the Constitution of the United States, and signed and sealed by the blood of our fathers."

The detective she called Mr. Peterson narrowed his gaze into sharp slits.

"As such," Mrs. Greenman continued, "I'm entitled to my own opinions and have the right to discuss the nature of our current political state."

After some grunts and the call for someone by the name of Seymour, the papers were again thoroughly examined. Seymour, a tall fellow with intelligent eyes and a pleasant expression given the circumstances, finally replaced Mrs. Greenman's papers inside her desk and turned to her with something akin to sympathy in his baritone voice.

"Well, madam, you have no reason to feel anything but pride and satisfaction at the ordeal you have gone through. For there is not a line amongst your papers that does not do you honor. It is the most extensive private correspondence that has ever fallen under my examination, and the most interesting and important. There is not a distinguished name in America that is not found here, and nothing that can come under the charge of treason." He lifted his hands. "Naught but enough to make the government dread and hold you as a most dangerous adversary."

Evelyn's mouth went dry.

"A woman will soon be sent to this chamber for further

searching." He gave a slight bow. "Good evening, ladies."

The intruders filed from the room, and in a matter of heartbeats, a rap came at the door, which still stood ajar.

A woman stepped across the threshold without waiting for a response. Evelyn didn't know exactly what she'd anticipated a female detective to look like, but this one seemed less interesting than she might have expected. Her face was neither unpleasant nor fetching, and she examined them with dull brown eyes. She gave them her Christian name, Susan, but did not provide a family name by which to properly address her.

The stiff woman ran her hands along the inner and outer seams of Evelyn's and Alice's gowns, and required they turn out their pockets. Finding nothing, she instructed poor Mrs. Greenman to unfasten her garments and hand each piece over for inspection.

Evelyn and Alice both gasped.

"Miss...um, Susan?" Evelyn asked, her nerves aflutter. "My companion and I would step from the room and afford our hostess the proper modesty."

"You may turn your back, if you wish, but you may not leave," Susan stated flatly, her gaze never lifting from Mrs. Greenman's shoe, as though she expected to find some great mystery engraved upon the leather.

Evelyn whirled around, humiliation and fury churning within. What manner of churlish fiend would subject a lady to such indecency? The only thing that kept this from being nigh on the same violation as Martinsville was at least they had not attempted to have a man perform such a task!

When at long last the ordeal had been thoroughly conducted, Susan strode from the room with nary a scrap with which to present the detectives. While the door yet stood open, a startled scream came from downstairs and made

Evelyn's heart skip a beat.

"What manner of inhumanity are you extracting upon my maid?" Mrs. Greenman demanded of the detective standing watch in the doorway, her eyes flint-hard. It seemed the last humiliation had finally unmoored the lady from her steadfast calm.

"Your maid is not being harmed," the red-haired man said flippantly, though he could not have known for sure, seeing as how he'd not moved from his position by the door.

Mrs. Greenman exercised the near royal extent of her station and bearing and insisted in no uncertain terms that someone go downstairs and report the precise circumstances that occurred.

Even a man who stole into homes and ransacked possessions could not deny the authority in her demand, and he mumbled something about shrieking females as he marched down the steps. In due time the disgruntled man returned, informing the stoic Mrs. Greenman that two colored servants had come by the house and were being held for questioning, but were completely unharmed. Mrs. Greenman made no response.

As dark descended on the house, gloomy perils seemed ever more to envelop them. Despite the evening chill, they were not allowed to stoke the fire. The detective said he would not risk Mrs. Greenman having an opportunity to burn anything yet undiscovered.

Evelyn's head ached. She should have never come here. But how was she to know she'd call upon Mrs. Greenman just as the government sought to accuse her? It would seem all of the rumors about the resourceful widow had been true.

Evelyn eyed Alice, who remained quietly watchful near the door. If nothing else, surely this ordeal would convince her friend to abandon ideas of clandestine activities.

Evelyn certainly had no wish to partake. All she wanted was to locate her father, and then perhaps he'd allow her to keep residence with him. Perhaps she could even find a paying position working in hospitals so as not to be a burden to him. She'd discovered that while the work was exhausting, it was also fulfilling in a way she'd not expected.

The women remained in the chamber to wait, the partially opened door not hampering the detectives' discussion about a continued search. Evelyn clenched her hands. When would she and Alice be allowed to leave? They were not suspects, were they? Having not been searched by the female detective, Evelyn had thought they would soon be released. However, as time stretched on, that seemed less likely.

Finally, the detectives left for the evening. Unfortunately, the subordinates remaining had somehow come upon Mr. Greenman's store of brandy. By the time full dark fell, the men outside the door of Mrs. Greenman's room had consumed enough drink that their loosened tongues began to wag and they turned their backs on their charges.

No longer under immediate scrutiny, Mrs. Greenman's shoulders sagged. "I am sorry you girls have been swept into this madness. However, it seems we have little choice but to keep our wits about us and avail ourselves of the inebriated state of our guards." She eased closer and lowered her voice. "Once they have relaxed themselves further, we shall steal through the house."

Relieved, Evelyn let out a sigh. "You have a plan for escape, then?"

Mrs. Greenman regarded her closely. "I don't think that will benefit us. Upon so doing we may instead find ourselves imprisoned at the Old Capitol rather than in the comforts of home."

"What are you going to do, then?" Alice whispered, her

large eyes more rounded than usual.

"I must go to the library and destroy every paper of consequence. I don't doubt they will not survive another day of searching, and if we are to have any hope of escaping these trials unscathed, those papers will have to be destroyed."

Unscathed hardly seemed possible at the moment.

"I'll help," Alice said, her smile bright.

Mrs. Greenman shook her head. "No, you stay here and keep watch on the guards to be sure they do not take notice of us."

Annoyance colored Alice's eyes, but she nodded her agreement.

"Evelyn, you come with me. I'll need your assistance."

Evelyn bit her lip. "Mrs. Greenman, I don't think I—"

"Do you wish to go to prison?"

"No, but…"

"They already suspect you, or you would have been allowed to leave by now. Nothing you say will change their minds. Should they discover these papers, then your fate is sealed with my own. Do as I say, and this will all the sooner be over."

Seeing no other option, Evelyn reluctantly agreed.

Mrs. Greenman instructed Alice that should the guards return to the chamber from their place down the hall in Mr. Greenman's bedroom, she was to commence a loud conversation with them by means of both distraction and warning.

The plan thus in place, Evelyn and Mrs. Greenman left the bedchamber as silently as possible. They maneuvered down the darkened hall, Evelyn intent on keeping Mrs. Greenman's shifting shadow separated from all the others that lurked in the hallway. It took every ounce of her concentration not to make a misstep and alert the guards.

With heart thudding and palms sweating, she crept along

behind Mrs. Greenman, the woman possessing a stealth Evelyn marveled at. They slipped across silent floors and into the quiet of the library. Mrs. Greenman secured the door and let out a wary breath, the only indication that the excursion had been as worrisome to her as it had been to Evelyn.

Mrs. Greenman scurried across the library, snagged a chair near the far shelf, and climbed upon it. Frozen with awe, Evelyn watched the elite woman's fingers roam the shelves like a cat in search of a mouse in the upper beams of a barn. Finally, the widow snagged a folio from the upper reaches on top of the bookshelf. With what seemed to be practiced ease, she slipped it up between her skirt and petticoat. For a moment, Evelyn could only stare. Aunt Mary would have fainted over such a scandal.

"What do you propose to do with those?" Evelyn whispered, wondering how exactly the widow thought to dispose of that many papers, especially without a single fire allowed in the house. "You can't burn it, and if any of us are ever allowed to leave, we most surely will be searched." The thought of undergoing the humiliating event Mrs. Greenman had been forced to endure sent a shiver down her spine.

Mrs. Greenman pressed one finger against her lips. Then she brightened. "That foul woman did not insist upon the removal of my stockings during her undignified search." Her eyes turned down upon Evelyn's feet, and she raised her brows.

Knowing what would come next, Evelyn shook her head. "You ask too much."

"Too much?" Mrs. Greenman quipped, her expression muddled in the dark but her tone evidence enough of her ire. "*Too much* when this very day you have seen the mannerisms of these brutes? Seen firsthand the terrors of this government?" She drew nearer, so close that Evelyn could smell her

French perfume. "What is *too much* to aid in the most noble effort to escape tyranny? Did not our revolutionary men and women suffer for the sake of freedom? Do you think so little of the cause that you cannot suffer a fraction of what others have endured?"

Thoroughly lashed by this revelation of her cowardice, Evelyn could only nod. It was a slight gesture, and not one done in earnest, but Mrs. Greenman accepted it all the same. In a matter of a few hurried moments, Mrs. Greenman had lowered Evelyn's stockings and wrapped several sheets of papers around her bare legs like bark around a tree. She then fitted and secured the stockings over them, and though she felt like she had trunks for lower legs, the papers were sufficiently hidden. So long as no one placed their hands upon them and heard a telltale crinkling.

What would she do then?

"When they finally allow you to leave my chambers, which surely they must, if they decide to search you, feign to be seized with compunction at leaving me and return. We shall come up with another solution then."

Evelyn muttered acquiescence and began the arduous journey back to the bedchamber. Every step seemed to crackle with guilt, each movement screaming for the guards to come arrest her. Fear amplified every sound she made. The quiet was then shattered by the sound of quarreling men.

Evelyn and Mrs. Greenman reached the top of the stairs to discover the guards had roused themselves into a heated argument over which of their nationalities was the best: Irish, German or Scottish. Evelyn had to wag her head. Even within their own ranks men squabbled.

Such an upheaval, however, provided ample distraction, and not one of them had yet noticed the two women had slipped free of their confinement, nor did they hear the hurried footsteps of the women bolting back through the door at the opposite end of the hall.

Safely enclosed, Evelyn scowled at Alice. "Were you not to keep watch?"

She huffed. "They seemed adequately preoccupied."

Alice's point made, they passed several hours in tense company, each apparently too overwrought to rest. Then, sometime around three in the morning, a knock sounded at the door.

Without waiting for the proper call to enter, the door opened and one of the fellows, Irish by the sound of him, pointed a finger at Alice and then Evelyn. "You two," he stated, his words slightly slurred, "can go."

Alice, much to Evelyn's astonishment, adamantly shook her head. "I shall remain here and keep Mrs. Greenman in respectable company."

If not for the gravity of the situation, Evelyn might have laughed. Mrs. Greenman, under any other circumstances, would have never deemed a young working class woman *respectable company*. Today, however, such barriers hardly seemed to matter, as Mrs. Greenman actually seemed relieved. Did she fear to be left alone with these men? Perhaps, but what protection could Alice offer?

"Alice, we must go."

Alice lifted her chin. "I've done nothing wrong, and cannot be charged with such. Therefore, I have nothing to fear. I shall keep Mrs. Greenman company." She let her gaze drift down Evelyn's dress. "You should go get some rest, though."

Evelyn, having the duty of removing evidence from the premise, had no option. She could not make Alice go, and she couldn't risk staying.

Casting Alice one last glance that pleaded she reconsider

this foolish endeavor, Evelyn stepped from the room. She walked carefully down the stairs, the pounding blood in her ears muffling whatever sound emanated from beneath her skirts.

The guard seemed to take no notice of anything, however, and she reached the lower floor without being arrested or manhandled. Then, with all the pomp and circumstance given a mongrel, Evelyn was all but tossed into the street, and the front door soundly shut behind her.

Alone in the cold darkness, terror clawed at her stomach. She turned to the left and right, seeing no one else lurking about at such a witching hour. Unsure what she would do unescorted in the darkness without her pistol to save her, indecision kept her rooted to the ground. She couldn't very well return inside, nor could she walk about like a lady of the night. And she hadn't paid any attention on the carriage ride here. How would she remember all the turns it would take to get her back to the hotel?

Oh, Lord. What should I do?

The prayer pounded in her skull, heaving with the rush of blood in her ears. She could not stay here, of that she was certain. That left only one option. With one final glance at the house, she searched for probing eyes watching her. For several moments she scanned the shadows around the house, forcing her quivering insides to maintain composure.

Then, seeing not a single curtain shudder, Evelyn lifted her skirts to a scandalous height and did the only thing her frantic mind could conjure.

She ran.

Sixteen

$\mathscr{B}$one weary, Samuel pulled his jacket around him and stepped into the cool night. Or, rather, early morning. This day seemed to be without end, bleeding from one rise of the sun to nearly the next. His body yearned for rest, and his footsteps fell heavily upon the quiet street. It had been a harrowing journey, if not an overly lengthy one, from the army encampment to Washington.

Wind skittered through the city, snagging on refuse and the ever-present rotting offal piled knee-deep near the monument. Only the thought of his feather bed and two smiling faces come morning kept him moving toward home.

Two days after the army surgeon arrived, Samuel had been given his leave to return to Washington. Strangely, leaving had been more difficult than he'd imagined. The army hospital ran smoothly, and he believed the men in his assigned regiment were better for having benefitted from the stringent way he kept things. His replacement, a sour-looking man with untamed whiskers, didn't seem adequately concerned with cleanliness, and he certainly didn't find mental rest and rejuvenation a proper component of healing. Samuel could only hope the men would not grow too discouraged during the long, monotonous months of winter.

He pulled his collar around his neck, weary feet picking their way around discarded papers that foretold ongoing trouble. Somewhere off to his left, a drunken man serenaded an alleyway, his voice bouncing on the brick walls and creating a haunting tune. Samuel quickened his pace. Would this day never end?

By the time he'd made it back into Washington through the multitude of barricades and checkpoints, it had been near evening. He'd considered shirking his duty and reporting to the infirmary in the morning, but had discarded the notion and continued to the hospital as he'd been instructed, though the hour had grown woefully late. Dr. Porter then insisted on taking him through the halls and explaining every minute detail about what had occurred in his absence. The doctor had seemed pleased with Samuel's report from the stone house hospital, and he couldn't bring himself to dampen the man's enthusiasm by requesting to return home.

He'd been somewhat dismayed to learn that all of the remainder of the medical students had left the infirmary. They'd been given their final paperwork and sent out to do a varying degree of assignments. His friend Marcus Hammond would be serving as a field medic. Samuel prayed he would do well in the position. Others had returned home or volunteered their services, but in one manner or another had advanced to the next stage of their lives. All except him.

Whether Dr. Porter doubted his abilities or exalted them, Samuel had yet to decipher. Regardless, he still lacked the one thing he needed to complete his medical license. He'd finished the hours, passed the final assessment, and now waited on the signature the primary physician remained reluctant to pen.

Amid the exhaustion, disappointment, and confusion, one blessing stood out. Dr. Porter had, indeed, treated the private with the amputation for infection as Samuel had requested prior to leaving Washington. The man healed fine, and though Dr. Porter claimed there was still no evidence that the soldier wouldn't have been fine without treatment, he'd administered it all the same.

Dr. Porter didn't complete his rounds until deep into the night, and then Samuel had stayed on longer when a soldier suddenly experienced an apoplexy attack. By the time the man had been stabilized and was resting comfortably, the clock had chimed twice. Now, he'd finally find some rest for the ache in his feet.

Something moved. Down the street, a shadow bobbed through the gloom, bouncing to and fro like a misguided spirit. Samuel slowed his steps, his eyes narrowing. The apparition gained speed, hurdling itself toward him at a reckless pace. He shook his head. Likely another poor fellow who'd thought he could erase his sorrows at the bottom of the bottle and instead found himself running from imagined foes.

Not in the state of mind to encounter one such as that, Samuel took three more strides and then tucked himself into an alcove in the shadowed entry of a haberdashery. He'd let the fellow pass by, and then he'd continue home in peace.

Evelyn's lungs burned and moisture stung her eyes, making it all the more difficult to see in the dark. Many of the street lamps had either gone out or hadn't been lit at all. She slowed, her heart hammering so rapidly it hurt. Pressing a hand into her aching side, she tried to get a sense of her bearings. Nothing looked familiar. How was she to find the

Halverson Hotel?

Washington in the dark was not at all what she remembered from her society days. Whenever she and Isabella traveled, it had been by carriage and with an escort. She'd never been out on the city streets alone. And certainly not at night.

The chilling wind caught a discarded newsprint, hurling it up in the air and sending it dancing. She glanced around at the unfamiliar buildings, the damp and crumpled papers stuffed in her stockings uncomfortable. She'd hoped to find her hotel, and then as that seemed all the more unlikely the longer she wandered, had prayed to at least locate a friendly establishment where she might find safety. But no such place was to be had at this hour.

She still had to get rid of the papers, but shy of crouching in the shadows somewhere and pulling them free, she'd not found an opportunity. What had those men been thinking? Tossing a woman into the streets at night was impermissible.

Why, when she told her father—

The thought cut off as a large shadow separated itself from the front of the building she passed and snaked toward her. Evelyn yelped and jumped back, tripping on her hem and coming down hard on her backside. Her teeth jarred in her skull and pain shot up her spine. A scream lodged in her throat as the shadow sprang forward, thrusting a paw at her as she sat helpless on the ground.

"Miss?"

She sucked air and tried to scoot backward, her infuriating skirts tangling her feet and ensnaring her in this nefarious man's trap.

"Miss? Are you all right?"

It took her a moment to realize that the shadow had not moved any closer, nor had it made any attempt to fall upon her. She stilled, something pricking at her senses that she could not place.

"Miss, if you are lost, I would assist you to your destination."

That rich voice, smooth as a river stone, washed over her with a keen sense of amazement. "Doctor Flynn?" She could scarcely believe it. Had she not left this man at the army encampment? And now he emerged from the shadows in her path? It seemed both impossible and, at the same time, an answer to a desperate prayer. Of all the men in Washington, he would be one of the few she would trust.

He stepped closer, disbelief in his voice. "Miss Mapleton? Good heavens, is that you?"

Relief, thick and sweet as honey, poured through her. "I'm afraid so." She lifted her hand. "Would you mind?" She was suddenly keenly aware of her skirts. Thank heavens she'd only worn layers of petticoats and not a crinoline cage! Having it fly up in front of Yankee miscreants had been humiliation enough. She would not have been able to stand the same happening in front of the doctor.

His large palm enveloped her hand and firm fingers gripped her tight. With his other hand he stabilized her elbow and righted her. He dropped her hand as soon as she gained her feet, but kept his grip on her arm. She found comfort in that.

"Miss Mapleton, what are you doing on the streets of Washington in the middle of the night?"

She blinked in the darkness, trying to get a better look at his face. "I could ask you the same question."

He chuckled, probably finding the circumstances as unbelievable as she. "I was on my way home after a late night in the wards."

A shiver fluttered down her spine that had nothing to do

with the chill in the air. "I was visiting a friend who was arrested, her home and person searched, and then I was tossed out on the streets with nary an escort or means of transportation." The words tumbled out, once more seeming incapable of staying properly confined whenever she stood in this man's presence. And the nearer to him she found herself, the worse the problem became. She stepped back, and he released her arm. She felt all the colder for the loss.

"That is quite the tale." He seemed more in awe than suspicious, though Evelyn would have expected the latter.

Still, she bristled. "I thought you were an army doctor out at Chain Bridge."

He leaned forward as though trying to make out her features in the paltry light of a waning moon. "I'm a medical student finishing my licensing procedure at the Washington Infirmary. I was merely sent to Chain Bridge for experience and to help until the assigned army surgeon could arrive." He stepped closer, and the faint scent of soap and shaving oil tickled her nose. "Miss Mapleton, as enchanting as this turn of Providence is, I would prefer to get off the street."

She wrapped her arms around her middle. "As would I. May I trouble you to show me how to get to the Halverson Hotel? I fear I've become turned around in the dark."

"I would rather take you home."

She gasped. "I beg your pardon?"

He chuckled heartily, a robust sound not suited for the shifting night shadows nor for a man who had spoken with great impropriety.

"Just because I stayed with the army doesn't mean—"

"Whoa," he said, as if quieting a spirited horse. "You jump to rash assumptions, Miss Mapleton. My home is naught but another few steps from here. I cannot in good conscience leave you alone but, forgive me, I'm far too tired to walk the half mile it would take to reach the Halverson."

Evelyn worked her fingers in the fabric of her rumpled skirt, feeling foolish. She straightened her spine, though she knew he could no better see her in the darkness than she could him. "Staying in the home of an unmarried man isn't proper." A sudden thought leapt up and surprised her. "You're not married, are you?"

"I'm not." He spoke straightforwardly, as he always seemed to do. "However, to ease your worry, we will not be alone."

"Oh?"

"Mrs. Tooley keeps residence with me."

She burned to ask more, but the itching papers on her legs and the weariness brought on by fear, flight, and the night's chill sucked the questions right out of her like starving leeches. "I thank you for your kindness."

He took her elbow and turned her back the way she had come. She must have passed his residence in her wayward run. Relaxing under his gentle guidance, she allowed her gaze to try to pick apart the features of the darkened buildings. Which of the neat townhomes belonged to a doctor? She didn't have to wonder long, because, true to his word, they traveled but a few more paces before he steered her to the left and helped her up a short flight of stairs.

"What of your friend Miss Avery? Has she had any lasting ailments caused by her fall?"

The thought of Alice still trapped at Mrs. Greenman's tightened her stomach. "She is well." Why did that feel like a lie?

The doctor patted around in his pockets for a moment and then produced a key. He led her into the pleasantly warm entry space. Her shoes clicked across the floor, and in a few moments, Mr. Flynn had located a lamp and struck a match.

He turned up the wick, and golden light bathed his features.

Reddened eyes studied her so intensely that she self-consciously placed a hand to her hair, wondering what state of disarray the lamplight had revealed. She'd not been given the option to retrieve her bonnet, which she'd taken off along with her gloves at Mrs. Greenman's this afternoon. Had it only been this afternoon? It seemed days ago.

"Miss Mapleton, I will request of you an explanation for the events that sent you into the streets."

She hesitated, knowing it would likely lead to a tangled thread of events she could not explain away to his satisfaction.

"But for now, I'm devoid of energy, and I suspect you feel the same. I shall wake Mrs. Tooley to prepare a room for you." He turned toward a staircase with carved banisters.

"Oh, but that is not necessary."

He looked at her over his shoulder, clearly befuddled. "You will not be returning outside."

"You don't need to wake your..." She searched for the right title, not knowing what position the woman held. "Your maid at this hour. I will be pleased to take rest in the parlor, if you don't mind."

He frowned.

"I'd rather not cause a fuss in your household. I'm fine resting upon a settee."

His eyes darted to the door to her right that likely led to the parlor. "It's not proper for a lady to sleep on a settee."

A laugh bubbled out of her. "Well, I daresay a settee is a great deal better than sleeping in an army tent." She snapped her mouth shut. Why couldn't she keep from revealing herself?

His jaw tightened, and her gaze skittered across the dark stubble that shadowed it. She'd laid her eyes upon him many times while Alice recovered, and not once had she seen the darkening of his jaw. An odd sensation to know what its roughness might feel like under her fingers had her clasping her hands behind her back.

A small smile tugged on his lips, and for one terrifying heartbeat, she thought he'd read her mind. "In that, it seems you would be correct. Another curiosity I would like satisfied. However, I still must insist." He turned to the staircase.

"Mr. Flynn!" A voice tumbled down the stairs, startling them both. A woman wrapped in a sage dressing gown with a cap haphazardly pulled over her gray tresses hurried to the foyer. "I did not know you were back from..." Her gaze fell on Evelyn.

"I've just returned this day but was occupied at the infirmary until this late hour. I didn't mean to startle you." He followed the stunned woman's gaze to Evelyn. "This is Miss Mapleton. She's in need of a room for the evening."

The older woman's eyes rounded, and she turned to the doctor for further explanation.

"I'm rather exhausted, Mrs. Tooley, and have a great longing for my bed. If you would kindly see that our guest also has a bed for the evening, I would be much obliged."

Evelyn dipped her chin to the befuddled housekeeper. "I would be exceedingly grateful, ma'am. I've had a harrowing day."

As though finding her senses, the woman came alive with a flutter of hands. "Oh, you poor dear! Come, now, let us get you settled!" She waved Evelyn toward the stairs like a wayward child.

Doctor Flynn bade them a good night and disappeared up the stairs, leaving Evelyn in the hands of Mrs. Tooley, whose rounded cheeks dimpled when she spoke a string of instructions and comments Evelyn could scarcely keep up with.

Keenly aware of the papers in her stockings, Evelyn walked gingerly up the staircase behind the housekeeper.

Light pooled in the hall where the doctor had apparently lit the wall lamp. It washed over burgundy carpeting that muffled her steps and glinted off two mirrors hanging from the papered wall. Mrs. Tooley opened a mahogany door and scuttled inside, lighting lamps and mumbling something about the cold.

Evelyn followed, her gaze darting around the room. The burgundy carpeting continued inside the chamber, offset by cream quilts and heavy curtains. The canopied bed was neither grand nor lacking, and the entire room seemed to be an interesting aggregate of simple and elegant. From the plain porcelain washbasin to the carved marble-top dresser, the room seemed comfortable and homey.

"We need to get you a fire going," Mrs. Tooley stated, eyeing the cold hearth. "I can fetch a few logs from the kitchen to take the chill out of the air."

Not only would she welcome the added warmth, the fire would make destroying Mrs. Greenman's papers all the easier. Tension eased from her shoulders. "I hate to trouble you, but it would be nice to warm myself."

Mrs. Tooley smiled, her features reminding Evelyn of a kindly grandmother from a children's tale. "It's no trouble at all, dear. I've always been an early riser, so an hour or two more to my day doesn't make much difference." She clasped her hands. "Oh! And since I've the extra time, I'll make those pastries Mr. Flynn is fond of."

The thought of pastries made Evelyn's empty stomach grumble, the afternoon's tea and tarts long gone. She wrapped her arms around herself to stifle the sound as much as possible as the housekeeper bustled out. Alone, Evelyn wasted not a moment untying her petticoats and letting them slip to the floor. Then, with quick fingers, she pulled the chafing papers from her stockings, stuffing the crumpled mess underneath the pillow on the bed.

She had finished the task and was retying her skirts when a tap at the door announced Mrs. Tooley's presence an instant before she stepped into the room. My, but the woman was fast! She had a woven basket draped over one arm filled with fire kindling poking out in all directions. In her hand, she carried a plate.

Evelyn's eyes snapped up to the woman's face.

Mrs. Tooley grinned. "You sounded a mite hungry. It's not much, just yesterday's bread smeared with a little jam, but perhaps it will hold you over till breakfast."

She accepted the offering with gratitude and followed Mrs. Tooley's instructions to sit and eat. The jam made from strawberries was sweet and delicious, and while Mrs. Tooley busied herself with the fire, Evelyn secretly licked her fingers.

Her task complete, Mrs. Tooley brushed her hands on her dressing gown. "Now then. That should take the chill out of the room." She stepped toward the bed. "We'll turn your bedding down and—"

"No!" Evelyn lurched into the woman's path, and Mrs. Tooley startled. "I mean, you've done plenty. I can see to my rest now."

Mrs. Tooley lifted her eyebrows, then merely shrugged. "Very well. I'll get on about the morning necessities, then."

Alone, Evelyn slid the door latch into place as quietly as possible and headed for the bed. She grabbed a handful of papers, eager to see what information the acclaimed lady spy had gathered. She quickly scanned one page and then another.

Line after line contained drivel about family visits, new clothing, and other mundane nonsense. For this she had risked imprisonment? Had run through dangerous streets? Disgusted, she tossed the leaflets one by one into the fire and watched them curl. Her second trip to the pillow cleaned out the cache, and with a final handful, she turned to the fire to see this mess finished.

She'd nearly tossed every letter in when one page caught her attention. Evelyn set the others on the brick hearth and stared at the one in her hand. Strange symbols, vaguely resembling the Greek lettering she'd learned in the female college, littered the page. She turned it one way, and then the other, but could not make sense of the meaning. For this, Mrs. Greenman had likely hidden the folio away.

Evelyn watched the fire dance for a few moments, and then with nimble fingers folded the slip of paper into a small square.

With a fling of her hand, the paper sailed into the fire. The remaining letters, of no consequence, were tossed into the flames as well. Why Mrs. Greenman had wrapped all of it around Evelyn's legs, she could not fathom. The one small paper would have been much easier to hide. But then, perhaps the letters only *seemed* mundane.

It mattered little now. She ached from head to foot, and her body longed to seek the comforts of the bed. She removed her mother's pearl necklace, then pulled off the russet dress and draped it over a chair back.

She slipped between the cool press of quilt and mattress. Before she even had time to allow her body to warm the bedding, she drifted into a troubled sleep.

Seventeen

*E*velyn stirred, something tingling in her senses. With some effort, she peeled open one eye against the enveloping sunlight…and found two eyes staring back at her. With a startled gasp, Evelyn shot awake, scurrying to a sitting position.

Next to her bed stood a small girl with large brown eyes and wispy brown hair. Evelyn clutched the blanket to her chest, taking a moment to remember where she'd fallen asleep. The doctor's house.

Another face popped up over the cream quilt. "Who are you?" A little boy, appearing somewhere around eight years of age, crossed his arms over his linen shirt and narrowed his eyes.

Not entirely sure what to do with the curious pair in her bedroom, Evelyn pulled the covers closer to her neck and glanced at the door, which stood ajar. Should she call Mrs. Tooley?

The little girl giggled, swinging her skirts around. The boy frowned at her and then glared at Evelyn. "Did you not hear? What're you doing in our house?"

Evelyn tilted her head. Tough little man. With as much dignity as could be gathered in such a predicament, she said,

"My name is Evelyn Mapleton, and Mrs. Tooley prepared this room for me."

The boy softened and uncrossed his arms but still seemed skeptical. "We was coming in here like we always do whilst Mrs. Tooley makes breakfast. Didn't expect to see someone in the bed." His cute little face scrunched. "You sure you're supposed to be here? She didn't say nothing about no lady in the guest chamber."

Never having had to explain herself to a child before, Evelyn couldn't help but grin at this little one's boldness. "It was rather late, and I'll bet she's been busy. I'm sure she merely forgot."

Cautiously stepping closer, the little girl placed a small hand on the quilt and peered up at Evelyn. She offered the girl a smile.

"And may I ask who you are?" Evelyn said.

"I'm Benjamin," the boy answered, "and that's my sister Emily."

"Pleased to meet you, Benjamin and Emily."

They settled into silence, as Evelyn had no idea what to do now. Finally, Emily leaned near to her brother and whispered something Evelyn couldn't hear. Benjamin puckered his mouth and shook his head. The little girl grabbed his hand and whispered again. Benjamin shook his head more emphatically.

"No, Emily. She ain't. Now you hush."

Intrigued, Evelyn lifted her eyebrows. "I'm not what?"

Benjamin's cheeks reddened and he looked down at his toes. "Nothing. You don't mind what she says. She talks like everything's gonna be a fairy tale."

"Oh?" Evelyn grinned at Emily. "Why, there's nothing I love more than a good fairy tale. Princesses and knights are my favorites."

Emily rewarded her with a grin and giggle before she spun around and hurried out the door. Benjamin regarded Evelyn for another moment, then his eyes widened. His gaze darted to the door, and Evelyn guessed the reason for his concern. Footsteps hurried down the hall, and before he could dart out of the door, the opening was shadowed by a much more stern-looking Mrs. Tooley than she'd seen last night.

"Benjamin! What in heaven's name are you doing in here?"

He thrust his hand toward the bed. "There was a stranger in the house. I was making sure it was all right."

Mrs. Tooley held out her hand, and the boy reluctantly grasped it. "A gentleman doesn't burst in upon a lady still in bed!" Benjamin hung his head and she softened her tone. "Come, now, and let's leave our guest in peace, shall we?"

He regarded the maid, or perhaps nanny, with narrowed eyes. "So you *did* know she was here?"

Mrs. Tooley laughed. "Of course I did." She drew him against her side. "As does Mr. Flynn."

Benjamin's face brightened. "He's home?"

"He is." She held tight as the boy tried to scurry away. "But he's not yet risen. You can wait to see him at breakfast."

Benjamin poked out his lip. "But—"

"Breakfast," Mrs. Tooley repeated, her tone firm.

Benjamin sighed. "Yes, ma'am."

"Good boy. Now off you go."

Benjamin dashed out of the room, and Mrs. Tooley put a hand to her chest. "I'm sorry they bothered you so early, Miss Mapleton. I had them in the kitchen with me, and when I turned around, they'd slipped off."

"It's quite all right." Trying to piece together the members of this household, Evelyn asked, "Are they your children?"

"Gracious, no!" She chuckled. "Merely children of my heart. I'm too old to have ones this small." Her eyes grew wistful. "But they've been a blessing, and I love them like my own, I do." She winked. "Even if they are a spot of trouble." She waved a hand. "But listen at me babbling. I have food to tend. Take your time, Miss, and come down when you're ready."

After the door closed, Evelyn waited for several moments, pondering the children the doctor had never mentioned. The pang it gave her was entirely irrational, since he had no obligation to discuss his personal life with her. Still, she had to wonder, what had happened to their mother? A familiar ache stirred, the loss of her own mother never truly fading.

She took her time dressing, wishing she could get some of the wrinkles out of the gown. They had taken cares to prepare for their visit with Mrs. Greenman, but without access to even her small bag of personal items, there wasn't much she could do beside run a damp cloth over herself and don yesterday's garments. At least she'd had a nice bed and a warm fireplace. How had poor Alice spent the night?

After seeing to all the morning necessities, Evelyn stepped from the room and was greeted by the inviting scent of cured ham and coffee. She descended the stairs, her gaze lingering on each aspect of the doctor's home. Like the chamber she'd spent the last few hours in, this part of the house seemed equally refined yet simple. She trailed her hand down the banister and followed the sound of childish laughter.

Just off the entry she'd barely glimpsed in her exhaustion last night, an open doorway beckoned. At the threshold, Evelyn paused to watch the scene before her. Mr. Flynn, his hair neatly combed back from his face, knelt beside the dining table with little Emily on one knee and an arm around

Benjamin. Not wishing to intrude on such a touching moment, she merely stood there, feeling decidedly out of place.

Delighted the children had not forgotten him in his prolonged absence and actually seemed thrilled to see him, Samuel couldn't help but drop down to embrace them. He gave Benjamin a good squeeze while he balanced Emily's doll-like form on his knee.

"So, young man, did you take good care of the house in my absence?"

Benjamin lifted his chin, his little spine as straight as a new sapling. "Yes, sir, I surely did."

"And you minded Mrs. Tooley?"

Benjamin's features faltered. "Well, we tried. I promise."

A chuckle bubbled up out of his chest. "Let us try a mite harder, shall we? Mrs. Tooley is a great blessing to us, and we wouldn't want to exasperate her."

"Yes, sir. I promise we'll try harder."

He squeezed the boy's shoulder, thankful he could no longer easily feel the bones underneath. "Good lad." He turned his focus on Emily. "And you, young lady, have you been behaving?"

Emily ducked her chin and nodded. Still shy and quiet, he wondered how long it would be before she opened up to him. The way she tightly clung to his lapel would have to be progress enough for the moment. Her brown eyes darted to the door, and an unexpected smile stretched across her face. Samuel followed her gaze to find Miss Mapleton standing in the doorway, watching them.

She shifted uncomfortably. "Forgive me. I didn't mean to intrude upon your family moment." The smallest hint of longing laced her words.

He rose from the floor. "No need for forgiveness. You're not an intrusion."

Benjamin cut a glance at her that said he didn't agree. "Who is she?"

Samuel placed a hand on the boy's shoulder. "This is Miss Mapleton."

"Yeah, I know that. She done told me. But I mean *who is she*, besides what you call her."

Samuel looked to Evelyn with surprise. "You've met the children?"

Humor sparked in her luminous eyes. "Indeed. They introduced themselves earlier this morning." She turned to address Benjamin. "To answer your question, I'm a friend who lost her way to her hotel last night, and Mr. Flynn was kind enough to let me stay here so I wouldn't be out on the street alone in the dark."

Benjamin's eyes widened, and understanding entered his gaze. He nodded in that serious way he had. "All right then." Seeming satisfied with the explanation, he hurried around the table and plopped into a chair, his hands reaching for a sweet roll.

"Benjamin." Samuel drew out the boy's name and he paused. "Are you not forgetting something?"

His face reddened. "Oh, right. Sorry." He scrunched his eyes tight. "Thank ya, God, for these nice sweet rolls Mrs. Tooley made. Amen." He snagged the roll and shoved half of it into his mouth.

A small laugh sprang out of Miss Mapleton before she hid it behind her fingers. Samuel pulled out a chair for her. "We're still working on proper table manners."

She took her seat then regarded him over her shoulder. The sweep of her coal black hair nearly distracted him from her words. "I find him enchanting."

Something in his chest tightened, and he turned away before he could ponder what caused it. Emily waited patiently for him to pull the chair out for her as he had done for Miss Mapleton. Withholding a grin, he slid the chair out and settled her next to their guest. Emily peered up at the lady with sparkling eyes that earned a smile from Miss Mapleton's too often stoic lips.

He'd watched her in the army hospital, always intent on her work and rarely smiling. This morning, the curve of her lips seemed to come easily, and as he took his own chair at the head of the table, he couldn't help but let his eyes linger upon her. She was lovely with her striking coloring, but when she smiled... Well, somehow her eyes nearly glistened, and she turned from lovely to downright beautiful. She caught him staring, and he had only a sheepish grin to account for his lack of manners.

Mrs. Tooley stepped in and offered both coffee and tea, and he was surprised to see her select coffee. She sat with the stiff posture and moved with the controlled grace of one who had been instructed on all the ways of being a lady. An odd combination, given he had seen this same lady sprint through the woods and tend dying soldiers.

"So, Miss Mapleton," Samuel said, "What brings you to Washington?" And, more specifically, what had landed her in such a predicament that she had been alone last night unescorted? But it seemed boorish to ask directly, especially in front of the children.

"I had hoped to find my father." She took a tiny bite of sweet roll and dabbed her rosy lips with a napkin. "But I've been unable to locate him."

"You don't have an address for him?" He didn't mean to sound accusatory, but not knowing her father's location seemed rather odd.

Her features remained smooth, but some of the warmth left her tone. "I do not. I was told he had come to Washington. I decided to make the journey to find him. I'd hoped a family friend would know of his whereabouts, but she did not."

The children seemed occupied with their breakfast and not particularly interested in the conversation, but he still chose his words carefully. "Would this be the friend you visited yesterday?"

Miss Mapleton watched Emily, who had her gaze riveted on the sleeve of Miss Mapleton's gown. "Yes. Since Mrs. Greenman is currently experiencing some difficulties, I'll fetch Alice this morning and then make other plans."

The statement contained several items he wished to question, but he chose the most immediate. "Alice is still with her? Is she in need of constant care?" Despite Miss Mapleton's assurance last night that the girl had healed, one could never be sure with head injuries if they would have lasting consequences.

"Oh, no, I assure you Alice has made a full recovery." A crease formed between her eyebrows. "She...well, she simply did not wish to leave."

"Miss Mapleton—"

"Please, Evelyn is fine," she interrupted, further perplexing him. Did the woman never cease to change direction? She was like a fickle wind, darting from one thing to another and shifting from balmy to frigid in spurts and sputters. At his silence, she continued. "After you rescued me last eve and allowed me to stay in your home, such formalities are hardly needed." Her face seemed earnest, and he sensed the invitation contained her gratitude.

He withheld a smile and merely tilted his head. "Then you must call me Samuel."

Emily now slyly watched the lady, who had returned her focus to her plate. Then she reached out a small hand and gently touched the fabric along Evelyn's arm. Evelyn noticed and shot Samuel a curious look. He could only offer a small shrug. His best guess would be that Emily had not spent time in the company of ladies. Nuns, yes, but that was hardly the same. And Mrs. Tooley certainly didn't dress in fine silks.

Evelyn remained still, watching as the little girl trailed a finger over a small ribbon on the cuff. Emily realized she'd been seen and quickly put her hand back in her lap.

"It's a pretty ribbon, isn't it?" Soft words soothed and coaxed, and he had the strangest desire for her to speak to him in such a tone.

Emily bobbed her head but kept her eyes on her plate. After a moment, Evelyn returned her attention to him, but her tone had returned to stringent formality. "Forgive me. I believe I interrupted you."

Samuel had to search back to remember the train of thought that had been derailed when she asked him to use her Christian name. "Oh, yes. Evelyn." The name felt smooth and solid, just as he'd first believed. "If you cannot locate your father, what do you plan to do?"

She eyed him as though he'd asked too many probing questions. Perhaps he had, but the mystery surrounding this woman intrigued him.

"I've not yet decided."

She seemed unwilling to elaborate further, so he chose another question. "And what of Miss Avery?" He glanced at the children and altered his words. "What if Miss Avery does not wish to leave her current establishment?"

"I hope to convince her to return to her home in Front Royal. Otherwise, we shall stay in Washington and continue to look for my father."

He set down his fork. "Are you sure that's wise?"

His words seemed to spark a fire in her, because she set down her fork as well and pinned him with a cold glare. "Sir, I am capable of more than you might imagine." Worry crept into her tone. "Besides, if I do not find him soon, I'll—" She shook her head. "Never mind. That's not of your concern." She became rigid. "I thank you for your hospitality."

"It's my pleasure."

"Is she gonna stay today, too?" Benjamin asked, seeming to have paid more mind to the conversation than Samuel thought. Crumbs clung to his lips as he spoke, little reminders that the child wasted no time in devouring anything set before him.

"No," Evelyn answered. "I shall return to my hotel today."

"And how long shall you stay in Washington?" Samuel subtly indicated Benjamin should wipe his lips.

Evelyn noticed the exchange but focused her attention away from the boy, who watched her carefully as he smeared the napkin across his face. "For a time," she answered vaguely, though if it was done to purposely elude him or she simply didn't yet know, he couldn't tell.

Deciding she would offer little more, Samuel let it be. "If you have need of anything, you may call upon me here or at the Washington Infirmary."

She tucked a strand of ebony hair behind a small ear, and her scent of honeysuckle drifted to him, sweetening the sugary aroma of the rolls. "Again, you have my gratitude."

The room settled into near silence, only the sounds of silverware and shifting children to distract him. Samuel kept his eyes lowered, but his thoughts rested on the fetching woman at his table. If what she'd stated was true, then why did he get the uncanny sense that he'd somehow said something to offend her?

Why must this man be so kind? It made a mess of her insides, the way he spoke with such concern for a woman he didn't really know. A woman he must surely realize was a Southerner. An enemy he would have never let into his house if he'd known she'd shot a Federal soldier or stolen supplies from them. Evelyn shifted in her seat, her appetite waning. She needed to get Alice out of Mrs. Greenman's house before the girl wound up in prison, and then she needed to put more fervent efforts into finding Daddy. She just hoped she could do so before her funds ran out.

When the awkward silence stretched for as long as she could stand it, Evelyn rose from her seat. Samuel did the same, and gestured for Benjamin to stand. The boy frowned but obeyed. Little Emily, seeming to think the same must be required of her, dropped her napkin and scrambled out of her chair, coming to stand rather close to Evelyn's leg.

"Thank you for the meal, Doctor. I'm indebted to your hospitality, but I must be on my way."

He rounded the table. "I shall have a carriage fetched for you."

And further obligate her? "No, thank you. It's a pleasant autumn morning, and I shall be pleased to walk."

The muscles in his smooth jaw twitched. "If that is your wish."

"It is." Must he stare at her with such perception? She

glanced away. "I should be going now." Without daring another glance at him, Evelyn turned to leave. But she'd no sooner made it to the threshold than a tiny hand slipped into hers and held fast. Surprised, Evelyn looked down at Emily, but the girl kept her focus ahead. She threw a questioning look over her shoulder, but the doctor seemed as taken aback as she.

Evelyn gave the little girl's hand a small squeeze and then attempted to extract her fingers, but the child would not let go. "Would you like to walk me to the door?"

Emily's lips curved, and she tugged on Evelyn's hand. Still, she did not speak. If she'd not seen Emily whisper to her brother, Evelyn may have assumed the child was mute. Not sure how else to proceed, Evelyn allowed the girl to pull her through the foyer, but instead of releasing her at the door, Emily led her to another room.

Painted a fetching yellow with cream-colored carved moldings, the room appeared to be both a music and reading area. Once inside, Emily released her hand, bounded to a bookshelf, and snagged a book. She clutched it to her pale blue dress and shyly approached Evelyn, who still stood rather perplexed on the yellow rose rug.

Tentatively, Emily separated the book from her chest as though it were attached there and cautiously held it out to Evelyn.

"You want me to read to you?"

The child stepped closer, the book still outstretched. Her eyes were large, much like Alice's, and her tiny face contained an odd mixture of hope and trepidation. Evelyn's stomach clenched. How could she explain to the girl that she could not sit here, cozy with the children as though she belonged in Samuel's house? This sweet innocent did not know the woman before her.

"She loves fairy stories," Samuel said from behind her.

Ignoring him lest she come undone, Evelyn took the book and turned it over in her hands. "Oh, I'm terribly sorry, Miss Emily, but I'm afraid I don't have time to read now. I must go find my friend." She fought against the sudden sorrow that wrapped cold fingers around her heart.

The light in the little girl's eyes dimmed, but she gave a small nod and then turned to go. Samuel watched her pass, worry and sadness on his features. What had happened to the child that she acted thus? Evelyn's heart wrenched, and she felt like a calloused heel. She did not fancy being the cause of such disappointment.

"She'll be all right. I'll read to her later." Samuel offered a kind smile. "We understand you have much business to attend to."

Evelyn wanted to ask questions about the children, but it wasn't her place. And besides, she did need to get to Alice. Samuel allowed her to pass and then opened the front door, further concern across his features though he remained blessedly silent.

Determined to exit without revealing more of herself than she already had, Evelyn stepped out onto the portico and resisted the urge to touch her uncovered head. She'd have to remember to fetch her bonnet as soon as she got to Mrs. Greenman's home. "Good day, Mr. Flynn."

"Good day, Evelyn." He said her name with a touch of humor, as though mildly chiding her for not accepting his invitation to use his given name. But to do so would further foster the dangerous stirrings in her heart, and she could not allow that to happen.

She made it down the three steps from the portico before she realized she wasn't entirely sure of her location. She turned to find Dr. Flynn still standing in the doorway, his hands in his pockets and his features painted in amusement.

Evelyn tried for one of Isabella's haughty tones. "If you would be so kind, would you mind pointing me in the direction of Mrs. Greenman's residence on Baker Street?"

"Continue down this street," he said, indicating toward the left, "until you reach Conner Avenue. Then turn right onto Baker. It's not terribly far. I'm not familiar with the Greenman residence, however, so you will have to find it from there."

She thanked him and hurried away. It took only a dozen steps before she regretted not letting him get her a conveyance. The autumn wind in Washington was colder than she'd expected, and her silk gown was hardly suited to walking. Evelyn stiffened her spine and lengthened her stride, distracting herself from the cold with the views of the city.

Men in jackets and snug caps went about their business, and as Mrs. Greenman had said, Evelyn did not see many women or children out in the crisp morning air. But neither did she see a lawless band of miscreants running amok. She reached Baker Street without incident and slowed as she neared Mrs. Greenman's impressive home. Stately with heavy block walls and rigid columns, it boasted of wealth and influence. Neither of which seemed to matter to the men who had created such upheaval within.

To her surprise, no guards stood outside the house, and if she didn't know better, she wouldn't have thought anything amiss. Gathering her courage, Evelyn walked up to the front door and rapped softly. It immediately swung inward on silent hinges, proving her suspicion that someone waited inside. Had they watched from the windows as she'd approached? What if she'd turned away before knocking? The thought of someone springing from a hiding place and grabbing her forced a tremble she couldn't suppress.

The man with the beard, whom Mrs. Greenman had called Peterson, lifted his eyebrows. "Miss Mapleton?"

She pushed her shoulders back and leveled her tone. "May I come in?"

He widened the opening and gestured her within, clearly surprised to see her.

"I've come for two reasons. First, Miss Avery has no business staying here, as she never laid eyes on Mrs. Greenman prior to our visit yesterday. Whatever it is you suspect of Mrs. Greenman, Miss Avery is merely my traveling companion and is not privy to any connections or interests Mrs. Greenman may have. Therefore, I have come to fetch her." The practiced words tumbled free with more momentum than she'd intended, like a careening carriage with spooked horses.

Mr. Peterson made no reply to this. "And the second reason?"

"I forgot my bonnet."

He chuckled. "Is that so?" He indicated toward the coat rack near the door. "Would it be that one?"

Evelyn plucked the bonnet from a peg. "Yes, sir. Thank you." Unable to keep his probing gaze, she let her eyes wander around what remained of Mrs. Greenman's home. The furniture had been stripped of its upholstery, leaving tuffs of cotton batting to drift across the hardwood floor. It seemed their investigation had become more fervent in her absence. Had they found anything of consequence?

"And I suppose," Mr. Peterson said, drawing out his words and recapturing her gaze, "you also wish to tell me that you would like to take Mrs. Greenman on an outing with you as well?" His tone held a dangerous mix of humor and threat.

Features schooled into an unconcerned calm, Evelyn

waved a hand. "Certainly not. I have no desire to interfere with your…investigation." She gestured toward the mangled settee in the hall. "I simply wish to take poor Miss Avery, who was merely too frightened to leave in the wee hours of the morning." She leveled him with a contemptuous stare. "And as your men deigned to set a lady out in the street without escort or transportation, it is little wonder she was too afraid to leave when requested."

Mr. Peterson merely shrugged. "You did."

"Miss Avery lacks my gumption."

He released another chuckle, this one containing more mirth than the first, and his countenance seemed to relax a measure. "Perhaps you are right."

She opened her mouth to thank him, but as quickly as the humor seized him, it evaporated. "You may have a few moments," he said, his features sharpening. "But *only* a few moments, to inform Miss Avery she may go with you."

Evelyn inclined her head. "I thank you." She headed up the stairs before the fickle man could change his mind, keenly aware that he watched her every move. *Please, Alice,* she silently pleaded, *don't be a fool.* She turned at the top of the stairs and continued to Mrs. Greenman's chamber, thoughts of sneaking about in the dark still fresh upon her memory.

She tapped on the door. "Mrs. Greenman? Alice?"

After a moment, Mrs. Greenman's startled face appeared. "Miss Mapleton?" She grabbed Evelyn's arm and wrenched her inside the room. She lowered her voice to a clipped whisper. "The papers?"

"Burned."

Mrs. Greenman closed her eyes for a brief moment. "Then what are you doing here?"

Evelyn extracted herself. "I've come for Alice."

Alice rose from where she sat at Mrs. Greenman's dressing

table, her gown rumpled but her hair tamed. "Whatever for?"

Evelyn stifled a groan, but tried to speak with caution lest Alice dig in her heels like a mule. "Alice, you've done nothing wrong. You shouldn't be imprisoned." She spoke the words as much for Mrs. Greenman's benefit as for Alice's.

"I wish to aid the cause." She lifted her chin with a determined air.

What had Mrs. Greenman said to her whilst Evelyn had been at the doctor's home? Had she promised Alice some kind of position? Did the woman think she could further conduct espionage while under guard? Evelyn tried not to grind her teeth. "And don't you think that would be better accomplished outside of a guarded room?"

Alice's forehead crinkled, as though such an obvious thought had not occurred to her.

"Actually, she's right," Mrs. Greenman stated, her eyes narrowing. Evelyn could nearly see the thoughts churning in her head. "It *would* be better for you to go."

Alice shook her head. "But I came here to help you."

Much to Evelyn's surprise, Mrs. Greenman stepped over to Alice and took her hand. She lowered her voice to whisper to Alice, but Evelyn heard her anyway. "I'll need you to gather information while I'm restrained. Our plan will be easier this way."

"Surely you don't think Alice can come here and deliver information to you unnoticed?" Evelyn said in a sharp whisper. She forced her clenched hands to relax. "And then what? You would send forth said information to whomever, under the careful watch of the detective police?" Was she the only one with any sense?

Mrs. Greenman studied her for a moment, her crafty gaze seeming to pick apart each statement. "Do not underestimate me, Miss Mapleton. You have not given me enough credit, and have heaped too much upon the heads of dimwits."

Evelyn turned to Alice. "Come, let us be done with this."

"We're far from done." She glanced back to Mrs. Greenman.

The lady smiled at Evelyn. "I'm aware your aunt did not provide you with adequate funding. I can supply your needs while you look for your father, and I'll also send word to my friends to aid your search." She lifted her brows. "All I ask is a few small favors in return."

She glanced at Alice, regretting confiding the situation. Feeling a weight settle, Evelyn asked, "Such as?"

"You'll start by working at the Washington Infirmary. Soon our captured boys will go through there before they are imprisoned. You and Alice will offer your services, and I'll send instructions when needed."

Blood pounded in her ears. Of all places.

"Surely that's not asking much," Mrs. Greenman continued, "as Alice informs me you already intended to seek a paid position. Perhaps in a hospital? Think of this as a solution to your problem."

A knock sounded firmly at the door, and it swung open before anyone had a chance to answer it. One of the soldiers who'd been arguing with his fellows in an inebriated state last evening frowned at her, looking much more intimidating this morning. "Miss Mapleton, your time has expired."

Evelyn drew a deep breath. "Come, Alice. Let's be on our way."

Alice darted a look to Mrs. Greenman, who inclined her head toward the door.

Then Alice stalked out, and Evelyn scrambled to stay on her heels. They hurried right past Mr. Peterson, who regarded them with far too much interest.

Evelyn offered a disingenuous apology for Alice, excusing

her rude behavior to exhaustion and the extenuating circumstances. Mr. Peterson accepted the explanation with a complacent nod that Evelyn didn't for a moment believe. Nonetheless, the detective graciously supplied her with directions back to the Halverson, and they somehow managed to get out the front door.

It was going to be an arduous walk back to the hotel, one that Evelyn was now certain would be trailed and documented by the detective police. She watched her friend stalk away, beginning to wonder if it would have been better to not have gone to fetch Alice after all.

Eighteen

Washington Infirmary
October 10, 1861

A man's howls echoed through the ward, slicing across Samuel's ears the moment he stepped into the infirmary. Concerned, Samuel's gaze swept over the room flitting from patient to patient. Men lay about in their beds, more sick than wounded now that the cusp of winter had fallen upon them. No surprise, as camp conditions were deplorable. How such a discrepancy between the civilization of Washington City and the near inhumane conditions of the camp could so quickly occur, Samuel had no explanation. Yet none of these, miserable as they might be with their cramped stomachs and yellowed complexions, produced the gut-wrenching sound that reverberated through his head.

He made his way deeper into the hospital, glancing at nurses and volunteers who saw to their duties as though the screams of a tortured man did not perforate the thick scents of waste and infection. That could only mean they had grown accustomed to it in the few hours since Samuel had returned home to find rest. He quickened his pace. Some of the men nodded to him as he passed. Normally, he tried to remember the name of every soldier under his care as he made his way past them, but today, he was far too distracted by the sound that had now become an enraged howl.

When he'd crossed the length of the main ward and had not yet found the man responsible for the unholy clamor, he turned to the hallway on the right that led to the hospital's office chambers.

The sound stopped suddenly, and the ensuing silence seemed somewhat eerie.

About halfway down the hall, a soldier stood posted outside an open doorway. Frowning, Samuel leaned around the guard to get a better look into the small room where he assumed the screaming man was being held. The once empty chamber was dark, but the thick shadows still revealed at least two men lying on the floor.

He turned to the guard. "What is the meaning of this, soldier?"

The square-faced fellow had a glint in his blue eyes. "Sorry, Doc. Blasted Reb won't keep his trap shut."

A Rebel? "Is this man injured?" he asked, once again trying to lean past the stocky man's frame.

The wailing had grown silent, though if because the poor man had run out of hope or had fallen unconscious, Samuel couldn't tell.

"No need to worry yourself," the unconcerned soldier intoned. "I'm just supposed to watch them three Rebs until they get loaded up to go to the Old Capitol."

"Why bring them here if they don't require medical care?" Impatience grafted an edge into his tone, and his hands clenched tightly at his sides. The man had the audacity to shrug, and Samuel's blood temperature spiked. "If they are meant for prison, then why not take them straight there?"

The soldier considered this for a moment but then merely lifted his shoulders once more. "Just following orders."

Samuel took another step closer, the distinct stench of waste, vomit, and blood flowing from the room and tainting his scrubbed ward. "Well, I daresay that if the men were brought to the hospital, it was because they need medical attention. Step aside, please."

The big man scowled. "Why do you care? If they die, then that's less we have to haul off to prison and fewer who can shoot at us."

"This is a *hospital*," Samuel snapped. "Not a prison or a battlefield. If there are men who need medical attention, it's my duty as a doctor to see to them."

"But they're Rebs." The man rubbed the back of his stubby neck and stared at Samuel in utter confusion.

"Soldier, were you given specific orders that these men were to be denied medical attention?"

"Well, no, but—"

"Then move aside." Samuel placed a hand on the man's shoulder and nudged him out of the way, then stepped inside the dim area that appeared more unused storage space than office. His stomach churned, and he swallowed down the familiar bile. Three men were huddled there, sitting on the bare floor without a single blanket or stick of furniture.

With the sweeping assessment the war had given him a knack for, Samuel slid his gaze over the captured soldiers. They were filthy, caked in mud and blood. The color of their uniforms was nearly indistinguishable. One cradled an arm, one lay curled on his side on the floor, and one sat with his back against the wall eyeing Samuel with open hostility.

In the corner, a single bucket contained the contents of what could only be bodily waste. He resisted the urge to put his hand over his nose and spun back toward the door. "Soldier! Get an orderly in here this instant!"

The man frowned. "What for?"

"Because these men obviously have not been allowed any basic necessities."

"They're Rebels," the man stated again, as though that were the answer to everything.

Heat gathered in Samuel's chest and burned its way through his veins. "I don't care who they are! I will not have my hospital contaminated!"

The soldier merely stared at him blankly. Samuel stalked out the door, shaking his head. Regardless of what the army thought, any man in his hospital would be clean, fed, and tended. And for heaven's sake, they would not keep waste in their room!

Evelyn shifted her weight from one foot to the other, wondering exactly how she had ended up here. Thinking back, it seemed a rather odd string of coincidences had piled upon one another, each step bringing her farther and farther down a path that, six months ago, she would have never believed herself traveling.

Not only had Mrs. Greenman made good on her promise by funding their stay at the hotel, but merely three days after they'd left her home, she'd had two trunks filled with petticoats, gowns of every variety, and other necessities delivered to their room. One thing was for certain. Evelyn had indeed underestimated her. How did she manage to do such things while still under guard?

Alice stood at her side, dressed in a plain gown matching Evelyn's own in simple function, without any adornments or feminine frivolity that might distract a man.

It had taken much longer for them to be ordered by unsigned missive to report to the infirmary as volunteers than she'd expected. Evelyn had spent the time afforded to her by Mrs. Greenman's funding to try to locate her father, but none of the Washington papers had claimed to have seen him. Worry over his condition had become an ever-present itch.

The door clicked and an elderly gentleman with a thick gray beard strode inside, a spindly woman on his heels.

"Ah, here they are. Mrs. Brown, these are your new volunteers," the man said, gesturing to Evelyn and Alice without an introduction. "Come with high recommendations."

Evelyn dipped her chin. "I'm Evelyn Mapleton, and this—"

"Alice Avery, sir, ma'am," Alice interjected, shooting Evelyn a harsh glare.

Evelyn snapped her mouth closed. What had happened to her sweet friend in Front Royal? Alice had grown more distant the longer they stayed in Washington. And lately, she hardly even saw Alice. Many days she didn't return to their shared hotel room until late at night. Evelyn had asked what she'd been doing, but Alice's vague answers had soon faded to cutting retorts that it was none of Evelyn's concern.

The pair didn't seem to notice Alice's rudeness. The doctor merely nodded. "I'm Dr. Porter, the primary physician at this hospital. Nurse Brown is in charge of the volunteers and will see to all of your needs and direct you in your duties."

The pinched-faced woman looked them up and down as though they were horses at the auction. "Experience?"

"I tended wounded in the Fifth Wisconsin near Chain Bridge," Evelyn said.

"How interesting!" Dr. Porter said. "One of my students served a time at Chain Bridge. Surely you know Mr. Flynn?"

"Yes, sir. I became acquainted with him during my time there."

"Excellent!"

The nurse seemed less interested in the revelation, and merely nodded for Alice to answer the same question. With smooth words and placid face, Alice replied, "I served at the Benvenue hospital as well, and before that helped in the tent hospitals under General Winfield. They were camped not far from our farm in Lewinsville, and as soon as our brave men arrived, I saw it as my duty to leave my own work behind to aid my country."

Evelyn pressed her lips together, wondering at what point the bright-eyed girl from Front Royal had become a cold and efficient liar.

"And what brings you ladies to Washington?" Dr. Porter asked.

"I came to find my father," Evelyn said. She'd not speak for Alice. If the girl wished to lie, she could do so on her own.

Nurse Brown studied Evelyn closely. "And where are you from?"

"I've lived for many years in Martinsburg, Virginia." The truth. Evelyn kept the woman's steady gaze until it darted to Alice.

"And you?"

"Front Royal." Ah, now Alice would try for a sliver of truth. How would she remember which things she'd told in earnest and which she'd fabricated?

The nurse's eyes narrowed. "I thought you said you were from Lewinsville."

Evelyn held her breath, wondering if Mrs. Greenman's entire plot would unravel because Alice easily forgot her story.

"Yes, ma'am. My grandparents have a farm there and I spend most of my summers with them. I consider it as much home as my own house. My parents are from Front Royal, though."

The nurse seemed satisfied with this blatant falsehood, and after they bade good afternoon to Dr. Porter, they were ushered into the hall, where the nurse peppered them with instructions.

They trailed behind her purposeful stride down a wide hallway as she gave a brief tour of the facilities. Alice cut a sharp glance at Evelyn that she pretended not to notice.

Alice grabbed her elbow. "Did you know that Yankee doctor works here?"

"Yes."

"And you thought not to mention it?"

She probably should have told Alice before they came today, but for some reason hadn't. But then, it wasn't as though the two of them sat and chatted anymore. Why, Alice hadn't even been very interested in what had happened to Evelyn the night she'd been thrown out of Mrs. Greenman's house! At least, not beyond what she'd done with those papers.

"Sorry."

Alice narrowed her eyes but said nothing more as they passed a soldier standing guard outside a darkened doorway, the stench of waste drifting around him and making Evelyn's eyes water.

"Oh, my," Alice said, placing a hand to her face. "What's in there?"

The nurse kept walking and spoke over her shoulder. "Just some captured Rebels. Don't worry. They won't be here long."

Alice and Evelyn shared a glance. No one had said anything about a guard for wounded men in a hospital. Nurse Brown droned on about the location of linens and where to take the wash, and as she rounded the corner, nearly collided with a scurrying young man clutching a mop.

Throwing a hand up to keep the boy from running her over, Nurse Brown shouted, "Peter!" and the boy lurched to a halt. "What are you doing?"

The towheaded boy glanced at the two women behind the nurse and then to the guard outside the door behind them. "Mr. Flynn said to clean the Rebs' chamber."

Evelyn couldn't see the woman's face, but she heard the scowl in her voice. "Whatever for?"

The boy shrugged. "He said enemy or no, he wouldn't have any filthy soldiers contaminating the ward. He said I had to clean it."

Nurse Brown considered this a moment and then nodded. "Very well. It is getting rather putrid in there." She grasped his arm. "But you be alert. Don't turn your back to one of them for a moment."

The youth's eyes widened. "I won't."

"Good lad."

Evelyn clenched her teeth as she watched the soldier step aside for the nervous boy. Did they actually think suffering men were going to assault a boy trying to clean for them? Under the watch of an armed guard?

"How many of them are in there?" Alice asked as they continued down the hall.

"Just three."

Alice quickened her pace to take the nurse's side. "Why are they here?"

"Captured officers. They were hauled in here last evening, waiting to be taken to the Old Capitol."

Evelyn found herself searching the area for Samuel, wondering what he would think of seeing her here. Would he find it another strange twist of fate?

"You can start by changing the linens on all of the beds. Then you can help the nuns pass out the evening meals. If any of the men need help with letters, you may do that as well, but only after every man has clean bedding and a full stomach." Without further instruction, the nurse hurried away, leaving Evelyn and Alice to their chores.

Surprisingly, it took at least three hours before Samuel saw her. She'd been watching him as he assessed a patient, inspecting a cut on the man's lower leg. The soldier had frowned as the doctor leaned close and then made a notation in a folio. Six beds away, Evelyn kept her head down and her hands busy tucking the ends of a sheet around the corners of the narrow mattress.

She worked too far away to make out the words Samuel spoke in low tones to his patients, but not too far away to hear the compassion in his voice. She was staring at him when he caught sight of her, and she didn't avert her gaze as a smile bloomed on his features.

Leaving the next man on the line, Samuel walked to her with purpose and a friendly intent that should not have caused such flutters in her heart. Evelyn continued smoothing the finished cot, making sure it would be ready should a new patient have need of it.

"Why, Miss Mapleton, this is a surprise."

She tried not to let herself be disappointed that he'd chosen to address her formally. Why should she expect anything different? "Good day, Mr. Flynn. I hope you are well."

He waited until she met his probing gaze. "What, may I ask, are you doing here?"

A nervous laugh escaped her throat. "Currently? Changing bedding." He stared at her as she gathered the rest of the linens and made for the next bed, the last of those she had to complete.

"I'd assumed you'd found your father or left the city, as I haven't heard from you." Disappointment laced his tone.

She'd often thought of calling on him again, but didn't have the nerve. She'd told herself if she'd spent too much time in his presence, he might have found out the truth about her. Better to remember his kindness the way it was and someday look back on the memory of him with fondness.

She shook out a sheet and spread it across the mattress, ignoring the faded red stain splashed across the center. "I've done neither."

"And so you came here. To my hospital." His voice contained equal parts skepticism and curiosity, and Evelyn continued to avoid his gaze.

"I might as well be useful."

"And you are still residing at the Halverson Hotel?"

With Mrs. Greenman's funds. "Yes."

He was quiet while she finished the bed and, with nothing else to occupy her, finally had to look up at him. He studied her as though she were one of his patients. Then he took another step closer, and she had to tilt her head back to keep his gaze.

"Why are you here, Evelyn?"

He spoke softly, and the way her name whispered across his lips sent a tingle through her that she could not ignore. She took a step back.

"I told you."

His eyes lowered into scrutinizing slits. "I find it interesting that you keep showing up in my life. I have concluded it must be one of two explanations."

"Oh?"

"Either Providence has thrown us together, or you have

set your sights upon me." Humor twinkled in his eyes as Evelyn felt the blood drain from her face. "Either way, I find it fascinating."

She blinked at him. "Why, I…you can't…" She snapped her spine straight. "What an ungentlemanly thing to say!"

"Oh?" He rubbed his smooth jaw, a boyish grin making him even more handsome. "I can find no other reason to explain you serendipitously finding your way into my path no matter where I go."

Evelyn clenched her hands. "And who's to say you have not been showing up in *my* path? I may very well accuse you of the same!"

He chuckled, and the blood that had retreated from her face now surged, heating her ears and most surely staining her cheeks a telling red.

Samuel turned his hands out, palms up. "I do live in Washington, and I am studying to be a doctor…" He let the rest of the sentence dangle, leaving Evelyn to fill in the fact that she was less likely to be in those places they'd met than he.

She spun away to put as much distance between herself and this confounding man as possible. Cool fingers wrapped around her wrist.

"Miss Mapleton, wait."

She paused but did not look at him.

"Forgive me. I should not tease you in such a manner. I don't know why I find it such a temptation, but for some reason…"

At his hesitation, she couldn't help but turn to look at him. The sensation of his hand upon her wrist tingled all the way up her arm. His warm eyes studied her, and once again she was struck at how open this man seemed to be.

"Well, that is not entirely true. I believe I do indeed

know the reason." His smile wobbled, and her heart seemed to drop to her feet. "I fear I'm most taken with you, Lady of the Wildwood."

Samuel watched as confusion broke through Evelyn's carefully composed features. He probably shouldn't have said any of that, especially revealing his secret nickname for her, but he couldn't help it. She would surely think him mad now, and perhaps that's exactly what he needed. He'd had a most difficult time erasing her from his memory even without the occasion to look upon her. Now she'd found her way to him once again, and this time he would take note of it.

He couldn't have her working in his ward and keep these stirrings to himself. Life was far too short. She was simply too intriguing, and all the more so now as her mouth worked to form a response to his wild musings.

"I'm sorry, what did you say?"

Realizing he still held her, and as they were in the midst of the listening ears of the patients, nurses, and volunteers, Samuel dropped her hand and motioned her toward the door. "Would you mind if I walked with you to gather more linens?"

"But I'm finis—" She shook her head, dislodging a lock of raven hair from the sensible knot at her nape. Then she laced her fingers and dipped her chin. "Yes, that would be fine."

He directed her out of the ward and hopefully away from the majority of the listening ears, and waited to speak again until they were in the quiet hallway. "Forgive me. I'm certain you'll find such blather the ravings of a madman, but the first time I saw you, you reminded me of a sprite from one of Emily's tales."

She peeked at him through her lashes but kept her face forward, slowly walking at his side, where he had the uncanny feeling she belonged. "I resemble a sprite? I'm not entirely sure if you mean to compliment or insult me, sir."

Despite the edge of sarcasm in her voice, Samuel laughed. "Believe it or not, it is a compliment. I saw this beautiful fairy queen emerge from the woods like something from a fanciful children's tale. When I would think of you after that, I didn't know what to call you, so I gave you the title of Lady of the Wildwood, or the Wildwood Queen."

She remained quiet for several moments, sealing Samuel's worry that she would, indeed, consider him either a halfwit or a fool.

"You thought of me after we first met?"

"Often." He shoved his hands in his pockets. They came to a stop by the linen closet. He glanced around the hallway, but they remained alone. "I still do."

She tilted her head back to look up at him, her eyes full of questions. "Why?"

A sudden nervousness swirled within him. It was not a sensation he often felt, as a doctor must be sure of himself, but this one little woman had an odd effect on him. He placed a hand on her shoulder. "I should think that would be obvious, Evelyn. I find you captivating."

She drew a deep breath that lifted her shoulder under his touch. "But you don't know me." She shook her head and gave a rueful laugh. "And I am certainly nothing from a fairy tale."

"Would you like to come to dinner tomorrow? I believe Mrs. Tooley is preparing a roasted lamb."

Something sparked in her eyes, but it quickly disappeared

behind another guarded expression. She stepped out from under his touch and clasped her hands. "I don't think that would be wise."

He could tell she'd appreciated the invitation, and in the moments when her eyes had found him when she'd thought he hadn't seen her, he could tell she found him at least somewhat appealing. Why, then, did she pretend otherwise?

"Emily would be happy to see you."

"She's a precious child, but I don't think it would be good. We don't need to form any attachments, since I won't be long in Washington. It would only cause..." Her throat seemed to tighten, and her next words came out pinched. "It would only cause unnecessary hurt later."

His forehead creased. Did she speak of the children...or herself? "I would say that none of us knows what the good Lord has in store for tomorrow." He took a step closer, and she didn't back away. He longed to reach out and see what her cheek would feel like under his fingers.

"Mr. Flynn!" Nurse Brown's voice hit him like a volley.

Samuel turned to find the woman scurrying down the hall. She shot a curious look at Evelyn, who quickly ducked into the linen closet, and then called to him again.

In two strides he met her. "What's happened?"

"They cleaned that room as you said, and one of the orderlies got them washed for you to examine. But Dr. Porter—" She pinched her lips. "Well, I told him he best take it up with you, seeing as how you gave the orders."

Stifling a groan, he cast one look at the linen closet. His conversation with Evelyn would have to wait. He gestured for Nurse Brown to lead the way and hurried on to his duty.

But for the first time, he found himself wishing he could ignore his patients and take hold of a woman instead.

Nineteen

ever in all his time at the infirmary or under the man's instruction had Samuel seen the distinguished doctor bathed in such emotion. Dr. Porter puffed and panted harder than a blacksmith's bellow. The air in the infirmary seemed warmed by the heat radiating from the man's face. A couple of orderlies and volunteers came down the hall, but upon seeing the attending physician's countenance, scurried quickly away.

He waved his hand through the air indicating the door where the beefy soldier stood watch over three pitiful Confederates. "What is the idea of this, Flynn?"

Samuel clasped his hands behind his back and kept his face passive. "I instructed the staff that the room, and the men within, were to be cleaned." And from the quality of the air in the hallway, it already helped.

"We are a *Federal* hospital," the doctor seethed, jutting his chin toward the door. "Or have you forgotten?"

Nurse Brown, who stood partially behind Dr. Porter's larger frame, folded her arms over her stained apron and regarded Samuel as though he had spontaneously sprouted another set of arms.

He tried not to let frustration slip into his tone, but the

lunacy of this conversation baffled him. "Would you prefer our soldiers become exposed to disease?"

Dr. Porter frowned. "That has nothing to do with your treatment of enemy soldiers. Why, it's bad enough they're being held in here without—"

"Begging your pardon, sir," Samuel interrupted, holding up a hand. "But they are indeed here, regardless of how, or why, or who sent them. And since they are, I would not have them contaminating my ward whilst they are forced to inhabit it."

"*Your* ward, is it?" He elevated bushy eyebrows, equal parts question and challenge in his eyes.

Choosing his words carefully, Samuel gave a slow nod. "Indeed, sir. As per your wishes, I've put myself to the task of learning to run this hospital. In so doing, I instructed the staff to keep the facilities pristine."

"He's got us scrubbing floors and changing bedding more often than we can keep up with," Nurse Brown grumbled.

Samuel ignored her. "Both the mental and physical condition of our men has improved during the past weeks because of my efforts. Is that not the case?"

With obvious reluctance, the doctor nodded.

"Then these men"—Samuel indicated the door behind Nurse Brown—"are brought into the hospital and tossed into this chamber with nary a bed or coverings."

"As is befitting traitors," the nurse quipped.

It took more than a little self-control to disregard her remarks, knowing that if he were to snap and send her away now, it would only antagonize Dr. Porter. "In this deplorable condition, these men have been kept with naught but a pot to keep their waste in." Accusation and disgust crept into his voice despite his efforts to keep a level tone. "A pot that had not been changed prior to my orders."

"Well, yes, but…"

He held up a hand to stay the doctor's words. In this instance, he would have his say. "The stench permeated the ward, carrying with it untold viruses and disease. You would put our men at risk?" Not to mention how the poor fellow had cried out in agony. But he would have to get the doctor to agree to cleanliness before he would ever consider treatment.

The doctor scowled at him. "You know it's not our intention for our men to contract further disease."

"Yet it's an inconvenient fact that if the enemy is not tended, then our own patriots will suffer as well."

They stood there for several moments, the doctor scowling, the nurse turning up her nose, and the soldier posted at the door darting glances at them all. Samuel kept Dr. Porter's gaze until the man relented.

"I cannot fault your logic." One side of his mouth curled up as he spoke. "And while it pains me to see good supplies wasted on men who would just as soon slit our throats, I concede that it is a predicament we must navigate."

Samuel inclined his head in thanks. He would take that for now and pose the need for treatment once Dr. Porter returned to a normal color.

Samuel motioned to the nurse. "Mrs. Brown, if you would, please send some volunteers to see to these prisoners' needs."

The disgruntled nurse speared Samuel with a contemptuous glance before scurrying off.

Dr. Porter pressed his lips together. "I cannot decide whether I commend your actions or not. You're doing well in taking charge, but I fear you've gone about it in the entirely wrong manner."

Another thing the doctor might hold over him. Samuel

forced his tight jaw to loosen. "Sir, I've done all that you've asked, and the other members of my class have long since moved on. When can I expect you to sign off on my medical papers and grant my license?"

The man stared at him for a moment, something working behind his eyes that Samuel could not piece together. "You will have it when I feel you are ready." With that, he spun on his heels and strode down the hall at an infuriatingly leisurely pace.

Blood spiked, Samuel stood in the hallway breathing deeply and dissecting the various scents that wafted in and out of his senses. He waited in the hall until one scrawny orderly completed all of his instructions, the boy's sallow complexion confirming that Samuel wasn't the only one who had been sickened by the room's stench.

When the boy was gone, Samuel addressed the guard. "I'm sending orderlies and volunteers to see that the men are properly bathed and fed. Please allow them entrance as needed into this chamber. I shall return later."

The fellow shrugged, and Samuel wondered if he were capable of more expressive communication. Blowing the remaining stench out of his nostrils with a derisive snort, Samuel stalked away. He paused briefly at the fork in the hallway, part of him wishing to return to the linen storage to see if Evelyn still waited for him there. But knowing it would be better not to speak to her in his current state of annoyance, he turned his focus on his duty to his patients.

In fixing them, perhaps he could forget about all the things he couldn't fix. The staff's animosity over having soldiers from the wrong portion of the country in his hospital, the waffling desires of the attending physician and, most notably, his perplexing feelings for one contradictory young woman.

Setting himself to his work, he grabbed his folio with patient notes, plastered an encouraging smile onto his face, and threw his energy into his rounds. All through the remainder of the day and past the evening meal, Samuel tended the men and made his notations, keeping special track of any time he detected the putrid smell of infection.

Sometime during the later hours of the evening, he scanned over his notations. With any luck, he would have adequate evidence to support his theory. Now, if he could only bring himself to make note of the early signs of infection and then withhold treatment until more obvious signs occurred. Perhaps he could detect the time between when the first signs appeared and the infection affected a man's health. Making note of the days in between seemed significant to the advancement of the medical practice.

But withholding treatment put his patients at risk. Was it ethical to study a man without his knowledge? He closed the folio and leaned over his next patient, a candidate for such considerations. How had he missed the first telling smells of infection on the torn bicep of this private from Wisconsin? He would administer treatment now, but the redness and swelling had already begun.

This man's wound hadn't been sustained in battle but rather had occurred while the private was on furlough in Washington. It seemed the situation involved some kind of misunderstanding with another soldier in a tavern. The gash had cut deep, flaying open skin and muscle and exposing bone. Samuel had been the one to stitch it and had thought he'd kept a good check on Private Morris's condition. But the reddened skin and yellowing substance around his stitches said otherwise.

"Can you believe such a thing?" Private Morris asked, interrupting Samuel's contemplation of the wound.

Samuel frowned and leaned closer. Why didn't this one smell as strongly as the others? "Believe what?"

He no longer bothered asking Dr. Porter about administering treatments. He doled them out whenever he deemed it necessary, and because of his particular sensibilities, he had found it necessary rather often.

Who would have thought that his curse could be useful? His nose had led him to treat many infections before they fully took root. It had alerted him to contaminated water supplies and had once spared the ward from what Samuel was sure would have been a detrimental case of food poisoning.

"War is men's doing," Private Morris continued, unaware of Samuel's galloping thoughts. "That's what."

"Umm hum," Samuel agreed, fetching a clean roll of linen from the crate of supplies and measuring off an acceptable length.

"Who ever heard the likes of women involving themselves in such?"

Samuel's attention sharpened on the patient's words as he wrapped the strip of linen around the wound. What was he going on about? "I'm sorry, what did you say? Women are fighting in the war?"

The patient snorted. "Of course not." He scowled. "But seems they have a notion to go about involving themselves in the conflict just the same. Why, I even heard tell that one woman was discovered trying to sneak into camp wearing trousers and acting like a man!"

Samuel smiled. The longer men spent in the hospital, the more they turned to idle gossip as means for entertainment. "I'm sure such things are merely rumors."

Private Morris wagged his head, sending sandy brown locks sweeping over his pale forehead. "No, sir. Lincoln himself is talking about 'fashionable women spies,' and it was written up in the paper that they have arrested a woman right here in Washington on the charge of running a ring of spies. They say she's directly responsible for our loss at Bull Run!"

"Is that so?" Samuel tied the end of the bandage off. "It seems farfetched, if you ask me."

"I thought so too at first, but sure enough, the detective police have imprisoned a high-society widow by the name of Greenman for treason."

The name slammed into Samuel, making him suddenly feel off balance. "I'm sorry, who did you say?"

"Mrs. Margret Greenman," the private repeated, growing excited. "They say she runs a spy ring, and they have her under constant guard. Rumor says she's still operating, but they can't prove it."

Samuel forced a chuckle. "And you've become so bored in the hospital that you've taken to fanciful gossip?"

The man made a sour face and plucked a newssheet from his rumpled blanket. "Look here for yourself. This ain't no gossip, Doc. It's right here in print."

Samuel accepted the newssheet. The *Albany Evening Journal.* He didn't have time for much reading these days, but the mention of Evelyn's friend stirred his curiosity. *The heavy business in the war of spying is carried on by women!* he read. *Is it not about time that an example is set which will prove a terror to these artful Jezebels? Is it not time to impress them with the conviction that they may presume too much upon the privileges of their sex and the gallantry of those in authority?*

Samuel's mouth dried, and he found it difficult to swallow. With increasing distress he continued to read about how the widow Greenman had been arrested for espionage. The newspaper called for trying the woman for treason. Samuel handed the paper back to the soldier.

He regarded Samuel with both satisfaction and concern.

"I'm telling you, this is a dangerous business, it is."

Indeed. More so if Evelyn were involved in such a thing. Her mannerisms at their first meeting returned to him, along with Mrs. Ida Johnson's tale of the two girls disappearing from camp. Then she'd come to Washington and met with Greenman, whom Evelyn admitted had been searched by the detective police.

At the time he had been too concerned with her emotional state to pay the story much heed. But could such things really be a matter of coincidence? He tried to keep his own worries from his voice. "Worry not on it. I'm sure these stories are only novelty to distract from the real issues of war."

The man settled himself on his pillows and took up the newsprint once more. "I'm sure you're right. What can a woman truly do other than try to charm a man out of his secrets?"

Evelyn kept her voice low as she bathed the man's brow. "She says to send Beauregard a word."

The Confederate soldier fluttered his lashes, the signal that he knew what she referred to and what it meant. She continued to wash his warm forehead, her back to the guard that stood relentless watch at the door.

"They are to move her to the Old Capitol." Another swipe of dripping cloth. "New methods of communication must be established."

He fluttered his lashes again, and Evelyn breathed a sigh of relief. She'd done as requested and passed Mrs. Greenman's message down the line of conspirators. How many links existed in the chain that connected the widow to the general, she would probably never know.

Alice murmured something behind her as she spooned broth into another soldier's mouth, but though Evelyn couldn't make out what she said, she knew it must be the same message. How did Mrs. Greenman expect to convey information from the Old Capitol prison? But then, Evelyn would have never figured the widow would work codes into color-coded needlepoint and slip it out of the house right under Peterson's nose, either.

Her work completed, Evelyn dropped the rag into the bowl and rose from the hard floor. Could the hospital not at least give the men a bed? She cast another look at the rumpled soldier as she gained her feet. If this was what they could expect in a hospital, what fetid conditions might await them in prison?

She turned and started for the door only to find Samuel darkening the doorway instead of the guard. Palms sweaty, she brushed them down her skirt. He could not possibly know the words she'd spoken. Yet he watched her with narrowed eyes, and the stiff set of his shoulders caused her breath to falter. His usually open face hardened into somber lines, and he folded his arms over his wide chest.

That first day in the woods she had thought him more blacksmith than doctor, and looking at him now, the idea resurfaced. She glanced down at the soldier lying at the hem of her plaid skirt. "Nurse Brown told us to tend these men."

"May I speak to you in private, Miss Mapleton?" His voice, while still rich, held none of its usual warmth.

She glanced at Alice, who pretended to ignore them as she fed the soldier propped against the wall. "Certainly." She pushed as much cool indifference into her tone as she could muster and followed him into the hall.

He spoke nary a word as she trailed his stiff form down

the hall, across the ward, and down another hall. He came to a stop in front of a closed door and glanced both ways, as though to be certain the hall remained empty. Then he produced a key to open the door, motioning her to step inside.

Evelyn frowned. "What?"

"It's the supply closet." Samuel waved his hand toward the shadowed recesses within. "What I have to say would best be kept from prying ears."

She opened her mouth to retort.

"For your own safety, it is best no one *else* begins to question your reasons for being here."

Setting her teeth and telling herself to maintain the same composure Mrs. Greenman had exhibited as her home had been pilfered, Evelyn slipped into the dimly lit room. She clasped her hands in front of her and waited as he closed the door and took a stance in front of it. Her heart hammered. If he meant to interrogate her, there would be no escape.

Windowless, the room was lined from the polished wood floor to the plastered ceiling with shelves of medicines and supplies. She took a step back, her skirts pressing up against a crate that smelled of wood shavings. She let her gaze return to Samuel's rigid features, determined not to be the first one to speak.

"Did you know that Mrs. Greenman is to be sent to the Old Capitol Prison for crimes against her country?"

Not *her* country. "I have heard that, yes."

The muscle in his jaw twitched. "And this is the same friend who was arrested while you were inside her residence, is it not?"

Something fluttered in her chest, and she had to force her breathing to slow. "As I told you before."

He rubbed the back of his neck. "I must admit I don't

want it to be true. And, therefore, I fear I have ignored more than I should."

Evelyn tried to swallow but found her throat far too dry. What information did he know? The way he looked at her now... Unwanted tears burned the back of her eyes, so she kept them held wide, lest they produce too much moisture and betray her.

He stood there with his arms at his sides, his shoulders stiff, disappointment and anger marring his usually friendly face. This was the look she'd tried to avoid. The one she knew would come if he ever found out who she really was. Why had she let herself develop feelings for this man, pretending that they were not enemies? Alice had once accused her of trying to stand with one foot on each side of this conflict, and it seemed she'd been right. But that gulf, that space as wide as eternity, still existed between them. And something like that could not be spanned.

Ignoring fissures that formed in her heart, Evelyn forced a look of contempt. "Sir, I do not see what business it is of yours whose company I keep. And, I do not see how the current predicaments of an old family friend have given you adequate justification to lure a woman into a closet."

Surprise widened his eyes for a moment, but then he shook his head. "I swear, Evelyn Mapleton, you would be a fine catch for the theatre. Tell me, is it hard for you to fabricate such a persona or does it come easily?"

Despite what he stated, Evelyn gaped at him, her mask of a fine lady's intolerance of impropriety slipping free. "I know not of what you speak."

Samuel snorted. "Come, now. Don't lie to me."

Completely unnerved by this man who seemed to have no trouble reading her, she crossed her arms. It would be only a matter of time until he had her arrested. Would the conditions in the prison be more than she could bear? And what of her father? Would he ever find her there?

Even still, she couldn't bring herself to lie to him. Samuel had been nothing but a friend to her, even though he had to have suspected her before now. He'd not only not condemned her, but he'd welcomed her into his home, rescuing her from what could have been a terrible fate that night on the street in Washington. He'd treated her with nothing but respect. He deserved the truth.

She hung her head, defeat both a slicing pain and a buoyant relief, and began the tale. "The Yankees stormed through Martinsburg. They pillaged like pirates and crashed through our homes. One of them tried to violate my cousin." The release of the information brought a kind of peace, and she allowed the lancing of her wound to continue. "I couldn't let him do such a thing, so I...I..." She straightened her shoulders, determined to tell it all, even if she would risk his condemnation. "I shot him."

As soon as the words were out, she gazed at the floor, unwilling to see the disgust bloom on his face. "General Patterson placed me under guard. I briefly thought I could send useful information from the Yankees to my father, and he would make good on his promise to let me live with him." She gave a little shrug. "But I soon gave up on that and found purpose in hospital work in Front Royal. After a disagreement with my aunt, I chose to come to Washington to find him."

Samuel watched her with curiosity and a wrinkled brow, but the words had broken free, and would not be contained. "Alice wanted an introduction to Mrs. Greenman, and the lady was an old family friend whom I'd hoped knew where to find my father. Hence why we happened to be at her home the day she was placed under arrest.

Samuel kept his arms crossed, his expression still rigid. The disappointment on his face seared her wounds. "Why not tell me the truth?"

She turned her palms out. "I believe I've never once told you a falsehood. I may not have told you everything, but I did tell you when we first met that I had tended the wounded in Front Royal. Surely you knew then that I had to be a secessionist."

To this, he merely grunted. Not knowing what to do with that, Evelyn continued. "We traveled to Washington by way of a detour in Lewinsville and Chain Bridge, because Alice was supposed to contact a man on the doctor spy line. I foolishly thought you were the contact I was supposed to find. That's why I ran when I figured out I'd gotten the wrong man."

She lifted her gaze to his guarded eyes. "The rest you know."

"Do I?"

Something deep within her felt cold. She didn't need to tell him about Mrs. Greenman asking her to pass info to those soldiers. It was done, and besides, all she'd said is that they would have to have new ways to communicate. She hadn't done anything important.

Samuel still studied her. "Why work here?"

"I intended to find work in a hospital and try to make my own way." He watched her, and her pulse fluttered.

"That's all?" He lifted his hand as though to reach for her, and then lowered it back to his side.

She held still.

Samuel's eyes darkened and he drew closer, so close now that she stared right into the buttons on his broadcloth jacket. A sound rumbled from somewhere in the chest behind those buttons, and she shivered, her vulnerability now on display.

She had to get out of here before she became completely undone. She tried to step around him, but he caught her.

"Evelyn. I must know. I must know all of the truth if I am to protect you."

Protect her? "Why would you want to do that?"

He ran his thumb along the edge of her jaw. "Why do you ask questions you must already know the answer to?" He leaned down, his face inches from hers. "I *must* know why you are in my hospital."

She couldn't think with him this close! "I...I had to deliver a message for her. To pay my debt. But it was nothing. She just wanted them to know they would have to find other ways to communicate." She nearly choked on the words, but they clamored out of her throat all the same.

He heaved a weary sigh, his breath warm across her face. "Oh, Evelyn. Do you not see what dangers you weave?"

She bit her lip and his gaze lingered on her mouth. "What choice did I have?"

"There is always a choice."

He was much too near. Her heart pounded, but she could not move away. Think! The only way to free herself from his spell was point out the divide between them. Her father, should she ever find him, would never approve of a Federalist. This skittering of her heart would only end in pain.

"I'm a secessionist."

"Are you? I've twice seen you work in Federal hospitals."

She shook her head. That hadn't changed the truth of the overreach of government power. "Can you not see that our homes and lands were invaded?" she said, trying to put steel into her tone. "This war is fought because we merely wished to be left alone and not have our businesses and lives taxed and overmanaged by a government that wishes only to increase its power."

Samuel tilted his head as though she spoke lunacy. "This war is about slavery, and slavery is an evil that must be abolished."

"There's more to it than that, Samuel."

Something flashed in his eyes, and she realized it was the first time she'd said his given name aloud.

She rushed on. "Lincoln would not concede to peace talks. He wanted this war to push for the taxes and for deeper government control. These things have been stirring for many years."

A small smile tugged on his lips. "You speak rather fervently on topics a woman is not often versed in."

She lifted her brows. "Just because I'm a female doesn't mean I'm uneducated in politics. My father reported for newspapers, and these are all things he told me. He feared slavery was merely a tactic Lincoln would use to cover his true intentions. Why, the man would rather the Negroes be shipped back to Africa than for them to come to the North. Tell me, if your president is such a friend to the colored people, then why send them away?"

The little muscles in his jaw twitched again and he took a step back. She could feel the loss of him, but it was for the better. He had to see the gulf between them now as well. Whatever affections she had hoped might exist could not span the rift caused by two different ways of thinking. Unless...he could see her side. "Do you believe the government should have more power than the states? That sovereign states that freely joined the Union should not have the same freedoms to leave it? Surely you can see that the removal of our raw goods from Northern factories goaded this war?"

His eyes darkened once more. "And what do you think of the slaves whose sweat produces those goods?"

"I don't believe in slavery." She huffed. He missed the

point. "It is an institution that has long existed in human history, but it is a deplorable one. No Christian should believe they have the right to own another." She shook her head. "But I still believe that particular issue could have been resolved without war."

"That's all I needed to know. The rest matters little."

In one sudden move, his arm slipped around her waist. He pulled her in tight against him, and she gasped. His dark eyes stared into hers, and a hardness in her heart softened. She relaxed and leaned into him, enjoying the warmth that spread through her.

He lowered his head, and with one sweet breath, brushed his lips gently across hers. She sighed into him and pressed a little firmer, and then the moment was over.

He raised his head, and a languid smile caressed his lips. "Would you like to come to dinner? Mrs. Tooley is making lamb."

Palms sweaty and nerves all aflutter, all she could do was nod.

Twenty

*T*he scents of succulent roasted meat and braised vegetables still hung in the air at Samuel's residence. The meal had been one of the finest Evelyn had ever consumed, even at the multitude of society parties she'd attended. Warm light cascaded from the parlor fireplace as she, Samuel, and the children settled down for tea.

Samuel, dashing with his neatly combed hair, freshly shaven jaw, and skillfully tied cravat, sat comfortably in a fireside chair. Emily twirled in a blue silk dress, and little Benjamin was precious in his pressed lapels and shined shoes. The house filled with the children's laughter and, for the moment, she could forget all the troubles that existed outside the walls of this one cozy townhome.

She settled on the settee and arranged her skirts, watching Samuel ruffle Benjamin's hair. What would it be like to have a family like this? To have a home filled with easy laughter? Despite her every attempt to keep her mannerisms in check, Samuel Flynn managed to tease silly giggles out of her. And for some uncanny reason, that only made her feel more comfortable with him. Almost as though she belonged.

His gaze found hers across the room, and the confident smile that turned his lips sent her mind aflutter. Did he share these uncanny stirrings? His kiss and tender words in the hospital said he did. But why? Why, when she'd confessed so much to him? Could he not see these feelings were impossible? That they were supposed to be enemies?

A tug at her skirt brought her gaze to the wide brown eyes of little Emily. The child clutched a book to her chest, wary hope on her face.

"Would you like me to read to you now?"

Emily's smile was sunshine breaking through the clouds, and before Evelyn could react, the girl climbed into her lap and snuggled against her. Evelyn glanced at Samuel, and the expression on his face nearly stopped her heart. She darted her gaze to Benjamin, who stood by his father's side watching Evelyn closely. He would not be as easily won.

She opened the book and began a tale of a heroic king, his fair queen, and the knights of a round table. The children sat in rapt attention, and for a time she lost herself in the adventure of the story. By the time she reached the end of the first chapter, however, Emily snored softly in her lap, and Benjamin had taken a place at her feet.

The little boy's eyes were filled with wonder. "Why, you read even better than Mr. Flynn!"

Warmth spread in her cheeks, but she didn't dare a glance at Samuel. "Mr. Flynn?"

Benjamin's little face scrunched. "Yeah, did you forget his name?"

Looking over the top of Emily's downy hair, Evelyn couldn't help but smile. "Of course not. I've just never heard a child call his papa by a formal name before."

The boy shifted back on his heels and tilted his head. "He didn't tell you?"

"Tell me what?" Evelyn caught Samuel's eye, but he merely offered a lopsided grin.

"Me and Emily are orphans. Our ma was sick and left us with the nuns when Emily weren't no more'n a babe." He tossed his thumb over his shoulder. "Mr. Flynn brought us home with him, and he's our guardian now."

She drew Emily against her, her hammering heart sure to wake the little darling. Her words came out breathy. "No, he didn't mention that." She spoke to Benjamin, but her eyes were on Samuel.

"He didn't want me and Emily to be separated," Benjamin continued, "so he's letting us live here. Emily says he's our new father, but I keep telling her she shouldn't say that."

"Why not?" Samuel's voice spread through the room, the first words he'd spoken since entering the parlor. "We could be a family, couldn't we?"

Benjamin turned and she could no longer see his expression. "You really mean that?"

Samuel regarded the boy with all the seriousness of an accomplished physician, a man whom anyone could take one look at and judge sincere and honest. "Nothing would please me more."

Benjamin shoved his hands in his pockets. "Well, all right then." He glanced back at Emily in Evelyn's lap. "I, uh, better go get Mrs. Tooley to take her to bed."

"A wise idea," Samuel agreed. "Thank you."

The child scurried away, leaving them in silence for several moments. Heat radiated in Evelyn's chest that had nothing to do with the child snuggled against her. She allowed herself the pleasure of resting her chin on Emily's head and tried to find a safe topic of conversation. "Does she ever speak to anyone other than Benjamin?"

Samuel sat back in his chair and rubbed his hand through his hair, tousling it. "She does, but I still haven't gotten her to say much." He lifted his eyebrows. "She's sure taken a liking to you, though."

"I'd say," Mrs. Tooley said, sweeping into the parlor. "Why, it took me nigh on two weeks to get that little 'un to sit with me like that."

Evelyn reluctantly handed over the child, an ache forming in her heart. "She's such a beautiful girl."

Mrs. Tooley scooped her up and then sent a questioning look to Samuel.

"The hour is growing late," he said, rising. "I shall escort Miss Mapleton to her hotel."

Evelyn bade the nanny a good evening and moved to the foyer, where Samuel helped her put on her cloak. She tied the strings around her throat and pulled on her gloves, telling herself she had no reason to feel sorrow. It had been a refreshing reprieve from the depressing nature of the hospital and the time spent alone in the hotel room, but it had come to an end.

Once outside in the biting wind, she pulled the hood over her head. Samuel offered his arm, and she looped her hand around his elbow, his touch immediately taking her back to the feel of his lips upon hers. Thankfully, he couldn't see the heat in her cheeks.

"Would you prefer to walk or take a carriage?"

Walking would further tire her aching feet, but it would afford her more time at his side. "I'm content to walk."

They strode in silence for a few moments before he spoke. "I would like to discuss some things with you."

He'd come to his senses and could no longer entertain such dangerous thoughts about a *Secesh* woman. "I assumed you would."

He placed his free hand over her fingers on his elbow. "Although Dr. Porter dallies in completing my licensing, I take my role as a physician very seriously."

Not where she thought the conversation would be headed. "As well you should," Evelyn replied. "It's an important role, especially with this war." She shook her head and drew closer to his side as she skirted a puddle. "I've heard tales of so-called doctors who read a field manual and think they are capable of tending the wounded."

Samuel chuckled. "My father is going to like you."

"Is your family nearby?"

"They live in Maryland, but they're scheduled to arrive in the later part of next week. With this war, their first visit with the children has been delayed much longer than anticipated. They were rather surprised by my new situation, but they are looking forward to meeting Benjamin and Emily. My mother, especially, is greatly anticipating fawning over the children."

The glow from streetlamps pooled along the path as they turned a corner and started down another street. Like giant fireflies, their light danced and swayed in the cool night air. "Not many men would take on two orphaned children."

"Ah, well, I can't explain it really." His hand tightened over her fingers. "There was just something about them I couldn't let go. It was as though God himself placed a love for them in my heart I could not ignore. They've been a great blessing to me."

Evelyn's heart fluttered.

"But that is not what I need to discuss with you," he said, a smile in his voice. "You have the most uncanny ability to derail my thoughts."

Unsure how to respond, she merely continued the simple pleasure of walking at his side. She had known the evening couldn't last. War would steal from her the irrational longings that she had known better than to let fester in her heart. Tears burned at the back of her throat, but she refused to let them take hold.

"As I said, I take my position seriously. I believe it is my duty to care for the wounded."

"And you do an exemplary..."

He squeezed her hand and slowed his pace, making her lose the end of her sentence. "Evelyn, if I may." At her nod, he continued. "I've made an oath that I'll do all in my power to bring healing, even as this war brings bloodshed. I will care for every person who comes to me in need of medical care, regardless of gender, uniform, or skin color." He stopped under a street lantern and turned her to face him. "Do you understand?"

Having seen him care for Alice, and knowing he'd angered Dr. Porter and most of the rest of the hospital staff by insisting the Confederate soldiers at the infirmary be properly tended, she'd seen that commitment in action. "Of course I do." It was one of the things she admired about him.

Perhaps even loved about him.

The thought nearly stole her breath. No! She could not love a Yank! She was merely infatuated by his generosity, kindness, and...oh, my, he was looking at her with that tenderness again.

Samuel placed a hand on her shoulder. "I need to know that you truly do understand what it means to me. Under no circumstances would I want to aid in causing more men to end up in my hospital. Or any other, for that matter."

She stared into his eyes, trying to get her fumbling brain to understand what he meant by such a statement. Of course he wouldn't want more men injured. None of them did.

"I need you to promise me."

Anything. The word stuck in her mouth.

He leaned closer. "Evelyn, I need you to promise me you will not do anything that will cause more men injury. That you'll work to bring healing and not death."

Her mouth was too dry. She swallowed. What did he think of her? "Why would you think I wanted to bring death? I have worked my body to exhaustion tending the sick and wounded. I would never wish them further harm."

Samuel's fingers clung to her shoulders, his gaze intense. "Then promise me. Promise me you will do nothing to further the war and will help me bring healing until it ends."

Heart hammering, she nodded. Of course she wanted to see this war end and healing come.

"Say it, then, please."

How could she deny any request that came from this earnest man? He spoke with such conviction, such honest care for his patients. "I promise, Samuel. I'll do everything I can to help you bring healing."

The flickering light of the lamp above him washed over his relieved features, and he heaved a sigh that expanded his chest and sent a puff of air across the fur rimming her hood. "Thank you." He lifted her hand to his mouth and pressed a kiss there, and she wished she weren't wearing gloves.

He threaded her hand around his elbow once more, and they continued to the hotel, the topic of conversation only occupying half of her thoughts. They purposely ignored the glaring issue that stood between them, no matter what noble promises were made. He was a Yank, she a secessionist. That gulf could not be spanned, yet with every passing moment, she longed ever more to build an impossible bridge. Couldn't they escape somewhere, just them and the children? Disappear out in the western territories, where war would be little more than words splashed across the newssheets?

"Evelyn?"

"Oh!" She turned to look at his profile. "Forgive me. What did you say?"

"I asked if I may call upon you, and if you would like to have dinner with my parents when they arrive."

How had she missed something that important? As they neared the doors to her hotel, Evelyn stopped a short distance from the doorman. Could she let her heart continue on this path? He would never leave his patients, and the West would be no place for two children who needed stability, not the frontier. Such wild, foolish notions.

"Samuel, how could you ask such a thing, knowing all you do about me?"

He stared at her, conflict evident on his face.

"You know I shot a man. I didn't kill him, but I certainly sent him to the hospital."

"You did it to protect, Evelyn. That's different."

"Still, I fear I may have let my father's ardent opinions and my family's disinterest in me grow into a hatred that I shouldn't have—" Her words caught, but she cleared her throat and continued. "Don't you see? You are a Yankee doctor, and I am…" Her voice trailed away.

"You're what?" Samuel said. "I've seen you work tirelessly by my side in two different *Union* hospitals. What exactly does that make you?"

A traitor. Her father would be sorely disappointed. "I'm still what you all venomously call a *Rebel.*"

"So is my sister."

His words hung in the air, and she stumbled over her next heartbeat. "What?"

Samuel rubbed his hands together. "My sister married a man from South Carolina. When the war started, her husband sided with the South. My sister had to decide if she stood with the family of her youth or the family she'd started with her husband." He gave a small shrug. "None of us blame her for siding with her husband. The Word says that husband and wife are to be one."

Evelyn wrapped her arms around herself. "That had to be difficult."

"Especially for my parents. It's hard to see families torn asunder merely because they believe different things about politics."

"Indeed."

"But this war is much more than government, taxes, and tariffs. It's about people who have been treated with a grave injustice. When the Israelites cried out, God heard them in their enslavement and brought about their freedom through the great plagues. Have you ever thought this war is our own plague for allowing our country, a country founded as one nation under God, to enslave and degrade our fellow man just because he has a different skin color?"

Evelyn opened her mouth, and then closed it. She'd never believed in slavery, but truth be told, she'd spoken with more conviction over taxes than she had people's lives. A pang of guilt pierced her heart. And how had she felt to learn that her own family looked down upon her merely because of her heritage? Something she was certain Samuel would never do. "Slavery is an ugly thing. And no, it should not be allowed to continue. If only we had been able to bring it to an end without war."

His hands warmed her shoulders. "And if only we were able to settle our differences about politics and tariffs as one nation. But the time for *if only* has passed. I believe the only way to bring healing is for the country to stay intact and for freedom to come to the people of this land."

"And you believe that marauders disguised as soldiers have the right to pillage and steal to make that happen?" She could not help the edge that colored her tone. Some things were not easily forgotten.

"I do not." Samuel's voice had an edge she'd not heard from him before. "Committing evil to end evil accomplishes nothing but further heartache. It is a deep shame there will always be men who do evil in the sight of the Lord."

Ida's words came back to her. It seemed the Confederate soldiers had committed atrocities as well, though she'd chosen to ignore it.

"War is unspeakably ugly, and it's out of our control." He eased closer, much too close for what would be proper in public. Especially at night. But she did not step away. She tilted her head to keep his intense gaze. "We can only control our own actions. We can only seek to follow God's will as best we can. And as Paul says, 'If it be possible, as much as lieth in you, live peaceably with all men.'"

He grabbed both her hands and gave them a squeeze. "Evelyn, if your father were here, I would like to speak my intentions to him. But until you locate him, I will speak them to you in his stead."

She could only blink. It was too much, too fast.

"I intend to try to spend more time with you and to get to know more about the wonderful woman I know you to be." A small smile tugged at his mouth. "I also intend to ask you once again if you will join my family for dinner."

She blinked like a hapless fool, offering only a nod.

"I shall accept that." He offered his arm. Samuel gestured toward the doorman, who did not attempt to hide his study of them. "But for now, it is best I return you to the hotel. We both need our rest."

She allowed him to guide her to the door and somehow managed to repeat his words of farewell before hurrying through the lobby. She barely noticed the sparkling chandelier, the polished floors, or other patrons turning in for the night. Evelyn hurried past the maid lighting a wall sconce on her way up the large central staircase.

Did that man know what he did to her? Why, he nigh on turned her mind to mush! The pounding of her erratic pulse swelled in the back of her skull, causing an ache to spread through her head and down her neck.

On the second floor, she turned to the right, locating the room she and Alice shared. After fumbling the key in her trembling fingers, Evelyn finally opened the door and slipped into the privacy of her room. What she wouldn't give for a tub full of hot water and—

"There you are." Alice rose from the dressing table, her hair lying in wild waves across her shoulders.

Evelyn placed a hand to her chest. "Alice. I wasn't expecting you to be here."

"Where have you been?"

Evelyn set her jaw and draped her cloak over the back of a chair. How dare she ask with such accusation as though *she* were not the one usually out until late hours?

"I asked you a question."

"No. You demanded an answer, and I don't have to provide one for you."

Alice dropped her wooden hairbrush on the marble-top dressing table. "My! Someone is defensive today."

The pulse in the back of her head began to throb. "I don't wish to quarrel with you. But as of late it seems that every time I do or say anything, you are immediately up in arms about it."

The young woman that Evelyn questioned if she could still call her *friend* eyed her coolly. "You were with that doctor, weren't you?"

Evelyn slipped behind the dressing screen and removed her petticoats. "What if I was? What does that matter to you?"

"It matters," Alice said with a haughty sniff, "because you're becoming too friendly with the enemy."

The pulse gained strength and throbbed behind her left eye. She was too tired to argue. She unclipped her mother's pearls and slid them inside a black velvet bag.

"Have you forgotten what happened to you in Martinsburg?"

Evelyn drew on her nightdress and stepped out, nearly bumping into Alice where she paced across the carpeted floor.

"What about in Front Royal?" Alice continued when Evelyn didn't respond. "Don't you remember our boys there? How terrible they looked?"

No worse than the Federal boys at Chain Bridge. "I've not forgotten."

"Oh? Well, while Mrs. Greenman was being sent to prison, *you* were out with a Yankee."

Evelyn turned down the heavy coverings on one side of the bed, then decided to stoke the fire.

"Did you at least deliver the message?" Alice grumbled.

It took Evelyn a moment to realize Alice referred to the detained soldiers at the infirmary. "Of course I did." Heavens, Alice had been right there in the room with her! "I told him everything Mrs. Greenman requested. Now my debt is complete."

Alice snorted. "Don't be ridiculous. You think delivering one message makes up for all of this?" She gestured to their clothing and then around the fine room. "That's hardly worth one meal and a night's lodging, and we've used far more than that." She grabbed a handful of her wild hair and twisted it into a braid.

"I don't wish to be involved further. If that means I can no longer stay, then so be it." Samuel would surely help her if she received a negative response to her inquiry at one last paper. It was her final hope of finding Daddy, and then she must face the choice of trying to return to Aunt Mary or starting a life on her own here in Washington.

Alice tied a ribbon at the end of the thick braid and tossed it over her shoulder. "We came here to aid the cause. Don't forget that."

Evelyn sat on the feather mattress and pulled the pins from her hair, allowing it to spill down her back. "Do you ever wish this war had never started?"

"It had to be done. And I think a lot of good will come out of it. The South will have independence, and I think women will gain more rights."

"And what about the slaves?"

She shrugged. "I don't give much mind to them. The abolitionists say the war is all about freeing the slaves, and the plantation men say it's all about representation, property, and taxes." She crossed the rug and climbed in on the far side of the bed. "None of that matters to me. I don't care if the colored people are slaves or free. I just don't want them taking jobs from hard-working men like my brother."

Evelyn reclined and drew the covers around her. "What do you think this war is really about?"

Alice blew out the candle. "All of that, I suppose. But the only people it matters to are the rich ones. People like me, we don't get a say in all of that. We just get to suffer the consequences of men's whims and folly."

Perhaps she had a point.

"So," Alice continued, "The way I see it, the only option left to poor folks is to try to save what we have and make the most of what comes our way. If the North wins, we could lose everything. If the South wins, then perchance my brother will have something to come home to. And maybe, at the end of it all, we women may have a few more options and a little more respect."

She closed her eyes. The pounding in her head drummed, and she wished for sleep.

"We shall go see her tomorrow," Alice said sternly.

"Who?"

"Mrs. Greenman, of course. We have something to do."

Evelyn laid a hand over her face. "No. I told you I'm finished doing things for her."

"She said you would say that."

Good. Then it wouldn't come as a shock.

"In which case, I am to withhold the letter from your father until we complete our visit."

Evelyn bolted upright. "You have a letter from Daddy? Give it to me."

"Once you go with me to the prison, it's yours."

Evelyn clenched her teeth, anger making her head ache more. "You have no right."

"Perhaps. But as soon as you go, then it will be done. Your debt will be paid and you can have your letter. Then after tomorrow you can leave and do as you please."

"That's extortion."

Alice turned on her side, leaving Evelyn to stew in the dark. She didn't want to go to the prison, but she needed to know where Daddy was. Something must have happened to him. Otherwise he wouldn't have left her for so long.

She drew a deep breath, letting tears slide down onto her pillow. As her skull throbbed, Samuel's words pulsed with each beat of her heart.

Promise me, Evelyn.

Twenty-One

November 3, 1861

*T*his one final task, and Evelyn would accept no more of Mrs. Greenman's aid or any of the woman's dangerous plotting. Once she knew what had become of Daddy, she would make plans for the future. Maybe find a paying position or ask Samuel if the hospital would allow her to work for room and board. One more task, and her debts would all be paid and this would all be over. She drew her wrap around her and repeated those words to herself as they neared the prison.

The Old Capitol Prison was made up of a cluster of dismal structures huddled along the east side of First Street, a lackluster jumble determined to be uninviting. The November wind plucked at Evelyn's hair and pulled it free from the hood she hoped would shadow her face. Alice had lied to Nurse Brown about their health today, and so by proxy, Evelyn had lied to Samuel. Neither had the stomach ailments Alice's missive had described. The only thing that ailed her this day was the sour taste of deception.

Did Samuel know yet about the letter? Did he worry over her condition while she traipsed through the mud on her way to visit a prisoner? She shivered, though it had less to do with the chill than her guilt.

They neared the looming structure at the center of the depressing compound. The three-story pile of brick had once housed Congress before the British burned it during the 1812 war. It hadn't performed any honorable duties since, and the façade seemed weighted with despondency. Its one notable feature, the large arched window on the front, could have been appealing if one could ignore the wood that had been nailed across it, barring any hope of escape for those condemned within.

Evelyn had heard enough about the place to know she had no desire to be anywhere near it. It was first planned to house Confederate prisoners of war, but now it collected an eclectic variety of malefic captives ranging from blockade runners to Southern widows with more bravado than sense.

They passed through the main door with only a nod from the guard, though Evelyn had no idea why. Then another man, as gloomy as the first, guided them through the drab chamber and to the office of the superintendent, one William P. Wood. Mr. Wood filled his small office with both girth and height, an impressive fellow surely able to keep his inmates in line.

Alice dropped into a curtsy and passed the man a slip of paper. He read it, narrowed his eyes, and then, to Evelyn's pure amazement, waved them back toward the doorway they'd just crossed.

"You have a quarter hour. No more. You are not to touch the prisoner, nor exchange anything with her. You will be under a guard at all times."

"Yes, sir," Alice replied sweetly.

Evelyn kept her hands at her sides, her pulse pounding furiously.

Alice twirled around and cast her a sly grin, then slipped

out the door.

Evelyn ground her teeth. This girl was no longer her friend. Holding Daddy's letter captive to make her come to a prison! And for what? How would that help the foolhardy widow and her overly enthusiastic apprentice?

They followed a guard down a series of winding halls, dread heavy in her stomach. She shouldn't be here. She should turn and run.

Could she even find her way back out?

The sounds of men grumbling and shouting grated on her ears as they passed row after row of barred chambers. The sounds chafed less than the smell. The overwhelming stench of the latrines permeated the brick walls and would certainly cling to her clothing long after she removed herself from this horrid place.

Near the back of the building, the guard opened the door to a narrow chamber, ushered them in, and then planted himself squarely in the open frame. The feeling of being trapped shortened her breath. It took nearly every fiber of her willpower not to bolt past the man and sprint free of this madness.

Stay calm. A few moments only, and then I'll have the letter.

And even if Alice refused to give it to her—or worse, it didn't exist—nothing else Alice said would make her continue this madness. If she kept taking risks for Mrs. Greenman, she most surely would find herself in this dank prison as well. And she couldn't abide being confined to a narrow chamber with crumbling furniture, a filthy single bed, and a cracked mirror over a tiny fireplace that did not hold enough of a flame to take the chill from the air. She shivered. The windows were covered in thick slats that choked out the sunlight and any fresh air that might have been found. In all, it was the most depressing place she'd ever set foot in.

Mrs. Greenman rose from a dilapidated chair that creaked with her movement and stood a few paces from them. Though pale and much too thin, her hawkish eyes still glinted with determination.

Alice inclined her head. "How do you fare, ma'am?"

Evelyn wrapped her arms around her waist and watched a mouse scurry into a hole in the corner. Then she concentrated on pulling fetid air slowly into her lungs and releasing it without haste. She took a step back toward the entrance.

Mrs. Greenman glanced at the window. "They are taking every precaution. I suppose I should be flattered that they think so highly of my resourcefulness that they cannot even allow me a nip of fresh air."

Alice shot Evelyn a glance, but spoke to Mrs. Greenman. "It is most dreadful that a lady be treated with such maliciousness."

"The language here scrapes upon the ear," Mrs. Greenman said, "and the sights that have met my eyes are too revolting to describe."

Evelyn glanced at the guard, who watched them closely, and then did the only part she had in this entire ridiculous plan. She subtly shifted herself to stand slightly behind and to the left of Alice. With her back to the guard, Evelyn's wide skirts blocked part of Alice's form from the guard's eye. He didn't seem to notice, however, as he kept his gaze riveted on the widow.

Alice quickly made a series of hand gestures where the guard couldn't see. Evelyn nearly rolled her eyes. For this they risked imprisonment? Making secret codes? How did the woman expect to do any of her spying from this chamber?

"Why, this very morning," Mrs. Greenman continued to lament as her sharp eyes followed the gestures, "they put me on display like a caged bird, parading Yanks through here to gawk at me as though I were some kind of animal."

Alice snorted. "Most horrendous." She made another set of signals with her fingers. "Are we allowed to bring you any manner of comforts?"

"Do not underestimate the determined nature of these Yanks. They will see that every comfort has been stripped from me until they can tease any incriminating lie from my parched lips."

Evelyn swallowed, wishing to moisten her own parched lips and be gone from this place as soon as possible.

Alice dipped into an odd curtsy and then backed toward the door, stepping on Evelyn in the process. "Good day to you, Mrs. Greenman. May the sun brighten your days and the moon comfort your nights."

A smile quirked one corner of the widow's mouth, and Evelyn frowned. What did Alice blather about? Before she could contemplate or make a move, Alice tripped on Evelyn's skirt and bumped into her, sending Evelyn stumbling forward. Mrs. Greenman suddenly reached out, grabbed Evelyn by the wrist, and swept her into a tight embrace, keeping her from hitting the floor.

"Hey! I said no touching!" The guard's thundering voice reverberated around the room.

Evelyn tried to right herself, finally gathering her feet under her as the widow pulled her close.

"I mean it!"

Evelyn struggled to release herself from the woman's grip, but Mrs. Greenman held firm. The guard sank his fingers into her shoulder and wrenched her backward. She stumbled, held up by the claws that felt like eagle's talons down into her bones.

Mrs. Greenman let go. "Oh, my!" She placed a hand to her heart. "I'm terribly sorry." She fanned her face. "I merely got caught up in the emotions of missing my dear friends. Do forgive me, sir."

The guard scowled at her. "You'll be granted no more visitors if you cannot follow simple instructions."

"I understand." She lowered her head, but not before Evelyn caught the glimmer in her eyes.

The guard snatched Evelyn's shoulder. "Come, you will have to be searched."

Evelyn planted her heels, wrenching herself out of his grasp. "What!" Indignation scorched through her veins, mingling with the fear that resided there. "You will do no such thing!"

He grabbed her by the elbow, nearly lifting her off her feet as he hauled her from the room, ignoring her cries of injustice. In the hallway, he pushed her against the wall, pinning her there with his forearm tightly pressed against her collarbone. Visions of Martinsburg filled her mind.

Clenching her fists at her sides, Evelyn forced her voice to remain low. "Release me, sir. This is no way to treat a lady."

He called for another guard, and lifted one side of his mouth. "But it *is* the way we treat Rebel spies."

Her heart pounded furiously. What would they do to her? Where was Alice? She glanced down the hall, but the girl was nowhere to be seen. She trembled, alone in the cold of the heartless prison. "What..?" The word stuck in her throat, terror clenching her voice into the squeak of a cornered mouse. "What will you do to me?"

The man's face contorted. "I told you. You have to be searched." He snarled. "If she passed anything to you, we will find it."

Squirming made him increase the pressure across the base of her throat, so she stilled. "Please, you must believe me. If that woman passed anything to me, it was entirely without my knowledge or consent."

"Of course you would say that, you little Jezebel." The guard released a dark chuckle as another fellow, more scabrous than the one before her, joined his side. "You vixens will say anything you think will prey upon men's decency."

Please, God, don't let her have placed anything on me.

While the first guard held her against the wall, the other knelt in front of her. His grimy hands skimmed down the folds of her skirts, pressing into her legs and hips. Tears burned and spilled over, sliding down her face in humiliation. Without restraint, he brushed over every curve she possessed and splayed his fingers through her hair and released some of her pins.

Evelyn caught a sob in her throat, determined not to let them see her defeat, but unable to stop it. She wanted to curl into herself and melt into a heap on the floor. Anything to end this disgrace.

Finally, the man stepped back and nodded to the other. The first one released his hold, and Evelyn's trembling knees buckled. She stooped forward, air burning as it came shuddering into her lungs.

"You will have to remove the garment," the second guard said, his nasally voice slithering over her like an eel.

She pulled her arms tighter around herself, sinking lower until she could press her kneecaps into her face.

"What's going on here?" The staunch voice of Superintendent Wood sluiced through her jumbled thoughts.

Get up! With a surge of desperation, she straightened her legs, scraping her back along the wall. She fixed her eyes on the superintendent's startled features and clasped the fabric at her neck. "Please, sir, I beg of you. Don't allow them to make me remove my dress."

The man's mouth fell agape, and he turned on the nearest

guard. "What foul intentions did you plan to commit?"

The fellow who had guarded Mrs. Greenman's chamber lifted his beefy hands, palms out. "She embraced the widow against orders. We had to search her."

The muscles in the superintendent's jaw flexed. "Was this embrace under your supervision?"

"It was." The man jutted his chin. "But I separated them immediately."

Evelyn's lips trembled. She had to hold herself together. "I've been thoroughly searched, sir, and swear upon my life I have no items from Mrs. Greenman upon my person." She steeled her voice. "And especially not *under* my gown!"

Wood's face reddened, and he pointed a finger at the two guards. "Has this woman been searched?"

"Yes, sir," the second man, the one with too willing hands, replied. "I searched the folds of her gown, but she could still be hiding something."

"Return to your post," Wood said, his voice nearly a growl.

The man scurried away.

"And Carter…" Wood pointed to the first guard. "Mrs. Greenman gets no more visitors."

"Yes, sir." The man turned and stood in front of the closed door.

"Now." Mr. Wood eyed Evelyn with caution, as though she were the one who had perpetuated her own humiliation. "I don't care who you women know in Washington or what politician wants to flex his influence. Those tactics will not work here a second time. If I ever see you in my prison again, you will not be leaving it. Do I make myself clear?"

Relief surged through her, making her press closer against the wall to maintain her footing. "I assure you, sir, you will never lay eyes on me again."

He extended his hand, motioning her ahead of him. Evelyn lifted the hem of her skirt, and heedless to any sense of propriety, broke into a jog. She could not reach the sunlight fast enough, and even after the Old Capitol's door slammed behind her, she did not ease her pace. Tears blurred her vision, making her twice stumble before she was far enough down First Street to take a full breath.

Where was Alice? What had they done? They'd clearly planned to do that, but why?

Evelyn scanned every face she passed and checked as many alcoves as she could on her way back to the hotel but saw no sign of a curly brown mop of hair. Hoping to find the perfidious girl, she hurried up the stairs and flung herself into their chamber.

The room was empty. She paced, willing her mind to focus. As she neared the bed, something atop the quilt caught her eye. A paper.

She snatched it up. The envelope's seal had been broken, but its dirty surface contained her father's writing. At least Alice had kept her word.

She pulled a single sheet of paper out and unfolded it, her father's neat penmanship jumping out at her. She placed a hand to her chest and sank on the bed.

Dearest Evelyn,

I received word from your aunt that you went to Washington after me. I wish you had waited, as I have not been in that city for some time. Just after the battle at Manassas, I traveled back south. I have been working an exciting position that is very crucial to our cause. I cannot give you details until I see you again in person, but suffice it to say, my work with the newspapers is a critical link to the information we need for our men.

I admit I was rather surprised to learn you tended soldiers in Front Royal. I am thrilled by your gallant and selfless actions. Your dedication to our great cause wells this old heart with pride.

Evelyn's eyes blurred, and she had to wipe the moisture away.

Despite your aunt's wishes, I am unable to come after you and must continue my way to New Orleans. My work there is very important and must be completed.

I pray this letter finds you well, as these are the most dangerous of times. If you do not wish to return to your aunt, I'm sure you'll do well in the fine company of a loyal lady such as Mrs. Greenman.

Evelyn's hand trembled and a tear fell, smudging the date on the bottom of the page under his signature. The letter had arrived in Washington several weeks ago. She rubbed the paper between her fingers. Had Mrs. Greenman lied about knowing where her father was? Or had the letter come after their first visit and she subsequently withheld it?

The line about the newspaper work niggled in her brain. Could he possibly be referring to the secret codes Alice used? It was a question she must ask when she had the chance to speak with him.

Oh, but how? She wouldn't follow him to New Orleans, and she wouldn't stay with Mrs. Greenman even if it was an option. Evelyn sank to her knees, the weight in her chest as solid as an artillery cannon ball.

She needed help.

Her friend now entirely lost to her, Evelyn had only one person she could trust. Girding herself with a whispered prayer, she gathered her petticoats and found her footing once more. Then she wiped her eyes and stepped back out of the room with new determination.

Outside the Halverson Hotel, the people on the street sauntered about their daily business, going to and fro from various appointments and errands. But Evelyn's life had no such simple luxuries. She kept her eyes moving, scanning people as she passed. Men with stovepipe hats cast her glances, while women with little children in tow kept their eyes downcast.

Evelyn held her spine erect, ignoring the lingering gaze of a fellow with a full beard, and made her way down the road. The clear sky held the warmth of a cheery sun, but none of its gentle touch chased the chill from her veins. The fine hairs on the nape of her neck stood on end.

Movement in the shadows between two buildings drew her regard, but whoever had been there darted away before she could get a good look. She quickened her pace. The streets seemed to grow farther apart the faster she tried to reach them. Every doorway seemed to contain a shadow, every lingering eye some hidden malice.

By the time she reached the comforting brick façade of Samuel's townhome, she was nearly out of breath. Lifting her hem to climb the stairs, she heard a rustling to her left. Pausing, she narrowed her eyes. Was someone kneeling behind the leafless branches of a puny shrub at the corner of the house?

Had her fear and imagination simply run away with her? Heart hammering, she took another step closer, telling herself this was all tomfoolery.

Giggles erupted from the bush as she neared.

"Emily!" Relief surged like a mighty wind. Evelyn clutched her cloak. "What are you doing out here in the cold?"

The little girl rose, her almond-colored dress perfect for blending in. She offered Evelyn a smile and a little wave, clearly pleased with herself for having given Evelyn a fright.

Evelyn extended her hand. "Come, let's get you inside where it is warm."

A shadow moved behind Emily. The world seemed to slow to molasses as Evelyn lifted her eyes from the child's delighted features to the form of a man in the alleyway. He wore a long coat and a dark hat. She opened her mouth to scream, but the sound erupted from Emily instead. The man swept the child into his arms and smothered her little mouth.

Evelyn lunged, but with a swish of tailcoats, he turned and disappeared between the houses, the earth exploding back into a deluge of scattered senses.

"No!" Evelyn hiked her skirts and rounded the side of the house. "Emily!"

Behind her, footsteps pounded, closing in on her, but she couldn't peel her eyes from the abductor's retreating form. *Please, God! Let me get the child.* An arm snaked around her middle, stopping her and forcing the air out of her. She gasped for a breath to scream but was released so quickly that she stumbled forward.

"Evelyn!" Samuel's frantic voice clawed past her terror. "What are you doing?"

She whirled around, gasping. "They took her!"

Samuel frowned, his movements infuriatingly languid. "What?"

"Emily!" She pointed down the alley. "He took Emily!"

Samuel's eyes bulged and his gaze darted past her. Evelyn reached for him, but Samuel was sprinting away.

Twenty-Two

*S*amuel's feet pounded down the narrow strip of ground between the townhomes, his mind whirling. Who had taken his child? He skidded to a stop at the rear of the house, scanning the small garden areas surrounded by a low brick wall.

Where had they gone?

There! Movement jerked past his neighbor's garden and into the alleyway behind the adjacent property. Samuel lunged, leaping over a heap of sour rubbish and hitting the narrow gap at a full run. A man jumped out of the shadows and fled, his coattails spreading behind him.

He could not let the miscreant escape. With a growl, Samuel pushed his body to move faster. The man was nearing the opening to the next street. If he made it, he could disappear into any street or crevice.

The man looked over his shoulder, fear in his eyes. Samuel's legs pumped harder. The offender reached the narrow opening.

Samuel leapt, hands outstretched. He grasped a handful of material, felt it rip. His other hand surged out, wrapping around the abductor's arm and giving a mighty yank. They hit the ground with a sudden jar, and his breath stuck in his lungs.

Scrambling, Samuel put his weight on top of the man, rolling him and pinning his shoulders underneath his knees. The man's hat rolled from his head, exposing sandy-colored hair. A hawkish face stared up at him as rapid breath flared his large nostrils.

"Where is she?" He grabbed the man's lapels, pressing him into the cobbles beneath them. The man groaned and tried to roll, but Samuel shook him. "Where is my child?" He drew back his fist. If he did not speak….

"She's fine!"

Samuel stilled.

"I assure you," the man said, nearly breathless, "she's safe with the detective police! No harm has come to her."

Samuel lowered his hand and narrowed his eyes. "Why did you take my daughter?"

"We are protecting her."

He snorted. "My patience is growing thin, man. Explain yourself."

The fellow struggled, then relaxed when Samuel leaned closer. "Easy, Mr. Flynn. We have the child's best interest in mind and simply removed her from a desperate spy who would use her for nefarious plans against our country."

What? The madman spoke in delusions. "*Where* is Emily?"

"She will be returned to you, sir, you have my word."

As though this man's word was worth a hastily printed Confederate Greyback to him. He pressed his weight into the man's sternum. "Then why run?"

He struggled underneath the unrelenting weight. "To lead you in a different direction."

The muscles in Samuel's jaw tightened, and whatever expression crossed his face caused the other man's eyes to widen. "She will be returned as soon as we get the information we need."

Samuel growled. "If you harm my—"

"We only wish to disassemble a spy network! It's your patriotic duty to aid us in this endeavor." His flat face hardened, though it appeared to be a forced attempt at bravado. "Now, let me up."

Samuel rocked back onto his heels and grabbed a handful of the man's collar, dragging him up as he stood. "I will do nothing until I see my child."

The weasel had the audacity to scoff. "And you'll not see her until we get what we need." The man spoke calmly, as though he couldn't sense that it took a great deal of restraint for Samuel not to further flatten his face.

He jutted his chin. "You are acquainted with one of the spies in connection with Mrs. Greenman. We've seen her at your residence on a couple of occasions. Just now we saw her outside of your house."

Samuel shoved the man against the rough brick wall. "What have you done to Evelyn?" If they dared to take her as well...

The man lifted his eyebrows. "We've done nothing to her. But we learned this morning that *young woman*"—he spat the words as though they were the foulest curse—"went to the Capitol Prison to meet with Mrs. Greenman, where she apparently exchanged information. It was the proof we were waiting for to warrant her arrest."

Samuel ground his teeth. Evelyn had promised to have nothing more to do with that slippery woman!

"The incompetent superintendent," the man spat, "was foolish to let her go. Fortunately, however, she returned to her hotel, and my men were able to follow her here."

Samuel's blood pounded in his veins, and the sticky scent

of sweat radiating from the man's greasy hair furthered his disgust. "None of this explains why you've stolen my child."

The man placed his hand on Samuel's arm. "I must insist you release me if we are to talk like civilized gentlemen."

Civilized gentlemen did not abduct children. And this conversation did nothing but waste precious moments. Instead of releasing the man, Samuel put his thumb and forefinger under his chin, taking hold of his windpipe. "All I have to do is squeeze."

The bravado left the miscreant's eyes as they widened. "Please!" The word vibrated against Samuel's fingers. "As soon as you answer some questions and we apprehend Miss Mapleton, we'll give you the girl!"

Rage boiled in Samuel's chest as he hauled the man off the wall and shoved him ahead of him. The man mumbled something the pounding blood in his ears caused Samuel to miss, but it didn't matter. He pushed the man forward, marching him back through the rear gardens of the town-houses and around to the front door of his house, where he'd left Evelyn.

He glanced around, but the street was devoid of a small woman with raven hair. Disregarding the stares of passersby, Samuel shoved the man up the steps and into the house.

"Evelyn!"

Mrs. Tooley scrambled out of the parlor, her face pale. "Mr. Flynn! What's happened?"

His mother, having arrived this morning, scrambled out behind her. "Samuel? Oh!" Her brown eyes grew large in her rounded face, and her gaze darted to the man secured in Samuel's grasp.

Samuel tightened his grip on the back of his captive's jacket. "They've stolen Emily!"

Mother gasped, her hands fluttering about her face.

He directed his words to Mrs. Tooley, who could hope-fully maintain more wherewithal than his mother during stressful situations. "Where is Evelyn?"

Mrs. Tooley twisted her hands in front of her. "She's not here, sir." Tears gathered in her eyes.

With an infuriated roar, Samuel threw the blackguard into the parlor.

Evelyn ran. She dodged startled people on the street, pushed past a dirty man with a cart, and darted around a hackney, startling the horses and earning a shout from the driver. Still, she did not stop until her feet reached the infirmary and her burning lungs could not gather another breath.

Heaving, she stumbled into the ward, her eyes skimming over the patients and across the faces of the nurses and volunteers. Where was she? She had to be here somewhere! What happened to Emily had to be connected to Alice. Whatever misguided plan Alice started in the prison must also include taking Emily. But to what avail?

Evelyn stalked through the ward, not pausing as nurses called her name. She was disgusted with herself for not seeing it earlier. Alice had deliberately planned to use her! Did she even care that Evelyn had suffered humiliation at the hands of the guards?

Worse, had she plotted to abduct a child?

Her only hope of helping Emily was to find Alice. Evelyn exited the rear of the ward and headed for the hallway to the offices, where they kept the captured Confederates. Surely she would find Alice there. And when she got her hands on her...The unfinished thought simmered.

How dare she? Whatever plans Mrs. Greenman and Alice concocted, they had no right to bring a child into it! Fuming, she made a line straight for the barrel chest of the Federal guard positioned in front of the small chamber housing the Confederates.

The soldier lifted his eyebrows and then stiffened in his stance. "Ho there, lady." He held up a hand. "What are you doing?"

"Where's Alice?"

The man's broad forehead wrinkled. "Huh?"

Evelyn flung her arm at the room behind him. "The girl with the curly hair who feeds them. Is she in there?"

He shrugged. "She was here earlier, but she's gone now."

With an exasperated groan, Evelyn put her hand against him and tried to shove him out of the way. "Let me in!"

As solid as the walls flanking him, the soldier remained firm. "What's got you up in a tizzy, lady?"

She drew a long breath, willing her nerves to calm. "Please, sir. I need to know where Alice is. It's a matter of grave importance."

"I told you, she ain't in there. She left a few minutes ago, and I haven't seen her since." His eyes shifted to something behind her.

Footsteps pounded down the hall, and Evelyn turned. Samuel! Relieved, she hurried toward him. "Did you get her?"

He snatched her arm, his face red. "Come with me."

"Samuel! What—"

Dragging her away from the soldier and down the hall, he made a noise low in his chest that stole her words. Seeming larger than ever, he made an imposing figure. Panic surged in her chest. "Where's Emily?"

"I intend to find out."

At the other end of the hall, he opened the door to the supply closet and thrust her inside, then slammed the door behind them. "What have you done?"

Had he roared the words, she may have been less frightened. Instead, his low voice sliced through her, an icy knife that plunged deep.

"I didn't do anything!"

He clenched his hands at his sides. "I will not take any of your lies, woman! They have taken my child and will not release her until *you* give them the information they want!"

"I didn't do anything," Evelyn repeated, though with less gusto. She'd done enough. She wrapped her arms around herself, her hands trembling. "This is Alice's doing."

Samuel's nostrils flared. "Explain yourself." She opened her mouth to respond, but he stepped closer. "I know you went to visit that spy this morning."

"Please, you must understand." She took a tentative step closer. "I didn't mean for any of this to happen."

"So help me, Evelyn, if harm comes to Emily because of your lies—"

"Alice purposely shoved me into Mrs. Greenman after they said we could not touch!"

Samuel scowled.

"Then she disappeared. They searched me." She shivered, the memory still too fresh.

Samuel's eyes darkened, and the heat in his eyes sparked once more. Did his heart rage for her humiliation or against her foolishness?

Her own heart wrenched. "I think Alice used me as a distraction. That must be why she coerced me into going to the prison with her. They used me to do something." Tears slid out of her eyes and burned tracks down her cheeks. She longed to reach for him but dared not. "That's all I know.

We have to find Alice."

Samuel closed the distance between them and gripped her shoulder. "You promised me you would do nothing more to bring destruction." Fury and pain warred in his usually gentle eyes. "Yet here you have brought it not to men in uniform, but to a little girl."

"Samuel, please," her voice quivered. "I didn't mean…"

He released her and turned away. "It doesn't matter. You will stay here until I find Alice and get my child. If you speak truth, then I suspect Alice is the one they truly want." His broad shoulders lifted and lowered with a heavy sigh. "Then I'll have to decide what to do with you."

Without another word, he threw open the door. Before she could gather her senses, it closed once more. Evelyn grasped the fabric at her throat, numb to all but the sting of loss that engulfed her.

The scrape of metal on metal shook her from her stupor. He meant to lock her in! She lurched forward, her skirt catching on the sharp edge of a wooden crate. She yanked it free and reached for the doorknob, only to confirm what she already knew. Sobs welled in her throat, twisting her insides. Sinking to the floor, she let tears wash over her.

This was all her fault! Why hadn't she refused to go to the prison? Daddy's letter hadn't even been worth it. All it did was confirm the truth she'd tried to deny. He'd not wanted her. Again.

Evelyn wrapped her arms around her knees and drew them to her heaving chest. No longer would her father, his opinions, or his lack of care for her hold sway over her life. Her desperation to earn his love had brought harm to Emily and torn apart the beginnings of the bridge that had linked her heart to Samuel's.

He would never forgive her. She could never forgive

herself.

Oh, forgive me, Lord. I should have prayed for wisdom. I should have asked for your guidance. I should have trusted in you and your love for me. You are the Father I need.

She gulped for air, the room stifling hot. Samuel's words came back to her. *As it has to do with you, live peaceably with everyone.* But she'd never really accomplished that. If she were honest with herself, she'd always tried to push Aunt Mary and Isabella to think better of her. She'd at first been subservient and then had caused dissension because she could not let them see she felt unwanted and unaccepted.

And what of her father? She'd tried to be the lady she knew he wanted her to be, always trying to live up to the impossible standard she imagined her mother had left behind. Then she'd gotten into a mess because she'd been determined to make him proud. Make him love her the way he should have loved her all along simply because she was his child.

Tears soaked the fabric at her knees. Now Samuel and Emily would suffer the consequences of her choices.

Forgive me. Help me to make it right.

Samuel stalked down the hall, his senses aflame with warring emotions. What kind of man took a child to make a point? And what kind of woman got herself so tangled in a web of deception that it nearly choked her?

He rounded the corner and headed for Dr. Porter's office. He had little time. He rapped twice on the door, and then entered without invitation. "Where's Nurse Brown?"

Dr. Porter raised his eyes from a stack of papers on his desk. "Why, come in, Mr. Flynn." He leaned back in his seat.

"Nurse Brown," Samuel repeated. "I need to know the location of one of her volunteer girls."

"You best have a seat."

Samuel ignored the man's gesture toward a chair. "I cannot. I have a matter of grave importance."

"As do I." He eyed Samuel. "I was about to come find you."

He didn't have the time to listen to any more exposition on the state of the country or the list of items he wanted Samuel to accomplish. "Sir, I—"

"It's come to my attention that you have had inappropriate relations with the staff at this hospital."

Samuel's thoughts stuttered to a stop. "Excuse me?"

Dr. Porter laced his fingers on his desk. "This young woman you seek, is she the one you were seen having a clandestine meeting with in the supply closet?"

"What?" He shook his head. "No, I'm looking for Alice Avery. Curly hair and large eyes."

The doctor grunted. "Another of your trysts, then?"

Heat seared up his neck. "I've had no inappropriate meetings with young women."

"Oh? So you did not take Miss Mapleton into your residence?"

Tension bunched the muscles in his shoulders. "I've invited her to eat with my children, the nanny, and myself. That's hardly a matter of consequence. Now—"

"And what of your times in the hospital? Surely you must understand those things are not to be accepted here."

"I only sought a private place to talk. Nothing more." The back of his neck tingled. That wasn't exactly true. He had kissed Evelyn.

Dr. Porter stared at him.

"Sir, I don't have time for this. I must find Miss Avery."

"Why?"

"I need to take her back…" His words trailed off. Even he could see how saying he needed to take her back to his house seemed entirely inexcusable. "I need to ask her about her involvement in a situation. I believe she has information that can help me locate my missing child."

Dr. Porter's mustache twitched. "What contact have you had with the Confederate soldiers?"

The man never listened! "I checked them for wounds and sickness. Now, Miss Avery—"

"Miss Avery was seen in the room with those soldiers, as was Miss Mapleton. Both young ladies were seen in your company on several occasions. Is there something you wish to confess to me?"

Samuel ground his teeth. "Sir, this is not what you think."

"It's not? The detective police seem to think differently."

"The detective police?" His blood churned through his veins. "The detective police took my little girl! And they will not give her back to me until I deliver the answers they want. Answers that I can only get from Miss Avery."

Dr. Porter seemed entirely unconcerned. "Then you admit to being involved with this?" He wagged his head. "I knew it was best to keep you in check."

"What?"

Tracing a finger along the lines of a paper on his desk, Dr. Porter cocked his head. "You didn't think that I postponed your medical license for no reason, did you?"

His gut tightened. "You said you wished to ready me to run a hospital."

"At first, I figured if I held out long enough, you would give up." He leaned back in his chair. "Then after seeing your determination despite the curse upon you, I came up with a better idea."

Samuel stilled, confusion crumpling his brow, then shook his head. It didn't matter. "I must go."

"I thought I could ignore the past and I could treat you like the son you should have been."

The words brought Samuel to a halt.

"Your mother loved me, you know. Your father stole her from me."

This man was insane! Samuel yanked open the door.

"We were to be married," Dr. Porter continued, his voice following Samuel into the hall. "But her father thought I wasn't up to his standards." The man hurried out of the office door. "William Flynn, oh, now, there was a man with ambition. A physician on his way to making a name for himself." Disgust dripped from his tone.

Samuel set his teeth as the man gained his side.

"Well, I could do that, too, if that was what it took. So I enrolled in medical school and worked tirelessly to earn my marks. But it wasn't enough. Dorothy still married William."

Despite his better judgment, Samuel paused. "This is ludicrous."

Dr. Porter sneered. "Then when he took a place on the medical board, he made sure that the criteria increased to make it even harder for a poor boy to earn his license."

Samuel stared at him, his mind stumbling to keep up. His father and Dr. Porter had both courted Mother? And for that he'd purposely sabotaged Samuel's licensing?

"But I would not be deterred," Dr. Porter continued. "For years I devoted myself to the pursuit until I became a professor of medicine at Columbian. Then I went to find your mother to show her all I had accomplished." His face reddened. "But still she would not have me. Said she loved your father and had made a family with him. I told her that didn't matter to me. I would raise the nitwit's children as my own. But she still wouldn't leave him."

Pain sharpened the doctor's gaze. This was not the man he had studied under. This man with wild eyes and a sneer was not the doctor he'd looked up to and sought to please.

Dr. Porter gripped Samuel's elbow, his fingers like a vice. "I never loved another. I learned to devote myself to my work and to excel in my profession. Imagine my surprise when the son who should have been mine turned up under my care. I thought I had been given another chance." He snorted. "But you were defective. Tainted by the blood of a man who steals another's love."

Defective. The word slithered over him and sank fangs into his tattered nerves. He snatched his arm free and stalked down the hall, but the man scurried along beside him, continuing his uninvited tirade.

"You thought I didn't notice. You thought no one knew you couldn't handle the smells. But I always knew the scent of blood makes you sick." His voice rose. "Fitting, I suppose. A curse worthy of the deeds that caused it."

Samuel stepped into the ward. Patients and nurses turned to look as he stalked by, the head physician sputtering beside him.

"But I was willing to wait," the doctor continued, un-concerned his voice carried for all to hear. "I wanted to wait to see if I could help you get past the curse your father placed upon you. But instead of growing under my leadership, you took advantage of me. You overstepped into my position, took sympathy on Confederate prisoners, and started womanizing like your father."

Samuel quickened his pace, skirting a nurse and ignoring a patient's call. The doctor scrambled after him.

"It's not really your fault. You can't help you have a

traitor's blood in your veins." He struggled to gain Samuel's side again. "But I cannot give you your license. Not with so many defects." He barked a dark laugh. "Ironic, really. Your own father is the one who pushed for the stauncher medical practices that ultimately led to thwarting your ambitions."

Samuel expanded his chest in an effort to maintain control. "This is an issue I will have to address with you later."

"Where are you going?"

Samuel ignored him and quickened his pace toward the front door. He couldn't focus on this insanity when Emily was still in danger.

Dr. Porter grabbed his sleeve. "Whoa, now, son. Wait a moment."

Samuel snatched his arm free. "I'm *not* your son."

Cold eyes glinted at him. "If you want my signature, you will do just as I say."

How had the man he'd thought was his mentor descended into such a state? Here, clearly written on his face, were the consequences of a heart that harbored bitterness. Bitterness he could not let overtake him as well. "Doctor, I'm truly sorry for the pain my family has caused you. But with respect, I must go. No matter what you think of me, there is an innocent child I must consider." He flung open the door.

"If you give them that spy, they'll return the child."

The words stopped Samuel's advance and sent ice through his veins. "How do you know about that?"

"I tried to tell you, boy, but you never listen to me."

Samuel's jaw clenched.

"As I said, the detective police came here. As any patriot would do, I told them all I knew about Miss Mapleton and Miss Avery. That led to a rather interesting conversation about you." He spread his hands. "Despite everything, I'm trying to help you. Turn Miss Mapleton over and let them do whatever they do to traitors. That will get your orphan back."

Pulse pounded in his ears. Dr. Porter didn't know Evelyn was here. Maybe the detectives didn't either.

"Don't be a fool, boy. Hand over the wench and be done with it."

Perhaps he was a fool. Evelyn had made her loyalties clear. But, God help him, he could not let her be taken to prison.

Dr. Porter's face hardened. "I will have no choice but to tell them you're involved."

"Then do what you must."

He left the doctor sputtering behind him.

Evelyn drew in shuddering breaths. Her body radiated heat, and perspiration slipped into her eyes. She wiped the stinging moisture away. How long had she sat here? She rolled her shoulders and lifted her head.

Something wasn't right.

Acrid air burned her raw throat, and a new panic stirred. She scrambled to her feet, her hem catching and causing her to trip. The fabric ripped as she wrenched it out from under her. The smell grew stronger, thickening the air and clinging to her nose. Her heart hammered.

Evelyn grabbed the doorknob and then pulled her hand back with a yelp. Why was it hot? Panic surged as her mind grasped the truth. She stumbled away from the door as tendrils of smoke crept underneath.

She drummed a fist against the door, her burned palm held to her chest. "Help! I'm in here!" She pounded harder, her hand aching. "Please!"

The door grew hotter, and Evelyn backed away as the dark curls of smoke gathered under the door and forced their way in. The smoke thickened in the room, a dark evil that had come to steal her breath.

She coughed, the smoldering air burning her lungs. She grabbed her chest, but the coughs overtook her. She would be trapped here, destined for smoke and fire. No one other than Samuel knew she was here. And he needed to get to Emily.

Please, save Emily.

Lungs heaving, Evelyn sank to the floor.

Twenty-Three

*S*amuel's feet pounded against the road as sweat collected at his nape and slid between his shoulders despite the chill of November.

He would find that girl.

By the time he reached the Halverson Hotel, both his anger *and* his lungs burned. He barreled past the doorman without so much as a cursory greeting and slapped his hand on the receiving desk. "Which room is occupied by the Misses Mapleton and Avery?"

The clerk, a spindly fellow with a sallow complexion, lifted his eyes from the desk. "And you are?"

"Mr. Samuel Flynn, friend and employer of Miss Mapleton."

He pushed his spectacles up on his pointy nose. "Hmm. And are the ladies expecting you?"

The way the fellow eyed him with suspicion made Samuel aware of his state of disarray. He squared his shoulders. "Sir, I'm a training physician at the Washington Infirmary. Both young ladies work as volunteers there, and it is urgent I speak to Miss Avery."

The man bobbed his head. "Oh, yes, sir. I've heard them speak of their work there." He ran his finger down the ledger. "Ah, room sixteen…"

He'd but spouted the room number before Samuel spun away and took the stairs two at a time. A brass knocker with an engraved number decorated the door, but Samuel opted to pound his fist on it instead. "Miss Avery!"

No reply. Clenching his teeth, Samuel pounded harder. Two doors down, a woman opened her door and peeked out, her wide eyes telling him he'd best soften his ways or the frightened girl would never open the door.

"Please, Miss Avery. It is of great importance." His words strained. "They have taken my little girl, and I must get her back."

No response.

He slammed his hand against the door and hurried back down the stairs to the reception desk. "Is Miss Avery here?"

The clerk sniffed. "You ran off before I had the chance to say so earlier. She and Miss Mapleton left early this morning."

He clenched his hands. The man might have led with that information. He dipped his chin. "My apologies. If you see her, would you kindly ask that she call upon my place of residence?"

"Certainly, sir," the clerk said dryly, handing Samuel a pencil and pad.

Samuel scribbled the address and returned the pad, then ducked back out the door. Where would he find her now? The hotel and the hospital were the only locations he knew.

Except for the Greenman residence, but why would she go there? He hesitated on the street, willing his mind to slow and put together the pieces. Evelyn had gone with Miss Avery to the prison. Something had happened with the widow Greenman, and Evelyn had come to his house. For what? Help?

Guilt scurried across his nerves, but he pushed it aside.

There would be time for explanation and forgiveness later. Evelyn had left his house and gone to the hospital, claiming to be looking for Alice. But why would Miss Avery be at the hospital? If Mrs. Greenman was a spy, and Alice had plans as Evelyn claimed, then why…?

The realization exploded upon his senses, and he bolted down the street. Startled pedestrians scrambled out of his way, and he called an apology as he sprinted past. How could he have been such a dimwit? He'd allowed two women of questionable loyalty to care for Confederate soldiers, knowing they had been in contact with a woman arrested for spying and treason.

He sucked a lungful of air, the usual putrid scents of the city grazing across his senses. He'd grown used to them—the press of people, the waste of livestock, the hints of smoke in the air as it wafted from chimneys. All of it common enough to ignore.

Something seemed different, but in light of the circumstances it hardly mattered. He kept running. But the farther he made it down Fourth Street, the more the scent of burning wood and smoke thickened the air. He coughed, not remembering when the chimneys had seemed this strong.

A niggling fear erupted. Something must be on fire.

As though in answer to his thoughts, the fervent toll of a bell sounded behind him, accompanied by the pounding of hooves. He didn't need to glance over his shoulder to know the fire engine would soon pass him. It hurtled down the cobblestones, men shouting as the conveyance made a hard turn. His spine tingled. They were heading the same direction as he.

As Samuel rounded the corner onto East Street, his fear blossomed into panic.

No!

Flames licked the walls of the infirmary, sprouting out of the windows like hellish fiends. The fire wagon jerked to a halt, and men leapt out, shouting directions. They operated the pump, but Samuel knew it would not be enough. Though already at a full run, he forced his legs to move faster.

Nurses and patients littered the street as people shouted in panic. Sick and wounded men were propped against neighboring buildings and trees, and those who could maneuver themselves did their best to help the others. Dr. Porter shouted orders, and his words broke through the clamor.

"That's the last of them!" he called to the firemen.

Samuel pushed through the crowd, ignoring the fingers that clung to his coat. Nurses called his name, but his mind had singled in on only one thought. Where was she? Surely someone had let her out. His heart constricted as he spun around, frantically scanning every face. But his Wildwood Queen was nowhere to be seen.

Disregarding the shouts of both the firefighters and hospital staff, he charged into the building, the heat hitting him like a furnace. Air smothered in smoke burned paths down his nose and throat.

Evelyn!

Hades engulfed the ward, gobbling up beds and smearing ash across the walls. Samuel leapt over a heap of blankets that had succumbed to the flames and headed for the door at the back of the ward. Fire scurried along the walls, and a curtain of heat shot out of the entrance to the back hall. He held his breath and jumped, praying he would not land in flames on the other side of the smoke-darkened doorway.

Pain seared through his arm, and his shirt caught fire. He beat against it with his palm as he sprinted down the hall to the supply closet.

The key!

Samuel thrust his hand into his pocket. "Evelyn! I'm coming!" Where was that key? His fingers fumbled, grasping in panic, until he finally wrapped them around the tiny shard of metal. He grabbed the doorknob, pain rushing up his hand. He released it with a shout. The metal had grown too hot! He plunged the key into the lock and turned it, using it to push the door in.

"Evelyn!"

Smoke billowed into the small room from behind him as though it had been waiting for him to give it entrance.

Thank you, God.

The flames had not reached the room, and only the smoke that had managed to work its way under the door tainted the air prior to his entrance. But where was Evelyn?

A shadow shifted, and he lunged forward, finding her in a heap on the floor. "Evelyn!"

She groaned as he turned her over, her beautiful face red and smeared with sweat. He drew her up against his chest and buried his face in her hair.

"My love, forgive me."

He gathered her in his arms and pushed to his feet. Her head lolled back over his arm. Her breath wheezed, and was far too shallow. How long had she inhaled the smoke?

Samuel coughed and ran down the hall. The fire had now wrapped through the doorway from the ward and plumed along the ceiling, a great mass of red and orange.

He would not get through the ward the way he had come.

He spun the other way, running past the room where they had kept the Confederate soldiers. He nearly left them to their fate, but his conscious would not allow it. Sending up a prayer for help, he stuck his head through the door.

Empty.

He whirled back around, heading for the rear door of the hospital. With a thrust of his foot, Samuel kicked the door open, and a wave of air sweeter and cooler than any he had ever breathed washed over him.

Evelyn stirred in his arms, groaning.

He pressed a kiss to her saturated hair. "Stay with me, darling."

Evelyn turned her face against his chest as he ran down the steps and into the cool of the gathering dusk. Shouts drew his attention, and there, in the flickering light of the flames, stood a small woman with wild hair. She was flanked by two men.

She froze, staring at Samuel. Then she waved her arms wildly at the men. "Go!"

The men bolted, one in each direction. The woman hesitated, giving him time to register her shadowed features. *Alice.* Then she spun around and darted after one of the men. Rage burned in his chest. He could not leave Evelyn to chase her, but he was loath to let her escape.

Evelyn coughed, rough and ragged, against him. Narrowing his eyes, he watched the traitors disappear. He would have to get Evelyn to safety. His mind now numbed to the panic, his feet found the familiar path back home seemingly of their own accord. Never had he been so glad to see the small townhome draped in evening's shadows.

"Open the door." he rasped as he neared. "Mrs. Tooley!" Samuel coughed and tried again. "Open."

He tromped up the steps, Evelyn's weight leaden in his arms. He rammed his shoulder into the door, and pain radiated up his arm. "Mrs. Tooley!"

The door flung open, and Samuel stumbled inside.

Mother gasped. "Oh! Heavens. What's happened?"

"Get Father." Samuel staggered into the parlor, past the detective he'd tied to the chair by the mantel, and gently lowered Evelyn to the settee.

He pushed the hair back from her face and lowered his head to listen to the ragged draw of her breath. "Forgive me," he whispered.

"It seems you found a way to capture the trollop after all." The detective's snide voice scraped jagged nails down his frayed nerves, and Samuel whirled on him.

The fellow's eyes widened, and he tried to scoot back in his chair. "Oh, now…wait!"

Arms wrapped around Samuel's middle and jerked him back before he could find the satisfaction of splintering the man's nose.

"Samuel. The patient." His father's voice crashed through his rage, and he paused long enough to regain his senses.

"We tried to question him," Father said. "He wouldn't give Emily's location, but insists she is well." He gripped Samuel's shoulder. "Let's first tend the patient." Father swung his gaze to the detective, fire glinting in his blue eyes. "Then I'll clean up whatever mess you make of this one's face."

Samuel gave a curt nod.

Father released him and dropped to Evelyn's side. "What are the injuries?"

"Fire." Samuel knelt next to her. "She was trapped inside. I think she breathed too much smoke."

Dr. Flynn, the best physician Samuel could hope for to attend to Evelyn, had, by God's grace, arrived with Mother this day, which had been the only reason he'd been home when Emily had been taken. Father gave him a reassuring smile and then tilted Evelyn's head back to further open her airways. "Do you know how long she was in there?"

"Too long." His chest constricted, and he gripped the

collar of his shirt as though he could dispel the guilt that lodged there.

Father checked over her, noting a burn on her palm that matched the one on Samuel's own. He clenched his jaw. She must have tried to break out. How panicked she must have been.

"The burn is not severe and should heal fine with a little salve." Father pushed her damp hair off her face and put his fingers on the pulse under her neck. "She seems otherwise uninjured. I suggest she receive plenty of rest and fresh air." Father rose and turned to Samuel. "As for you, I shall need to see to your arm."

Samuel shook his head. "It can wait."

Father seemed dubious, but stepped back. He put his hands in the pockets of his wool trousers, his expressive eyes assessing Samuel with customary calm.

Mother, however, could not be contained. "Samuel! You must have your father see to that. Why, it looks right awful!"

He made a low noise in his throat that silenced her, and he turned toward the captive detective. "I have come from the Washington Infirmary, where I saw Miss Alice Avery aid two Confederate soldiers escape the fire. There was a third, but I didn't see him with her. Were I to guess, I would say that fire wasn't an accident. It would seem to me Miss Avery is the lady you'd wish to question. Not this one."

His hawkish face twisted. "You are sure of this?"

Samuel took a step closer and flung his arm at Evelyn. "Evelyn also informed me she was coerced into going to the prison today, where she was then used as a distraction for something Miss Avery and Mrs. Greenman planned. After being searched, she went looking for help. That's why you saw her here."

The detective glanced back at Evelyn, his features conflicted.

"As you can see," Samuel continued, "the lady has suffered from breathing smoke, and I myself have a wound from the fire. Do you think I would inflict such injuries merely to deceive you?"

The man's features softened, and…was that a slight pang of regret that crossed his face? "No, I can see you are not the type of man to do so." The detective's shoulders lifted with a long inhalation. "I fear this plan has gone terribly awry. I intended to intercept Miss Mapleton and question her. Then we saw the child talking to her, and my subordinate, well, he is an impulsive fellow."

The muscles in Samuel's jaw twitched.

"I'm Detective Fredrick Mallow, by the way. I'm sure you'll want to speak to my superiors."

"Undoubtedly," Father said. He smoothed the thinning hair on the top of his head, then took hold of Mother's hand.

Detective Mallow cleared his throat. "Anyway, he took the girl to question her about what she might know."

"That's asinine!"

"I fear I must agree with you. I was rather surprised myself and had to leave my position to go after him. Unfortunately, that put me in your path instead. In that moment, I decided to mislead you. I thought I could get enough distance to come up with a plan." He nodded to the rope around his wrists. "That didn't go well."

Samuel glared at him.

"But, please, believe I had no intention of the situation coming to this. In the brief exchange I shared with my associate, I improvised and told him to take her away, but not far. I merely thought we could use the threat to get information that has thus far been exceedingly frustrating to obtain."

Father snorted. "What sort of immoral man takes a child for his own purposes?" Mother clung to him, her rounded form in sharp contrast to Father's lean one.

Samuel stepped closer to his captive, his words coming out in clipped measure and tainted with the unrestraint that would usually be unbefitting a physician. "Where. Is. Emily?"

The fellow darted his gaze from Father to Samuel and then to Evelyn draped across the settee. "He took her to the eatery around the corner. He is not to go any other place without my say."

As though such a statement were adequate assurance! With one last glance at Evelyn, Samuel bolted out the door. There could be only one eatery the man referred to, and he wasted no time reaching it and barreling inside.

At this hour, patrons filled the tables, and their chatter clamored over his ears.

There!

Against the wall, his little Emily sat perched on her chair, primly eating a bowl of ice cream. Across from her, a young man of no more than seventeen years wore a rather perplexed expression. Samuel wove through the crowd, trying to contain his emotions lest they scare her.

Emily grinned. "Hey!"

Relief surged through him as thick as molasses, and he dropped to one knee. Emily scrambled down and launched herself into his arms.

"Are you all right, little one?"

Emily nodded and then frowned at the young detective. "This strange man made me come here and asked me lots of funny questions. I was mad about it at first, 'cause I wanted to see Miss Evelyn." She lifted her shoulders. "But he gave me lots of ice cream, too, so I guess I don't mind too much." She scrunched her little face. "Mrs. Tooley don't let me have many sweets."

He'd never heard Emily string together that many words at once in all the time he'd known her. He shifted his gaze to the nervous young detective. The fellow fiddled with his cravat and rose from his place.

Samuel stood with his daughter safely in his arms. "Do not think to leave so easily," he said with a growl.

The young man paled.

Emily giggled. "Oh, Papa, don't be cross at him. He didn't mean to frighten me. He said so. And he did seem right sorry about it." She gave the fellow a little wave. "And thank you for my ice cream."

The boy bobbed his head. "Please, sir. I meant no harm."

Had Emily called him Papa? The shock of it melted some of his fury. He pointed a finger at the boy. "This matter is not settled. I will be certain your superiors and the law are made aware of what occurred today. And you should expect word from my family's solicitor."

The fellow squeaked a reply and bolted out the door. Samuel watched him go and hugged Emily. "I was sorely worried about you."

She smiled sweetly and placed a kiss on his cheek. "Thank you, Papa."

His heart constricted. He'd not been mistaken. "For what? I lost you, and it took me a long time to find you. I don't think that makes me a very good guardian...or father."

Emily wrapped her arm around his neck as they made their way back through the restaurant. "But you came looking for me and got me back. You didn't forget me or leave me. That makes you the best Papa."

The back of his throat constricted, and he didn't trust himself to speak.

"Did you find Miss Evelyn? She was outside with me."

Emily frowned. "Did they take her for ice cream, too?"

Samuel stepped out into the cool night air and turned toward home. "I did find her." He measured his words carefully. "She's a little hurt, but will be fine with rest."

"That's good. I like her."

Samuel couldn't help but chuckle. "I do, too."

Emily's giggle felt like a balm to his raw nerves. "I told Benjamin she should be our new mama."

His heart skittered. "You think so?"

She bobbed her little head emphatically and snuggled closer in his arms. "Of course. She's perfect."

Samuel mounted the steps to the house, realizing nearly everyone he loved was encased inside. "Do you think Benjamin will agree?"

"Sure. He likes her too. He just don't want to admit it."

He chuckled and opened the door. "Then I guess that only leaves one person to ask."

Twenty-Four

November 5, 1861

*P*ain stirred in her chest, and each breath she drew came as a scalding wave. Evelyn moaned. *Fire!* The thought pricked through her muddled senses. The hospital was on fire. She had to get out! She thrashed against the floor, which seemed far too soft.

"Shh now. You're all right." A soothing voice lapped at her ears. "You're safe now. Not to worry."

She shivered, realizing she was no longer on the hard floor of the storage room but snuggled into something warm and soft. She pried her eyes open, blinking against the light.

"Ah, there you are! I was beginning to wonder if you would ever want to wake up." The voice belonged to a woman with a rounded face and chestnut hair streaked with gray. She smiled, revealing dimples. "I want you to drink now."

The words awakened a sudden and voracious thirst, and Evelyn nodded, pulling herself to a sitting position in a fine feathered bed. Where was she? The bed was draped with a deep blue covering that matched the curtains hanging from the open window. Evelyn accepted a mug of water and raised it to her parched lips, shivering as the cold air slipped over her shoulders.

The older woman chuckled. "The doctor said you need-ed plenty of cool, fresh air." She waved a hand at the window. "I told him you would catch your death of cold, but he insisted." She sighed dramatically, but a smile still played about her lips. "I suppose since he is such a fine physician of considerable standing"—she wriggled her eyebrows—"we shall have to do as he says."

Evelyn blinked at her, unsure how to take the woman. The cool water flowed down her throat, soothing away some of the sting. She gulped it and then handed the empty cup back to the woman.

"More?"

Evelyn nodded as the lady filled another cupful from the pitcher on the carved bedside table.

"Oh, where are my manners?" The woman handed her the cup. "I'm Dorothy Flynn."

Evelyn drank half of the cup and then handed it back. "Mrs. Flynn?" Her voice was reedy and thin.

"I'm Samuel's mother." Her eyes twinkled. "And I'm quite pleased to meet you."

Alarm erupted. "Emily!" She struggled free from the covers.

Mrs. Flynn placed a hand on her shoulder. "Emily is fine, dear. Rest easy." She gently coaxed Evelyn deeper into the covers, pulling the quilt up under her chin.

"What...?" She tried to clear her throat, but the pain made her wince.

"Shh. Don't talk too much now." Mrs. Flynn patted her arm. "Samuel found her right around the corner, happy as a lark and eating her third bowl of ice cream."

Evelyn's forehead creased.

"Seems some intrepid young fellow thought he would

abscond with her and get Emily to give him some information. That, or somehow use her to get Samuel to convince you to tell them something they wanted to know." She lifted her expressive brows once more. "But I don't believe he realized Emily had no intention of uttering a word to him. When Samuel got there, he says she scrambled down from her perch, nuzzled into his arms, and then politely thanked the detective for her treat."

Evelyn almost wanted to laugh. Mrs. Flynn accomplished it for them both. "Now my Samuel, he was hot as a heap of coals, and believe you me, those detective police are due for quite the dressing down. We've already had a fine visit with some nice policemen."

"Is Sam...Mr. Flynn, here?"

Mrs. Flynn grinned. "Of course. He's been sleeping on the settee in the parlor. It makes him act like a bear in the mornings, but he insisted you take his bed."

Evelyn's breath arrested. She was in Samuel's bed? Mornings? How long had she slept?

"He had no other option, you see," the lady continued, "since his father and I have taken the guest chamber."

She had no response to this and willed her heart to slow in its rapid hammering. Mrs. Flynn patted her shoulder. "I'll let him know you're finally awake. He's been rather concerned."

"How long?"

Her face crinkled and then opened with understanding. "Oh, he brought you back from that fire, and you slept all through the night, all through yesterday, and then he said he would wake you himself if you didn't rouse this morning." She gestured to Evelyn. "But here you are."

The elder lady slipped through the door, leaving a wide view of the hall. What had happened to the hospital? Had they been able to save all of the patients from the fire? Had Samuel rescued her? She remembered flashes of heat, and then a warm embrace through her fears.

A few moments later, heavy footsteps sounded on the stairs. There would be no escaping the wrath that would come now. Why had he taken her to his house?

And worse, put her in his bed?

Samuel entered dressed in charcoal pants and only a linen shirt and bracers. His sleeves had been rolled to the elbow, and a thick bandage encased his left forearm.

"You're hurt." The words slipped free. Did he know she referred to more than the wound on his arm? "I'm terribly sorry." Tears pricked her eyes, but this time she didn't bother to hide them.

Samuel pressed his lips into a line and stepped into the room. He snagged a ladder-back chair from a small writing desk and pulled it over to the edge of the bed. "It is I who should apologize. I never should have locked you in a supply closet. If I'd gotten there any later…" He let the words trail off, but his eyes spoke more.

Evelyn swallowed hard and forced her raspy voice to form words. "You wouldn't have had to if I had not caused all of this mess. I know you will never be able to forgive me for what I've done—"

"I already have."

She blinked the moisture from her eyes, startled when he reached up and brushed the tears away with the pad of his finger. "You were not responsible for what happened with Emily, though once you are recovered you will have to speak with the detective police."

Evelyn nodded.

"Based on my account, they are looking for Miss Avery and will take her into custody." He leaned closer. "Have you anything more to tell me?"

Other than the fact that everything within her strained to close the divide between them? More than revealing her heart was filled with a love that could never be? Tears welled anew. "No, I have told..." She coughed, her lungs burning. A fitting penance, perhaps.

Samuel handed her the cup and she drank, the cool water soothing. She handed it back to him, suddenly aware she was entertaining a gentleman in naught but a borrowed nightdress and bedclothes. Heat—which had nothing to do with the fire still in her chest—simmered in her cheeks.

Gathering herself, she tried again. "I've told you all of it, Samuel. I promise."

He smoothed her hair, letting his hand cup her cheek. Her heart hammered. Why must he be so tender? He should scream at her, blame her for all that had happened. She deserved no less. Instead, warmth pooled in his eyes. Eyes that held none of the malice they should. Instead they seemed almost...

A giggle from the doorway made Samuel drop his hand. Evelyn leaned forward to look around him, relieved to see Emily beaming. Evelyn smiled and offered a little wave, pleased to see the child happy and well.

Emily bounded into the room and jumped up on the bed.

"Hold on there!" Samuel reached for her, but she scrambled across Evelyn and plopped down on the other side of the bed, then gave him a triumphant smile.

They both stilled as Emily snuggled up to Evelyn, her wide little eyes bright. "Mama? You all right?"

The world stilled, the breath from her seared chest leaving her. She stared at the girl, a new ache forming. "Yes, darling. I'm fine." She didn't dare look at Samuel.

Emily patted her cheek. "Good. I wanted to come before,

but Papa wouldn't let me."

Samuel made a funny noise in his throat, and Evelyn's gaze darted to him. His Adam's apple bobbed. Then a strange little smile tugged at one corner of his mouth. "And I told you that was because she was still sleeping."

"Well, she looks fine to me." Benjamin's voice came from the doorway as the little fellow entered the room, eyeing Evelyn.

Emily giggled. "She just needed lots of sleep. And water." She turned serious. "Did you drink lots of water like Mr."— she grinned—"I mean, like Granddaddy said?"

Evelyn could only nod.

Benjamin came to stand next to Samuel. Emily jutted her chin at him. "Granddaddy says Mama will be good as new in a week or two."

Benjamin's mouth fell open. "What did I tell you 'bout saying stuff like that?"

Samuel ruffled Benjamin's hair. "Let her be, boy."

Benjamin crossed his arms. "But she can't go getting her hopes up like that. She's always saying we are going to be a family and"—he shrugged—"we ain't even asked her yet."

Evelyn's heart hammered. How would she handle this? "Well, Benjamin, I don't—"

"I haven't had the chance yet," Samuel interrupted. "But when I do..." He gave the boy a look. "I'll let you know. Now, you two get downstairs and ask Mrs. Tooley to bring up some broth."

Benjamin gave Evelyn a tentative smile, and she received a rather exuberant hug from Emily before the children scurried from the room, twittering to each other. The silence they left in their wake had Evelyn fiddling with her blanket.

She swallowed, her raw throat burning anew.

"Evelyn, there is something we must discuss."

"I know. I'm sorry I have put you in a most awkward situation with the children. I didn't mean—"

He placed a finger over her lips. "May I continue?"

Evelyn pressed her lips together.

Samuel removed his hand. "There's something I need to know." He leaned closer. "Did you have anything to do with the fire?"

"No." She stared deep into his eyes, willing him to believe her.

"I didn't think so, but I had to ask." He braced his elbows on his knees. "It would seem Alice used it as a distraction to get those Confederate soldiers out of the hospital. To what end, I still don't know."

She hung her head. "I'm sorry. This is all my fault. I should never have agreed to take Alice to Mrs. Greenman."

"You're not responsible for her actions."

"Still, I acted rashly and foolishly, and I must beg your forgiveness. For everything."

"And you have it. As I hope you will forgive me for not taking the time to listen to you and for locking you in the closet."

"Forgiven." Tears wet her lashes, but she didn't wipe them away.

He drew a breath. "Now, secondly, I must know if you have any further plans to associate with Mrs. Greenman, any of her accomplices, or in any way whatsoever plan to continue *any* sort of spying, treason, or other dastardly deeds."

Evelyn pulled her lip through her teeth. "I allowed desperation to please my father and earn his acceptance to steer my actions." She frowned. "Though I am separating my beliefs from his, I do still believe the government is overreaching its power."

His mouth twitched. "I expected no less."

Somehow her beliefs about state's rights seemed less stringent than they had before. Not in the light of the suffering people faced. "I suspect that opinion will still have many labeling me a traitor, though." She twisted the sheets. "If I ever find my father, he and I have much to discuss."

"I understand the desire to please one's sire. For mine's encouragement and faith in me, I never gave up seeking my medical license. It wasn't until it was denied me that I realized my father was proud of me no matter what I did."

Evelyn looked away.

"Your father should love you because you are his. Maybe he hasn't realized the hurt he caused and thought he did what was best." He squeezed Evelyn's hand. "In my short time of practice, I've learned parenting is a most difficult endeavor. You owe it to yourself to speak your feelings to him. Then perhaps you will find healing. And if it doesn't go the way you hope, then you will be able to move on."

Wise words. It would take courage to reveal how her father had hurt her, but Samuel was right. She nodded.

"I'll help you find him if you wish it."

"Why?" The word squeaked out against her raw throat. "Why would you want anything to do with me? After everything I've done?"

"Ah, well." He cleared his throat. "I suppose that brings us to my final question." Samuel slipped from the chair and knelt at the side of her bed, looping his hand around hers. "Evelyn Mapleton, would you set aside political differences, and would you join me in the quest to bring healing, rather than pain, to as many as we can who are affected by this war?"

"Yes, as best as I—"

He grinned. "And would you promise to help me as we both try to live peaceably among everyone, even as the fires of war rage around us?"

She nodded slowly.

"And would you do these things by my side? Would you take my name and become a mother to my children?"

Tears burned in her eyes. *Yes!* But how could she marry him in name only, knowing she loved him while his heart merely sought her protection and security for the children? "I..." Her throat would not form the refusal.

He squeezed her hand. "I realize you may not feel the same as I do, but marry me, and I promise I will spend the rest of my days trying to earn your love in return."

"My...my love?"

"Yes, dearest. Don't you know that you have snuck into my heart and taken possession of it?"

She shook her head, but her raw throat wasn't the only thing making her words stick. He couldn't possibly be saying what she had longed to hear.

"I love you, Evelyn." Earnest eyes stared at her. The same eyes that had always been open and full of life. A life she longed to share.

"Oh, Samuel!" She flung herself into his arms and buried her face in his neck. "I love you, too."

He chuckled and pulled her tighter. "Is that a yes, then?"

She pulled back, her face inches from his. "With all my heart." Then she pressed her lips against his, enjoying the strength and warmth of him.

Samuel pulled her closer and tangled his fingers in her hair, deepening the kiss. Just when she thought she might float away, he pulled back and smiled.

"She said yes!"

A squeal erupted from the hallway, followed by the pounding of feet. Evelyn extracted herself from his arms and sat back on the bed as the children and Samuel's parents flowed into the room.

Mr. Flynn, who shared his son's good looks, smiled at her. "Ah, so it would seem we are to acquire another Rebel." Before Evelyn could gain the chance to be offended, he winked. "My daughter will be glad to know the scales have become more balanced." Despite the humor in his eyes, there was a sadness as well.

This war caused division. Between states, between friends, and between families. She reached out and took Samuel's hand. Perhaps love was enough to bridge the divide.

Emily twirled and stuck her finger out at Benjamin. "See? I told you she was gonna be our new mama."

Benjamin puckered his lips and made a show of assessing Evelyn, who most certainly was not looking her best. "Yeah, I reckon she'll do."

They all laughed. Surrounded by a family that cared for her despite her mistakes and her disheveled appearance, Evelyn marveled at the blessing God had granted. In the middle of a war that sought to divide, love had found a way to unite. Where pain wounded, hope mended.

And where her heart had felt abandoned, it now over-flowed. With her new children close, her new parents smiling down at her, and the man she loved at her side, she was finally home.

Epilogue

May, 1862

Pounding hammers disturbed the cool of the morning, and the scent of freshly hewn lumber hung in the air. Evelyn watched as the beams for the new hospital were set into place.

"Are they almost finished, Mama?" Emily looked up at her with wide eyes. "It sure is big."

Evelyn gave her little girl's hand a squeeze. "It is. They are going to call it the Judiciary Square Hospital now."

Benjamin wrinkled his nose. "What do they want to do that for?"

Evelyn had no answer, so she merely shrugged. It seemed fitting that it would have a new name. Because the place where the children had first met their father, and the place where she had first learned she could love a Yankee, was gone. And in its stead, something new would come.

Just like the little family they'd built in the midst of war. A new beauty from the ashes of what once was.

Her father had not even attended her wedding, but it had hurt less than she'd expected. They'd had a small, simple ceremony with Samuel's parents, the children, and Mrs. Tooley in attendance. All the people God had given her to love that loved her in return had been glowing with happiness during her nuptials. And for that, Evelyn was exceedingly grateful. Who needed to wait for months to prepare pomp and frivolity? She greatly preferred being a wife and new mother in their cozy townhome to spending that time planning.

She turned the children back to the carriage and found Samuel waiting for them there.

"They say I'm to be the head physician." His words were somber, but the exuberance in his eyes gave him away.

"And to think that horrible Dr. Porter tried to keep your license from you. Good thing your father had the college set it to rights. I do hope he contemplates his actions during his retirement." She tsked. "Your mother says he was out of his mind. She never wanted to marry him."

Samuel chuckled and placed a sweet kiss on her cheek. "A man will do all sorts of madness for the love of a woman."

Evelyn ducked her head, but Emily still giggled and Benjamin shushed her.

"Papa, will you be taking care of all the soldiers in there?" Benjamin asked, gesturing toward the giant structure.

Samuel put a hand on the boy's shoulder. "Yes." His eyes found Evelyn's. "Your Mama and I have promised we will care for as many as need us." He knelt in the dust near their carriage. "But we'll always be sure to take care of you and Emily."

Benjamin grinned. "I know that."

Samuel ruffled his hair. "Good then." He looked back at Evelyn. "How did it go?"

"They wouldn't let me deliver any food or blankets."

"Well, you can understand why."

She could. She'd promised never to step foot in that prison again, but as the wife of a prominent Washington physician and with her signature on a Federal loyalty paper, they could hardly throw her inside.

From what she understood, Mrs. Greenman and Alice now shared the same narrow chamber, and conditions had not improved since Evelyn had first seen it. While they deserved imprisonment for the fire that had destroyed the hospital and could have taken lives, she still felt that all within the prison should at least be warm and well fed.

Samuel kissed her forehead. "I'll see if we can convince some of the women's charitable organizations to help us gather relief for all of the prisoners."

Evelyn's heart constricted. Blind to blue and gray, Samuel heaped his kindness upon them all. She looped her arm through his. "I love you, Dr. Flynn."

Samuel chuckled. "And I you, Mrs. Flynn, but you've told me that twice today."

"Have I?"

"Aye, but I never grow tired of hearing it."

The End

If you enjoyed Evelyn and Samuel's tale, please take a moment to leave a quick review on your favorite online retailer or book group. Thank you!

Historical Note

I'm often amazed at the stories that exist in history. One of my favorite parts of research is reading first-hand accounts of people who lived through the era I'm writing about. For this book, a lot of my characters' adventures are based on the first-hand accounts of Belle Boyd and Rose Greenhow. Many of Evelyn's thoughts on how and why the war started are reflected in the contemporary letters and documents of an array of Southerners at that time.

Evelyn shares some adventures with Belle, most notably those first scenes when the Union Army occupies Martinsburg. Belle gives an account of what she saw and how her family felt that day. Her book *Belle Boyd in Camp and Prison* gives a detailed account of how Belle shot and killed one of the men that broke into her home and how the Federal soldiers tried to burn it. Belle also tells stories of hiding supplies under her skirts. Belle's flamboyant personality and loyalty to her cause show up in Alice and her determination to be a spy. All of these exploits, though historians believe Belle's accounts may have been exaggerated, made for great adventures for my story.

Margret Greenman is based on Rose O'Neal Greenhow, renowned Confederate spy in Washington. Her account of Detective Pinkerton (the man I based Detective Peterson on) and the search of her home were elements I weaved into the story. Mrs. Greenhow tells about a young companion of hers who happened to be in the house when Mr. Pinkerton came to arrest her. Rose stuffed papers into the young woman's stockings, and strangely, the friend was allowed to leave in the wee hours of the morning. Mrs. Greenhow also gives a detailed account of her time in the Old Capitol prison, and I used several of Rose's personal opinions as dialogue for Margret Greenman. You can find Rose's full story in her book, *My Imprisonment and the First Year of Abolition Rule at Washington.*

Evelyn's first day of nursing is inspired by the account Louisa May Alcott gives in *Hospital Sketches*, and Evelyn's reaction to washing the men matches how Louisa felt that day. I also used the US Central Intelligence Agency's report on historical espionage during the Civil War, which gave insights into how Rose Greenhow hid and delivered information, including hiding coded messages in mundane letters like the ones Evelyn burned, the message transports on the Doctor Line, and how she continually found ways to send and receive information even while under guard.

The Fishback Inn is a real place where Belle Boyd stayed with her family and served as a nurse in Front Royal. McClellan's army did create Camp Griffin during the time Samuel is there, and across the Chain Bridge, the Benvenue house was used as a hospital under General Winfield. There was also a skirmish with a survey team in Lewinsville.

The Washington Infirmary first cared for the poor before becoming a military hospital. It burned on November 3, 1861 and was rebuilt as the Judiciary Square Hospital. The cause of the fire is unknown.

Those are the main elements I put into the story, though there are several others (like the New Albany Journal's report on women spies). If you are interested in learning more about the real-life women who did some amazing things during the Civil War, I recommend *Liar, Temptress, Soldier, Spy* by Karen Abbott. She weaves the historical lives of Belle, Rose, and others into a tale of intrigue.

Thank you for taking this trip back into history with me. Isn't life full of so many amazing adventures? It's fun to use them to spin tales and add a little authenticity to my characters and their stories. It's one of the many things that makes this writing adventure so much fun!

Acknowledgments

Writing a book is always a journey, and while it can feel solitary at times, it's never a journey traveled alone. This particular novel took me on a different path than any of my others, and as such, has blessed me with quite a few people to thank.

Our Lord has a way of taking our plans and turning them in a new—His!—direction. Just when I thought I had it all figured out, *Eternity Between Us* managed to upend everything. And I'll admit, it became exceedingly frustrating at times when nothing seemed to go the way I thought it would. But God had a new plan and used the year-long journey to teach me a few things. I'm thankful for a Heavenly Father who leads His children by the hand on new adventures.

During the ups and downs of this story, I'm thankful for the friends who supported me along the way. Becky, I'm forever grateful for your encouragement. You listened and prayed with me each time things got difficult, and you were the first person to see this tale unfold. To my agent, Jim, thank you for your confidence in this story and your enthusiasm for my work. Your faith in me is a huge blessing.

I'm humbled by the incredible authors who took time to read the early version of this book and bless it with their endorsements. It's exciting to see the names of writers I have long admired grace a page in one of my own tales. Jocelyn, Dawn, Patricia, Pam, Misty, Andrea, and Sharlene, I cannot thank you enough.

Thank you Momma for reading all of my stories, even though at times it's difficult. Your support means the world to me. Thank you Jason for always supporting my writing dream, and to my two little monkeys, whose excitement over Momma "making a new book" always fills me with joy.

And finally, to my wonderful readers. Where would I be without you? My amazing team of Faithful Readers are dear to my heart. Thank you for your encouragement, enthusiasm, and willingness to review and share about my books. You help more than you know. To every reader who picked up this novel, thank you. We are a team, you and I. For a story is never truly complete without you to bring it to life. You have my forever thanks.

So now we draw the curtain closed, and open the page for a new story to begin and a new adventure to unfold. And I pray the Lord brings us together again for another exciting journey.

Stephenia

Discussion Questions

1. Evelyn tries to protect her cousin but ends up further straining her relationships and putting herself in a precarious position. Do you think she could have done anything differently?

2. Samuel suffers from a sensitivity to smells that he believes could ruin his dream to become a doctor. Later, he learns it could actually help him. Do you have an example of something else God ended up using for good?

3. Evelyn longs for acceptance. How do you think this affected her actions?

4. In the beginning Evelyn supports the Confederates, but in the end signs loyalty papers to the Union. Why do you think she made that change?

5. Evelyn takes supplies from the Union camp and delivers them to the Confederate camp. Why do you think she did this? Were her actions justified or not?

6. Southern thoughts and feelings on the war were often more complicated than most modern people realize. Other than slavery, what issues do you think concerned the non-slave owning population?

7. Samuel entreats Evelyn to live at peace with everyone. By doing so, he equally cares for men from both sides. How might this same concept translate to your own daily experiences?

8. Samuel adopts two children in order to help them. How do the children end up helping Samuel and Evelyn as well?

9. The divide between Samuel and Evelyn at times seems impossible to span. Have you ever experienced a situation that seemed impossible to overcome?

10. It's your turn! Where do you think Evelyn and Samuel's story goes from here? Where do you see them after the war is over?

Other Books by
Stephenia H. McGee

Ironwood Plantation

The Whistle Walk

Heir of Hope

Missing Mercy

★Ironwood Series Set

★Get the entire series at a discounted price

The Accidental Spy Series

*Previously published as The Liberator Series

An Accidental Spy

A Dangerous Performance

A Daring Pursuit

★Accidental Spy Series Set

★Get the entire series at a discounted price

Stand Alone Titles

In His Eyes

Eternity Between Us

Time Travel

Her Place in Time

(Stand alone, but ties to Rosswood from The Accidental Spy Series)

The Hope of Christmas Past

(Stand alone, but ties to Belmont from In His Eyes)

Novellas

The Heart of Home

The Hope of Christmas Past

www.StepheniaMcGee.com

Sign up for my newsletter to be the first to see new cover reveals and be
notified of release dates

New newsletter subscribers receive a free book!

Get yours here

bookhip.com/QCZVKZ

About the Author

Stephenia H. McGee writes stories of faith, hope, and healing set in the Deep South. After earning a degree in Animal and Dairy Sciences, she discovered her heart truly lies with the art of story. She put pen to page and never looked back.

Made in the USA
Middletown, DE
11 February 2023

24608360R00213